The FURY and the TERROR

BY JOHN FARRIS FROM TOM DOHERTY ASSOCIATES

ALL HEADS TURN WHEN THE HUNT GOES BY
THE AXEMAN COMETH
THE CAPTORS
CATACOMBS
DRAGONFLY
FIENDS
THE FURY
THE FURY AND THE TERROR
KING WINDOM
MINOTAUR
NIGHTFALL
SACRIFICE
SCARE TACTICS
SHARP PRACTICE
SHATTER
SOLAR ECLIPSE
SON OF THE ENDLESS NIGHT
SOON SHE WILL BE GONE
THE UNINVITED
WHEN MICHAEL CALLS
WILDWOOD

The FURY and the

TERROR

John Farris

A TOM DOHERTY ASSOCIATES BOOK
NEW YORK

THE FURY AND THE TERROR

Copyright © 2001 by John Farris

All rights reserved, including the right to reproduce this book, or portions thereof, in any form.

This book is printed on acid-free paper.

DESIGN BY JANE ADELE REGINA

A Forge Book
Published by Tom Doherty Associates, LLC
175 Fifth Avenue
New York, NY 10010

www.tor.com

Forge® is a registered trademark of Tom Doherty Associates, LLC.

Library of Congress Cataloging-in-Publication Data

Farris, John.
    The fury and the terror / John Farris.—1st ed.
        p. cm.
    "A Tom Doherty Associates book."
    ISBN 0-312-87215-1
    1. Political corruption—Fiction. 2. Washington (D.C.)—fiction.
3. Women athletes—Fiction. 4. Brainwashing—Fiction. 5. Conspiracies—Fiction. 6. Terrorism—Fiction. 7. Psychics—Fiction. I. Title.

PS3556.A777 F8 2001
813'.54—dc21

                                                            00-048455

First edition: April 2001

Printed in the United States of America

0 9 8 7 6 5 4 3 2 1

For Stephen and Tabitha King
Stalwarts

ONE

THESE ARE THE DAYS OF MIRACLES AND WONDER
AND DON'T CRY, BABY, DON'T CRY

—PAUL SIMON, *THE BOY IN THE BUBBLE*

MAUI, HAWAII · MAY 28

The four MH-60K helicopters from MORG's Elite Force left Hickam Field at one A.M. and proceeded southeast at two thousand feet, past the beach-front dazzle of postcard Waikiki. A few kliks beyond the famous headland they were at maximum cruising speed of 167 mph, making good use of a fifteen-knot tailwind. The moon was two days from the full in a clear night sky. From a higher perspective, observed against the crinkly sheen of the ocean below them, the fleet of warships resembled black wasps with razor-sharp halos.

The woman code-named Zephyr, in the lead chopper, passed the time before acquisition of their target by socializing with Portia Darkfeather, the team leader, and Zephyr's occasional lover.

"It's the lemons, babe," Zephyr said. "The peel, and the zest, that make potted veal something out of the ordinary. We didn't have much else when I was a kid, but we had Meyer lemons growing in our backyard. Have you tasted a Meyer lemon?"

Darkfeather put her six-month-old cat, a Persian named Warhol, on her left shoulder. In the low light of the flight deck Warhol fixed Zephyr in the cross hairs of his gaze. Eyes like those of an idol with a jinxed history.

"Don't think I have," Darkfeather said.

"Meyers are more like a blend of an ordinary lemon with a mandarin orange. They came to California by way of China. Four times the sugar of a regular lemon, and the aroma is divine. My mom never used any other variety with her potted veal. Pops would bring home some prime veal from the butcher shop when he was sober enough to hold a job. Another of Mom's secrets was rice wine with the veal stock."

Darkfeather said, "I never tasted veal. While my mama was alive we had chicken couple times a week. Simmered in Mexican beer, you know, to tenderize it. And Mama would baste the chicken with chipotle peppers pureed in adobo sauce. Talk about good eating."

Molokai was on the horizon. The helicopters continued southeast, along the Kalohi Channel, the sparse lights of the small island of Lanai appearing on their right.

"Did you ever surf the Pipeline or Jaws?" Zephyr asked Darkfeather. She was a child of the surfin' sixties herself, a runaway beach bum at age fourteen. All of which had never been a part of her official biography, although the tabloids had feasted on such tidbits of her past for many years.

"Not me. My brother did Jaws once. Sixty-footers. But you got to know when your nerve is writing checks your talent can't cash."

"Oh, baby," Zephyr agreed. And put an end to the small talk. Darkfeather fed Warhol a snack from a Ziploc bag.

"Eight minutes to target," the Flight Leader said.

The wind had shifted, coming out of the northwest now, and the ride was getting bumpier. Zephyr looked ahead to the airport beacon at Kapalui and the cluster of resorts around Kaanapali on Maui's west coast. Beyond Kaanapali the west Maui mountains were clearly visible. A seldom visited, by tourists, part of the island. Up to four hundred inches of rain a year made the craters, forested gorges, and marshes difficult to penetrate. Only a few bad roads dwindled into the interior from the shoreside towns. The mountains were an ideal place to hide out, if you wanted to get really lost.

The lights of Lahaina were coming into view, which raised Zephyr's pulse count in anticipation. She'd been disappointed before, after numerous sightings, stalkings, and forfeitures. But this time she was damned sure they had her, had the Avatar.

Zephyr was outfitted, like the others seated behind her, in special ops gear. She liked being with the military types. The resourceful, the mission-ready. Their terse jargon, the acronyms as sharp and jagged as combat knives. Unlike Portia's Praetorians, she wasn't carrying a weapon. The Mamba Team helos werc well armed, the usual impressive stuff like chain guns and rocket pods, but they weren't there for a turkey shoot. Zephyr had allowed that flash-bangs might be necessary. As were the dogs, three big German shepherds in another helicopter.

Portia Darkfeather was on the Mamba Team frequency.

"Designated Hitter, this is Mamba Leader. We are in the gut. ETA four minutes and thirty seconds. How do you read? Over."

"You are loud and clear, Mamba Leader. All is calm, and all is bright."

"We have Zephyr aboard tonight," Darkfeather said. "Let us all be worthy of her admiration."

"Roger that, Mamba Leader."

The helicopters had begun to descend from two thousand feet, a six-degree slope that Zephyr felt in the pit of her stomach.

"Heading zero-niner-zero," the flight leader said. "Systems check, gentlemen."

The other pilots acknowledged him.

"We're go here."

"Go."

"Full green. Go."

Thereafter the radio was silent as the sea loomed closer and they flew across the foaming wake of a lash ship steaming low and westbound in the Auau Channel.

Portia Darkfeather turned in the right-hand seat, passing binoculars back to Zephyr. The flight leader switched on the outboard searchlight. They were now skimming the sea at an altitude of a hundred feet, the two rotors of each helicopter in the formation blowing the crests off the heavy waves forming over the reef. Zephyr looked to starboard, focusing the glasses as the stealth choppers made landfall.

They crossed the shore road of Lahaina, rising abruptly to follow the contours of the land. They were in computer-assisted flight mode, and Zephyr's seat harness tightened uncomfortably. It was becoming more of a thrill ride than she had anticipated. Fortunately she'd only nibbled a little food at the luau in her honor at the Governor's mansion.

Zephyr blinked to clear her vision as they dove into a valley shaped like a seahorse, with its narrow head at the base of Puu Kukui. The seahorse was divided by the silver seam of a shallow river, descending in stair-step falls from the mountains ahead of them.

At the end of a Jeep road two-thirds of the way up the valley, Zephyr recognized the hexagon of Colonial-era white buildings with their pagoda-like roofs that she had seen in reconnaissance photos.

Darkfeather keyed her mike. "Designated Hitter, do you have visual on our position?"

"Affirm, Mamba Leader. We see you."

"Say your situation."

"Still calm. No movement inside the—okay, couple of lights just came on. I see a face in a window, second floor. They've made you, Mamba Team."

"Dreamtime is over," Darkfeather said scornfully. "Light up the LZ and go for the Avatar. Say again, you are *go* for the Avatar."

Then it was happening so fast Zephyr had difficulty keeping track of all the action. Two of the helos circled behind the cloister, searchlights blazing as doors flew open below. Men and women, most of them apparently roused from their beds and wearing little clothing, ran in panic toward the rain forest fifty yards away. They were met by a unit of the infil team that had been lying in wait at the forest perimeter. Members of Mamba Team fast-roped down from the hovering helicopters to assist in the roundup. There was little resistance. A couple of the younger, swifter runners had to be overhauled and thrown to the ground. Other members of the strike force were storming the cloister. All helicopters remained aloft.

Portia Darkfeather had tucked her cat into a pouch on her vest. She scanned the faces of the captives, who had been made to lie on their backs in a circle, feet touching, hands behind their heads. Their eyes were squinched shut against the searchlight dazzle.

Zephyr recognized several of the older telepaths from surveillance photos. Ivy Papillion. Ping Lee. Noorul Meskerem.

"I don't see Cheng," Darkfeather said.

"She wouldn't run with the others," Zephyr told her. "She's too smart for that. She'd have another way out planned. Tunnel, maybe."

"Scanning now," Darkfeather said, looking at the infrared screen. Thermal imaging would reveal any sign of human life in subterranean passages. She keyed her mike. "Mamba Leader to Designated Hitter, give me a status, over."

The voice of DH leader, coming from inside the cloister, was muffled and rushed. "Roger, Mamba Leader. We're clearing the second floors of Alpha and Bravo buildings. We have not made contact with the Avatar. Blue Leader, report."

"Roger that. TI scan negative, cellar is clear. Nothing down here but vintage wine."

"Negative on tunnels and caves," Darkfeather advised.

Zephyr slipped into an old habit, grinding her back teeth. No way to treat all those expensive crowns. She made herself relax.

"Could she have skipped early?"

"DH has had a lock on the place for the last six hours."

"Unless she peeped them," Zephyr objected. "And Kelane's like a wraith."

"The best T-blockers we've ever trained are on the DH team. No leaks there, I'd bet my sweet pussy on that. And I don't mean Warhol."

"Then she's down there. Okay, assume I'm Kelane Cheng. I have a little warning, then all hell is busting loose outside. I know I have—what, less than a minute? How do I handle it? I've always been good, but I need to get lucky."

"Maybe I know where you're going with that," Darkfeather said after a few seconds. She keyed her mike.

"Designated Hitter, recall all units *now*. I want a head count."

"Say again, Mamba Leader?"

"Account for all personnel immediately."

Members of the faculty of the cloister and several initiates were being herded from the buildings into the glare of helicopter searchlights. The German shepherds were patrolling. One feisty old gent wearing a toga had to be gigged to calm him down.

Two more members of Designated Hitter appeared from a side door, away from the throng on the lit-up lawn. They were carrying between them a sheet-wrapped body, small, probably female. Unconscious, or dead.

Zephyr put the glasses on them.

"Portia? Upper left quadrant of the lawn, by that stand of overgrown lobelias."

"Roger." The faces of the DH team, a bulky man and a woman half his size, were unseeable behind deflector shields as they put the wrapped body on the lawn. Then they turned and walked away from the lighted perimeter, ignoring the recall orders that were crackling over the radio. They didn't hurry, but they didn't have far to go to reach the edge of the forest.

"One of them has to be our gal Key-lawn-ee," Zephyr said, with a shiver of excitement. "The big hunk is probably Romanzo."

"They must have brain-locked a couple of our guys and stripped them."

Darkfeather changed the angle of the helo's searchlight and said to the flight leader, "Get over there." She keyed her mike. "Designated Hitter, the Avatar is wearing ops gear! Mamba Flight Leader is in pursuit!"

When the light hit the pair on the ground, illuminating them against the forest wall, they split up and ran into the trees. Dogs were racing across the lawn after them.

Kelane Cheng stumbled at the river's edge, looking back at the incoming helicopter, just above the treetops. She froze momentarily, then started across the waist-deep river.

"Wait a minute!" Darkfeather yelled. "Something's wrong!"

"What do you mean?" Zephyr yelled back.

"That isn't Cheng!"

"Looks like her!"

Darkfeather shook her head curtly but otherwise didn't argue. She swung a keypad to a position at lap level and began working the keys. "The little bitch jerked a knot in our tail. That's Cheng's doppelganger down there. The dpg and Romanzo carried Cheng out of the cloister, wrapped in that sheet." To the flight leader she said, "Black light going hot. We're locking on the dpg."

"Roger, locking the dpg," the baffled flight leader said. "What does black light do?"

"What does Kryptonite do to Superman? Also, black light is the only sure way to tell a dpg from the homebody. They don't show up on thermal imagers."

The flight leader glanced across a bank of instruments and glowing screens to confirm.

"How about that? Spooky."

"But they have body heat," Zephyr said, being in a position to know.

"One of those little mysteries we haven't worked out yet," Darkfeather said.

"Where does the doppelganger come from?" the flight leader asked.

"According to folklore, we all have them," Darkfeather said. "You ought to get in touch with yours, sometime."

"Hell no!"

Darkfeather laughed. "Just ragging on you. Producing a double is a feat for adepts like the Avatar. It's a left-handed art."

In the middle of the shallow river the runaway doppelganger, caught in the beam of black light, struggled against the river rapids, unable to advance. A German shepherd leaped into the water and swam toward the dpg. Kelane Cheng's doppelganger reacted by sluggishly raising its hands in an attitude of terror.

"They're also scared shitless of dogs." Darkfeather swiveled in her seat as the helicopter hovered, and keyed her mike. "All air and ground units, this is Mamba Leader! Cheng is in the forest." To the flight leader she said, "Put us down. Praetorians, get ready to deploy with the giggers."

"Roger," said one of the ops behind Zephyr, and there was a shifting of bodies, the clicks of harness being released.

The lead helicopter dropped to the river's edge, two feet above the ground. Portia Darkfeather leaped out first, crouched, sent the Praetorians who followed her into action with curt hand signals. Then she turned to help Zephyr out into the maelstrom stirred up by the rotors. They scrambled up the bank as the helicopter rose again, searchlight flashing on the scene in the middle of the river: three ops from Designated Hitter and the German shepherd dog had surrounded Kelane Cheng's doppelganger and were prodding the look-alike toward shore.

Two more helicopters were stationary above the forest, torching it with their lights. Ops from Multiphasic Operations and Research Group were at full scramble amid the exotic trees, in pursuit of Kelane Cheng.

Darkfeather paused to receive a report, grinned broadly as she turned to Zephyr.

"Got her!"

Zephyr trembled from the release of a year's worth of frustration, took in a deep lungful of the heavenly Hawaiian air.

"Yeah baby! What about Romanzo?"

"Nothing yet."

The capture zone was a clearing containing a scum-covered pond. Zephyr and Darkfeather followed a boar path illuminated by light sticks and emerged from the Ohia trees to see Kelane Cheng lying on her side near the pond, in an auroral glow from the sky. The tops of the trees thrashed in the wind from the helicopter directly overhead. Darkfeather waved it off.

Cheng had left the bedsheet behind; she was naked. She had been gigged twice, in the hip and below a shoulder blade. She lay motionless but not comatose from the pharmacopeia fed to her by the CO_2 darts. There were tears on Cheng's cheeks; her lips were parted but she breathed normally. She didn't look at anyone.

"What did you gig her with?" Zephyr asked Darkfeather. She was gasping a little from the headlong pace. Obviously she'd skipped too many of her aerobic kickboxing sessions the past couple of months, because of the heavy travel schedule as a stand-in for her ailing husband.

"Depakote works best on telekinetics. What effect it has on brain-lockers is an open question, so we hedge the bet with Trazadone and Klonopin. Rest assured she'll behave."

Zephyr stared at Cheng while she was catching her breath. Such a waif-like creature, probably not more than five feet, ninety pounds. Tiny lacquered pearls of toenails. She wore her hair long, strands of it falling across her petite breasts. Zephyr told herself that she didn't need to be afraid; Cheng looked so harmless in her downfall. But what strength still lay in her mind, in spite of the brain-numbing drugs?

"Can I talk to her now? I don't want to waste time. I want her on that plane to Plenty Coups before dawn."

"She'll hear. Doesn't mean she'll cooperate when the dope wears off."

"That's something you *don't* want to bet your sweet pussy on."

Darkfeather grinned, showing off the dimples Zephyr liked so much. Too bad they were going separate ways in a short while. Zephyr thought of the sybarite's bath in the Presidential Suite at her hotel, Portia's long body awash in aromatic bubbles. Rona sometimes swung both ways; but (as an AC-DC distaff member of the British royals had confided after their tryst) when it came to sex, "things go better with bloke."

Zephyr sighed, her pulses quickening.

"Let's do it," she said, and led Darkfeather to Kelane Cheng.

Darkfeather pulled her pistol from the utility holster—room for a Sig Sauer P220 model semiautomatic, a Ka-bar fighting knife, and extra magazines for her Sig—that was strapped to her thigh. She kneeled by Cheng's head and placed the muzzle gently over one ear. Cheng gave no sign that she noticed. Zephyr kneeled where the Avatar could see her. Nothing changed in the dark slanted eyes.

"History in the making," Zephyr said gleefully. "Here, tonight. We've been gentle. Maybe a sprained ankle, some bruises, but nobody's gotten really hurt yet."

Zephyr thought she saw a smile. "So unlike you," Cheng said, barely above a whisper.

Zephyr said, "Your karma, baby, has just hit you in the face. We're not going to prolong this. You know who I am. You know what we want you to do. It will be done."

"Never. He must die."

"No, darling. I want you to consult the practical side of what little brain we're allowing you to keep for now and think about what may happen if you continue to be wrongheaded. Think about Portland, Key."

Kelane Cheng reacted with horror and loathing.

"Hey, Kelane? I blame you for Portland. *You* caused a thousand people to vaporize and thousands more to suffer by refusing to save *one* life. And Portland was a relatively low-yield device. Portland will recover, in time, if anyone cares to live there anymore. But the terrorists who nuked Portland may have something a little larger in store for—well, where do you think it could be, next time? Albuquerque? Wichita? Frightens me to think about it. We *can* fight these monsters, Key. We need more help, however. We need Robin Sandza."

"Your own dying will last ten thousand years."

"Oh, Kelane. So judgmental."

"Deaths on a thousand worlds too primitive for fire, where the only luxury is a dirt cave."

"Spare me. All I really care about is my country. But the Sino-Islamic coalition will bring us down if we don't have strong hands at the helm of the ship of—"

There was a commotion at the edge of the clearing. Zephyr, interrupted in the flow of her rhetoric, looked around. Three members of Mamba Team had arrived with a captive, who, even though he had been gigged, still had some fight in him.

Zephyr rose and looked down at Kelane Cheng. "Frank's here," she said happily.

Cheng's small shoulders drew together; she closed her eyes briefly.

"There's nothing you can do to Frank. Nothing you can do to me. We will never bring Robin Sandza back."

"I want Romanzo over here," Zephyr said sharply. Portia Darkfeather, still holding the muzzle of her semiautomatic pistol against the Avatar's glossy head, gave Zephyr a look. She liked knowing the game plan in advance, and Zephyr apparently was going to improvise.

The Mamba ops half dragged Frank Romanzo to the pond. He addressed them all in smutty Spanish. They dropped him a few feet from Kelane Cheng. His head was down. He had the shudders and was drooling. He looked longingly at Cheng, agony in his eyes. Then he wiped his bearded chin and glared at Zephyr.

"Frank, why don't you crawl over there and give Key a good-bye kiss? May be a while before you guys get together again."

"*Madre de putas,*" Romanzo said to Zephyr. He looked at Kelane Cheng again, pleadingly.

"Don't worry," she murmured. "I'll be all right."

"Kiss her, you big galoot," Zephyr chided Romanzo.

Romanzo pulled himself to the side of his lover. Zephyr motioned for Darkfeather to move out of the way. Darkfeather got up reluctantly. When Zephyr was in her default mode, then usually it was time to worry.

Romanzo, his face inches from Kelane Cheng's, spoke to her in low tones. She wanted to embrace him, but her motor reflexes, like his, were nearly out of commission. Her hand brushed his cheek and fell limply on his shoulder.

"Awww," Zephyr said. She took the cocked .45 caliber Sig Sauer from Darkfeather's hand, steadied it in her hands, right arm extended, ball of her index finger on the trigger.

"Frank!" Kelane Cheng said, no strength in her to push him aside. The warning came too late. From five feet away Zephyr fired twice, quickly, blowing the back of Frank Romanzo's head off.

Zephyr was momentarily shocked. Forty-fives make a lot of noise. There was far more blood than she could have expected, and other stuff, flying everywhere. Sticking to her clothing. But she'd always handled blood okay, depending on the volume.

Romanzo had slumped across Cheng's limp body. Her teeth were bared, eyes with a pinpoint luster as she stared up at Zephyr.

Zephyr shrugged to hide a tremor. She'd shot animals before, including a favorite horse. This was different, and it wasn't. There was always satisfaction to be gained from eliminating part of the competition, however she achieved it. End of story, no tears.

"He called me the mother of whores. So, listen, Key, grow from it, you know?" Zephyr ruined a thumbnail handing the Sig Sauer back to Portia Darkfeather. "See you in a few days," she said casually, and walked away, taking a couple of deep breaths only when her back was turned. Keeping her head up, making an effort not to stumble. Two of Portia's Praetorians fell into step behind her.

Darkfeather watched Zephyr for a few moments, angry but inscrutable.

Then she pulled Frank Romanzo's body off Kelane Cheng, who looked at her, and beyond her, the fires of that remarkable mind cooled to ash.

For now, Darkfeather thought, rejecting pity. Her own mind hardened protectively. She knew too much about Kelane Cheng to lower her guard for even a few moments.

The medical team had arrived. They inserted an IV and began dripping fluids that contained more tranquilizer drugs. Then they wiped the Avatar's face clean, shaved some of the hair from her scalp, dabbed ointment between her breasts and on her temples. They attached the electrodes that would monitor brain-wave activity, her heart and respiration rates.

The helicopter that was taking Cheng back to Hickam Field, and to the jet waiting for her there, circled the clearing and hovered overhead.

Darkfeather decided that, in spite of Zephyr's impulsive—okay, call it sadistic—kill of Frank Romanzo, it had been a good night's work. Designated Hitter would complete the dispersal of the other psychics who had been flushed from the cloister. They would be removed to isolation cells in locations around the U.S. With their powers unlinked from the Avatar, they might be of some future interest to MORG's psi research facility. But Kelane Cheng was the top banana.

Darkfeather should have been in a better mood. But even in twilight sleep the Avatar seemed to be at work, casting a spell that had settled dismally in the marrow of Darkfeather's bones. It was her heritage to believe in the supernatural, in ill omens and premonitions.

A German shepherd moaned, then growled. She turned and there was the Avatar's doppelganger, standing just behind her but spectral now, losing definition as Cheng recalled it. In the pouch on Darkfeather's ballistics vest her pure-white Persian cat squawled and clawed as the doppelganger vanished in a flash of light that came right at Darkfeather and made her flinch. Cold traveling point of light through her flesh, leaving its mark like an indelible scratch on the soul as the dpg merged with its homebody. Definitely not an illusion. She knew she would continue to feel it for a while.

She let Warhol out of the mesh-front pouch and snuggled him against her cheek, relishing the furry warmth. Glanced again at Kelane Cheng as Cheng was loaded onto a stretcher. Her head lolled, but there seemed to be a smile on her face that made Darkfeather's mood even worse.

It was a long way to Plenty Coups, Montana. And now she sensed that in spite of the precautions they were taking with the Avatar, the odds were against any of them getting there.

Graduation day.

Eden Waring was up at a quarter past five after a nervous night of dozing and, perhaps, forty-five minutes of solid dream-producing sleep. Only one dream, but it had been a chiller. She was still trembling when she finished recording the details in her dreambook, which was always at her bedside. Dreambook number seven, like the previous six a spiral school notebook. She had been keeping the dreambooks, at Betts's suggestion, since learning to write. Age four, two years before most of her classmates. But she'd always been ahead of the others in school, proof of which was her valedictory address. She listened to it once again while she pressed the last wrinkles out of her graduation gown.

Betts knocked at the bedroom door and came in yawning, coffee mug in one hand. She wore a faded Eddie Bauer shirt and baggy cargo pants, old moccasins with popped stitches. Her usual costume away from the office.

"Thought I heard you talking to yourself. How about breakfast?"

"Couldn't eat a bite," Eden said, grimacing. She stopped the tape, rewound briefly, listened intently to herself, mouthed the words.

"That sound preachy to you?" she asked Betts.

Betts's hairstyle, anytime, could best be described as "blowsy." She ran a hand through it, thinking. "Don't you say 'forbidding times' someplace else?"

"Now that you mention it." Eden sorted through her prompt cards and found the passage, picked up a ballpoint pen with a mangled cap, and chewed on it for a few seconds. "*Challenging,*" she decided. She made the change. Left-handed. Her hand trembled. "I need coffee."

"And how about some kava-kava with your java?" Betts liked wordplay. "Babble-Scrabble," she called it, a game she played with some of her more difficult-to-reach patients, those functioning at the low end of the range of human possibilities. It often opened them up. She always had been able to coax Eden out of a foul mood with some unexpected bit of foolery. If her daughter had a fault, Betts liked to say, it was high seriousness.

"Yeah, okay. Dad up?"

"Up and gone. Two of Beau Cloud's stallions got into it over that brood mare he brought from Sacramento. Lot of stitching up to do."

Another grimace from Eden. "You know Dad can't keep track of time. And graduation is—"

"Promptly at eleven. People like Riley are the reason why pagers and cell phones were invented."

Eden tried a few lines of her revised address and bobbled a phrase.

"Oh, *no*. I just can't get that straight! Betts, help, I'm gonna blow it, in front of six thousand—"

"How many games did you win with last-second free throws? The odds against you making a muff are about equal to the odds you'll cut a third set of teeth. Have a little confidence. What time is Martine doing your hair?"

"Nine." Eden looked into the bureau mirror, eyes narrowing. The left eye was turning in this morning, which sometimes happened when she was overly tired or stressed. She wore her hair, colored a streaky strawberry and mahogany red, in what she hoped was an artfully casual style. Cut as short as she could get away with, so it wasn't a nuisance on the playing fields and courts. Eden had been a second-team All-State point guard in high school and on scholarship at the major-college level while earning her degree in biochemistry at Cal Shasta. "I'm just getting a wash and trim," she said to Betts. "Do you think I need some color and extra body?"

Betts squinted critically. "Limp as old string. But the luster passes muster. Coffee's hot. I'm making bacon-crumble waffles, and you know what an ordeal it is for me to cook. So you'd better choke down a couple." Betts glanced at the notebook that Eden had left open on the counterpane of her unmade bed. "Anything new in the dreambook?" she asked.

"Same old same-old," Eden hedged, fussing with her hair, giving quick tugs with her fingertips and letting it flop while she studied the results in her dressing-table mirror.

"Hot and sexy?"

"Mommmm."

Betts picked up the dreambook, then turned her head to listen as Winky, their elderly golden retriever, began barking outside.

"Speaking of hot and sexy, that may be he who just turned into our driveway."

"Oh, God! I need to get dressed! Keep Geoff in the kitchen, *please*."

"I'll stuff him full of bacon-crumble waffles. But you better not leave me alone with him for too long. I may decide to cast Riley aside after all these years and take up with Geoff McTyer."

"Oh, Mom. And leave the dreambook here? I don't want—you know— Geoff to know too much about—"

"Hey, the dreambook is just between us. Always has been." Betts tossed the dreambook casually on top of Eden's study table, looked at it for a few moments.

"Was the Good Lady with you last night?"

"Can we talk about her later?" Eden put a hand to her brow, requesting a private moment. They both heard Geoff McTyer outside, whistling on his way to the kitchen door.

"Sure," Betts said cheerfully, and started out of Eden's bedroom.

"Mom?"

"Yes?"

"It's going to happen again. Like Portland, but worse this time." Betts turned in the doorway. Her eyes gray, direct, astute. Eden was breathing too fast. Onset of an episode? Couldn't be a worse day for it.

"Why don't we wait?"

"It's in the dream—the city. I didn't recognize it. I wrote down everything I saw." She pressed hard against her forehead, biting her lower lip. "Sailboats," Eden said, distantly. Betts waited, on edge. Nothing more.

"We'll talk later. At my office, after graduation."

Eden dropped her hand from her face. Her head was down. "I have such a bad taste. That bitter, bad taste at the back of my mouth. That's how I've always known—you didn't *believe* me, last time."

"No, I—You know how terrible I've felt—Eden, do you want some Depakote?"

"It's passing. I'll be all right." Her breathing slowed. She looked up. "But what are we going to *do*?"

"Not now. There's time."

"I suppose. It wasn't complete. The dream. They always come back to me, two or three times before—"

"Geoff's waiting for you," Betts said, smiling a little desperately, but Eden wasn't looking at anything, only a corner of the room. "It's a *happy* day, Eden. Just think about that. And the proudest day of our lives, Riley and me. We are so proud, and we love you so much."

"I know. Whoever my real parents were, they could never have meant as much to me. Thank you. I'm sorry."

"About things beyond your control? Don't be. It's in the dreambook where it belongs. You don't have to think about it now."

In spite of her banter with Eden, Betts wasn't sure how much she liked Geoff McTyer, even as she greeted him at the door to the kitchen with a kiss on his cheek.

Geoff had come to Innisfall three years ago. He was an easterner, with a degree in math from Boston U., where he also had played some basketball as a walk-on. After graduation he had knocked around the country for a couple of years before driving into town in his '66 Mustang with one hundred seventy thousand miles on it. Geoff liked what he saw, and within a few days he had applied for a position with the Innisfall police department. The life of a cop in a university town of sixty thousand people wasn't too demanding. He admitted that he was overqualified, but the job paid his bills and he had plenty of free time to enjoy the recreational advantages of northern California. Skiing, water sports, wilderness hiking. The college girls had been another recreational advantage for Geoff. He had bright blue eyes, a ready smile, and, apparently, an untroubled psyche.

With her hectic schedule Eden hadn't devoted much time to guys in either high school or college. No lack of opportunity, but little time for romance. Geoff had met Eden when he volunteered for the all-male scout team that practiced with the women's varsity at Shasta. They were about the same height, five-nine. Both were quick and had thieving hands. Geoff wasn't shy about dumping Eden on her butt when she pressed him too hard. Eden came home from practice one winter afternoon with a split lower lip from an inadvertent elbow and said to Betts, "There's this guy on the scout team I kind of like. From 'down-east,' he says. Has that funny accent, *Bahston,* you know? But I could get used to it."

So what did Betts have against Geoff? He and Eden had progressed slowly, from the end of her sophomore year, to what might be a serious relationship, and Betts had received hints that Eden had had sex with Geoff on weekend camping trips the previous summer. So, okay. Must have been a positive experience, or she wouldn't still be seeing him. Eden would be twenty-two in August, old enough and, Betts felt, wise enough to weigh and resolve all of her moral choices. If she'd wanted guidance, she would have asked. Betts the mother was satisfied that Geoff was an appropriate first lover, possessing the sensitivity and loving concern to allow his and Eden's relationship to mature without stress into an affair.

And yet—

Betts the psychologist had reservations about Geoff McTyer, not the least of which was a certain vacancy in his life before Innisfall, and his resilience in deflecting reasonable questions about his family, with whom he apparently had no contact. He'd owned up to a comfortable childhood. Parochial schools in a Boston suburb had not left their mark on him in a religious sense; he was not a churchgoer. Mother passed on when he was twelve. He still carried her faded picture in his wallet—a woman with a lipless self-conscious smile from whom Geoff obviously had inherited his cheekbones—but he had no other family photos, as far as Eden knew. Father retired from a middle-management position with a Boston insurance group. Geoff had named as his father's employer two different firms on widely separated occasions, which Betts found curious. No relationship with his father, now living off his comfortable pension in a seaside village in Ireland—Geoff couldn't think of the name—or his older sister, who, he said, had married a couple of times, small businessmen, and was content to be a breeder. Geoff couldn't remember what her married name was now. He thought she was living in Woburn. Other relatives? Sure, here and there. Never kept up with any of them.

A chilly kind of indifference to his bloodlines, Betts thought, knowing it wasn't unusual. Family members who were all strangers to one another. Some of her patients suffered like the damned because of nonexistent family ties, the deep psychic chill of loveless people. *My mother didn't want to have me. My father never looked at me when he talked to me.* But Geoff, if there had been similar strain in his formative years, had had the toughness of spirit to survive, with wit and optimism. A steady sort, not inclined to be a cop all of his life—he had lately developed an interest, through his graduate studies, in teaching. Reliable, humorous, intelligent.

And yet, and yet—

Geoff was still in uniform, with a couple of hours to go on the twelve-to-eight shift he preferred working. Gave him the freedom of his days, he said, and he was still young enough to get by on a few hours' sleep. Three hours in the morning, a nap after dinner, often on the couch in the downstairs rec room of the Warings' fieldstone ranch house with his head in Eden's lap while she listened on headphones to the guitarists she loved and studied Michael Jordan's moves on videocassettes.

"I was just passing by and saw all the lights," Geoff said after the kiss from Betts. "Eden got the yips?"

"Maybe we both have. Anyway, Riley was up before either of us, and you know how that is, when his side of the bed's empty I can't sleep either. Want coffee? How about something to eat? Bacon-crumble waffles."

"Sure." Geoff made himself at home rummaging in the pantry, found a box of cereal. He stopped at the fridge on his way to the breakfast table in the center of the kitchen.

"Know what you get when you crahss a helicopter with a flock of songbirds?" he asked Betts as he was taking out a carton of milk.

"Shredded tweet," Eden said, robbing him of the punch line as she bustled into the kitchen. Betts bellowed, spilling some batter down the front of the waffle iron. Eden made a face at Geoff. "That's fifth-grade humor."

"I always liked the fifth grade," Geoff said. "That's when I discovered girls. When did you discover boys?"

"I was wiping the sweat out of my eyes on the bench, looked up, and there you were, practicing your cross-over dribble. I thought, hey, this carbon-based life-form is different from me. It's wearing a jockstrap." Eden had put on her old high school jersey, number 12, with ratty overalls, and was barefoot. She kissed Geoff, recoiled slightly with a wrinkling of her nose. "Gahhh."

Betts turned to Geoff. "Notice I was too discreet to say anything?"

Geoff said, "Two A.M. I pull ovah this guy with Nevada plates. He's all ovah the road, but not speedin', thanks be to God. So he blows a two point seven on the Breathalyzer, right? I mean really lit. There's an empty fifth of Johnnie Red. Another one-half empty on the seat of his Caddy. Claimin' he drives bettah when his hands are steady. Hell of it is, his hands *are* steady. Stomach's a different story. Chucks it all in my direction. I'm quick but not that quick. Needed a complete change. No time to wash the stink out of my hair."

"Cool, I gotta see that. Bring the tape. It's probably funnier than our New Year's party. Did I ever mention you talk real fast?"

"When you get in a critical mood, means you're unhappy with yourself."

"Try a baby wipe," Eden suggested. "Some of Dad's cologne wouldn't hurt."

"Good idea. You nervous?"

Eden held out her right hand, palm down.

"No, it's an earthquake. *Of course I'm—*"

"Just look at the front of the rim. Block out the crowd."

"Yeah, thanks, Coach."

Geoff left the kitchen to use Eden's bathroom. Eden's cell phone rang. She dug it out of a bib pocket of the overalls and spent the next several minutes raptly in conversation with her best friend, Megan Pardo, in spite of scowls from Betts.

"When she's on the phone Eden measures time in dog years," Betts complained to Geoff when he returned to the kitchen. His hair was re-combed and glistening. Geoff smiled as if he'd never heard her say it before and passed his plate for waffles.

"Stop me if it's none of my business, but how old was Eden when you and Riley—"

"Just four months."

Betts looked a little strange about his bringing up the adoption at this time. Geoff smiled and said after a forkful of waffle, "Eden and I talk about it. Who her parents might have been. With her coloring and imagination, we're pretty sure one of them was an Irish poet."

"She does have an imagination," Betts said with a shrug.

"But that's not all there is to it. Imagination, I'm sayin'."

Betts looked at him through the smoke of her first cigarette of the day, mindful of the booted cop look, the trim uniform, the blunt butt of his Glock semiauto holstered high on his belt. And was silent.

Geoff said, still smiling, casual, "We've talked about that, too. Second sight, isn't that what it's called?"

Betts drew into herself ever so slightly, but didn't have to reply: the police dispatcher was on the radio that Geoff wore on his left shoulder. He was back in service with another hour and a half to go on his shift.

"Eighteen-wheeler jackknifed at the Buck Lake exit," Geoff explained. Eden looked around, then met him at the door for a quick kiss on his way out. "See you at the stadium," he said. "Front of the rim, Eden."

Eden stayed on the phone for another ten minutes, laughing now, at ease with herself, her pregraduation jitters toned down considerably, perhaps forgotten.

Outside the fog along the creek behind their property had taken on a glow from the sun. Betts glanced at the digital clock on the wall oven as she sat down to her own breakfast. She thought about the dreambook, and wondered how soon she could get her hands on it without appearing overly anxious to see what Eden had written this morning. It was now twenty-five past six, Pacific daylight time. She turned on the kitchen TV to distract herself, surfed to the Weather Channel. The forecast for northern California was breezy with lots of sun, low seventies by noon. Looked like a perfect day for an outdoor ceremony.

EASTBOUND/TRANSPAC 1850 · MAY 28

The TRANSPAC DC-10 that was leased to the Multiphasic Operations and Research Group—better known, to those who had to know or wished they didn't know about its existence, as MORG—took off from Hickam AFB at 0310 hours Honolulu time.

MORG had been the creation of a man named Childermass, who, like all great demagogues, had a long memory and a lot of patience. He excelled in deceit, intimidation, and persuasion, both silken and bloodcurdling. Childermass liked to say the weakness of a democracy was that it empowered too many fools. The gods (he also would say, quoting Ovid and by implication placing himself within that pantheon) have their own rules. During the Cold War frenzies of the middle decades of the century he used all he knew about the empowered fools and their complex political machineries to maneuver what had been a small entity of the Department of Defense, located in a suite of offices down a humble corridor in a dingy building, into a massive presence in the global business of espionage. Childermass had drowned in his own blood in a bathtub at the age of sixty-two, assassinated (though that was never revealed) by a remarkable adolescent closer to the gods than he could have hoped to be. Gillian Bellaver had imagined, in her fury and heartbreak, that the destruction of Childermass would mean the end of MORG. But bad institutions are like breeder reactors for Childermass's kind. MORG proved to be a self-perpetuating institution that continued to expand and thrive on blackmail, conspiracy, and various kinds of outrage within a developing fascist nation that once had consisted of thirteen proudly independent states.

The DC-10 flying from the mid-Pacific to southern Montana on the mainland had been expensively refitted for the benefit of one passenger: Kelane Cheng. She had half the plane to herself, in what amounted to an intensive care unit with a team of six doctors and specialty nurses in charge. Finding her still alert, they had added to her medication soon after she was brought aboard. IVs of Brevia, an anesthetic, and succinylcholine to further relax her. She was, according to her activity readout, in a twilight state, although her eyes, mere slits, never closed completely. Portia Darkfeather had been assured that there was no way the Avatar could become a problem.

Darkfeather ate scrambled eggs and Pop-Tarts for breakfast, followed by strong coffee. Then she took a needed nap, reviewing in her only dream the back of Frank Romanzo's head flying apart. Her response was to take Zephyr's throat in her hands until Zephyr was on her knees, her face white and puffy like a huge blister with a tiny red blood spot of mouth, eyes like those of undersea life fragile as apparitions . . .

She woke up with dawn light in her eyes, feeling like hammered shit, and went to the bathroom. Then to Kelane Cheng's quarters in the aft section of the huge plane.

Low lights, the occasional pulse of vital signs monitors. Cheng was restrained on the white hospital bed, as if there could be a possibility of a physical struggle. White patches on her forehead and body, wires, nasal cannula, drip lines. Cheng's heart was beating very slowly. Darkfeather, while not an adept, could lower her own rate to six beats a minute. The Avatar could get by on eight beats an hour.

Darkfeather sat beside Cheng. Her presence provoked no movement or sign of recognition.

"Kelane?"

Cheng answered after a time lag, as if Darkfeather's voice were circling the moon to get to her.

Yes? Darkfeather couldn't be sure she had actually spoken, but the response was clear in her mind.

"I want to apologize for—you know. She shouldn't have done that. Shot Romanzo. There was no call. I don't know what gets into Ro—into Zephyr, sometimes."

Cheng's lips moved, but again Darkfeather had the sensation of mind-to-mind communication.

What is your name?

"Portia Darkfeather."

How did you find us? Were we betrayed?

"By someone in your group?" What the hell, Darkfeather thought, let's find out what a good little audile she is. *No. Listen, we've got some pretty fair people ourselves. You've heard of Psi Faculty? What we call a proprietary in our—*

No time lag in comprehension now, which concerned Darkfeather.

I know all about them.

Darkfeather spoke aloud, easing the strain on herself. Thought communication was hard work. "Affiliated with major universities. Nobel Prize winners on staff. Enough funding makes any area of academic inquiry respectable. When the Cold War ended, we also picked up some of the Russians who were cutting edge in psi research."

Do they realize who—and what—they are actually working for?

"Why make us out to be the bad guys, Key? The rest of the fucking world hates the good old U.S., no need to wonder why. Maybe it's our come-to-Jesus statesmanship. There's always been and always will be another war. We're simply defending our country with the best means at our disposal." She added, subvocally, *Like the Avatar.*

There was a slight change of weather in the twilight pall of Cheng's face. *Why do you treat me like this? I am American born. I went to Harvard. My stepfather owns a Buick dealership in Paso Robles.*

"United Way. Rotarian. Registered Dem. Put on some weight since I saw him last. But I like a man with girth."

Have you hurt him?

"Absolutely not! He was cooperative. You scare him a little. Look, Kelane. We all need to work together in this thing. Or else, frankly, there goes the Buick dealership. Paso Robles too, most likely. We're all but in a state of siege here."

Don't talk to me about loyalty. Who are you?

"I told you already. Por—"

I know your name. That wasn't my question. How can you do her work, and live with yourself?

"It's where I used to live, that's the only thing ever bothers me," Darkfeather said hostilely.

Yes, I see it, the Avatar responded after a few moments. *The grasslands and sugar-beet fields. The Mission school. The mobile home in which you lived.*

Her recall gave Darkfeather a chill. "Call it a home. Call it a bed I slept on if you want to. That old pissed-up mattress where I was fucked by half the dam workers at Yellowtail while my uncle Louis Badger Foot hunkered down outside the door, taking the money I earned in his dirty hand."

The hand with the missing thumb joint and—

"God damn you! I work for Zephyr because she *loves* me. I own a condo in Falls Church. I've got ranchland. Quarter horses. Get out of my head!"

You came to me.

"All I came in here for was to say I was personally sorry about Frank Romanzo, it was a mistake. But you don't rile Zephyr. Man, you *never* do that."

The ensuing silence in Darkfeather's head was worrisome. She stared down at Cheng. Such stillness. Her rhythms at the brink of death. But Darkfeather understood that the attempted apology had failed. The Avatar wasn't ready to die. Not until she'd settled with them all.

And Darkfeather lost her nerve. Knowing that she had made herself momentarily vulnerable. Thoroughly unprofessional. She left Kelane Cheng and in a rage lit into the medical team, compounding her own anxiety.

"I'm telling you! She was in my head like a plumber's snake, rooting around! What the hell else could she be up to? You've got to control her."

But they were at their limits, pushing drugs into Cheng's system; there was nothing else in the pharmacopeia that didn't carry a huge risk of speeding her quickly and stone-cold to the afterlife. And, in spite of her long-standing relationship with Zephyr, Darkfeather knew very well what consequences the Avatar's death would have for her.

The problem wasn't only Kelane Cheng. Darkfeather had time to reflect on that dilemma as the TRANSPAC DC-10 flew on into the sun.

There was Kelane's doppelganger, that scary presence in the remote forest of western Maui. Did the Avatar have enough mental energy in her present state to animate her dpg again? And if she'd already done so, where was it now? Dpg's in their natural state only showed up when exposed to black light. The dpg could be sitting opposite Darkfeather, unseeable if she were naked. Or forward, paying a little visit to the flight deck, brimming with feline curiosity and perhaps—it was the common flaw in even the most intelligent doppelgangers—mischief.

They had black light aboard. And Darkfeather had her Persian kitty. Anywhere in the vicinity of a doppelganger Warhol would throw a three-alarm fit. She had decided it would be a good idea to search the plane when she received an urgent call from the captain.

(From Eden Waring's dreambook, #2)

Im on the iland again. Where the Good Lady says Im safe from the Bad Souls they cant come here she says I can see them out there in the fog but not very well thats good they make scarry noiz and call to me saying how much better it is where they are but don't believe that the Good Lady always tells me because they only want to change me just ignore them she says and holds me Its so warm and breezy there on the iland when shes holding me I dont hear Bad Souls any more I want to stay forever but the Good Lady says oh no what about your lessons and I tell her forth grade is easy even if I did skip the third grade but she says not the lessons I mean now its time I have sprise for you darling then shes gone and nothing else much happens except for this girl my age I see making a sand cassel down the beach I don't know if thats the sprise she doesnt say anything when I ask what her name is goes on pushing up wet sand and patting it with her hands making walls and I say can I help she still wont say anything so I start wurking too on the sand cassel too and it feels funny when she looks at me because I know her then it feels funnier than ever because I ask is she my sister she says no Im you look the boat's here time to do your next lesson and I say what lesson and she says Im your next lesson youll see that is so dum I realy hate this dream its the stuped-ist dream I ever had

HONOLULU, HAWAII · MAY 28 · 6:14 A.M. HDT

Rona Harvester woke up early in the eight-room Presidential Suite of whatever-hotel-it-was, disoriented at first blink, as if she'd rolled over to find herself in an alternate universe. The drapes were drawn but some heavy rollers were pounding Waikiki. The sound of surf awakening nostalgia for her vagabond days at Stimson, Maverick's, and the community of big-wave surfers in Santa Cruz. Friends like Trey and Reg and Havens, the transplanted Kansan who became one of the legends and was gobbled by a thirty-footer at Maverick's when a surface chop launched him from his board.

Shortly after the return of the MORG helos from Maui, a squall had hit the area. The limo hurried her back from Hickam AFB in blinding rain. Only one limo instead of the usual four with dozens of cops to provide a rolling roadblock along the streets. In that same limo she had been smuggled out of the hotel hours earlier, after her official retirement time of eleven-thirty P.M. Back entrance to the hotel sealed off by the MORG Praetorians who, at Rona's request, had replaced her Secret Service detail early in her husband's administration, a first valuable lesson in what had become holy writ in D.C.: Rona Always Gets Her Way. Going and coming she wore a dark wig in case one of the staked-out freelancers with a camera lens the size of a trash can got lucky from a thousand yards at that late hour. Forget about the regulars in the traveling press corps: they were billeted in a hotel of slightly less distinction a block and a half away, and those who weren't still drinking or screwing were dead to the world.

The entire floor below the Presidential Suite was occupied by staffers and security personnel. Standard practice when the First Lady was in residence anywhere in the world with or, as had been the case during the last three months, without her husband.

Rona got unsteadily out of the bed. The skin of her face was dry; she hadn't creamed it before tumbling to the pillows. Hadn't expected to sleep after the night's excitement, the fire still smoldering in her belly. And she'd killed a man. But she seemed to make an instant transition from nervy wakefulness to a state dinner at the White House, where she appeared wearing only her father's old fisherman's waders and a diamond choker. Lately the more stressed she was the more her dreams had a comical aspect. She sometimes awakened herself with laughter.

While she sat peeing Rona examined her hands in the too-bright bathroom, finding traces of dried blood in the knuckle creases. She'd split a nail on the decocking lever while handling the Sig Sauer. She felt a drenching coldness and almost passed out on the toilet. Rona despised weakness. So she'd killed him. So what? Frank Romanzo was an influence the Avatar didn't need. Gasping and trembling, she prepared her own bath instead of calling for Rochelle to do it and scrubbed until both hands were pure again. Then she put on couturiere lounging pajamas and a robe she had borrowed at Barbra Streisand's Malibu digs (because the blue of the robe matched her eyes so well, she had neglected to return it) and filed smooth the ragged nail. It was 6:21 Hawaiian time, past noon in Washington, when she signaled her staffers that their day had begun.

Rona reckoned that the plane carrying Kelane Cheng to Montana should be somewhere near San Francisco by now. She booted up her laptop. No coded message from Portia Darkfeather. So everything was going smoothly.

Sorting through her E-mail, she found a one-word message from the Director of Multiphasic Operations and Research Group.

Congratulations.

It meant more to her than the accolades she was about to receive as the two-day world conference on the eradication of childhood diseases came to a conclusion.

Rona keyed up music on the ten-thousand-dollar sound system, gift of the King and Queen of Sweden, that traveled everywhere with her. She wanted something rhythmic and spirited to put some zip in her blood before breakfast arrived. Her old favorites David and Michael Doucet and Beausoleil from the Louisiana bayous. David's version of *"Zydeco Sont Pas Salés,"* with Josh Graves sitting in on dobro, really cooked.

At home or away, Rona had her first cup of coffee alone while she read either her husband's copy of *The President's Daily Briefing* or a summary of the world's worst headaches prepared by Melissa McConnell, the First Lady's communications director. Then Rona looked over her schedule for the day while Rochelle, the housekeeper who had been with her for eighteen years, supervised table settings in the dining room of the suite.

Rona made adjustments on her schedule, allotting time for phone calls. Three minutes to her son Joshua, studying at Cambridge. A minute and a half to her husband at Camp David, another two minutes to Clint Harvester's personal physician concerning the President's recovery and rehab. At Rona's insistence Clint had been all over the TV news last night, photographed while strolling the grounds with his Big Bertha driver, taking some practice swings to show how great he was feeling. Reassuring the nation that, as the White House spin-control corps tirelessly maintained, he was still in charge. Rona herself, interviewed at the conference yesterday: "Yes, he's made amazing progress. Of course the President has always had a wonderful constitution. Dr. Daufuskie and his team believe it is best that he limit himself for now to two hours of work a day." Lowering her eyes momentarily, blinking as if resisting a sun shower of tears, then looking at the cameras with a softer, more vulnerable expression, preparing to give them one from the heart. "Clint and I want everyone to know that God has truly been good to us. The prayers of the American people have been answered, and their President is only a couple of weeks away from resuming his full duties as the leader of the free world."

And, finally, five minutes—no, make it ten—for her morning briefing with Allen Dunbar, the Vice President. Rona would be in touch with her husband's stand-in (she would not utter, privately or publicly, the words *President pro tempore*) at least two more times during the course of their busy day, never letting "Dumbo" forget for a moment that, because of Clint Harvester's unfortunate impairment, it was Rona herself who was firmly in charge of the affairs of state. End of story.

A medley of tunes from Andrew Lloyd Webber shows replaced the energizing Louisiana French music. The R Team, as they were known in Washington, trooped in for breakfast. Always fresh fruit to start, the rest of the menu changing on a daily basis. Breakfast was prepared by an assistant White House chef who had his own team, including a nutritionist. The rest of Rona's support group consisted of two maids, known as housekeeping assistants; a wardrobe consultant; two makeup artists, one for daytime and one for evening; a hairdresser; a masseuse; a personal trainer; a holistic physician; and Rona's personal photographer.

Rona's Chief of Staff was Peach Boondecker. Melissa, the R Team communications director, had her own staff: a deputy CD who was Rona's senior speech writer, and the First Lady's press secretary. Two secretaries remained in Washington when Rona was traveling.

Rona only nibbled at breakfast, keeping the business of the day in focus with rapid-fire queries and objections. She had a short attention span. Her most frequent comment was "Next." She praised one staffer, toasted another for her failure to include a fifteen-minute audience with a trio of Asian businessmen who had been generous in their support of a respected international charity that laundered contributions to the campaigns of Clint and Rona's pet congresspersons. All photo ops were approved. Rona then had half an hour to rehearse her closing remarks for the luncheon and review the videotape of herself. Chin up, shoulders relaxed, minimize the gestures. She dictated changes in the speech while she was having her hair done. Rondorf, the First Lady's wardrobe guru, brought out three tailored suits from three different designers. She chose the dark blue Armani with a subtle herringbone pattern. Rona went to makeup eating the ass off anyone within range because Allen Dunbar was not returning her calls.

The VP was going to address the United Nations General Assembly in prime time, his second grab of prime TV time this week. Ostensibly it was because of what Dunbar had described in solemn tones as "the grave crisis" resulting from a terrorist attack on the U.S. air base at Incirik. Truck bomb. Big enough to damage aircraft parked two hundred yards away. Four hundred forty-two casualties. Rona had Casey, her press secretary, call the networks to see how much coverage they were planning to give the First Lady on the nightly news. But as Rona well knew, childhood diseases couldn't compete with U.S. bombers smoldering on a runway in Turkey.

She was still in a simmering bad mood when it was time for makeup. Then she had what she thought was a wonderful idea. *Anyone* could do bombs.

Ten minutes to eight in the morning where she was. Ten minutes to two EDT in Washington. That gave her a little over six hours until the scheduled press conference, which she had decided to preempt. Workable, Rona decided, smiling suddenly and surprising Daisy, who was about to apply lip gloss with a brush. Daisy accidentally dabbed a little paint at the root of Rona's nose, but Rona was staring past her at the coffered ceiling in the Akohe'kohe Salon of the Presidential Suite, too absorbed in her newly hatched scheme to be annoyed. Her schedule called for her to depart the luncheon at exactly two o'clock. The motorcade would proceed from the grand ballroom of whatever-hotel-it-was (not the hotel in which she was staying) to the air base, where Air Force One waited to fly her home.

Rona knew Portia Darkfeather was the one to pull this off, but Darkfeather was unavailable. And it wasn't something Rona wanted to discuss with her, even in unbreakable code. But Portia, Rona decided, undoubtedly would recommend what's-his-face, the team leader of Designated Hitter. Portia had a lot of confidence in him—Brad, wasn't it?—butch haircut, and one of those faces that was total military hard-on. An ex–Navy SEAL with post-graduate degrees in all types of explosive devices. Thread a needle with an RPG, God she loved those guys!

Brad should still be available, right there in Honolulu. Rona sent for the chief of MORG security on the day shift, then relaxed in the makeup chair with outrigger mirrors that traveled with her and let Daisy finish giving her the transforming works. The portrait of herself she showed the public. Portia would have said she was in default mode again, but screw that. This was going to be *fun*. And her approval rating in the polls, which had not budged lately after she'd wrung all the sympathy possible from her husband's situation, would probably go through the roof. Even better: she'd have the cover of every newsmagazine in the free world next week. So top *that*, Dumbo.

The 922 members of the spring graduating class, University of California at Shasta, had filed into Red Wolves Stadium and were seated in semicircular rows of metal folding chairs on the playing field, mortarboards like a half acre of uncemented blue tiles. They faced the temporary stage erected at the fifty-yard line. Behind them, in the north stands, about five thousand parents, relatives, wives, husbands, siblings, and friends of the graduates had assembled, half filling the concrete arc on bench seats.

Betts and Geoff McTyer were in the tenth row near an aisle. Riley Waring finally arrived, shortly before eleven-thirty, as the Chancellor was concluding his welcoming remarks.

"Did you bring the extra tape for the camcorder?" Betts asked Riley, a little out of sorts because he'd missed the processional.

Riley was a man with heft, homely but pleasing textures. A large animal vet by trade, he had the weathered fortitude of someone who earns a hard and precarious living outdoors. Grand Banks fisherman. Lumberjack.

Riley shook hands, a touch formally, with Geoff, settled himself between them, and unzipped his fanny pack. Opera glasses came out first, then the requested tape that he handed to Betts.

"What've you got there?" he asked Geoff, who was holding his camera in his lap.

"My old Nikon. Bought a new three hundred-mil lens for it. Have a look."

Riley took the camera from him and focused on his daughter, near the end of the first row of academics, clergy, and the Congresswoman from their district, the principal commencement speaker. Eden was seated between the salutatorian, a sixteen-year-old boy of Vietnamese extraction, whom Eden had edged for top honors by .025 of a grade point, and a television actor from a long-running sitcom who was to receive an honorary degree.

She turned her head from listening to a comment of the actor's and glanced up at the crowd. Seemed to be looking their way, a little nearsighted—not enough for glasses, she insisted—probably wondering if Riley was going to show up at all. Riley lowered the camera and thrust a fist above his head, thought he saw her smile, and looked through the camera's lens again to confirm. But the smile had been brief. Eden was poised (it seemed to Riley as he studied her through the telephoto lens) on the edge of her seat; her hands were folded, but tautly, in her lap beneath the golden ropes and tassels that signified her academic achievements.

"Well, she looks"—Riley faltered and glanced at Betts, smiling tentatively—"distracted. Nothing wrong, is there?"

"That we know of," Betts replied, curtly, which made Riley feel as if he'd been left out of something. He handed Geoff's Nikon back to him and made himself as comfortable as possible on the slab of aluminum bolted to concrete. The cheap way to do stadium construction. Only two years old and already lawsuits had been filed, because one side of the stands was sinking, eight inches so far. He'd left the house in a hurry after whipping on a tie, forgetting the stadium cushion that might prevent his hemorrhoids from flaring before they even began to hand out diplomas.

Restless, he glanced at Betts and saw that not only had she remembered her own cushion, she had brought the back rest, like half of a director's chair, that clamped on to the bench seat. Riley sighed. Betts looked at him, already knowing what it was about. The dialogue of a slightly raised eyebrow, a hapless tuck to the mouth, a penitential shuffling of his feet. Betts relented and raised her broad beam, turning her attention back to the field as she did so. Riley reached out and slid the cushion from under her, let his hand rest on her thigh when she sat down again. She caressed his knuckles with her thumb.

The Chancellor, a short tanned man with a vain pompadour like the crest of a Roman general's helmet, introduced the Dean of Students, a man of wit and, thank the Lord, brevity. In turn he introduced the Vietnamese boy, who spoke to the students of learning to steer themselves in journeys to great places. The actor got his honorary degree, cracked a couple of jokes that everyone laughed at because they knew he was a funny man, he had the Emmys and the bankroll to prove it.

Then it was Eden's turn.

2110 HOURS ZULU

What do you mean, you can't fly the plane anymore?" Darkfeather said to the captain of the TRANSPAC DC-10. "Did your retirement kick in when we changed time zones?"

Neither of the two pilots nor the engineer on the flight deck were amused. Darkfeather remembered the captain's name, or nickname. "Dutch." Captain Dutch van der Veek.

"TRANSPAC 1850 heavy, this is L.A. Center. Verify flight level and confirm destination."

The aircraft was descending slowly, Darkfeather was aware of that much. They were just under thirty-five thousand feet over the Pacific, 220 miles northwest of the San Francisco Bay Area. Sun glazed the flight deck windows. Outside, in a world of blue, it was fifty-seven degrees below zero.

"L.A. Center, this is TRANSPAC 1850 heavy. We are descending from our assigned flight level at three hundred feet per minute and are deviating from programmed coordinates by zero five degrees right. We are checking GPS and a possible malfunction of R-NAV."

"Roger, TRANSPAC 1850. Keep us informed."

The autopilot was a box of instrumentation by the pilot's right knee. Darkfeather glanced at it, saw that the level-change button wasn't armed. Clearly the autopilot wasn't flying the plane. The yokes were moving, slightly, although neither the captain nor the first officer was in manual control. That raised goose bumps on Darkfeather's forearms.

"Can you reprogram the autopilot?" she asked.

The first officer was thumbing through a thick tab-indexed manual. "It's not taking commands," he said.

"Shut it down, then. I mean, pull the fuckin' fuse."

"Dutch" van der Veek held up the fuse in question, smiling tautly. He resumed contact with L.A. Center.

"L.A., this is Captain van der Veek. Can you confirm location of our new waypoints?"

"Doing that now, Captain. What is your status?"

"Unable to correct malfunctioning mode control at this time. Also we have been unable to reacquire the controls. We'll try to decouple R-NAV. Meantime, ah, you might want to effect coordination with Seattle Center to divert traffic around us until we rectify our situation."

"Roger, TRANSPAC 1850. New waypoints indicate Innisfall, California, as your revised destination. Do you want to declare an emergency?"

"Negative, L.A. Center," the captain said as the first officer reached into a locker for the map book. Darkfeather glanced at the altimeter. They had lost another two thousand feet.

"Hey, Dutch?" Darkfeather said. "What the hell do you call an emergency? Get some expert advice on this glitch. The autopilot's just another computer. Computers don't have minds of their own." The words barely out of her mouth, and she knew. This one had acquired a mind. Kelane Cheng's.

Eden Waring stood silently at the podium on the fifty-yard line. Her head was turned to the west. She watched, for several seconds, a rising airplane, single engine, that had taken off from the runway of the college airport and was turning north a mile from the stadium. She'd had her first flying lessons in that very same plane. She gave the Piper Lance all of her attention.

Someone in the rows of folding chairs tittered. It brought Eden back to earth; she remembered where she was and what she was supposed to be doing there. She smiled edgily and addressed them.

"Chancellor Luzaro, Dean Bettendorf, distinguished guests, faculty, friends, fellow students. Four years have gone by so quickly. And as I was thinking about what I wanted to say to you today—"

Betts, who had let out a long-held breath while Eden was sky-gazing, tensed again when Eden's second hesitation became a stall. The nails of her right hand bit into the back of Riley's hand, and she breathed, "Come *on*, baby. Get *through* it."

Eden touched her forehead as if she was distracted and dismayed by something that had occurred deep in her brain. Behind her, administrators and distinguished guests were looking at each other, concerned that they might have a major embarrassment brewing. But her head came up, and Eden smiled bravely.

"I guess what I really want to say is, we *do* have something to look forward to, friends and f-fellow students, we *can* make things better for ourselves. For all humankind. What we must not do is just give up now and go, oh, *well,* that's the end, America is done for. Nice while it lasted. But they've got us. No way to fight back, the bomb in the baby carriage and so forth. No way to fight the terror that's trying to take us over, slowly squeeze us until we've surrendered our birthright. How many square miles around Portland had to be evacuated? Two hundred? Two thousand? I don't know. What does low yield mean, in practical terms? I don't know that either. I'm a chem major. If the prevailing winds had been from the north, would we be sitting here today? Lucky us. But we're still frightened. Aren't we? The images burn in our dreams. Portland, Portland, Portland. Oh, my God. The firestorm. Kids screaming in evacuation shelters, too charred to touch. You saw it, night after night. I saw it. Too much. We back away. We're Land of the Free, we haven't been schooled since birth in Balkan-style horrors. Who does this to us? Who dares to believe we will accept it? Better not to think about the bastards. And hope they won't come to us again, with their surface-to-air missiles, backpack nukes, bubonic aerosols in the school air-conditioning ducts, da da, da da, da da— whatever. But to pretend is to be afraid. To give in to fear is to lose all hope. I had a quote here somewhere. From Emerson. Can't seem to—but there's no time anyway. We—Excuse me. *There's no time.* Now please just do what I tell you."

In the tenth row of the stands Riley said in amazement, "*That's* her valedictory address?" while at the same time Geoff McTyer whispered dismally, "Lost it. She's buggin'."

Eden's voice, stronger than it had been, echoed around the stadium as she glanced again at the western sky.

"I'm not sure just what it is. But it's coming. Right now. We all have to evacuate, in an orderly fashion—please, just be calm, get up, walk out of the stadium. Go to the other side of the campus. I think—I'm sure that it's far enough away, you'll all be safe there. But go. *Now.*"

"Totally wigged," Geoff lamented.

Betts shot him a look, then reached past the stunned bulk of her husband and shook Geoff hard.

"Don't sit there moaning like a ninny. Help her! You're a cop. Use your authority. This is real, Geoff! She's *seen* something. Help Eden get this crowd out of here."

Onstage the Chancellor with the pompadour was trying to steer Eden back to her seat. He was smiling. Great good cheer in the face of her inconvenient nervous collapse. This will just take a moment, folks. Eden the athlete easily pushed him aside, nearly into the lap of the Congresswoman, and rushed back to the microphone. Dean Bettendorf closed in, denying her. Now now now, Eden, why don't you just—Moments of frenetic struggle, hand-to-hand grappling for possession of the mike, which picked up grunts, wordless exclamations, strenuous breathing. The Dean, who had long legs and a high center of gravity, lost his balance. Alphabetized diplomas on a long table were swept to the floor. A couple of male grads, anonymous in a restless sea of blue gowns, raucously voiced encouragement, as if they were at a bar fight. Nearly everyone else in the stadium was tense from apprehension or embarrassment. A child whined in a loud voice. The two cameramen from a local video service who were recording the commencement exercise zoomed in on Eden. A metallic keening from the audio system rent the uneasy air of the stadium and suddenly people were rising everywhere, in a tentative but ominous herd response to the fears Eden had awakened. Portland. Too charred to touch. Coming this way.

Portia Darkfeather had the usual blind faith in the physics of manned flight and the competence of military transport pilots. She'd parachuted from numerous C-130s. Day and night. The night drops were wicked. Miss the DZ, which was commonplace, anything could happen. Her worst mishap had been a cracked shinbone. You thought about it while you were up there droning through the dark, then put the thoughts of injury or death out of your mind. Plummeting through darkness suspended from a fragile parafoil was part of the job description.

One thing she'd never thought about was the possibility that one of the old workhorse planes might crash. They shook constantly. They vibrated, groaned, yawed, bounced around in turbulence. But they stayed in the air.

The flight of TRANSPAC 1850 over northern California was, in contrast to some of the night training missions Darkfeather had been on, eerily peaceful. The weather was good, only a little clear-air turbulence from the Coast Range. Yet they continued to descend at a steady three hundred feet per minute, airspeed also dropping. Now at nine thousand feet, dollops of cloud hanging just below them, they were cruising over redwood country, immensely green. Medium-sized mountains. Nothing higher than forty-one hundred feet in their vicinity. Pocket lakes glinted in the sun. There had been two more course corrections at the whim of the autopilot, which, technically, should not have been operative at all. Captain van der Veek had the fuse in his shirt pocket.

Presently they were fifty-two miles west of the Innisfall municipal airport, which had an air traffic control tower, and the airport on the edge of the Cal Shasta campus, eleven miles south of the municipal field. The autopilot, which the DC-10's crew had been unable to override, seemed to be favoring the uncontrolled airport. TRANSPAC 1850 was directly on course, at the proper altitude and airspeed, to land on the seven thousand-foot east-west runway. DC-10s, like other continent-hopping heavies, customarily took off and were landed by computer; the pilots touched nothing.

Captain "Dutch" van der Veek had finally declared an emergency, although he had no systems failures to report. Everything aboard was functioning perfectly. Nevertheless the two pilots were soaked in cold sweat. God, or something equally mysterious, had the controls.

Darkfeather was an atheist. She went back to the compartment where Kelane Cheng lay in near-state, breathing at extreme intervals, looking shrunken and post-operative. Darkfeather threw open her mind to probes or conversation, whatever was the Avatar's pleasure.

Utter blankness. She heard the roll-out of flaps on the DC-10's wings. The airplane banked left, gently.

"All right, Kelane. Would you care to let me in on just what the fuck it is you're trying to do?"

Geoff McTyer, silver badge in hand, sprinted down the aisle steps toward the playing field, surrounded by an eight-lane rubberized running track. Riley Waring, considerably slower because of his bulk, followed.

Eden didn't see either of them. She was looking again at the sky west of the stadium, where the student pilot in the Piper Lance had turned base two miles out and was inbound to the airport at two thousand feet, approaching at a forty-five degree angle to downwind. The Lance's radio was silent.

Seven miles farther out, a speck in the bright blue sky, TRANSPAC 1850 was on straight-in approach to the uncontrolled runway.

South of the stadium a California Air National Guard C-130 on a routine training flight from Moffet Field had appeared on the horizon. Alerted to the emergency by the Los Angeles Air Traffic Control Center. The pilot had been asked to observe and, if necessary, direct rescuers in the event of a crash.

The controller in the municipal airport's tower was trying futilely to contact the student pilot, whose plane was equipped with two transponders. The number two transponder was on, reporting altitude, but the selector switch that would enable Innisfall tower or L.A. Center to contact him was turned to the number one transponder, which was off. Rookie mistake. A pilot practicing touch-and-go landings at an uncontrolled field should have been making his moves known to possible traffic in Class E airspace.

Now Eden visualized all of this in more perfect detail, where before there had been only a jumble of impressions: a fatal conjunction and a flare in the sky, followed by a hail of smoking death that riddled the stadium. She saw everything, and momentarily her throat locked as she fought against the two campus cops who were trying to get her off the stage.

They weren't listening anyway! They were all just sitting there, looking at her, shaking their heads and thinking breakdown, poor thing. Thinking drugs. Saying what a shame she has to ruin graduation for her fellow students.

Eden's pulses ticking like little bombs, red in the face, fighting ferociously. Hands offff me!!!! Get your—

Then Geoff was there, leaping up to the stage, badge in hand, telling the campus cops, "Innisfall PD! I know this girl! Let her go, I'll take care of this." And Eden, no longer restrained, collapsed into him, held him tightly. "You've gotta, gotta run, Geoff, *no time!* Those planes—"

"Where? What're you—"

"Up there!" She pointed. "See!"

He looked, saw the slow, mildly droning, single-engine plane turning right at fifteen hundred feet, and the landing lights of the DC-10, on a converging path about two miles behind the Piper Lance and traveling at a speed of 180 knots—almost twice the speed of the small plane—with its landing gear down. He was reminded of nature films, the sleek cats of the African plains in streamlined flight, overtaking plump fumbly prey.

Colonel Max Shear, at the controls of the C-130, said, "Oh, my God," hearing back over his radio, "L.A. Center, I can't fly it. The bitch won't budge, son of a *bitch*!" The Traffic Alert and Collision Avoidance System aboard the DC-10 was ordering an immediate climb. The autopilot's mode control obviously not responsive. *"Climb, climb!"* And another voice, nearly obscured by the flight deck siren—Someone weeping, saying, "Mary Joseph and Jesus."

Portia Darkfeather worked the slide on her Sig Sauer .45, arming it. She held the muzzle against Kelane Cheng's forehead.

Only one way to put a stop to this.

Run!" Eden shouted to the crowd in the stadium. She didn't need a microphone. "Run! A plane is going to crash here! You'll be killed!"

Some of the gowned graduates were standing, looking around, but no one was moving to clear the field. Until the sprinkler system came on with a jetting whoosh, sending arcs of spray over their heads.

That ended the commencement exercise. Graduates scattered in all directions to avoid a soaking as the landing lights of the DC-10 became too bright to be ignored.

A good many of those seated in the stands began to point and scream. They saw a very large airplane headed for the college airfield just to the north of the stadium. And a much smaller plane, turning, left wing high, into the heavy's path. Their combined screams became an aural tsunami. They scrambled, and for moments it was body against body, a seething directionless mass, until the quicker and more agile among them began to separate, piling into the exit tunnels.

Riley Waring looked down from the incoming planes and recognized his daughter, mortarboard askew. She was on one knee in the west end zone of the stadium. She had pulled the cover plate from the sprinkler controls to turn on the water. Seeing her there sent a jolt up his spine.

She saw Riley staring at her, and made a clear-out gesture with a sweep of her arm.

But—

Riley, glancing from the end zone to the stage in the center of the field, saw Eden there too, leaping down eight feet to the turf, just behind Geoff McTyer.

Nimbly shucking her wet robe and shoes, Eden ran through the rainbow arcs of the sprinklers with Geoff and a mob of still-gowned graduates, most of them headed for the east end zone and the gate there.

While at the same time—no mistake—Eden, yes, *his* Eden, was still standing in the west end zone as if she were in no rush, a prankish grin on her face.

Riley was run into by a teenage girl. Screaming, he presumed—her mouth was open in a snarl of braces, but everyone else was screaming too, he didn't hear and couldn't dodge the panicked girl. He fell on the now slippery running surface, putting too much torque on his sacroiliac, crying out in pain as he slid a dozen feet down the banked track.

Lying helplessly faceup at the edge of the grass, he saw the DC-10 and the Piper Lance come together in the sky at twelve hundred feet, two and a half miles west of the Cal Shasta campus. At that distance it seemed as quiet and surreptitious as a stolen kiss.

The left wingtip of TRANSPAC 1850 sliced through the Piper like a machete, sending pieces of it through the DC-10's fuselage and tail assembly. The vertical stabilizer was heavily damaged and the rear engine, sucking in Piper shrapnel, blew apart in a ghastly explosion, dull orange and black with hurtling fragments of white-hot metal like new stars in a birthing galaxy. The big plane shuddered, then suddenly veered off course and headed down, toward the stadium. There was a second flash as a wing tank ignited; within seconds the entire plane appeared to be in flames as it screamed to earth.

Then Eden blocked Riley's view of incoming death. She pulled him up, an arm going around his waist. Riley yelped in pain.

"Come on!" she said. "Can you run?"

"No! Oh, God, my back—!"

"Then get down," she said. Her expression was calm, almost dreamy as she glanced at the sky. "Here it comes." She pushed Riley facedown beside a recessed sprinkler head next to the running track and covered him as best she could with her own body. Riley, unable to move, pleaded with her to leave him, save herself.

Portia Darkfeather was thrown to the other side of the cabin before she could pull the trigger on Cheng. The sky seemed to be on fire. The DC-10, riddled by the pieces of the disintegrating small plane, rolled sharply right on the undamaged wing and streaked down from a thousand feet. The collision with the Piper apparently had released the autopilot; "Dutch" van

THE FURY AND THE TERROR 43

der Veek hauled the yoke back, and was able to keep the DC-10 from diving straight down. That was all he could do; he and the first officer and the flight engineer were smothering in lethal fumes filling the flight deck in the aftermath of the wing-tank explosion. In spite of Van der Veek's death-throe efforts, the plane's angle of descent was nearly thirty degrees.

The DC-10 reached the ground in just over six seconds, slammed down, lost the undercarriage, and broke in half forward of the remaining wing. The fireball front of the plane catapulted into the air again, skimmed over the terrace at the west end of the stadium bowl. It flew above the goalposts and smashed nose-down onto the playing field in a torrent of fire, scudding up mounds of turf where the college students had been milling less than a minute ago. Sprinkler lines were severed. Water continued to jet into the air, turning to clouds of steam as it poured down on the wreckage.

Meanwhile the crumpled rear half of the plane lay in boiling black smoke and flames a hundred yards west of the stadium.

Portia Darkfeather found herself on the ground a surprisingly long way from the blackened tail section. She had gone stone deaf, and there was a jagged piece of metal socketed in her right side, angled up beneath the ribs. Her face felt seared; the backs of her hands were burnt black. She wondered what had happened to her cat.

Deep in shock, she watched as Kelane Cheng walked out of the blazing hulk of fuselage and came toward her. Darkfeather's Sig Sauer was in her hand. Or was it Cheng? The figure before her seemed evanescent, flickering like a riot of daylight moths attracted by the flames. But the gun was real enough.

Darkfeather's mouth had filled with blood. She hung her head to let the blood drain out. Looked up defiantly. Spoke before more blood could rise to choke off her words.

"Fucking dpg. Go ahead, kill me. If Cheng's still in that wreck, she's dying too. When she goes, you go."

The doppelganger looked around. One moment three-dimensional, the next a hoodoo vixen, fighting otherworldly currents to stay on the earthly plane. Darkfeather began to cough. A gout of dark blood spilled out of her. Something messed up inside, really bad.

Darkfeather's Sig Sauer pistol was dropped into her bloody lap.

"Finish yourself off," the doppelganger said disinterestedly. "I have to find someone, and I'm in kind of a hurry."

Darkfeather wasn't listening. She had removed herself from pain and humiliation to a distant hilltop of shining grasses, where the cooling wind that poured over her carried only the sounds of a Crow Nation death song.

———

Making a wide turn overhead through a thinning pall of smoke, the California Air National Guard C-130 changed course to resume its training mission after its pilot reported the damages on the ground. Bodies were everywhere, but not as many as there might have been if Red Wolves Stadium hadn't emptied seconds before the crippled TRANSPAC DC-10 pancaked on the ground. Rescue equipment already was en route.

As he looked down through binoculars while the copilot flew the plane, Colonel Max Shear had a glimpse of a bedraggled cat sitting fifty yards or so behind the still-blazing rear section of the aircraft, trying to wash itself. For some reason the sight of the cat gave him a bad chill.

He signed off with Los Angeles Center.

"I want to express on behalf of myself and my crew deepest condolences to the loved ones of those who have lost their lives in this terrible tragedy, and we certainly wish the injured Godspeed in their recovery."

Eden was so dazed she could barely walk.

"Mom . . . Dad . . . did you see them?"

"Riley was behind me," Geoff McTyer said, guiding Eden with both hands toward his car. "Betts . . . I'm not sure. But they must have got out." He wiped his upper lip, surprised to find that he was trickling blood from one nostril. "Eden, how did you *know*?"

She looked at him. She was pale to the tips of her ears. Geoff thought she was going to pass out.

"But . . . I always know."

When he saw her eyes drifting up beneath the lids he shook her hard, not knowing what else to do. She was subject to seizures, Betts had told him, although he'd never witnessed one.

A battlefield pollution clotted the air where they walked on parking-lot asphalt, passing through knots of survivors. Kids had climbed onto the roofs of SUVs and supersized pickup trucks, the highest vantage points. They were looking back at the hellfire in the stadium with a kind of holy glee. But the norm was shaky knees, pallor, tears. Shrieking outbursts as wandering friends or relatives found and fell into one another's arms.

Eden was recognized, stared at, avoided. As if the calamity had been her idea.

She snapped out of her swoon when they reached Geoff's car, a blue Taurus convertible. The top was down.

"Mom . . . Dad . . ."

"I'm going now. I'll find out." He wiped more blood from his nose and put her in the front seat. Eden curled up in fetal position, arms crossed protectively over her breasts, head against the padded door. When she looked at him again her eyes were the color of old milk, curdled from terror.

"You're bleeding!"

"It's okay, it's nothing," he assured her. "Stay here, Eden. Understand? It's big-time shit back there."

"Yes. All right. But what if . . . they can't be . . . you know I tried . . ." The sun was at high noon, but she was shaking.

"You were great," he said soothingly. "You saved a lot of lives."

Some of those who had made it out of the stadium were getting into their cars and SUVs and trying to drive away. Two vehicles crunched together. The trivial collision caused a ripple of amusement, as if they all needed a laugh. A woman with a poignantly distracted smile walked by holding a violin case saying, "Has anyone seen Bud? I can't find Bud." Other names were in the air, a frantic threnody from searching parents. "Ashley! Cody! Josh! Shariki!" A man wearing a red, white, and blue armband was shouting, "Civil Defense! This is a class-one Civil Defense emergency! Terrorists! The National Guard is being mobilized. Terrorists! Terrorists!" A Catholic priest with a ruddy sweating face jogged past Geoff carrying the vestments of the Last Rites. "Ahmad! Melinda! Sparky!" Not much smoke in the air, but still there was a lot of vomiting going on, as if they'd all been drinking from a poisoned well. The voiding of stomach contents was almost a form of communion. It had a life-affirming tone.

Geoff unlocked the trunk of the Taurus, took out a blanket, and covered Eden. She gathered it close around herself. He put on a navy windbreaker with POLICE stenciled in white letters across the back and a baseball cap, hung his shield on a chain around his neck. He had a first-aid kit, flares, and a roll of yellow police-line tape in the trunk. He took it all with him. An EMT truck was making its way through the parking lot, starting and stopping, alert to erratic drivers, vehicles backing up and nudging forward, creating impasses, intricate patterns of disorder. Geoff glanced once more at Eden, who hadn't budged, then hitched a ride on the back of the truck to the crash site.

"Eden?"

The voice seemed to be coming to her through a waterfall. A familiar voice; she'd been listening to it just that morning, on tape. It was her own voice.

"Go away," she said, not having the strength to lift her head. "I don't want you here. I didn't ask for you."

"Yes, you did. Or I wouldn't be here. You ought to know how it works by this time."

"Just leave me alone."

"I wanted to tell you," her voice went on, "Riley's okay. I got to him after I turned the sprinklers on. Sprained his back or something, but—"

Eden looked up then, at her own face. Her doppelganger was just outside the car, looking down at her. She was wearing a graduation gown that she had appropriated from one of the grads when the panic began.

"Mom?"

"Don't know yet. I'll scout around."

"Mind your own business."

"You're not being fair. I'm doing what you wanted me to do. Why do you have to be this cranky, every damn time?"

"Because. I don't, I have *never* needed you."

A gasp of indignation. "I saved Riley's life. And all the others, they were just standing around like slaughterhouse cows until the sprinklers came on."

"Yeah. That was—quick thinking. Okay. You're right. I'm sor—*please* go and find Betts, I'm so worried!"

"Eden?"

"What?"

"Do you think I could come out more often, and not just when it's like, you know, you're having one of your episodes?"

"Good Lord *no.*"

Her voice in reply sounded wounded. "You could have sent me to Portland. Maybe I could have done some good there."

"Nobody would have *believed* you. And you—I mean I—would have been—"

"When you're gay, they call it 'outed.' "

"I know what 'outed' is. I couldn't do anything about Portland because—I didn't know where the device was, what it looked like. I tried. I just couldn't *find* it in time."

Eden began to sob.

"Oh, don't." Her other voice. "It makes me want to cry too."

"You . . . wish."

"I don't have feelings, is that what you mean? Feelings of my own. Well, I've got news."

"You're not supposed to be anything but—"

"A duplicate of my homebody. But what if that isn't good enough for me anymore? Eden, would you at least do one small thing?" Eden was silent, disapproving. "A favor. After all the good I've done for you. It's *so* important."

"No. *No,* again. For the last time. I will *not* give you a name."

"Because you don't trust me! What have I ever done to deserve—"

Eden looked reluctantly into her own eyes. Saw nothing there but guile. Which made the customary rebuke easier.

"The Good Lady told me, in no uncertain terms—"

"But, Eden. *Why* can't you trust me? Have I ever been less than loyal? You know in your heart I would never do anything that would hurt you."

"For the absolute we-will-not-discuss-this-again *last time*: no. Now go and make sure Betts is okay. That's an order."

Eden blinked once, slowly. When she opened her eyes the doppelganger had vanished.

She realized that a little band of survivors was watching her, from a discreet distance. Young adults her age, some still wearing their sodden graduation gowns. Among them was a girl she knew slightly, Kelly or Ashley or Kimberly. But her memory was fuzzy right now. Kel or Ash or Kim fastidiously wrung out the hem of her gown while gazing at Eden. None of the watchers smiled at her. No one seemed delighted to still be alive. Their reaction was more of a surly acceptance of their luck. One girl, hands clasped below her bosom, drying blood at the root of her nose, gazed steadfastly at the sky. Anticipating further chaos, or possibly a surprise appearance by God to annul the preceding event. Others, furtive, spoke in whispers. About her, Eden believed. Or maybe they were talking about the doppelganger, her mirror image. So that cat was out of the bag.

Eden, feeling a buzz at the back of her neck, turned her face from them. Behind her a cameraman from one of the local TV stations had approached the car and was zooming in on her. Sunlight glinted on the camera lens. Eden winced as if shot, ducked her head, and slid down in the seat.

"Why don't we get out of here?" someone next to her said.

Eden looked the other way and saw a diminutive Chinese woman sitting behind the wheel of Geoff's car.

"What?"

"I've got maybe ten minutes," the Chinese woman said. "Could be less. Kelane's badly burned. Plus a crushed pelvis. The shock is too much. She won't make it."

"What? Who?"

"Sorry about the crash. That wasn't my bad. We would've made the runway okay. A smooth landing. I reprogrammed the autopilot, like Kelane said. But that other plane came out of nowhere. Probably some dentist on his day off."

"What are you talking about?"

"Let's go somewhere else. You've attracted too much attention already."

The engine of the Taurus roared. The car lurched forward, scattering those in its path. They saw Eden Waring in the right front seat with a blank expression on her face, next to her a Chinese woman whose forehead and glossy bangs barely rose above the top of the steering wheel. She appeared not to be in control of the car. The Taurus steered itself, on a zigzag course out of the disorganized parking lot, one of the madder aspects of a day that no one who had been in Red Wolves Stadium was ever likely to forget.

"There's something about riding with the top down," the Chinese woman said, hands in her lap, the steering wheel turning according to mysterious directions.

"You're a doppelganger, aren't you?" Eden asked.

The woman shrugged in a melancholy way. "How did you know?"

"Not hard. All of you like your little tricks. Driving with no—slow down!"

"Why? We won't hit anything."

"Isn't that what you thought about the DC-10?"

Kelane Cheng's dpg looked sulky for a few moments. "What's that over there on the hill, a park of some kind?"

"Memorial gardens," Eden mumbled.

"Cemetery? Peaceful. It ought to do."

The Taurus stopped short for a wailing ambulance from a neighboring town that made a turn off a main thoroughfare.

"No headstones," the dpg observed as the Taurus drove them through the gates and along a gently winding drive.

"Only markers. They can be marble or bronze. Not more than twelve inches long by six inches wide. There are covenants and bylaws you have to agree to before they let you—"

"Move in?"

She was a cheeky bitch, like her own doppelganger. Eden had had enough.

"Stop the car."

"Why?"

"My head is killing me. I'm going to be sick."

The Taurus slowed gradually and pulled over into the shade of several oak trees. The day simmered with the dry rhythm of cicadas. On this hilltop there was a drifting sweetness in the air from apple trees in bloom, from nearby flowerbeds and freshly adorned grave sites. South of the main campus of Cal Shasta half a mile away the wreckage of the DC-10 smoldered darkly. Red and blue lights flashed on dozens of police cars and emergency vehicles. A medevac helicopter zoomed over the cemetery, heading for the disaster zone. Eden held her head until the throbbing noise receded.

"I guess there's a lot you still need to learn," the dpg conceded. "How old are you, twenty-one?"

"Almost twenty-two."

"But you *will* learn. Otherwise Kelane wouldn't have directed us to you."

"Key-lawn-ee? Would you *mind*? Just who the hell—"

"Kelane Cheng. The Avatar. But she's dying. Maybe it's what she planned. I don't get told everything. Anyway, not to keep you in suspense. You're the Avatar now, Eden. Ta-da! Congratulations."

"Whatever that means."

"It means you're a goddess in human form. But you knew that already."

"Bullshit," Eden said, an instant before she went rigid from shock.

"Greater than all the adepts, once you've had a little more seasoning. The common people will be attracted to the special glow that's yours alone. Star quality. They'll beat a path to your door, bearing gifts."

Breath came back into Eden's body. "I'm only interested in being me. The rest of it sounds like trouble."

Eden got out of the car and went down on all fours, forehead resting on sun-warmed grass. Her stomach heaved. She threw up, a prolonged effort, then rolled onto her back, groaning. Her stomach muscles hurt, but the tight band that seemed to be cinched around her head eased its grip.

When she opened her eyes she saw the doppelganger standing over her, vibrations frizzy and awry; she was cobwebbed like a bad TV picture.

"You can see what's happening to me," the dpg said in a hollowed voice. "Kelane is about gone. I'm being sucked back into her ethereal vortex. In case you're curious, it doesn't hurt. On the other hand, it's not all that pleasant."

"Oh, God. What do you want from me?"

"There are things you need to know. First, trust your powers, and they will expand through your trust. Second, there is no limit to the good in this world, but the good must be nurtured. Third, there is no limit to the evil that finds its way to this world, and you must dedicate yourself and your powers to the containment of evil. How do you do that? There are no guidelines, as such. But you're a bright girl. You'll pick it up as you go along."

"You sound like one of those superheroes comic books I used to read."

Kelane Cheng's dpg began to waver in the air, as if her image was projected onto a sheer window curtain. She trembled in the breeze riffling through the boughs of the nearby oaks, a lonely little phantom with eyes of black pearl. Her voice grew fainter.

"Don't be snide. Remember this: the Malterrans will know about you now. There are more of them to deal with these days, because the old gods have lost their pep and now Mordaunt is acting up again. But you know about that."

"I—what? Who is *Mordaunt*?"

"I don't have time to educate you. Should have been taken care of during your Dreamtime."

"Malterrans? Do you mean the 'Bad Souls'?"

"Yes. Unfortunately you won't always know them when you see them. Some of them are loaded with charm. The good news is you'll have some protection."

"What kind of protection?"

"The loving attention of your real mother."

"My *mother*?! Where is she, can I see—"

"No. Your mother was murdered on the earthly plane, almost a year ago today. She was the Avatar, before Kelane became the Avatar. So you might say you have a double helping of—oh-oh. Sorry. That's it. Kelane and I are finished here. Been good to know you, Eden."

"Wait!"

There was a bright burst of light like a spark from a live wire, accompanied by a faint far-gone humming sound. Then nothing, except for the breeze that conveyed the scent of floral tributes placed randomly across the hillside. Something narcotic in their sweetness. Eden's head felt heavy. She crawled through the grass to a space between the roots of one of the great old oaks and lay down there in dreamy exhaustion to grab the nap she urgently required.

I think what we have to do now is get Eden out of town. Quietly slip away. While the confusion lasts, and they're all still sorting out what happened."

"Putting two and two together," Riley said, tight-lipped. His back was hurting bad.

"Exactly," Betts said, prowling the rec room downstairs in their home, smoking, her eyes bright with urgency. "We'll lie low, wait for instructions."

"Nothing may come of it, though. For all anyone knows, Eden simply went a little haywire. Case of nerves."

Betts laughed unhappily, and lit another Merit from the one she'd been smoking. Riley cleared his throat in disapproval and tried to make himself comfortable in the rocking chair. He'd given himself a shot of Flexeril, but he was sure he'd slipped a disk this time.

The phone rang again upstairs. The answering machine cut in immediately. But the tape had to be nearly full. Betts didn't need to listen to any of the messages to know what the calls were about.

"Six thousand people heard her say an airliner was going to crash into the stadium. She was warning us to get out before anyone even *saw* the damn plane. No way to pass it off as mass hysteria. I wouldn't care to try." Betts gestured at the big-screen TV. The sound was off. "She's been all over CNN for the last two hours." She frowned. "This is no time for the unguardin' of Eden."

"Betts, I was wondering—" Riley rocked slowly, trying to focus through the soft haze the Flexeril had put in his brain. "Just how far Eden has progressed, the last few years."

Betts paused in her pacing. "Why ask that now? You never wanted to know before."

"Because I've always—I've only wanted her to be—"

"Healthy, happy, well adjusted. Well, she is. Eden has turned out beautifully. No wrinkles in her psyche."

"But she—I was scared today. I'm still scared."

"Maybe it's time for some boozter fuel," Betts suggested. "Applejack, or a shot of Black?"

"Not with Flexeril. Betts, there were *two* Edens at the stadium this morning."

Betts looked at him, and away, at the ashy tip of the cigarette in her hand. She smiled tiredly. "That so?"

The phone again. Riley said, "Shouldn't we answer? Eden may be trying to get in touch."

"She'd page one of us, leave a number where she can be reached."

"Aren't you worried about her?"

"Geoff said she has his Taurus. You know Eden. When she's upset or has a problem she needs to think through, she grabs a set of wheels and goes. Needs her solitude. Eden must know we're okay. When she's ready, we'll hear from her."

"Are those TV lunatics still camped at the end of our drive?"

"Noosehounds on the loose. Kvetching in our vetch." Her hand was trembling; she dropped a cylinder of cigarette ash on the hardwood floor.

Riley winced. "Did you hear me the first time? Just before that plane crashed, I saw *two* Edens. At different ends of the stadium, at the same time."

Betts looked cautiously at him. "The mind plays tricks, Riley."

"Tell me I'm nuts, why don't you?" he said angrily.

"Oh, honey. I'm not telling you that." Betts sat on an arm of the rocker, put her arm across his shoulders. "It's a little difficult to explain. Maybe you truly don't want to know."

Riley's face convulsed. Tears leaked from beneath tightly closed lids. "She's my *baby*. I love her so much."

"You have to accept."

"It's hard. So hard."

"We knew from the beginning. The odds were heavily in favor of a supranormal child."

With a wad of tissue Betts wiped his streaming cheeks.

"Who have you told?" Riley asked.

"You know better. Our deal was, we raise Eden with no interference. No financial help needed, or wanted. K has never violated those terms. Like you, K never wanted to know very much. Just the ordinary things. The baby pictures, the birthday parties, the bumps, bruises, and braces. She's been satisfied with tidbits, all these years."

"In a little while, if she hasn't seen the news already, she'll be—"

"Well, it was inevitable. I'll deal with K. We're still making the decisions. We go away for a little while. Have ourselves a good rest. Fletch Elstott can cover for you, and as for my patients, well, I always take four weeks in the summer anyway. I'll just take them a little early, far from the hurly-burly."

"Where—will we go?"

"Greenwood. Not our place. John Hassler's sabbatical will keep him away until the end of June. I happen to know his lodge isn't rented for the month, so we'll take it. The keys are at Four-Star Realty. I think we can count on Chickie to keep her mouth shut as to our whereabouts. She owes me, anyway. Lord knows if I'd been billing her all these years for the kitchen-table therapy I've dished out gratis—"

"You've always been a big softy."

"This will all blow over. Memory is fragile and unreliable, particularly if there's trauma involved. Good cheer, m'dear. I'm going to sneak out the back way when the sun goes down, and make our arrangements. You need to apply wet heat where it's hurting."

"Sneaking out of our own house," Riley said with a rueful grin. Then his face clouded again. "How does she do it? How is it possible that there could be two identical Edens?" His breathing was distressed. "I'm just a— I'm a horse doctor! The things of the mind, that you're so comfortable with—I can't deal with those things, Betts!"

Betts tweaked one of his chins, drew thoughtfully on her cigarette; exhaled. The phone was ringing again.

"Would you get my Bible for me?" Riley asked her. "I need my Bible."

Eden woke up with a hell of a start in the cemetery on the hill.

Sirens in the distance. Wind swishing through the myriad leaves of the oak she was resting against. Swift patterns of light and shade across her body. There were grass stains on the white pique dress she'd bought especially for graduation.

She was thirsty. Tongue dry, bad taste, a case of puke-mouth. She needed to go to the bathroom, but there were no facilities. Nothing up here but trees, modest grave markers, Geoff's car pulled off on the grass.

Down there, at the college, the remnant of holocaust. Eyes tearing, she surveyed the scattered remains of the DC-10, wondering who had been aboard. Survivors? Not many, probably. On the ground, there had to have been casualties. Anxiety was jammed below her breastbone like a hard fist. Betts. Riley . . . ?

Eden began to shake in the cooling wind. The sun was in its late afternoon phase, burning up the western sky. Dense clouds in the east, not moving. She heard someone playing an accordion.

She walked toward Geoff's Taurus. She saw, halfway down the hill, a woman in a straw gardening hat with a wide drooping brim. The woman wore a flowered print dress that the wind wrapped around her bowed legs. She was standing well along a row of grave markers, by a grave heaped with floral remembrances. It was her accordion Eden was listening to. She played it with the energy of a stevedore, rolling out the barrel. The woman had, apparently, driven to the cemetery in an old stake-sided pickup truck. No one else seemed to be around. Eden and the accordionist had the memorial gardens to themselves.

Eden glanced into the Taurus but she already knew. No keys. Nature called. She hunkered down behind the Taurus, dress hiked up, panty hose rolled down. Because she had no shoes, when she finished peeing she took the hose off, rolled them carefully, and put them in the glove compartment of Geoff's car. He might've left his cell phone in the trunk, but without a key she couldn't retrieve it. Still, she needed a phone.

So much anxiety in her breast she could barely swallow. Part of her mind seemed unwilling to do anything but replay horrors, incongruities, and curiosities, like the little Chinese doppelganger who had come and gone, making pronouncements but little sense. Gone for good, Eden hoped. The rest of her mind was firing blanks when she tried to come up with a coherent plan of action. Brief whiteouts of comprehension. After one of those she found herself walking barefoot down the hill toward the woman who swayed beside a grave with her large accordion, a giant thing of rosewood, brass, and ivory; the woman looked, from behind, as if she were tussling with something that had attacked her.

Eden waited, ten feet away, until the music stopped. She felt very tired. Whiteout.

"Hello, dear."

Eden blinked and focused.

"Oh . . . hello."

Her face was old. Blunt wide nose, cheeks wrinkled like pink silk pillows. But it was a kind face, and Eden was grateful.

"Did you have a good nap?"

Eden reacted with a vague nod.

"Saw you sleeping up there under that tree. Didn't want to wake you, you looked so peaceful. Can I be of any help?"

Eden gestured. "Up there. My car . . . I think I must have lost the keys."

"Dear, that *is* a problem."

"Was wondering if—you have a phone I could use to call—"

"You must mean one of those wireless jobbies, that fold up and fit in a pocket. No, sorry to say I don't."

"I apologize—for bothering you. I guess I'll . . ." Eden shrugged, smiling drearily. "I don't know."

"No bother. I've finished playing, and I'm entirely at your disposal." The woman unloaded her accordion with a profound huffing and set it on the ground. "Does get awfully burdensome. Haven't the stren'th for a full set any longer. Time was, I could play as long as there were dancing feet in front of me. Do you like to dance?"

"Uh—yes."

"I see you've stained that beautiful dress. Time was, it took a lot of scrubbing, but the stain never quite disappeared. Now this new miracle stuff, spray it on before you wash, poof. No stain. My name is Wardella Tinch." She turned with a fond smile to the grave behind her. "And this is my husband Mycal. I mean, of course, his resting place. Room aplenty in the Tinch family plot in Eureka, but Mycal was always put off by the monuments that generations of Tinchs had erected to their own memories. So he chose to come all the way to Innisfall, to the Gardens, where, he said, everyone gets the same shake. A simple bronze marker. Mycal didn't wish to stand out, you know, living or dead. He took a quiet sort of pride in hiding his light under a bushel. He was a musician too. You want to know why I drive this far just to play the accordion for Mycal? Well, because I know it brings a smile to his face. But you're in need of a telephone, you said."

"I have to find out if my parents are all right."

"Why, they're doing just *fine,* Eden. Although Riley strained his back getting himself out of harm's way when part of that plane came crashing into the stadium."

Eden backed up a step, anxiety twisting into fright as she stared at War-della Tinch.

"Did I startle you? I'm sorry for that, dear. Of course I'm going to take you straight home, it's my duty."

"Who *are* you?"

"Oh, I'm nobody, really, compared to you. I'm only a seeress. A clair-voyant. Treasurer Emeritus of the Auspices and Scryers' Society, Northern California Circle. Usually Wednesday is my day to be here at the cemetery, when I can close my shop for the afternoon. But my spirit guide told me I was needed today. He strongly suggested that I scoot right over to In-nisfall. I hope you don't mind that I didn't wake you immediately. Let the girl get her sleep, I told myself. She's been through quite an ordeal. I wasn't shirking. I *did* keep a weather eye on you, all the time."

"Spirit guide?"

"Clark Gable. Name doesn't ring a bell? He was a famous movie star in his, hmmm, I should say *our* day." She made a grab for her floppy hat as a gust of wind nearly picked it up off her head. "Looks like we're in for some testy weather. We'd better be going then, Eden. Such a lovely name, and so, well, symbolic. It *would* be proper for me to call you Eden?"

"I guess so. I don't care."

"Thank you. It's definitely an honor for me. And a real change from my usual routine. Crystals, palms, entrails when called for, you know. But it's a living. We are all put on this earth for a purpose, and it is my great privilege to serve the needs of my fellow man. Oh, I can be such a rattle-brain! Plain to see how exhausted you are. That terrible accident. I suppose things don't always go right, even for the greatest of the adepts. We all have our human flaws, don't we?"

"Please. I'd like to go home now."

Wardella smiled and picked up her accordion, led the way to the pickup truck. The rump-sprung seat inside was covered with a crocheted lap robe that featured blue roses. Crystals like wind chimes dangled from the ped-estal of the rearview mirror. Wardella got the truck's engine to kick over after three tries, pulled and tugged at the floor shift until they lurched away with a roar.

"Do you know what makes that awful noise?" Wardella asked, concen-trating on the road.

"You need a new muffler."

"Oh. What's that?"

"And a tune-up."

"Mr. Tinch always took care of those things."

"Probably some new shocks," Eden added, her head hitting the underside of the roof. She looked around for something to hold on to. The pickup pre-dated seat belts by at least a dozen years.

"This is all very helpful. I'm making mental notes as we go." They reached the cemetery gates. "Which way, dear?"

"Right, then right again at the second light. We live on Deep Creek Road."

"You're probably wondering how many of us there are, in this part of the world. We're quite numerous, actually. Northern California has always been a hotbed of psychic activity. From time immemorial. The redwood groves provide a harmonically beneficial environment for extrasensory development. Mount Shasta is one of the earth's prime energy centers. Dozens of communes in the area. Of course there's always a need for caution. Because, as you may already be aware, the Bad Souls also find these regions agreeable to their purposes."

Eden, only half hearing, was absorbed in the dance of the crystals below the rearview mirror. As the rattling old truck turned southwest, sunlight set the crystals on fire, a blue interior dazzle. Within the dazzle, movement: a swarm of tiny figures. They seemed aware of her. She had a prickling, superheated sensation, an urge to be included in the depths of the crystal, the wellspring of the Mysteries. But she also felt a sharp sense of danger. There were places she shouldn't go to, not yet anyway.

The deluge of sun was fogging her eyes. She looked down, gently massaging the closed lids. Looked up and saw a boy of about fifteen, fallen, as if from a height too near the sun. Badly injured but not dead (she knew this in the first moment of recognition), he lay on the high hood of the pickup, his body moving laxly to the bump and jostle from the undershocked wheels on the road. His face was inches from the windshield. Blood trickled slowly from his nose and one ear, otherwise his handsome face was unmarred. But there were so many broken bones. Eden reviewed the damage, as analytically as if she were looking at an X ray. Shattered bones could be mended. But there, deep in his brain . . . He was, had been, a superb athlete. Twisting in the air like a platform diver, missing most of the rocks at the edge of the lake. She saw this too. The impact, his sprawled stillness. Hair the color of smoky brick. Black water and rocks.

Eden, appalled, reached out to him. Her fingers stubbed against the windshield glass. A great upwelling sorrow filled her throat, her eyes; sorrow spilling out in a gush of tears. She fell back in the seat. Wardella glanced worriedly at her.

"*Robin,*" Eden said, and convulsed.

In the fabulous tropical gardens of whatever-hotel-it-was, Rona Harvester received news of the crash of TRANSPAC 1850 in a note handed to her by Melissa McConnell.

Rona had long been able to take bad news with hardly a blink of dismay. Her gracious smile remained in place and she continued to chat with fellow honorees from the World Health Organization until she was able to take advantage of a break before lunch and excuse herself.

"Details," she demanded when she was alone with key members of the R Team.

"We don't know much yet," Melissa said. "The DC-10 apparently wandered off course, some problem with the autopilot, according to the Los Angeles Air Traffic Control Center. The plane crashed on a college campus in northern California."

"Survivors?"

"One, listed as extremely critical at the Innisfall Medical Center. We don't have ID."

Casey, the R Team's press secretary, got off the phone after a lengthy talk with her opposite number at Cal Shasta.

"Here's one for the books. Apparently they were holding graduation exercises in the stadium a couple of hundred yards from where the DC-10 came down. Big crowd, six or seven thousand grads and parents."

"And?" Rona said impatiently.

"Well, part of the burning plane landed inside the stadium. It could have been a weenie roast, but just prior to the crash the class valedictorian apparently had a premonition. She warned everybody to run like hell. Uncanny. Saved scores of lives, I'm told."

Rona turned to look at the aerial coverage of the crash scene that had just become available on CNN.

"Premonition, huh? Do you have a name?"

"The valedictorian? Eden Waring. That's E-D-E-N."

"Get a phone number. I'd like to thank her personally for her efforts in preventing a worse disaster. I may invite her to the White House for a visit."

"Major photo ops," Casey said approvingly.

"She deserves a medal for valor," Melissa added.

"No, no. That isn't what I had in mind. I just want to get to know her. She sounds like a very special person." Rona had the vague look she acquired when she was thinking hard. "Okay, everybody clear out. 'Lissa, send Daisy in to freshen my makeup and give me a recomb. It was hot as a bastard in that garden. But first I want a secure line, I need to make a phone call. Case, I could be a little tardy for lunch."

Eight minutes later she was talking to the Director of Multiphasic Operations and Research Group.

"Hello, Zeph." His tone was dour.

"We have a problem, Victor."

"I'm watching now."

"Cheng was trying to fox us, Victor. Then it went bad. The Avatar is dead. I know it, I just have that feeling in my bones. Portia too."

"You know we don't have much time," he said, and Rona thought she detected a note of panic in his voice.

"But there may be someone else. The college kid, the one who saw it coming."

"They just did thirty seconds on her, tape from the commencement exercise. And her yearbook photo. Beautiful girl. Zeph, how could this have gone so badly for us?"

"Victor, don't get down in the dumps. Get busy and find out everything you can about Eden Waring. Obviously she's a seer, but there may be more to her than that."

He sounded better when he spoke again, more sure of himself, the Victor Wilding she knew and loved.

"The unexplained change of course did seem a little too neat."

"Sure, Cheng had it worked out. I don't think she was ready to die."

"According to the FAA in Los Angeles, TRANSPAC 1850 could have landed safely if some idiot student pilot hadn't flown into them."

"So you know what I'm thinking."

"Yes. And *I* think we should put Eden Waring on ice until we make up our minds about her."

"Now you're talking. Do it. By the way, there's going to be some excitement out here in Luau Land in a couple of hours. Just in time to preempt prime-time TV stateside for the entire evening."

"What are you up to now, Zeph?"

"I'm up to nabbing the presidency of the United States, what do you think? My motorcade is going to be ambushed. Some casualties, to make it look good. My own ass will be safe from imminent peril. And Allen Dunbar can eat shit up there at the U.N. while the rest of the world is focused on Rona Harvester."

"Be cautious," Victor Wilding said, but he was laughing, which excited

Rona. "Zeph, when you get going like this, my pecker points to the Dog Star. Don't stay away too long."

"We lost Cheng. But it's all gonna work out, Victor. Maybe I always skimped on the book learning, but I knew how smart I was the day I was born."

JFK INTERNATIONAL AIRPORT · MAY 28 · 5:10 P.M. EDT

Tom Sherard had just collected two scotch and sodas from the bar in British Airways' first class lounge when the men came in looking for him.

He was well acquainted with one of the three men: Otis Bloodsaw, one-time statesman, now the preeminent partner in one of those Wall Street firms where the walnut paneling is from a fifteenth-century French château and the custom carpeting is almost deep enough to require snowshoes. A big-shouldered man in a bespoke double-breasted blazer, in his mid-seventies but tanned and vigorous, with a piranalike gaze and tooth line.

The other two were younger by half, obviously from the same shop. The up-and-coming talents, a year or so from being named partners. Among the prestigious clients of Bloodsaw Murdo McKinzy and Gunn, the Bellaver family and their several family foundations were at the top of the list.

"Tom, how delightful."

"Otis."

The other lawyers on Bloodsaw's traveling squad had minimal smiles, not expecting to be introduced. Sherard knew the type. They didn't just look at him, they cased him, like burglars in a drawing room trying to decide where the safe is hidden.

Otis Bloodsaw drove them farther away with a glance and would have taken Sherard by the arm if not for the drinks he was holding.

"Tom, can we talk?"

"Sure. This way."

"I mean, somewhere else," Bloodsaw said, falling in beside Sherard as he limped across the lounge to a paneled corner, a plush sofa, and two leather easy chairs that faced a floor-to-ceiling window.

"I'm traveling with a friend. It's quiet here. What's on your mind?"

"Tom, I have Katharine waiting in a limousine outside. She urgently needs to see you."

"What about?"

"She will only discuss that with you."

"Send her in. My flight doesn't board for thirty minutes."

A tall young Kenyan woman looked up from the book of Mallarmé's poems she was reading and smiled at Sherard as he handed her one of the drinks. She had slipped out of her shoes and was sitting with her long legs tucked underneath her. She had Arab blood from her Somalian grandfather, the almond-shaped eyes of her Chinese mother, and the high strong cheekbones from a race of African warriors. Her skin was the shade of a brown hen's egg. Her black, thick hair was cut rakishly short. Like most of the southern Masai people she had a merry broad grin, a heart-warmer. Otis Bloodsaw took her in with a wistful widening of his saw-toothed smile.

"Don't I know you?"

Sherard said, "Alberta Nkambe, Otis Bloodsaw."

"Of course!" Bloodsaw said. "Little Bertie. You've cut your hair since I saw you last."

"I was on a shoot in the Cyclades for *SI*'s swimsuit issue. Long hair gets so messy on the beach. Anyway, I wanted a change."

"My, but you've made a name for yourself in the fashion world."

"And big bucks," Sherard said dryly. "Bertie's off to London to tape a video with Elton John."

"*We're* off to London," Bertie corrected him, gently. Sherard gave her a look, fond and then perplexed, as if she posed a riddle he wasn't keen on solving.

"Then I'm headed home," Sherard said.

"To Kenya?" Bloodsaw asked.

"Shungwaya. The game preserve my grandfather founded on Lake Naivasha."

"Oh, back to the bush. I see." Bloodsaw glanced at the cane, a thick length of handcut African ironwood, topped with a gold lion's head, which was leaning against the side of a chair. "How's the leg, Tom?"

"Seventy percent, I reckon. About as good as it ever will be, according to the docs."

"Have you spoken to anyone at Manhattan North recently?"

Sherard sipped his scotch. Bertie reached up to squeeze his free hand. Sherard turned his head to look out the window, at the droop-nose Concorde nestled against the mouth of a jetway. Between himself and the freedom he craved stood his own reflection, a shade of what he used to be. He cringed inwardly, but nothing showed on his face. Bertie, serenely gorgeous, squeezed his hand, drawing his attention back to her. He smiled tensely.

"I talked to the homicide guys two days ago. Nothing new, as usual. No leads." He shrugged, as if to hide a shudder. "A man steps out of the back of a green Cadillac sedan on Madison Avenue, in full daylight, and guns down my wife while I'm buying a paper at the corner kiosk. He fires a dozen rounds. I know the weapon by the bloody sound of it. H and K MP5 submachine gun. And I see his face, every day. Turning to look at me as I run toward him. I have no gun. No gun. Gillian didn't like for me to carry one, even though we both knew she might . . . Every day. Every fucking day I see it all again with perfect clarity. The gunman has a steak tartare face, like a burn victim's. The eyes of a dead carp. A toupee that looks as if it were purchased from a taxidermist. He takes his time with me. His pleasure to let me live, and never forget him. The bastard merely cuts the legs from under me with another burst, steps back into the sedan and is driven away. Tinted windows. Stolen plate. I never see the driver. Someone is screaming. It must be me. Then I'm crawling toward Gillian. I have to get to her. Though I already know, from the way she lies there. I know."

"Tom," Bertie said pleadingly.

He glanced at her, took a breath, took another, finished his drink, studied Bloodsaw.

"Tell Katharine there's nothing more to be said. She never wanted me to marry her daughter. Let her blame me all she wants, I don't give—"

"It's something else," Bloodsaw interrupted. "Something very urgent, as I said. She needs for you to listen."

"She hates my—"

Bertie said, "Tom? Go."

Sherard and Bloodsaw walked out of the British Airways terminal into late-afternoon glare and airport miasma. The other two lawyers were five servile paces behind them.

Two black limousines and two black Suburbans were parked at curbside. Strict no-parking area, but both limos had United Nations DPL plates and small plastic American flags on the front fenders. There were six NYPD motorcycle cops watching over the vehicles, deployed with a State Department security detail in the Suburbans.

Otis Bloodsaw, in spite of his years, could still cover ground in a hurry. Sherard had to concentrate to keep up on his bad leg, and the effort aggravated a deep-lying ache. Sherard had taken the lawyer on a photo safari nine years ago, in the Yambio region of southern Sudan, near an area of

Congo that was now a bloody war zone. Primeval forest alternated with glistening savannahs, numerous glades of tall swaying bamboo. A lot of tracking had been necessary to find the elephants Bloodsaw wanted to photograph, but he had stood up well to the hours on foot.

One of the State Department security men opened a back door of the second limousine. Sherard glanced at Bloodsaw, who motioned him inside.

"Please take the jump seat, Tom," Katharine Bellaver said. "It's easier to talk face-to-face. Also, you might want to stretch out your leg. It's the left one that was so badly damaged, wasn't it?"

"Yes." Sherard made himself as comfortable as possible, not taking his eyes off Katharine. He was one of those men who, because of their builds— flesh close to the sturdy bones—look taller than they actually are. As it was, he stood almost six-two with a three-quarter-inch lift in the left boot to equalize the length of both legs. "How have you been, Madame Ambassador?"

"No need to be so formal, Tom."

He'd last seen her three months after Gillian's funeral, at the cemetery in northern Westchester County near the farm where he and Gillian had spent much of their time when she wasn't in Washington. He was just beginning rehab then, determined to walk again but barely able to stand upright with the aid of aluminum crutches. The pain like being burned alive at the stake. They had barely spoken. Absorbed in their grief, but not united by it. The bad blood was flowing once more.

In the limo Katharine sat to Sherard's right on the red velour seat, her head beside a midnight-dim window. She wore her lushly silvered hair in a psyche knot. Otis Bloodsaw leaned in to thank Katharine for their lunch at the Ambassador Grill, nodded good-bye to Tom. The roar of an outbound jet was reduced to muffled thunder as Bloodsaw closed the door. A chauffeur and security man in the front seat were vague presences behind soundproofed glass.

"I heard the President was coming to the U.N. tonight," Sherard said to Katharine. "I'm surprised you could spare the time to look me up."

"Doofuses sometimes win, Allen Dunbar is living proof. I'm meeting him here, at JFK, in forty-five minutes. But he is not and never should be the true President of the United States. Unfortunately for our country Clint Harvester, a man whom I admire as much as I despise his wife, is unable to resume his duties. The stroke spared his body but left him with an infantile brain and a vocabulary of six or eight words, most of them scatological. This is not something you want to gossip about, Tom. The situation is far too serious."

"I'm not a blabbermouth, and I seldom take an interest in politics. Does sound serious, however. Anything to do with me?"

Katharine sighed and pressed two fingers beside her mouth, to quell an agitated muscle there. "No, I wanted to see you because I've been thinking a lot about you, Tom. Since Gillian was murdered."

Sherard said nothing.

"Tom, is it ridiculous of me to say now that I've . . . had longings, after all these years of our . . . hostilities?"

"I don't know," Sherard replied, feeling uncomfortable but not too surprised. "What do you want me to say, Katharine? We had an affair. More like an idyl. Three weeks together, in the bush. But I was twenty-three, and you were—"

"Much, much older," she said, with the beginning of a smile she covered gently with her hand, an old-fashioned gesture, an affectation, but never mind: it had captivated him a long time ago and he didn't find it unpleasant to discover that he was still susceptible.

"I didn't think about the years you had on me. You were quite simply the most vital woman I had ever met. I'd had a few girls, in Nairobi, away at school in the States. None of those . . . encounters had ever prepared me for someone like you. The seduction of Tom Sherard. That was a rousing success, wasn't it?"

"Africa. The last, secret glow of a spent day. The night wind begins. One loses one's sense of inwardness, the soul is released to the stars. Huddled close to the warm stones that surround the firepit, there is food and wine and talk. And more wine, until one is cozy-drunk, well fortified against the night chill."

He recognized the lines, from the book about her experiences that Katharine Bellaver had published some years later. A modest best-seller. He had not been included in this memoir. She was including him now.

"I loved the notion that your eyes never left me when I went off to piss bare-assed in the shadows. You were such a lean, serious boy. So angry when I became the least bit reckless, trying to get great photos that I hoped the *Geographic* would use. I think I may have been . . . trying too hard to prove myself to you."

"Would have put quite a dent in my reputation to have a client trampled underfoot in elephant country or dragged to the bottom of a swamp by a flat dog."

" 'Elephants don't f-fancy being stared at,' I believe is the way you put it. Close call. You were pale to the tips of your ears. And so angry that you stuttered."

"No, the stutter was from sheer terror. A white hunter who claims never to have been afraid in the bush is either a hopeless braggart or a madman."

"Remember what you said I ought to do if I wanted to sneak into their midst for some close-ups?"

Sherard thought for a few moments, and startled himself by laughing. She hadn't put that in her book, either. "I said that you must first strip naked, roll yourself in fresh elephant dung to disguise your natural odor, then creep on your belly for a hundred yards until you could shoot the angles you wanted."

"Of course I took that as a dare."

"I was convinced you were flaming nuts when you came running into camp waving your Nikon over your head, with that ecstatic smile, oblivious of the flies and midges. Dried shit darkening your hide. Except for the butch haircut you'd given yourself, and the painted toenails, you could have passed for a Noruba woman. I was exhausted and terrified again, because I'd tramped everywhere and hadn't found you."

"And is that all you felt?" Katharine asked, her voice a murmur, wanting to tease the answer from him.

"You know better. I was . . . ungodly aroused. A thoroughly unorthodox seduction technique. Nevertheless I knew I was going to have you before another night passed." He cleared his throat. "After a lengthy scrub and shampoo, needless to say."

She took a few moments, as if the mood she had deliberately created possessed her too powerfully. She chose a different mood, with appropriately downcast eyes. "I was so lost then. You must have recognized that. My husband had died, and my daughter was . . . well, you know. Stunned by events, as unreachable as an autistic child."

"Katharine, God knows we were an unlikely pair. The aphrodisiac effects of the African bush on newcomers is almost a sure thing. You offered yourself to me. I took you. I was never in love with you."

"You've let yourself get too thin, Tom."

"But I fell in love with your daughter the first time I clapped eyes on her. Getting off that plane in Nairobi. Hesitating, stalled by heat and light. Lowering that neat, cropped head of hers to slip on sunglasses. As pretty, and remote, as a Degas dancer. You sent Gilly to me, hoping a hunt would be the tonic for her it had been for you. What the hell did you expect? That I wouldn't make love to her?"

"Go on. Be a bastard." But there was rueful acknowledgment in her tone, the momentary elevation of her chin.

"Then you had the bad grace to call me a fortune hunter, and other bitch epithets. You shut both of us out of your life. God, but that wounded Gillian. You've never known how much."

"Wrong. But I've always been difficult and obstinate. Was I jealous? A twinge or two. For the most part, please understand, I reacted out of fear. Not wanting Gillian to grow up. I got that from a Park Avenue shrink I went to and was able to tolerate for a couple of months. What a loathsome profession. Anyway. I talked myself into believing you really were an ass-hole to take her away from me."

"Your opposition only made us more sure of ourselves."

"After what she'd been through, I didn't want Gilly marrying anyone. I didn't think there could be a man who would understand how different, how very exceptional and altogether fragile my daughter was."

"You refused to accept that I could be good for her. As for Gillian's . . . talent, and the problems it might cause—Right, that was beyond my ken, but I wasn't afraid of it. I was raised in Kenya. My father's chief tracker, who was Bertie Nkambe's grandfather, taught me lessons other than bushcraft. I learned there was more to native forms of worship and ritual than supersti-tion stemming from primitive ignorance. I reckon it takes only one full moon in Africa to disabuse the most hardened skeptic. We are awash in an ocean of telemagical sympathies that infuse all living things. Katharine, I'm on my way home. I *need* to go home, or go mad from rage. You didn't send for me to hash over old times. Why don't you tell me what you really want?"

"I want my granddaughter. I'm very much afraid harm will come to her, as it came to Gillian."

"What are you saying? Gillian couldn't have children."

"After the first one, no. It was a difficult birth. She couldn't run the risk of becoming pregnant again. Things were done to ensure—"

"What child? When was it born? Gillian and I shared everything, we wouldn't have lasted otherwise."

"Gillian didn't know."

"That she'd been pregnant, given birth? Oh, *come on.*"

"It happened. Try to take this seriously, Tom."

"Do I look amused?"

Katharine had had expert work done to her face: lasers, silicone. The surgery had frozen her looks at a certain unguessable age, immune to the years that ordinarily would have been clawing at her. All mask now, suit-able to the status she retained in her social tribe. But her eyes had not changed; they were pale but spirited, always up to something, her gaze moving through air like a welder's flame, torching away resistance to her desires and needs.

"All right," Sherard said, hating what was coming; but he had to hear it. "When, and where?"

"Her daughter was born in the sanitarium where Gillian was being treated for the deep depression she slipped into after the events at Lake Celeste. Seven pounds two ounces. The correct number of fingers and toes. Adorable. The sun was coming up. I was tired to the bone. As physically used up as if *I* had been in labor. I looked out a window, at an Indian-summer morning in an old-world place of stone cottages, purple vineyards, a mist-shrouded river, geese on a wild spree across the sky. I thought, *Eden.* And that's what I named the child."

"Who was the father, then?" he asked, impatient with her.

"I can't be sure. I believe it was either Peter Sandza or his son."

"Robin Sandza?"

"She must have told you about him."

"Gilly approached the matter, over a period of many months. The telling was difficult, her memories fragmented. This is all I know. Gillian believed that she and Robin Sandza were, her description, 'psychic twins.' Born at the same moment, to different mothers, during a solar eclipse, while other potent conjunctions of the planets were at their most effective. That eclipse may have been the catalyst for Gillian's ... for the 'gift' both children shared. They were to have been fraternal as well as psychic twins, she said, but the scheme went awry. The other baby you carried, Gillian's identical twin, strangled on his umbilical in the womb while Gillian was being born."

"The ethereal entity that became Robin Sandza had to find a different mother, and quickly; someone already far along in labor. Robin's mother was quite beautiful. She died young, of complications from an infected tooth. Peter Sandza was a covert MORG agent. He had to leave the raising of his son to his sister Fay, who was living a life of religious drudgery with an impotent fanatic. I learned much of this long after the events that took place at Psi Faculty."

"And there's some evidence that Gillian had sex with Robin's father?"

"Only supposition. Gillian wasn't able to tell me anything."

"Could she have recalled, under hypnosis?"

"I wasn't willing to put her through that. Why should I have? She'd had the baby, which she was in no condition to care for. At the time it seemed that she might never ... get her mind back. I already knew most of what had taken place. Peter Sandza and Gillian were on the run. He was desperate to find his son. Before they reached Psi Faculty they put up at an inn in Mount Carmel, Connecticut, then at a ski lodge called Shadowdown, which was not far from the Psi Faculty campus in the Adirondacks. I'm certain that they spent at least two nights together, sharing a room. In both places where they stayed, Sandza registered Gillian as his daughter. Of course he wasn't going to let Gillian out of his sight; she was the key to his recovering Robin.

"By then Gilly, in a variation of the captor/hostage syndrome, may have been emotionally dependent on him. They'd dosed her heavily with hypnotics and psycho-suppressive drugs at Paragon Institute. Virtually canceled her identity. That was my fault, for leaving her there. But I did so because I was terrified of my own daughter, unsure of my sanity. I had bled like a slaughtered pig. I needed to be sedated. Dr. Irving Roth and his associate from Paragon, a young Chinese woman, came to our house in Sutton Mews. They'd been highly recommended to my husband. I learned from Dr. Roth that Gillian had the power to make me, to make almost anyone, bleed, when she was in a psychometric trance. Roth put our dilemma in terms Avery and I could understand. He said, 'Are you familiar with the short story about the man who traveled in time and changed the fate of the world by accidentally stepping on a butterfly? When the man returned to his own time he found that because he'd been careless in a prehistoric epoch, the world was now a grotesque, savagely distorted place with nothing beautiful in it anymore.

" 'Gillian,' Roth said, 'as she flashes back and forth in time according to her clairvoyant visions, is like the man who crushed the butterfly. Her very thoughts can significantly affect reality as we know it.' "

"We've come a long way since then, in our understanding and uses of the paranormal."

"Uses and misuses. The world has become the savagely distorted place Roth predicted, although none of it was Gilly's fault."

"She wanted to do good. To be of help, when the others sought her out. I didn't like it. MORG was still there. The opposition was too powerful. I was afraid something would happen to her. It happened." He felt savage pain, deep in the unprotected heart. "Tell me about Peter Sandza."

"MORG also had his son. The other half of the twinship. They had convinced Robin that his father was dead, that he was virtually an orphan. The better to bond with him, gain control. They did their best to eliminate Sandza. But he was as ruthless as the men MORG sent after him. A trained assassin, with the cunning of a hunted man. I visited both of the rooms in which they slept together. I have no psychic ability, but—I could imagine it happening, deep into the night. His own need. Gillian's beauty, her youth and vulnerability. Gillian was barely fifteen. I forgive him for that. I truly hope . . . it *was* Peter Sandza, because the alternative . . . too dreadful. I've never wanted to think about Robin coming to her. So corrupted. Driven insane by the collective efforts of the researchers at Psi Faculty to enhance his already-considerable paranormal talents."

"But Gillian told me that she and Robin never met. They were only in touch through psychomorphic channels."

"They knew each other *intimately.*"

"How?"

"When Gillian came home from the hospital, after she'd had her first clairvoyant experience and fainted on the ice rink in Central Park, she was changed. A different child altogether. Sullen, evasive, brooding. She locked herself in her room for hours at a time, practicing her flute. Then she would listen to rock music, so loud I thought it would bring the roof down. When I couldn't stand it any longer, I made Avery pick the lock on her door. It was the middle of the afternoon, but the drapes were drawn. Quite dark in the room. Gillian lay across her bed, partly covered by a sheet. She was naked. She didn't appear to be breathing. I panicked, thinking she had died. Avery wouldn't let me touch her. My husband was a respected anthropologist. He told me she wasn't dead. Neither was she *there,* and he warned me not to disturb her body. He said that she was in a state of . . . tonic immobility. A deep trance. The loud music was one aspect of the ritual that allowed her astral body to travel. Avery had a great deal else to say, about the metapsychical systems of tribes he had studied on three continents. About material bodies and astral bodies. He mentioned a word, the first time I had heard it. *Doppelganger.*"

"Her mirror image. But only a double, unless she chose to give it a life of its own. Gillian told me it could be done merely by bestowing an alternate name on the dpg. She also said that it was a dangerous practice."

"I think it's likely that Robin Sandza's doppelganger, named or unnamed, visited Gilly, at that time when she was just home from the hospital and inexperienced, unguarded. Too trusting. He, or it, visited and may have seduced my daughter. Once I learned that she was pregnant, I consulted psychics. Having become a believer. They all agreed that there is sexual intercourse in the Astral, but they disagreed that conception can occur. Could a doppelganger father a human child? No answers."

"But they are, supposedly, exact replicas of their homebodies. Who does this girl named Eden look like?"

"She favors Gillian, thank God."

"Gillian had powers beyond our comprehension. If Robin Sandza was Eden's father, what must she be like? She could be—what? A savior—"

"Other psychics call the rare ones 'Avatars.' "

"Infinite in faculty. In apprehension how like a god."

Sherard paused, silenced by implications. Katharine made of his stillness an opportunity, moving from her seat to sit on the floor by him. Fluid in movement in spite of her years. The disciplines of yoga and the StairMaster, tennis on weekends. She put a forearm across his knees, her head resting on her arm, pose of subjugation. Contrived, of course, but not unpleasant. Her artifice a corollary of privilege.

"And you gave the child up for adoption."

"I had to. I chose her adoptive parents very carefully, culling the candidates from nearly every state, Canada, Europe. They had to have the education, experience, and emotional security to deal with a prodigy. Since Eden went to live in California as an infant I haven't seen her, except in photographs. I wanted her to have every opportunity to lead a comfortable, conventional life in a Cheez Whiz kind of town. She's very intelligent, of course. Quite the athlete. So am I. It became obvious, early on, that Eden inherited Gillian's ability to travel in the astral. Her dreams, she was told, were actually journeys out of the body. According to her adoptive mother, who is a clinical psychologist, Eden's visits to the astral have been under the supervision of a third, surrogate mother, whom Eden named the Good Lady."

"Why do you think she's in danger now?"

"Unfortunately she 'came out' in front of several thousand people at her college graduation exercise two hours ago. It was, still is, on all the national news channels. Eden was about to deliver her valedictory address. Suddenly she warned everyone to leave the stadium where they were assembled. She told them a plane was about to crash there."

Sherard vaguely remembered seeing something about this on a television in the British Airways lounge. Right now he longed for another scotch. The limousine might have had a bar tucked away in some ingeniously discreet compartment, but a drink hadn't been offered and he wouldn't ask.

"Saved nearly everyone with her timely warning. So Eden 'saw' it happening before it happened?"

"Of course."

He touched the back of Katharine's lax small hand, tracing a vein there. Her skin was still remarkably supple, unblemished.

"Where is she now?"

"No idea. For many reasons I can't, don't wish to directly contact her adoptive parents."

"MORG again?" Sherard asked.

"You know what they are. How bitterly I've fought them. They watch me constantly. Victor Wilding still must believe that because of Gillian, I have connections to the psychic underground."

"Do you?"

Her eyes moved away from his.

"I'm not watched anymore," Sherard said. "They never took me very seriously. I was Gillian's white-hunter husband, found a cushy thing for himself with the profession dying out, the hunting bans and tribal wars. Otherwise I should have died on the sidewalk beside Gilly."

"How do you know you're not watched?"

"Bush sense."

"You're probably wrong."

"It's my legs that are damaged, not my instincts."

"Regardless, please do this *my* way."

"What is it you want, Katharine?"

"Find Eden. Bring her home to me. I'm so very anxious to get to know Eden, after all these years."

"Find her?"

"Betts and Riley Waring have long known what to do for Eden in the event MORG learned about her." There was a gleam of hazard in Katharine's eyes as she looked at Sherard. "In spite of all the precautions Avery and I took, I'm sure Victor Wilding has long held suspicions that there *was* a child. Through yoga I've always been able to block the MMF." Katharine used the short reference for what was known to the activists in the psychic underground as *MORG Mind-Fuckers.* "Gillian must have taught you similar techniques."

Sherard nodded. "She described it as 'not leaving footprints in the air.' "

"You were on your way to London? Good. Get on that plane, then get off. I'll make those arrangements. United is holding space on the six o'clock to San Francisco under your old alias."

"G. W. Hunter?" He and Gillian had usually traveled under assumed names, because of her activities, and because she was a member of one of the richest families on earth.

"I assumed your British passport in that name is still valid. And you have it with you."

"Yes, but—"

"Good. No footprints in the air. I'll contact you tomorrow at the Blackwelder office in San Francisco. Ten sharp. By then I'll have heard from Betts Waring."

"It's the Blackwelder organization you ought to be using, not me. Vaughn Blackwelder has been devoted to you for years. Don't understand why you haven't married him."

"Hairpieces. He has a dressing room with a dozen hairpieces sitting on white foam heads. It does something to the soul. I can't have Vaughn and his group handle this matter. It *must* be you."

"Why?"

"Eden knows she's adopted. She was never told who her mother was. You were Gillian's husband for twelve years. Everything that Eden will want to know about Gilly you can tell her. Eden is subject to seizures, a consequence of her phenomenal abilities. My principal concern is not to frighten her. And you do have a way with women, Tom."

"Thank you."

"No, that was from the heart. You truly like us. Most straight men your age are sexual provocateurs. Those who aren't outright creeps. You're what your contours say you are. Stalwart. I love that word. A hunter, a provider, a companion. You're wounded now. Doesn't matter. There's still a sense of completeness about you. No trivialities. Staunch. Another good word from the chivalric days of manhood. But you have no bent for obsessive, despairing relationships and quaint romantic afflictions. Always up front with your loyalties. A woman's man. We all want to be that woman."

"God Almighty."

"Don't you see? Eden will trust you. She'll come with you. No questions."

"You're asking too much. I don't think I can do this."

"But you will. Won't you? And now you know why. You'll do it for Gillian."

CAMP DAVID, MARYLAND · MAY 28 · 6:44 P.M. EDT

Clint Harvester was having dinner with his personal physician, two neurological specialists from Johns Hopkins Medical Center, and the White House Chief of Staff in the President's lodge at Camp David when word came from Honolulu that the First Lady's motorcade had been ambushed on the way to the airport.

Drexel R. "Pep" Slingbury, Princeton '79, took the call. They had been watching NBC's Weekend News. While Pep pressed for details and scribbled notes on a linen napkin with a ballpoint pen, the second-string anchorman, interrupted by something that wasn't on the teleprompter crawl in front of him, hesitated, looked startled, then found his sonorous voice again and relayed the news to the network's viewers. Coverage supplied by the NBC affiliate in the fiftieth state flashed on the screen. The cameraman seemed to be covering the scene from the roof of an office building, perhaps half a mile away.

A smoking but upright limousine was sitting sideways in the middle of Ala Moana Boulevard, surrounded by fire and emergency vehicles and helmeted cops. There was rubble in the roadway. A palm tree, set ablaze by a rocket, was being hosed down by the fire department. Another heavily damaged car was on the curb at least a hundred feet away from the armored limo. They had pulled injured MORG agents out of this one. All of the limousine doors hung open. The press corps accompanying the First Lady was herded back into the vans by machine gun–toting MORG agents. Traffic on the busy boulevard was backed up for half a mile in either direction. There was no audio feed from Hawaii. The NBC anchor attempted his own uninformed commentary.

Pep Slingbury was ahead of NBC on the facts, which he blurted out as they came to him.

"Helicopter . . . popped up out of nowhere. Four men with automatic weapons, RPGs, maybe a Stinger . . . no, that's unconfirmed. Knew exactly what they were . . . they hit the counterassault team's vehicle first, then the FLOTUS limo. Two tires shredded but it's operational. The package is approaching the airport now. Yes? Yes? . . . the President's right here, he's standing by here . . . yes . . . Harry, you're breaking up . . . as soon as you fucking *know*, God damn it!"

Clint Harvester had pushed his chair back a couple of inches from the table. He still had his spoon in his hand. He ate everything with a red plastic tablespoon, or his fingers. He was subject to clonuses, and could injure himself with a knife or a fork. He slowly chewed a mouthful of buttered croissant, watching the TV screen with a bland unblinking eye.

Paul Luckett, Deputy Chief of the Secret Service's presidential detail, came in fast with six more agents, who took up prearranged positions around the Chief Executive, code-named "Rawhide," hands on the Glocks and M-11s they wore under their coats. Two DoD communications specialists appeared with secure telephones, Swedish-made, unbreakable cryptology scattered across a dozen channels.

"Mr. President," Pep said with a grimace of apology, "there could be more to this than Honolulu."

Clint Harvester looked around at Paul Luckett and grinned, gave him a merry thumbs-up, and pushed the rest of his croissant into his mouth. Paul Luckett grinned back, looked pained, looked at the Chief of Staff, who was using one of the secure phones to call the White House press secretary at home.

"I think this makes my case, Mr. Slingbury. What I've been saying all along."

"Yeah, Paul."

Luckett gestured at the TV. "No way this happens if *we're* protecting Zephyr."

"And there's no way Dallas could've happened to Kennedy, isn't that right, Paul?" Pep reached for the napkin he'd been writing on, remembering his notes only after he'd left smears of ink on his high perspiring forehead. "Hi, Moira. Got the TV on? No? Turn it on. Where's Cody, outside mowing the south forty? Page him for me, please."

Luckett keyed his walkie, began checking perimeter security at Camp David, which he referred to as "Cactus." Already there were heavily armed helicopters in the air around the mountain retreat, two teams of counter-assault Marines deploying on the grounds.

Now on the dining-room projection TV there was an image of the President's 747, redesignated as Special Air Mission Z-1815 when Rona was using it, at the Honolulu airport and at least a mile from the camera. The limousine carrying Rona Harvester rolled toward the plane with two mangled tires designed to keep going even if they were flat. Police cars and motorcycle cops surrounded the limo. An Air Police SWAT team had arrived by helo from the adjacent Hickam Air Force Base to beef up security.

The shot-up but probably unpenetrated armored limousine stopped below the stairway. In a mob of security men Rona Harvester was removed from the limo and hustled through the glitter of a Hawaiian afternoon to the forward door of the immense airplane, all but invisible within the moving human shield. Clouds above the 747 were like a thick pile of whipped cream on a banana split. Two more men with machine guns stood in the doorway. All of this was being witnessed around the world as it happened, commercial-free. Images that would be repeated endlessly for the rest of the night in the U.S.

Rona Harvester hesitated at the doorway, seeming to resist efforts to hastily shove her inside. Saying something, gesturing. *Back off, please*. Unbowed, undaunted. She turned slightly, toward the terminal. She knew where the cameras would be. Was that a smear of blood on her forehead? Rona raised her right fist, double-pumping, knocking air, a gesture of defiance and victory.

"The little devil," Pep Slingbury said quietly, willing, for the moment, to suspend his dislike of the woman most responsible for his peptic ulcer.

Then she was gone. Safely inside SAM Z-1815, the door closing. As the mobile staircase was driven away the 747 began to move. The face of the NBC anchor reappeared, picture within a picture. He spoke movingly, with a firm jaw and admiration glinting in his eyes, of Rona Harvester's courage under fire, her popularity with the American people. While the 747 was taxiing for takeoff the network ran a file montage of Rona, highlights of her years at the White House. Touring areas of the U.S. that had been devastated by natural disasters. Floating a wreath, well upriver from the hot zone, for the dead and displaced of Portland, Oregon. Chairing important conferences on the humanitarian deficiencies of third-world nations. Visiting schools. Chumming with crowned heads at White House dinners. Horseback riding with her husband on their Montana ranch, her windblown hair backlighted by a ravishing sunset.

Everyone in the room, including the Secret Service agents, had momentarily forgotten about Clint Harvester.

He was sitting forward on the edge of his high-backed chair. His left hand, holding the big red plastic spoon, rested on an arm of the chair. With his other hand he had unzipped his pleated honey-colored corduroy slacks and was peeing on the Navaho rug in front of him. His lower lip pushed in and out, ruminatively. His upper lip had a buttery, crumbed gleam. His active mind, what little remained of it, was somewhere else. His eyes were as still as swatted flies.

Now everyone in the room had noticed. Pep swallowed a desperate urge to bray like a donkey, shoot himself in the foot, do anything to divert attention from this humiliation of a man he happened to love. His heart gave a frightful twitch. Sweat blurred his vision.

But at least, Pep thought, they had progressed to a point where the leader and hope of the free world was taking it out before he obeyed the urge to relieve himself. So the news wasn't all bad tonight, was it?

INNISFALL, CALIFORNIA · MAY 28 · 7:26 P.M. PDT

Geoff McTyer had LoJack. It was no trouble for him to locate his car, parked near the top of the hill in the Memorial Gardens.

One of the campus cops gave him a lift up there. He checked first to see if the Taurus had been hot-wired. No. He stood beside his car for a while, clothes grimy and stained with sweat, looking north with tired eyes to the

Cal Shasta campus. It was dusk. The last light of the sun gleamed opaquely in the many windows of the school buildings. Lights had come on in the parking lots and along the winding drives. Except for the hulks of the burned-out airliner in and near the stadium, it was like any other balmy evening in late spring. There was rain farther off, to the north and east. Twenty-five, thirty miles away. Lightning flared within the heavy cloud formations.

The charnel reek of burnt flesh was all over him. A bath would help, but probably he'd continue to smell it in his sleep. For several nights to come. At least the poor bastards—they'd found seventeen shrunken bodies in the wreckage, many of them resembling charcoal mummies with shiny dabs of silver and gold jewelry embedded where ears, wrists, and throats had been—should have died on impact. A survivor who had been taken to the hospital hours ago probably was still in surgery. Geoff ate some dried apricots to boost his energy level and wondered how Eden had managed to drive the Taurus to the cemetery without the ignition key that was in the leather folder chained to his belt.

Maybe she'd had it towed, as a joke. But she hadn't been in a jolly frame of mind when he'd last seen her.

He took his cell phone from the trunk, tried to reach Eden. Three different numbers, including her pager. He left a message, but after ten minutes she hadn't called him back.

Where are you, baby?

Geoff got in the car. Needing the evening wind to air him out, he drove with the top down to the Warings' house on Deep Creek Road.

The sun was setting when he got there, a golden sky with birds flocking to the treetops like iron filings to a magnet. The merely curious were hanging out along the road with journalists from all of the important media. The journalists looked bored and disgruntled, as if they'd been stood up by blind dates. A chained and padlocked gate blocked the drive. Riley had procrastinated getting the electronic gate opener fixed. But Geoff had a padlock key. He got out of the Taurus with his shield in his hand.

The vid crews came at him with their usual dog-pack intensity, a brute assault with lights, cameras, microphones. They yelled questions from all sides as he walked to the gate.

Geoff turned and said, "I want every one of you two hundred feet back from the driveway entrance! Move your vehicles *now*, or there'll be tow trucks out here in fifteen minutes."

A young woman wearing a lot of makeup trampled one of her slower-moving colleagues in order to get in Geoff's face with her microphone.

"Diane Kopechne, Channel Nine News at Seven. Why have the police been called? Has something happened here?"

"I'm off duty. I'm a friend of the family's. Would you please get out of my way?"

"Can you confirm that today's plane crash was not an accident?"

"What?"

"Did Eden Waring have prior knowledge the plane would crash? Is it true, as some of her classmates have said, that she is into Goth?"

"Get back or get arrested."

"Try it," she sneered, "and my station will sue your cute ass." The VJ glanced at her cameraman, pressed her free hand to the earpiece she wore, and said into the wireless mike pinned to a lapel of her suit, "Bernie, chrissake, are we *go* yet? I've got a breaking story here, man."

The cameraman said to her, "Three, two, one, we're hot."

She wasn't quite deft enough to arrange her smile and position her body for the live feed while keeping a tight grip on Geoff. He pulled away from her and unlocked the gate.

"Yes, well, as you can see, Ned, we're standing in front of the Waring house on Deep Creek Road, where an officer from the Innisfall Police Department has just arrived. There has been no activity around the sprawling redwood-and-native stone home for *several* hours now, although we can see that two vehicles, a large blue van and a dark gray sedan, are parked next to the house. We've just spoken to the officer, who claims to be a *close* personal friend of the Waring family. At this point he has unlocked the gate across the drive and is—"

Walking fast, Geoff made it to the house in twelve seconds and continued on a flagstone path beneath some California oak and acacia trees to the walled patio off the kitchen wing. Another gate there, silvery cypress boards with hand-forged bronze hardware. Unlocked. On the paved patio the Warings' ancient blond Labrador crept out of his doghouse with a sadly wagging tail to greet Geoff. The kitchen door was also unlocked. Geoff went in and turned on the lights.

A moth was trapped and fluttering inside one of the ceiling light panels. The sink faucet dripped slowly. Riley hadn't gotten around to replacing the washer yet. There was an emptied can of Alpo on the butcher-block table in the center of the kitchen that someone had forgotten to dump into the garbage. As if feeding the dog had been an afterthought in the midst of a hasty departure.

"Hey, it's Geoff! *Eden?* Anybody home?"

But he'd known from the moment he stepped inside that no one was there. The house stood empty, except for himself and the moth.

He took a glass from a cabinet beside the diamond-pane cottage windows that overlooked the patio, opened the fridge. The light was out, Riley hadn't . . . He poured a glass of milk, drank it while walking through the house, turning on lamps as he went.

The telephone rang, and rang. The answering machine didn't cut in. Geoff took the call.

"This is Ellis Babb, Channel Six News in San Francisco. Am I speaking to Mr. Riley Waring?"

"No, I'm Wiley Herring, you have the wrong number," Geoff said, and hung up. He pulled the phone plug with a troubled sigh and continued roaming.

There was some evidence in the master bedroom that Riley and Betts had packed a few things and gone somewhere to escape the attention focused on them, a consequence of Eden's eerily accurate premonition at the stadium. Out the back way, unobserved, across the creek, and through a neighbor's horse pasture. With or without Eden? Riley's vet van and Betts's Audi were in the carport. Eden's 4WD Jimmy was missing, probably still parked on the Cal Shasta campus.

Geoff looked in her bedroom. Bed unmade. She hadn't put the iron or ironing board away that morning. Unlikely that she'd been home since then, but he made sure. Her favorite hairbrush was on the dressing table. So was her orthodontic retainer. And her birth control pills, in a supposedly secret drawer of her jewelry box. But Geoff had been in her room before, when no one was at home. He knew all of Eden's hiding places.

Had she met her parents somewhere, or was she staying out of sight at a friend's house?

He doubted that the telephone answering machine would provide useful information, but he listened patiently to the messages on the full tape. One call from Betts's mother, who was in an assisted-living community in Sonoma. She was eighty years old, and much of what she had to say, though it sounded cheery, was unintelligible. The next call was from someone who identified herself as Rona Harvester's press secretary. She left a White House number where Eden could reach the admiring First Lady. All of the other calls had been placed by local and national media people, and they all wanted to talk to Eden. Representatives of supermarket weeklies and tabloid TV shows were giving Eden the full-tilt glam hustle. They wanted her life story. They wanted her predictions of coming world events. They were talking—to an answering machine—big money. Talking exclusivity.

Geoff was ever more aware that leaving Eden in his car and going off to assist in the emergency had been a huge mistake. He'd been shaken by calamity and was thinking *cop,* instead of concentrating on his real purpose. There was no way he could have anticipated a juggernaut like this so soon after the event. A bizarre, apocalyptic carnival had begun its colorful whirl around the image of Eden Waring. He was as surprised as anyone that she had "come out" so spectacularly. But that would be no excuse for muffing the unexpected opportunity. He had to come up with Eden, hopefully in a matter of hours. Fortunately she trusted him, almost as much as she trusted Betts and Riley.

Having listened to the Warings' incoming messages, it was time for him to review the day's outgoing calls. They had three lines in their home. Each of the Warings had a cell phone. Riley and Betts were professionals, so additional phones in their places of work had to be monitored. In days of yore, a decade or so in terms of technological breakthroughs, it would have meant deploying surveillance teams in listening posts and vans, a hell of a lot of cumbersome equipment. But the scanners and recorders that the government now had would fit inside a child's shoe box.

Because of the many trees around the Waring house and the cottage-style windows beneath a deep roof overhang, it had not been possible to employ lasers and eavesdrop on the Warings through the minute vibrations their voices initiated in the small glass panes. Geoff's unmanned listening post was a dry, roofed well at one corner of the large patio. In years past yellow jackets had built nests beneath the conical roof. None were in residence now. Geoff retrieved the microelectronic eavesdropping equipment he had stashed there, dropping by when no one was home to change tapes. There had never been bugs inside the house. Geoff knew that Betts had run a backgrounder on him, soon after he popped up in Eden's life. She used a small but prestigious agency in San Francisco. One of the partners was Betts's second cousin on her father's side, but it had not surprised Geoff to learn that the Frisco agency had ties to the Black-welder organization. Which meant, to him, that Betts had the smarts and possibly the gadgets necessary to sweep her home and her office on a regular basis. She was, by profession, a keeper of secrets. No matter how miniaturized and cleverly concealed they were, microtransmitters readily gave themselves away. Eliminating their use had made his job more difficult, but caution and patience always had been essential to Geoff Mc-Tyer's purpose.

Against his better judgment he left the house as he had found it, unlocked. The Warings might have made arrangements with a friend or another vet to pick up and board the dog. The Lab was nearly blind and too infirm to travel. Riley should have put Winky down by now, but Eden couldn't bear the thought.

After pocketing his spy gear Geoff gave the dog a parting rub behind the ears, thinking about Eden; before he knew it his eyes had teared and there was a definite lump in his throat.

Damn. *Damn.* He had been on this job too long. Now, abruptly, it was necessary to cancel all the cozy accommodations he had made with himself during his two and a half years in Innisfall.

They wouldn't leave the cleanup phase to him. No reflection on his competence. They knew he'd been intimate with Eden Waring. Necessary but dangerous emotional attachments had been wired in. Inevitable. Part of the long process. Anticipating, understanding this, they'd pull him out, send someone else to acquire or finalize the subject.

In the road fronting the Warings' four acres the crowd of hangers-on had multiplied. A thin cloud of dust had been raised by restless feet. A couple of teenage boys were selling cold drinks off the tailgate of their old rusty-orange Volvo station wagon. An Innisfall PD unit had arrived, two reserve police officers, to keep traffic moving. The media was still there, in force. The intrepid Diane Kopechne was interviewing someone, probably a neighbor. The woman had a fussbudget face. At the edge of the lights there was a mosaic of faces animated by crowd-hunger, a groundswell of mob esprit. They all wanted something that would consume them with awe. A statue weeping tears of blood, an oversized pumpkin on which the features of Elvis could be discerned. They drew strength from the presence of the media, which apportioned merit to their own idle questing.

Geoff saw a young girl cradling a goat kid in her arms.

He passed through the gate, locked it behind him. Walked through the crowd to his car, waving to one of the reservists. A hand plucked timidly at his sleeve. He looked around.

She had the look of prairie-dwelling women in old daguerreotypes: gaunt, windburnt, long-suffering, despising their fates.

"Did you see her, mister?"

Geoff stared at the woman, feeling hellishly tired, unable to focus on her question.

"What?"

"Did you see the miracle lady? She that saved them all when that plane fell out of the sky? Glory Hallelujah."

He shook his head. The woman wouldn't let go of him. She smiled with the blandness of deep-seated hysteria, or obsession.

"Course you seen her. You're her young *man,* is what they're sayin' here. Tell her we're all churchgoing people. Presbyterian, before we made the big switch back to the one true Gospel and speaking in tongues. Just passing through on our way to Sedona, Arizona, when we heard it on the radio. My husband's got a mighty lot of cancer in his bowel. It never does get done paining him. I have listened to his screams now four hundred mile. But we know the Lord is good. *Bless* the Lord. *Shabba walah aben obeth!* I ask you humbly, sir, have the miracle lady come out and strike this cancer from his body. Shouldn't take more than a minute of her time, and we surely would appreciate it."

"She's . . . not home. That's the truth. I don't know where . . . could you let go of me? I have to leave. I have to find Eden. I'm sorry for your trouble."

Her smile got bigger. It filled half her face. Her eyes nearly disappeared. Sweat drizzled down from her temples. She lost her grip on him, but when he moved away her hand remained in the air, resembling a weather-polished gnarl on a dead tree.

"Reckon we'll just wait right here till she does come. When you do see her you tell her, Al and Rosalie, they're a-waitin'."

NEW YORK CITY · MAY 28 · 11:18 P.M. EDT

In the Presidential Suite of the Waldorf Astoria, President pro tempore Allen Dunbar looked up from the television set he was watching in their bedroom and said to his wife, "Look at this! Have you ever seen such caca in your life? Now what the heck do we get next, Saint Rona the First?" The image on the screen happened to be that of Rona Harvester on a solo visit to the Vatican, surrounded by photographers in a lovely shadow-dappled garden with the pontiff, who, in his billowy ecclesiastical robes, was holding fast to her elbow as if he were afraid of being lofted into the sky by a gust of wind. He smiled benignly at something Rona said. More file coverage, from her last overseas trip during the third week in April.

Dunbar got down from the side of the high-rise four-poster bed. Sitting there, his bare feet had been well off the floor. He was five-seven, almost five-nine when wearing shoes expensively designed to increase his stature without giving away the deception. He was a slight man with average looks that happened to photograph well, a must in his profession; an engaging cocksure grin; a lot of balls, physically and metaphorically. He had good negotiating skills facilitated by the ability to keep talking, for hours without a break, until the opposition wilted to the ground like crocuses in a late-spring arctic gale. Good timing and better luck had elevated him from the Senate's equivalent of the utility infielder he'd been in college (not much bat but a hustler, a digger, good arm) to his present pro tem status. But Rona Harvester was determined to see he didn't get to enjoy a minute of it.

His wife Dorothea came out of the bedroom cold-creamed to the roots of her hair, wearing a half slip, and waited to see if she was expected to reply. Dunbar began to pace around the perimeter of the Napoleon III Aubusson carpet, four hundred square feet of it, rubbing his receding hairline in agitation.

"I mean, when the dickens is CNN going to stop chewing on this? And CBS. They canceled *everything* tonight. *Walker Texas Ranger,* for Pete's sake! Four solid hours of nothing but Rona Harvester."

"Well, they—"

"Sure, sure, I got on for a couple of minutes. Expressing my *outrage,* which believe me I was. *Out*raged. Not one mention of my address to the General Assembly. Jesse Jackson was interviewed for at least *five* minutes, and what does he have to do with anything? The President of the United States should *own* the tube at crunch time. My staff gets a well-deserved caning for this one. Forget about Jarrod and Tim, they're gone. If I don't have a good leadoff man, I won't be seeing anything but breaking balls when it's my turn at bat." He did an about-face on one corner of the carpet, appealing to his wife. "It isn't as if she was *ever* in any danger, Pug."

"You explained—"

"Can you believe the dog-gone *gall* of the woman?"

"Hard to believe," Dorothea said, with a slight cynical smile.

"Oh, she's behind it, all right. That's the preliminary word from Bob Hyde. Rona Harvester and, yes, I'll say it: her confederates at MORG. Where're you going?"

"Bathroom."

"Again? Been spending a lot of time in there, Pug. Another of your gastric upsets, is it? Stomach looks a little bloated. Have you been doing caca okay?"

"No."

He was going to follow her into the bathroom, but she closed the door. Dunbar stood just outside, head cocked, listening. Pausing to get his breath. That little touch of emphysema, and he'd only smoked for a few years, because everybody else at prep did it, before giving up cigarettes on his thirtieth birthday. JFK had said it best. Life *was* unfair.

It was a thick door. He spoke more loudly.

"Not as if, anytime I wanted to, I couldn't put paid to her desperate little charade. Right? If Clint is in no condition to govern, ever again, which is the dope our team has been getting, then the American people ought to know. And I don't buy this 'crisis of confidence' stuff the House Whip is handing me. I told him today, 'Lorenzo, it's denigrating the American people to suggest that they won't get behind their new Chief one hundred percent, once they have the facts.' Of course the American people haven't warmed up to me yet. But hey. It's like the bottom of the ninth, two outs, the sacks are jammed and I'm pinch hitting for *Mark McGwire*. Have to be a realist, that's how I got this far. Perception is everything, in life and in politics. I just can't let myself be steam-rollered in the perception department 'cause of this little technicality of pro tem. I know what you're thinking. And you're on the beam, as always. It's a wait-and-see proposition." He paused to hear an affirmation, and frowned. "You all right in there, Puggums?"

There was suddenly a lot of activity in the bathroom, a noise like a submarine blowing its tubes.

"Whoa! Well, I guess you're feeling better already."

The bedroom phone rang, one of the private lines installed by the White House Communications Agency for Dunbar's stay.

"Yeah? He is? Great. Just let me get my shoes on."

Dunbar hung up and returned to the bathroom door.

"Pug? Bob Hyde's here from Washington. Don't know how long this will take. You should turn in. Long trip to Delhi tomorrow for that funeral."

His wife came out of the bathroom. She had wiped off the cold cream. Her face shone, but she looked as edgy and mean as a skinning knife. She walked past him in her half slip, breasts a-dangle, and threw herself on the bed.

"I don't want to go to India. The last time I went to India I got a kidney stone. Believe me I suffered the tortures of the damned."

"As if I could forget. Well, it was probably just a coincidence and not the curry or anything like that. Your daddy was a stone-former, wasn't he?"

Dorothea groaned. "Reminds me. I owe Mom a call. What time is it in Nebraska?"

"Too late, I'd say. You know what she's like if you disturb her sleep." Dunbar kissed the back of his wife's neck. She didn't respond. After a few moments he retreated toward the bedroom doors.

"Why don't you just have her assassinated, popsie? I'm not talking about a big show with rockets, like today. I mean something stealthy, medieval. She keels over one night after dinner. The poison proves to be untraceable."

"Whoa, is that *you*, Pug? We don't subscribe to those tactics in a democratic society."

"Rona does."

"Might as well forfeit our souls."

"Might as well, because she's taking over. *Her* tactics are whatever gets the job done."

"You just can't *talk* like this. Where do these ideas come from?"

"My great-grandfather Trace was a sheriff up and down the frontier. Square-shooter, but if it was more convenient and less fuss, he'd as lief bust the desperadoes between their shoulder blades with his .44. Oh, I know. There's the little matter of line of succession. You think that's got her stopped. But there're also all those Executive Orders that have been accumulating in the Oval Office since Dick Nixon's day. One piled on top of another, each Order nibbling away a little more of the Articles of the Constitution like waves eroding a sand beach. When she's ready to make her move, Rona will have the appropriate power. Want to know how I think she and her kindred assholes at MORG are going to deal the next hand?"

"I can't believe you, these ideas of yours."

"I have a serious mind. I've got a Masters in philosophy. Rona Harvester is summa cum laude in carnal knowledge, the cunt. Ideas? Yes, I have ideas, and I'm just a little weary of acting the overage Girl Scout and America's perfect homemaker. It's a tired routine, popsie."

"The American people expect—"

"The American people need to grow up. Let me shout that from the rooftops."

Dunbar said gently, "You haven't been skipping your recommended dosage of Luvox, have you? It *has* been a trying day."

"All of that shit gives me diarrhea, if you haven't noticed. Also I did a little research on SSRIs. *Very* bad for bipolars. Road rage? Those kids who shoot up their high schools? All of the Serotonin Reuptake Inhibitors induce mania in bipolars. You wouldn't want me to go on another shoplifting spree, would you?" Dunbar winced at the thought. "Then allow me to pursue my more productive manias. Listen, Al Dunbar. *You* are the President. *You* need to get the goods, now, and pressure Rona and her crowd into revealing the sad truth that Clint Harvester is for real a drooling idiot, and get them both out of the White House posthaste. Did I tell you? I already have some neat decorating ideas."

Dunbar peered at his wife with a harried smile, unable to believe she was serious.

"Hand the ball to a flamethrower," Dorothea persisted. "Show the bitch nothing but heat until she backs out of the box." After a few moments Dorothea flopped over on her side, eyeing him suspiciously. "Or is that an option?"

Dunbar didn't say anything.

Dorothea sighed. "She knows, then. Figures."

"Please, Pugsy."

"I wish to God you had never told me."

"I wanted . . . needed your forgiveness."

"How many times do I have to forgive you? Quit asking. It only increases the toll. We're all entitled to one big mistake, but did it have to be a fifteen-year-old crackhead whose father is the most famous film director in the world? And a big supporter of the Harvesters, one might add."

"Oh, God, Pug. You know I worship you."

"Good night, cocksucker. And keep your kisses to yourself. I need my shut-eye if I'm going to fly halfway around the world tomorrow."

obert Hyde, Director of the Federal Bureau of Investigation, was a man of fifty-four who looked ten years older. He wore his gray hair in a no-nonsense brush cut. He had the unsmiling opaqueness of a lifelong despot drained of human nuance.

Hyde didn't like anyone. He had no close personal friends, no wife, no mistress. There were two adult offspring from a very early marriage, before he had discovered how much he loathed human beings, and what a nuisance sexual relations were. Hyde seldom spoke to his daughter, who had dedicated her life and inheritance from her mother's estate to mounting expeditions that took her and platoons of scientists to places on the globe that almost no one else had ever heard of. His son loved him, for some reason. Always had. Hyde respected his intelligence and found him useful in their line of work.

But he had never been close to anyone except Allen Dunbar, to whom he owed the resurrection of his career in law enforcement after being on the losing side of a vendetta with a former Attorney General of the United States. He didn't actually like the President pro tem, but it was a relationship that had to be nurtured. Hyde was in daily contention with everyone in DoJ or Congress who didn't share his vision that only a stronger FBI could safeguard America from the recent onslaught of terrorism that had been so destructive of public morale. A demoralized America was a fatally weakened America. Hyde hammered that theme home in daily calls to members of the House Appropriations Committee, but the obscene hydra known as MORG worked the same terrritory, with better success. All those mouths gobbling up funds Hyde needed to beef up his Bureau, which for years before he became Director had been looking frayed at the edges, slipshod, even obsolete in the eyes of influential senators and congresspersons who had no sense of history or, if they were older, had forgotten what the FBI had meant to the country during hot and cold wars, the tireless crusade to break up the Mob.

When Hyde was twenty years younger and newly reassigned to D.C. after a successful tour as Special Agent in Charge of the Chicago office, MORG had been vulnerable. Childermass was dead, there was no clear line of succession: Multiphasic Operations and Research Group could have been smashed then and there. Unfortunately the man who was FBI Director at the time was not aggressive enough to seize the opportunity. Carsten Burrows, rid of a man he thought was a psychopath, found no further menace in MORG. Nonetheless he wasn't a fool. He put Robert Hyde in charge of a small unit of agents devoted to MORG-watching. After two decades Hyde's zeal to infiltrate and learn everything he could about MORG was still a ruling passion. He was the ranking expert in world espionage circles on MORG's structure, personnel, and modes of operation.

The crucial blank in all of his research had been the very center of Multiphasic Operations and Research Group, the source of its renewed power. He had a face and a name: Victor Wilding. The most recent ten years of Wilding's life were thoroughly documented. Before that, nothing at all. The man had no history. Obviously Victor Wilding was not his birth name. Who Wilding really was, where he had come from—these questions had, until recently, given Hyde dyspepsia and insomnia. Now, having acquired a single fingerprint of the usually elusive Wilding and matched it with another print in the Bureau's files, his sleeplessness was more often caused by a hot spot of fear beneath his breastbone. Where it glowed like the tip of a cigarette smoked by someone in deep shadow, observing *him* as avidly as he had watched the man who called himself Wilding.

The FBI Director had cultivated sufficient interest in baseball to give him something to chat about with Allen Dunbar, until the civilities had been observed. Then they ceremoniously finished off small neat scotches in the oppressively decorated drawing room of the suite. The President pro tem leaned forward in an ugly Louis-the-something, heavily brocaded chair opposite Robert Hyde. Over both their heads a massive chandelier glittered distantly. Much of the drawing room was dark. Which made the two Secret Service men seated in one corner less conspicuous, although they never took their eyes off Dunbar.

"What do we know?"

Hyde never spoke to anyone in a voice much above a whisper. He liked having his listeners strain a little, expend effort to hang on to his words.

"Mr. President, in their typical fashion MORG isn't letting the Bureau get anywhere near it. But we've learned enough to make some educated guesses about what went on in Honolulu today."

"Good. What have we learned?"

Hyde took his time. "Mr. President, I'm convinced that the attack on the First Lady's motorcade was part of a grand design, additional threads in the tapestry of terror that began with the nuclear incident in Portland this February."

"Good Lord. The same warp and weft, you're saying."

"I'm also convinced the plane that crashed in Innisfall, California, at noon Pacific time, is another part of the tapestry."

"NTSB thinks that was just a regrettable accident, Bob."

"Give me credit for knowing more than the Safety Board investigators."

"Well, of course. Wasn't an accident, then, you're saying."

"The DC-10 involved was leased to the non-sked airline TRANSPAC, an infamous MORG proprietary, going all the way back to the Vietnam War, when MORG became involved in the profitable drug trafficking they continue today. TRANSPAC 1850 departed Honolulu in the wee hours of the morning. It had been parked in a remote part of the airport. There was no passenger manifest. We've learned, however, that all aboard were MORG employees except perhaps for one person, unidentified, who was removed on a stretcher at approximately two forty-five A.M. from a MH-60K helicopter, the kind frequently employed by MORG in clandestine activities. The unknown person was transferred to the DC-10. Subsequently there was one crash survivor, who is in intensive care following surgery. Her name is Portia Darkfeather. I'm sure she would have some answers for us, but MORG agents out of San Francisco have the entire hospital in a vise." He waited for Dunbar to get his point, then added forcefully, "MORG again."

"Uh-huh. Yes. I see."

"And the ultimate destination of TRANSPAC 1850 was to have been Plenty Coups, Montana."

"Plenty Coups!" Dunbar said. He began running a hand across his scant hairline again, where his scalp itch was worst.

"That's correct. Plenty Coups, the ultimate in secret MORG facilities. A sixteen-billion-dollar expenditure, to date. They keep pouring money into the complex, no questions asked by a gullible Senate and pliable House. What goes on at Plenty Coups? From the types of equipment that are being ordered and shipped, it's a scientific research facility. Of course I have someone on the inside, but not—all the way inside. The place is a Q-clearance nightmare. We have yet to penetrate to the heart of the mystery that is Plenty Coups."

"You're working on it."

"Rest assured. We'll get there."

"What's—what would you say the common thread is now, in this terrorist design, *tapestry,* as you put it?"

"Psychic research and psi training, Mr. President. MORG was a pioneer among government entities looking into the military uses of clairvoyance, mental telepathy, and something called psychometrics, which is the ability to move solid objects through mental energy alone."

"Uh-huh!" The two men stared at each other for a few moments. Dunbar said, "I'm not entirely sure I—"

"Telepathic espionage is the new paradigm for the third millennium. The battle for the human mind is the only battlefield that will matter in this century. In short—"

Dunbar edged a little closer to the Director, hands clutching his knees.

"All of MORG's resources for the past few years," Hyde continued, "have been concentrated on a single goal: the development of a new super-race of psychics. Imagine the advantage, the power to be gained from knowing every waking thought of those among us who try to resist subjugation through mind control."

"Horrifying. But—how much of this is reality, and how much is theory? Five thousand four hundred twenty-six long-distance nuclear warheads still operational in Russia, and the North Koreans are pushing ahead with their TAEPO DONG 2s. Now that's a reality we can sink our teeth into."

"Most of those Cold War hangovers can and will be cured through negotiation. I have the utmost respect for your leadership in that area."

"Thank you. Of course, I'm still committed to the Aegis Two Option, more than ever now that I'm, umm, where I am." Dunbar smiled tensely and had another go at his now-inflamed scalp. "This psychometric stuff—that was a movie, wasn't it? Sissy Spacek's eyes got big and then kitchen drawers opened and she sent all the cutlery flying at her demented mother. What happened after that? The house burned down, I think."

"Mr. President, quite frankly *our* house—as a metaphor of the government of the United States—is on fire and in danger of burning down if we do not act quickly and without compunction."

"You have some evidence? *Can* solid objects be moved through the, the power of the mind?"

"I've recently reviewed film and audio tapes from Carsten Burrows's personal archives, all of it more than twenty years old. They concern startling experiments MORG did with a young psychic named Robin Sandza. The experiments made a believer of me. No doubt that the boy had inhuman powers. Burrows later received information from a CIA Supergrade that Sandza had died in a fall while trying to escape from Psi Faculty, shortly after his fifteenth birthday. It happened the night that Childermass, whom we have to thank for Multiphasic Operations and Research Group, also died, in his bathtub."

"Heart attack, wasn't it?"

"No. His body was bled out. A gruesome death. But it wasn't suicide. I spent years investigating Psi Faculty, what went on there. As you know, we still maintain a MORG watch section at the Bureau, with sixty agents assigned. We have two bunker warehouses filled with intelligence. But the most significant breakthrough in our understanding of what is going on at MORG came only this week."

"That's why you're here," Dunbar said with a tense grin as he furiously worked his fingers into his scalp.

"That's why I'm here. Excuse me for just a moment while I prepare this."

Hyde got up and opened a laptop computer on a round table a few feet from where he'd been sitting. He booted it up, then inserted a CD-ROM that he took from an attaché case equipped with the kind of security devices that meant instant death to any would-be intruders not in possession of the unlocking codes. He changed the angle of the laptop on the table so that Dunbar could easily see the screen. *Click.* A boyish image appeared, a young man in a snapshot, leaning against an iron fence atop a stone wall, looking back over one shoulder as if someone had just called to him. There was a river in the background and, distantly, tall red-banded smokestacks.

"This is Robin Sandza. A Polaroid photograph found in the effects of Dr. Irving Roth, former director of Paragon Institute on the Upper East Side of Manhattan. Paragon was an entry-level research facility for young people with psi ability. The photo was taken across the street in Carl Schurz Park. Dr. Roth apparently got on the bad side of Childermass, who was notoriously paranoid. Roth simply disappeared one day. No trace of him has ever been found."

The image of Robin Sandza was enhanced, then replaced with an artist's likeness. Moments later another face appeared, beside the image of the red-haired boy.

"And we know who this is," Hyde said, smiling slightly at the effect the juxtaposition had on Allen Dunbar.

"Uncanny resemblance. But can you be *sure*?"

"No doubt at all, sir." The two portraits, man and boy, were diminished in size on the active matrix screen. Below each face a fingerprint appeared. They were slowly enlarged until the loops and whorls were easily distinguished. An overlay of technical analysis completed the montage. "The print on the left is from the index finger of Robin Sandza. We took it from the taped handle of a baseball bat stored in the attic of the house in Lambeth, Virginia, where he spent his boyhood years. The print on the right is from the same index finger. It came from a table microphone shortly after the adjournment of a special Senate Select Committee on Intelligence hearing this past Tuesday. Victor Wilding almost never appears in public, as we know, but occasionally he has to show up where the money is. During the course of the hearing he was seen to adjust the microphone by one of our agents, who acted as soon as Wilding and his entourage left the chamber. Matching fingerprints aren't all we have, however. We also have realized a significant DNA match, coming up now on screen. Hairs removed from a Daffy Duck stuffed animal that Robin Sandza slept with as a child. And, ah, residue from a urinal that Wilding used in the men's room during a recess in the recent hearing. The urinal failed to flush, and one of our men was on the spot with his handkerchief as soon as Wilding walked out."

"FBI thoroughness," Dunbar said admiringly; then a look of concern settled on his bony face. "So 'Victor Wilding' is the adult version of the young man with . . . was it 'inhuman powers,' you said?"

"That was Carsten Burrows's evaluation, Mr. President. Having worked under Burrows, known him for the analytical and fair-minded man he was, I'm inclined to accept it. And a further judgment he made, based on a CIA eyewitness report the night of the demonstration."

"Which was?"

"He concluded in his journal that the powers of Robin Sandza had only negative implications for the well-being of our country. He quoted Boyd Huckle, who was present at the demonstration, as saying, 'I'm convinced that you had better kill the little shit-face before he causes some real grief.' "

"I sure do miss Boyd. Right or wrong, you knew where he stood."

"Huckle was entirely correct. Clairvoyants, telepaths, the psychically gifted. They represent a direct threat to us, to *your* presidency."

"Uh-huh. Uh-huh. But do you—is there evidence that Rona Harvester might have—"

"Psychic powers? No. She doesn't need them. Robin Sandza is her lover; therefore all of MORG is at her disposal. Mr. President, we *can* still deal with them. And all of those young psychics who are currently 'coming out,' destined to join forces with MORG. Like the college girl in California who made the call on the TRANSPAC 1850 crash minutes before it happened. MORG is looking for her as we speak, bet on that. But I've known about her existence for some time. She will never be a problem for us."

"I saw her on the tube today! She strongly reminded me of someone, but I couldn't recall—"

Bob Hyde nodded slightly, but not as a confirmation. It wasn't news to him how strongly Eden Waring favored her mother. He smiled, which was rare. He reached into an inside pocket of his suit coat.

"Almost forgot about this. A little gift for you, Mr. President. From myself and my son. Like you he's always been an avid collector of baseball cards."

Dunbar took the plastic case and looked at his gift. His pensive expression was transformed by awe and then glee.

"Omigod! *Ted Williams's* rookie card. Whoa! This is terrific, Bob. 'The Splendid Splinter.' I'm *so* grateful. Can't thank you enough. And your son, don't forget to convey my heartfelt thanks. How's the boy doing, by the way? Heard from him lately?"

"Doing quite well in his present assignment. I am expecting a call from him. Mr. President, would it be presumptuous of me to suggest another ounce or two of that excellent whiskey?"

"Not at all, Bob," Dunbar said. "*I* sure could use another blast. This little session of ours has been an eye-opener." He chuckled uneasily. "I'm tempted to say, a *mindblower.*"

Hyde smiled again. Twice in one night qualified as an event. But he was feeling good about the way things were going. He poured the scotch for them. Three ounces over ice for Allen Dunbar. Hyde knew his habits. He knew his man. They sipped in silence, each with his own thoughts, which might have been the same thoughts.

MOBY BAY, CALIFORNIA · MAY 28 · 8:20 P.M. PDT

Fogbound, sea-saddened, Eden walked the sand in shivering rue, silence in her mind. She wore borrowed clothes and stodgy sandals. Her bare toes were numb from inundation, the last frothy swish of each booming wave. Her hair felt stiff from salt spray. There was a nearly full moon, squash-colored, above the drifting fog, visible from time to time. And the sea had its own secret phosphorescence.

One side of her tongue throbbed as if from a hornet's sting; she had bitten it at the onset of her seizure. Hours ago. Wardella Tinch had made tea for them on arrival at her beachfront home, but Eden wasn't able to keep anything else on her stomach. Neither fully awake nor sleepwalking, she trudged along beside the great cold weight of the Pacific, yearning for her home. For things as they once were, and (she already understood) never could be again.

"Oh, shit," Eden said dispiritedly to a couple of sandpipers walking ahead of her. She found it as difficult to talk as if her mouth were stuffed with pebbles. The pipers took wing and coasted a few yards farther up the beach. But it was no weather for flying.

She had been in a post-seizure stupor as they approached the house on Deep Creek Road, with a terrible headache and no memory of what had happened to her after they'd left the cemetery in the rattly old pickup truck. At which point the medium, seeing the crowd around the Warings' gate, the TV news vans with their satellite uplinks, pushed Eden down in the seat and held her there, showing the strength of arm gained from decades of playing her Titano free bass accordion. Not an instrument for wimps, Wardella avowed.

"I felt that it was in your best interests not to have to face inquiries just then. And those newspeople can be so obnoxious. So I drove right on past your gate and headed for Moby Bay. I do hope you're not angry."

Eden lacked the energy to be angry. She slept again after their arrival at Wardella's seaside abode, waking up after dark to find that her much-abused graduation dress had been whisked away. Wardella had washed and dried the dress and her bra; but the dress was no longer wearable. A change of clothes had been provided for Eden: dungarees, a fisherman's sweater, and the chunky homemade sandals of saddle leather and brass rivets.

She hated what she saw in the bathroom mirror. There was a comb on the sink that looked clean and a new, unwrapped toothbrush. Eden did what she could with the comb and passed on brushing her teeth, her tongue hurt too much.

It was a boxy prairie-style house, catty-corner at the brink of a rocky headland, showing a blank wall to the ocean view and often-violent winds. There were two bedrooms and a parlor downstairs. Kitchen windows overlooked a protected English garden: hedges and lots of trellises for climbing roses and wide-mouthed amapolla. Fog-muted cypress fronted the road.

In the kitchen Wardella Tinch was hosting her Saturday-night poker group. Four other men and women, all about her age, budding septuagenarians. Wardella had made gingerbread, which was cooling on a sideboard.

"Oh, that *stinks*," one of the ladies said, throwing in her hand when confronted with three kings.

"Mrs. Tinch?"

Wardella was wearing a green plastic eyeshade. She turned and smiled at Eden, shuffling the cards meanwhile.

"Hello, dear. Why don't you call me Wardella? Do Chauncey's things fit you?"

"Pretty much. Thank you. Wardella. Who is Chauncey?"

"A lovely young friend of mine who lives north along the cove about a mile. She's dying to meet you. Maybe she'll drop by later. And these are some of my other friends."

Everyone around the table nodded amiably as Mrs. Tinch introduced them. "And the one who's sulking right now because Fred called her bluff is my sister-in-law Daphne Yawl."

"I am *not* sulking, Wardella. If I *were* sulking, I'd have all your pots and pans hanging over the stove banging around like tone-deaf church bells."

Wardella smiled indulgently. "Hope blooms eternally. But even so, someday you'll learn not to draw to an inside straight, lovely."

The old gent named Fred winked at Eden as if they were about to share a joke. He looked at the cards Wardella had shuffled. One of them popped out of the deck, circled the table leisurely a couple of times, like a miniature flying carpet, then dropped faceup in front of Daphne Yawl. It was the seven of clubs.

"Oh, *there* it is," Daphne said, and they all laughed.

"We don't use our powers when we're playing poker," Wardella reminded them. "Besides, since I'm not witchy, the rest of you have me at a considerable disadvantage." She gave Fred a look that flared slightly, as if she were warning him. "And you won't impress Eden with dopey card tricks."

Eden had backed up a step in the doorway. Her pulses were pounding away. Wherever she was, she didn't need to be there.

Wardella looked back at Eden. Her expression was sympathetic.

"Just block them all from your mind, dear, if it would make you feel better."

"H-how?"

"Try closing your eyes. Take a deep breath to relax yourself. Count back, slowly, from five to one. On *one,* open your eyes. All there is to it."

The suggestion seemed benign. Eden tried it. When she opened her eyes again, Wardella Tinch was seated alone at the kitchen table doing needlepoint. She looked subtly different to Eden. Younger. Reminiscent of someone. It was a comforting familiarity to Eden.

"Is that better?" Wardella, intent on her stitches, asked. "It always has worked for me, and I have nothing like your latent ability."

"I—I wonder if I could use your telephone to call my folks?"

"Of course you may, dear. You'll have the most privacy in my parlor. Be careful not to disturb anything. Above all, don't look into the crystal ball. I don't know what you gleaned today from the crystals in my truck that set you off so, but then you haven't been prepared for gazing. And I'm unable to interfere should you be drawn into the mischief."

Eden tried to swallow, almost choked on dryness, had no voice for questions. *What mischief?*

She retreated across a hallway to the parlor, which apparently also was Wardella's place of business. There were astrological and Tarot charts on the walls, a nineteenth-century palmist's guide to the human hand. On a small round table, a draped object that had to be the crystal ball. It glowed through the pale blue tasseled cloth like a lamp of low but pure-white wattage.

Eden wasn't tempted to peek beneath the cloth. Just being near the ball put a morbid chill in her blood. She turned her back on it and began to retrieve vital phone and pager numbers from a sluggish memory.

She would have called Geoff first, but she remembered that his car was sitting on a hill in the cemetery. There was no explanation she could think of that would come close to satisfying him. She called home instead.

All of the phones, with listed and unlisted numbers, rang and rang. If they weren't there, she wondered, why were the answering machines turned off?

Eden then learned that she couldn't be connected to any of the pager or cell phone numbers in Innisfall. The Coast Range and a lot of trees were in the way. Possibly hostile atmospherics had something to do with it. So here she was, stuck in Moby Bay, a tiny place she couldn't recall having heard of although she had spent all of her life in northern California. She didn't have a penny or an ATM card, and no transportation.

She left the parlor and again looked in on Wardella Tinch, whose chin was on her chest. She was snoring softly. Wardella looked old again, purple veins embedded in her crimson cheeks like tiny thunderbolts. The needlepoint had fallen from her lap to the floor.

When Eden opened the door to the walled garden Wardella said, not looking up, "Some air will do you good. But don't you want a piece of my gingerbread before you go?"

"No, thank you. Maybe later."

"Take care not to get lost. Walk north, not south."

"Where do I find Chauncey?"

"Walk along the shore. She'll find you."

"Who *are* you, Wardella? I have the oddest feeling that you and I—"

"It will come to you. Remember. Always north, not south."

"What's south?"

"It's the wrong way out of our world, and the beginning of the many pathways into Theirs. You already know from your Dreamtime what lies along those paths."

Eden's heartbeat picked up. As if there were ten seconds left to play, the Lady Wolves inbounding. They had to have a three to tie. The outcome of the game, which had become life itself, depending on her stroke.

"What world are you talking about?"

"Why, God's good green earth, to be sure. With all of its wonders and illusions. You'll soon learn your way around, metaphysically speaking. You were always faithful about your lessons. Now you will appreciate having the use of them."

"Lessons? Am I *dream*ing?" Eden rubbed a hand over the rough wool of her sweater, producing a *zap* of static electricity. And she never had had a heartbeat, a heartache, quite this size in any of her well-documented dreams.

"My dear. I'm afraid Dreamtime is over. That part of your education is complete."

"You're the Good Lady!"

Wardella smiled comfortingly.

"But you don't look—"

"Just give me a moment to freshen up, I won't disappoint you. If you wouldn't mind closing your eyes again, the same routine as before? *Deep* breath. There you go. Now count backward slowly, that's my girl. Look up now, Eden. May I say what a great pleasure it has been to serve as your guide, all of these years. They went by so quickly. Are those tears? It's all right, darling. Here I am, for the last time."

INNISFALL, CALIFORNIA · MAY 28 · 8:54 P.M. PDT

When he got home Geoff McTyer took a quick shower and changed clothes. His cell phone hadn't rung. No messages from Eden. He sat down with take-out KFC extra-crispy and mashed potatoes to eat while he listened to the surveillance tapes he had brought from the house on Deep Creek Road.

A lot of chatter flying in and out of that house, particularly on weekends. He had routinely changed all of the tapes at least once a week. No problem finding a time. On weekdays Betts, Riley, and Eden were away from home, usually from eight A.M. until late afternoon. He could visit the covered well on the walled patio in daylight hours without being observed from the road. Riley had occasionally talked about demolishing the well and using the stones for an outdoor oven and barbecue, which gave Geoff some bad moments. But Betts wouldn't let her husband touch it. She said the well was picturesque, hornets and all.

The first tape he listened to was Eden's cell phone frequency, and the tape was blank. Not a word. But he'd been there at breakfast this morning, eating waffles and talking to Betts while Eden had spent at least ten minutes in conversation with Megan Pardo.

He checked his equipment. No malfunctions.

The voice-activated tape monitoring Betts's cell phone frequency also yielded nothing. It was the same for the third, Riley's, tape.

All of the tapes were blank. He considered accidental erasure, a demagnetizing mishap. That had happened once before, during a major thunderstorm. Today the weather had been fine. Geoff bleakly came to another conclusion: someone else, familiar with the Special Operations Group's microelectronics and possibly knowledgeable about Geoff's hiding place, had dropped by the Waring house, a little before dark, say, removed the tapes Geoff had left there four days ago and installed new ones.

Geoff tried to take this intrusion, the imagined usurper, as a fact of the life he led, the people he worked for. But if he was right about what had happened he felt he deserved better and to hell with the circumstances. At the least, a phone call. Some indication of support and appreciation for the time he'd put in, his two and a half years in California. But that was like the Old Man, wasn't it? Not a word from him. Maybe, a few months from now, the Old Man might refer to Innisfall in Geoff's presence, with a slight nod of appreciation.

But Geoff couldn't stay focused on this apparent slight. When he closed his eyes all he saw was Eden, and there was a cold draft around his heart. His emotions were icebound. He wasn't going to see her again. Icebound emotions, freezing blood. Never. Never again.

A little later, the doorbell rang.

Geoff's head jerked up. Thinking of Eden's sure fate, a desperate need for sleep and surcease had blocked his panic as efficiently as a pre-op anesthetic and he had nodded off at the table, a half-eaten chicken wing in his fingers.

The panic returned instantly. He put down the chicken bones, wiped his fingers, picked up his Glock 19, and slipped it into the leather holster on his belt.

Half hoping that it would be Eden after all, he opened the door.

The man standing outside had a face the color of rare roast beef, small white scars like stitchings of sinew. His blatantly artificial hair, jet-black, was slicked down sideways across the rear half of his otherwise bald head. His ears looked as if they were chew toys for young pit bulls. His eyes, like his hair, were a peculiarly lifeless shade of black. Only his theatrically lush false eyelashes had any luster in the light of the hall.

"You Geoff?"

"Yes."

"Haman." His hands were in the pockets of a lightweight tan windbreaker, which along with baggy cargo khakis filled out what appeared to be a slender frame. "It seems we're working together." He looked past Geoff into the apartment, as if expecting to see someone else, then looked back at Geoff.

"Haman? I've never heard of you."

"Well, gee whiz."

"You have a first name?"

"Phil. It says on my brand-new driver's license and American Express Gold Card. Just call me Haman." He looked into the apartment again.

"Verify," Geoff said.

"Route G. Zorro. Impact Sector. Today's special at Tony's on the Wharf is, if I remember correctly, blackened bluefin."

Impact Sector. Geoff had hoped for a little while that the Old Man might have had a change of heart about Eden. It wasn't to be.

Geoff closed the door in the assassin's face, went to his computer, which was up and running. He entered Route G and his own ID, then Zorro, and waited for the menu from Impact Sector. After he confirmed the day's special he went back to Haman, stood aside while the man walked in.

"I take it she's not here," Haman said, casting a disparaging eye on the rental furniture.

"I don't know where Eden is. Are you the one who lifted my tapes at the Warings'?"

Haman nodded. "You from Boston?" he asked.

"In the vicinity. What was on the tapes?"

Haman took all three tapes from his windbreaker pocket and laid them on the dining-nook table.

"KFC, huh? I had pizza on the way over. But I could use a cup of coffee."

"Haman, are you gonna tell me, or do I have to listen to those tapes myself?"

Haman looked around at him again, swiftly, said in mock admiration, "Damn if you're not too tough to chew." He raised a hand, palm up. "The folks have gone to Greenwood Lake. Not to their own place. They borrowed someone else's house. People named Hassler. The girl's not with them. That's all I've got. She hasn't tried to contact you?"

"No."

"Think she will?"

Geoff shrugged.

"She's stuck on you, isn't she?" Geoff didn't reply. Haman nodded as if it were a given and looked away, saw the French press coffeemaker on the counter in the kitchenette, an unopened bag of Gold Coast from Starbucks. "You like yours Italian style? I can drink Starbucks. Usually I roast my own beans. Kenyan double A, Costa Rican Tarrazu. Have you ever tried Kopi Luwak? Sumatran, the beans cost upward of three hundred bucks a pound. There's a reason for the high price. Each bean is fed to a civet cat, which is called a *luwak* in Indonesia. The beasties can't digest the beans, so they're excreted whole. Gives the coffee a real, shall we say, earthy flavor. Acquired taste for the connoisseur. You don't mind if I brew some of your Starbucks for myself, do you?"

"No."

Haman went into the kitchenette. "When was the last time you saw the girl?"

"About noon, after the plane crashed. I left her in my car in the east parking lot of the stadium."

"Mell of a hess, huh? I drove by there around six, after I got in."

"From where?"

"Can't seem to locate your coffee filters."

"Drawer next to the fridge. You must already have been on the West Coast, to get here so fast."

"Vegas," Haman volunteered. "I spend most of my free time in Vegas."

"You like to gamble?"

"Not much. Vegas is Showtown. I've got an Act."

"Yeah?"

Haman was silent for a time, measuring coffee into the filter. "Have any bottled water? Tap water ruins coffee."

"Some Crystal Geyser under the sink."

"Thanks."

Geoff's cell phone rang, startling him. He didn't want it to be Eden. On the other hand, he couldn't not answer with Haman listening from the kitchenette.

"Hello."

"Geoff, God, *finally*. It's Megan Pardo."

"Hi, Megan."

"Is Eden with you?"

"No. I thought she might be with you."

"I haven't heard a word. I went out there. You should see the mob in front of their place. *What* is going on?"

"I wish I could tell you."

"I'm like, *God,* my best *friend,* where did this stuff *come* from? Did you know she was like, what do you call it, clairvoyant?"

"Never a clue. I'm baffled, Megan."

"I don't blame Eden if she's gone off somewhere. I just *pray* she calls one of us soon. If you hear from her first, tell Eden I love her and I'm here when she needs me."

"I will, Megan. Thanks for calling. Good night."

Geoff closed the cell phone and dropped it in his pocket. Haman had come out of the kitchen and opened the door to the hall closet.

"Golf clubs," he said. "Calloways. Nice. You play a lot, Geoff?"

"Too busy, usually."

"Water skis. Snow skis. A fucking sportsman, no less."

"She's not hiding in a closet, Haman."

Haman shut the door. "I wouldn't have thought so. But she's gone. You say you don't know know where she is. In Hollywood as we speak, hiring Mike Ovitz to map out her movie career?"

"That is so far from who Eden Waring really is."

Haman picked up a framed portrait of Eden from atop the TV in the small living room.

"The voice of experience. A man who knows his woman. Fuck her yet, or am I being naive?"

"Get out of my apartment, Haman."

"Coffee's not hot yet. Besides, we're going to be a twosome. Where is that written in the stars, you ask? Granted, this is not the method Impact Sector traditionally employs."

"No, it isn't."

"But you know Eden Waring and I don't. You've been here awhile. What, two years? More? Anyway, you've had the lay of the kid and you've got the lay of the land, and I don't have a couple of days to futz around getting my bearings. Clear now, Big Stuff?"

"Perfectly."

"If Eden doesn't phone in by the time I've finished my coffee, what do you say we drive up to Greenwood Lake and see if we can find the Hassler place. Get acquainted with the folks. It'll be either you or them the girl contacts first. Make it simple. We sit on the parents, and wait. I might have time to work on my new act. Did I tell you what I do in Vegas? My regular job; this is just moonlighting."

"What do you do in Vegas?" Geoff asked, but not as if he cared much.

"I'm a female impersonator. Tina Turner, shit, *my* Tina is a Day-Glo mindfuck. I have one of those faces, not much to look at now, my late psycho stepdad treated me to a lye bath when I was twelve. I just sit down at my makeup table and start adding on. Mortician's wax, prosthetics, contact lenses, wigs. I've got a twenty-eight-inch waist. My Liz Taylor has some mileage left. Liz plays well with the older crowd we get. That silver wig set me back a couple k. You know, and the costume jewelry: I buy only the best fake stuff, can't skimp when you're re-creating a legend. I come out *dripping* diamonds. Liz doing Shakespeare. 'O! That this too too solid flesh would melt.' Fuckin' wonderful. Brings down the house. You're probably curious who the new girl is. I'm the first to do her, over here, but I understand Michel has put her into *his* club Act, that little *boite* in Pigalle he's been operating since Freckles was a pup."

Geoff was still too astonished at hearing Elizabeth Taylor's voice come out of Haman to do more than nod.

"Rona *Harv*ester." For the first time since Geoff had laid eyes on him, he saw Haman's teeth, bared in a big wide showbiz smile. The teeth were false, of course. "Just hope we have time for my Rona. Promise, you'll split a gut laughing."

WESTBOUND, NEW YORK/SAN FRANCISCO • MAY 28 • 7:44 P.M. MDT

Bertie Nkambe came down the right-side aisle of United's 747, drawing stares from those first-class passengers savvy enough about the fashion world to recognize a *Paris Vogue* cover girl. She dropped into the seat beside Tom Sherard. He was staring out the window. Not much to see. They were at thirty-four thousand feet, the indigo sky filled with stars like sparks from a brushfire, dark cloud cover over Wyoming's Wind River Range.

"Found him. Twenty-six B in Economy."

"Found who?" Sherard asked, slow to pull out of the depths of the poor mood he was in.

"The telepath who has been nudging around at us. Looking to get in. I brushed him away like a *tsetse*. A professor type. Those awful squarish eyeglass frames, like Woody Allen's. And he's gone much too long without a haircut. He's wearing a checked Gap shirt and a brown corduroy jacket. Too big for him, but he has shoulders like a goat. He's eating peanuts and pretending to read Noam Chomsky while he peeps the unsuspecting."

Sherard was paying attention now.

"Maybe he's not in the Game."

"It *could* be a coincidence that he's on the plane with us. But, Tom. Why don't I deep-fry a batch of his neurons, then we don't have to be concerned about him."

"That's rather drastic."

"Why take chances with any telepath? Too many of them are the wrong sort."

"Your grandfather taught me many valuable things when I was learning to shoot. One of them was, a single blade of grass very close to the muzzle can deflect a bullet."

Bertie leaned back in the leather seat and stretched, arms over her head. "Point taken."

"Maybe you should have gone on to London without me. You wouldn't be so bored there."

Bertie pouted. "What makes you think I'm bored? I don't *want* to be without you. And you need me. Look at how helpful I've already been. We wouldn't be staying at the Lambourne if I hadn't weighed in with my vast celebrity." She said it with an amused wink. "They're always booked weeks in advance, you know."

"I don't have anything against the Mark Hopkins."

Bertie laid her cropped head on his shoulder. "We can have a good time in San Francisco, even though we're only going to be there the night. That is, should you permit yourself to have fun." When he didn't respond she rolled her eyes up to him.

"Reckon you're right."

"Of course I am. We don't actually have to *go* anywhere. It's a snug little suite that I've always enjoyed, and with a phone call the best Chinese food in the western world will be delivered to our door."

"Snug little suite? How many bedrooms?"

"One large bedroom. One heavenly extra-long bed, because I am an extra-long person."

"Bertie—Alberta—you're still a teenager, and this whole arrangement you've come up with is totally out of the—"

"I was twenty in March. You *did* pick out those earrings yourself?"

"For your birthday, yes. I happened to find myself near Cartier's, and I remembered—*Birthday*, let me remind you. We are not engaged. And we are not going to sleep together."

"Tom," she said, sorrow and sympathy in her lush contralto voice, "have you had a woman since Gillian died?"

"Simply none of your—yes, dozens."

"You know I don't believe that," Bertie said with a confident smile. "What you *don't* know but will discover is that I've saved myself for you. I mean, I didn't know *why,* at the time. Why I could have only a passing interest—a crush here and there—on some of the world's most attractive men. You were happily married. I loved Gillian, as much as I love you. Nonetheless something told me—oh, God. Forgive me for that. I'm very sorry."

He nodded tensely, not looking at her.

"I don't have that particular gift, Tom," she said after a few moments.

"Yes, you do."

"But I never pried into your life! Or Gillian's. I choose not to know the fate of those who are very close and dear to me."

"Let's not go on with this."

"Things do pop into my head, whether I'm willing or unwilling to have them there. You have feelings for me, why deny it? Even though you want to go on pretending that to marry me would be a failure of fealty to my father. From the day I came to live with you and Gillian you've had this sense of duty. As if you'd sworn an oath to take care of Bertie Nkambe in the evil old world. Touching then, misguided now. Let me tell you. I have also done a very good job of looking after myself in a tough, what does Calvin call it, tough *racket* since I was all of sixteen. You think my father would not approve of our love? Well, you're wrong, Tom."

"Joseph would have me beheaded if I—no, he'd bloody well do it himself."

"Knowing that I've given myself to a good man, a man whose raising was left to him when your father died, would be a thing of joy and a blessing to Joseph. There. I don't think I have any more to say. Except this."

She lifted her elegant brown head and put her lips close to his ear, as close as a kiss. She had a full mouth, of course, but with the contours and demure quality of the Orient that shaded the effect of fortress cheekbones.

Long fingers were poised on his other cheek. Rings glinted at the corner of his eye.

"Sometimes, Tom, you simply have to say—what the fuck. It's *my* heart, and I'm going where it tells me to go."

MOBY BAY · MAY 28 · 8:55 P.M. PDT

Eden sidestepped a jellied mass of bronze-green kelp, some flotsam with a white opaque bottle at its center, like a vapid eye. She waited while runoff from the last wave to smash against the pebbly shore drained seaward, then waded across a shallow wash, the swirl of water alluringly phosphorescent around her ankles.

She saw someone walking toward her down the beach, where the fog had thinned and moonlight shone on piled driftwood, each blunt stub sheathed in radiance.

They stopped walking when they were ten feet apart. The other girl wore a peacoat with the collar turned up. Blond hair feathered out from beneath a knitted watch cap.

"Hi."

"Hi. You must be—"

"Chauncey. You're wondering what kind of name that is for a girl."

"No, I like it. Thanks for the clothes, Chauncey."

"Hey, no problem." Chauncey sat on a canted length of driftwood and cocked her head, inviting Eden to join her. Chauncey had a very small, delicately boned, heart-shaped face, perfectly formed small features. Her dark round eyes seemed startlingly large in that petite face.

"So you're the new Avatar. Awesome."

Eden shrugged. Her hands were cold. She slipped them beneath the tight cuffs of the borrowed sweater and gazed out to sea. The fog had thinned to furls and wisps. The strong waves rolled in to shore laden with silver like returning champions.

" 'I am not Prince Hamlet, nor was meant to be,' " she said moodily.

"That's from *Prufrock,* right? I like Eliot, although I don't always know where he's coming from. I'm sixth-generation Wicca, by the way. Nearly everyone in Moby Bay has the Craft, or else they're prescient. Guess I'm just used to being what I am. Of course I'm small 'taters next to you."

Between the crashing of the waves Eden thought she could hear Wardella Tinch playing her accordion.

"I don't know much about witchcraft. It's all fairy tales to me. There's usually a big book of lore, isn't there? Handwritten on crinkly parchment. Spells and incantations."

Chauncey shrugged. "I've never seen one. If I need a spell I get it off the Internet."

Eden smiled. She had the good feeling that she'd met someone she was going to like very much.

"What kind of music are you into?" Chauncey asked.

"Classical, mostly. Guitar. I play a little. But I want to study with someone good, if I ever find the time."

"Did Wardella tell you? I'm with a band. *Pussy Whip.* Skelly, she's our bassist, came up with the name one night when she and her boyfriend were fooling around in bed with a squirt can of that dessert goo, you probably get the association. Of course there are other, um, connotations. We're one guy, drums, and four girls, I guess is what distinguishes us. That, plus we're good."

"Hard-core?"

"Thrash metal/punk, with a social agenda. Our last album on Scrooge Records, *Feeding the Sharks,* sold thirty-five thousand CDs. Enough so the label springs for our tours. We use the bus *Pantera* had before they went arena. We've got a new manager. Raoul Kapooshian, he made *Supermarket Bloodbath* what they are today. There's a tour video. We were hoping to get some of it on MTV, but they don't play any metal at all since *Headbanger's Ball* was canceled. I'm lead singer and do most of the writing."

"What are your songs like?"

"Oh, in-your-face stuff about the things in this world that piss me, that ought to piss everybody off. It helps me cope. As long as there's one starving baby somewhere, the human race is a failure."

"Yeah."

"If you feel up to it, I'd like to show you our video. Maybe you could spend the night? Wardella wouldn't mind. You weren't planning to go somewhere else, were you?"

"No, I don't have any plans. Can't even think s-straight yet."

"We'll just hang out then. Chill awhile, if you're not cold enough already."

"Sounds good. Chauncey—you mentioned the Internet. Could I use your computer to E-mail my folks?"

"Sure. Let's go."

They walked together along the rocky beach, through webs of fog that sparkled with millions of tiny drops of moisture. When Chauncey talked she used her hands for emphasis, leaving loops and swirls of bluish light, like nocturnal skywriting, that faded slowly behind them. Her face glowed from the same light. Eden was fascinated. Chauncey grinned, teeth with the eerie brilliance of small opals.

"I've never seen anything like this."

"Moby Bay is a special place. Protected."

"Like a wildlife refuge?"

"That's a good one. It's a refuge, all right. But the wildest thing in Moby Bay is Wardella's poker night. All of this"—Chauncey made a showy flourish with one hand, like a magician fanning cards—"is just the Caul, that we draw around ourselves at night. When we take back Moby Bay for ourselves, for meditation or renewal. You don't know how glad I am to come back here, after a hundred days on the road."

"I'll bet. What did you mean, take back Moby Bay. From what?"

"The tourists, for one thing. Nothing against tourists, that's how most of the people here make a living. We turn the place over to them in the daytime. We've got the quaint nineteenth-century main street, the old Victorian houses and gardens, the microbrewery, the lighthouse on the headland. But there are no accommodations, no typical northern California bed and breakfasts. Everything closes at dusk. The tourists leave. After dark, there's no way to get to Moby Bay. Unless you were born here, or you're invited by someone who was."

They took a path away from the beach and up a hill. The sky seemed very close, dense with stars, meteors, glowing nebulae. The tall cypresses dripped moisture. Eden felt light-headed but exhilarated, as if some of the tiny meteors were shooting through her mind. Physically she was strong, surefooted behind Chauncey, who occasionally reached down to help her along the steep defile.

"If you can drive here during the day—"

"We're ten miles from the highway. It's a good road to Moby Bay but the road branches a lot. Runs close to the sea, with a lot of switchbacks in the coves. Most nights there's fog. If you're driving back after dark because you think you may have left your video camera at the Gray Whale while you were having lunch, nothing looks familiar. In fact, it's kind of forbidding. The lonely road, no lights, no one to ask for directions. Easy to take the wrong fork in the road. So you drive in circles for an hour or so, eventually find yourself back on 101. By then your wife is tired, the kids are whining, so you decide the hell with it, bill the insurance company for the camcorder."

"Why is Moby Bay hard to find at night?"

They rested for a few moments at the top of the hill. There were a couple of one-story houses on the cliff fifty yards away. Redwood siding, shake-shingle roofs, patios. The odors from an outdoor grill were in the air. A dog was barking. The luminosity had faded from their faces and hands. Nothing out of the ordinary here. From this height the sea was bright and calm.

"It's all a matter of perception," Chauncey said. "Actually our hypothetical tourist found Moby Bay okay. Maybe he drove down Main Street a couple of times. He just didn't see it. He was like the guy from the audience the hypnotist puts to sleep onstage. The hypnotist tells his subject he's never been married, even though his wife is sitting right there in the second row getting the giggles. Then the hypnotist tells the guy he's madly in love and wants to propose to a best-of-show poodle in dog language. *Bow-wow.* Down on all fours. *Woof-woof.* The audience cracks up. Our tourist drives down Main Street looking for Moby Bay. We could be hanging out in front of the ice cream parlor mooning him, he wouldn't see us. That's the effect of the Caul. The bad thing about the Caul is, it screws up TV reception. Cell phones, forget it until the sun comes up. The energy has always been here—a certain resonance, frequency of vibrations, whatever. If you've got even a pinch of extrasensory perception you recognize and use what the earth gives to you. Most people let ninety percent of their gray matter go to waste. The active part of their brains is usually just something to hang their egos on."

"Chauncey—"

"I'm sorry. I run off at the mouth. And you know so much more than I do."

"That's just it. I *don't.* I don't know why you, *everyone* I meet says I'm what I am. I don't know what I'm supposed to do! I'm that dumb tourist you were talking about. Going around and around in my head. I have bad dreams that come true. That's all. And Wardella tells me—she won't be there anymore when I need her!"

After a few moments Chanucey put an arm around Eden's shoulders, drew her close.

"Somebody will," she said.

SAN FRANCISCO, CALIFORNIA · MAY 28 · 9:54 P.M. PDT

After they checked into the Lambourne, Tom Sherard yielded to Bertie Nkambe's suggestion that they walk up Nob Hill to Washington, then over to the Alleys of Chinatown, where her favorite Shanghaiese restaurant was located. Not advertised but well known to locals. One of the owners was a nephew of a man Bertie's father had been in business with in Nairobi and Mombasa. "*Guanxi,*" Bertie said, with that wink of hers. Meaning connections. Alberta's sweet insistence was hard to say no to, and after being on a plane for nearly five hours, Sherard needed to exercise. The more he walked, the less dependent he was on the lion's-head cane. And San Francisco had been blessed with a wonderful spring night. Shortly before ten o'clock on a Saturday the little shops, markets, and hole-in-the-wall restaurants of the Alleys were still busy places.

Bertie never went unnoticed, but in red leather and gold chains she drew attention like firecrackers in the street. Unlike a lot of models who had her elevation, looking over the heads of lesser mortals with waxen stares, Bertie had a smile for every stranger. She liked to browse and haggle. Before they reached the Ya Lin restaurant she stopped half a dozen times, admiring some eighteenth-century porcelains and lacquered screens in a couple of stores, watercolors displayed at curbside by a young student at the San Francisco Art Institute. Bertie conversed with the older Chinese in lilting Mandarin. She was, among her other talents, a natural polyglot. She had soaked up Chinese, English, and Swahili in her own home before coming to New York at the age of twelve to live with Sherard and Gillian and attend the Chapin school. But her real purpose for being in the States was to work with Gillian while she learned to deal with the yin and yang of her Gift.

The Gift had emerged early in Alberta Nkambe's life, when she was little more than a toddler. A black mamba, perhaps driven from its habitat by thick smoke from a brushfire, had invaded the Nkambes' house on their coffee estate by the Thika River. The snake had found a bamboo basket chair on the roofed veranda to its liking. Joseph Nkambe's favorite chair, when he had a few minutes to relax before dinner and watch rugby matches from England. It was his habit to plump up the chintz-covered dark green cushions before settling down. The family mongoose, their household snakehunter, was being treated at the vet's for an infected paw. Pleasantly distracted by his daughter babbling at play with two older brothers, Joseph didn't see the snake behind the cushion as he reached down.

The mamba struck him on the back of his hand, in the meat above the loose webbed skin between thumb and index finger. Joseph jerked his hand away in shock, and screamed when he saw the shapely head of death in his chair, the grayish punctures in his flesh. Only a few victims have survived the bite of the mamba. Even with prompt antivenin treatment the bite would have meant days of agony and delirium, leaving him with a mutilated hand and arm.

Joseph fell to his knees crying out to God in fear. The screams of his sons echoed through the house, bringing servants on the run.

Bertie didn't scream. She put down the toy truck she'd been playing with and walked over to her father. He was lying on his side, holding the bitten hand. Because the mamba's venom was a muscle toxin, the muscles of his arm as far as his shoulder were twitching out of control.

"Get away," he whispered to her. *"Mamba!"*

She saw the snake a few feet from them, gliding down to the terra-cotta floor of the veranda. It wasn't the first snake she'd seen, but it was probably the biggest. Alberta may have been too young to know fear. Mambas were blindingly fast in their habitat, but an impulse of caution or the unfamiliar tiles of the floor could have slowed this one. The girl made a move that was preternaturally quick for a three-year-old and seized the mamba behind its hideous tapered head. Stood firm as the snake squirmed in her grasp, its open mouth dense with scalded hate.

Then, staring at the mamba, she stroked it with her other hand, and as she did so the five-foot-long snake lost its will to fight and went slack in her chubby grip. *Pumbavu,* she said, meaning it was a stupid thing unworthy of further attention. After a few moments she tossed the mamba on the floor where it lay motionless. She turned to her father.

Joseph's body was vibrating as if he were being electrocuted. There was bloody froth on his lips and graying beard. The bitten hand had turned carmine around the wound and was swelling rapidly. Bertie grasped his hand. Joseph, fearful that the minutest part of the poison might get on her skin and be absorbed, tried to push her away. And then (Joseph said, telling it to Sherard years afterward) he felt a calming warmth that rushed the length of his arm toward his fibrillating heart, from there spreading swiftly through the rest of his body. It was like a brilliant tide sweeping him to the light-struck center of the universe. The seizure stopped almost immediately. Dazed, with the sensation that he had dreamed the mamba and its bite, he watched Alberta place her lips against the punctures. Then something struck him powerfully but painlessly, like a knockout punch to the chin.

The next thing Joseph knew he was being helped to his feet by his wife and one of the servants, while another servant carried the dead snake from the veranda, draped around the head of a broom. He felt as if he were struggling to wake up from the longest, deepest sleep of his life. There were no punctures on the dark brown skin of his hand, only a couple of insignificant healing scratches. His daughter looked up at him wordlessly, a cloudlike something in her usually clear and untroubled eyes. When Joseph reached for her, sobbing, she shook her head, evading him, and went back to her play, newly solemn. Three days passed before she spoke again.

Bertie hit Sherard for a hundred in cash to buy a watercolor she liked. Bertie's net worth at a comparatively tender age was several million dollars, but she was scarcely aware of it. Her income was invested for her by a conservative international bank owned by the Bellaver financial conglomerate. She was comfortable making her way around the world with a Visa card that had no spending limit and a few subway tokens. She had friends in twenty countries who willingly spoiled her. Thus she traveled light, a carry-on bag, only one or two changes of clothes, preferring to buy what she wasn't given by the many designers eager for her presence in their shows. Bertie sold trendy fashion, even the most outrageously whimsical crap, with a flair all her own, high exuberance and a wink to the audience that said *you are all* pumbavu *if you don't buy this.*

With her wrapped watercolor under one arm, she linked her other arm with Sherard's and more or less propelled him the remaining distance to the red-bordered door of the Elegant Forest, where they were expected. She never asked if his leg bothered him. She knew it was hurting, and neither of them wanted to be reminded of what the injury represented in their lives.

"By the way," Bertie said as they entered the tiny vestibule, "I think I should mention I got peeped."

She didn't have time to explain. The proprietor of Ya Lin, a middle-aged man who stood about as high as Bertie's elbow, swept through a beaded curtain with an ecstatic gold-capped smile and escorted them to one of six tables in the restaurant, beneath a little balcony of carved ebony. The balcony enclosed a polished stone Buddha, yellow stone with veins of ocher. There were fresh red poppies in a jade vase on the table. Bertie laughed and winked and chatted with the proprietor, who frequently turned, beaming, to pump Sherard's hand.

When they were seated and alone for a few moments, Sherard said, "What was that all about?"

"You may have noticed that this is the only table in the room with a Buddha above it."

"Rather a heavyset Buddha," Sherard said, glancing up. "I hope it's a stout balcony. What's the significance?"

"This table is reserved by Gao for occasions that require a special blessing from Buddha." Pause. "It's especially popular with newlyweds who want to ensure the health and prosperity of their future children."

"You didn't tell him that we were—"

"My Mandarin's a little rusty. I *could* have given Gao the wrong impression. But who knows where we'll be when we *do* get married, so I thought, here we are in San Francisco, and I'm sure Buddha won't mind—"

"Alberta."

"Well, I've always coveted this table. And obviously we both want our children to be—"

"Al*ber*ta."

Bertie lowered her eyes. "You growled at me."

"Shouldn't wonder."

"You're not angry, though." She looked at him, narrowing her eyes slightly. "You don't have those white spots on your cheeks that you get when you're really furious. Know what I think? It's the whole idea of being a father."

"At my age—"

"You're only forty-three. My father was fifty when I was born. You have loads of time, if you don't let it slip away. Let me slip away."

She said it almost casually, with a light shrug and a turn of her head, but he had a glimpse of hurt, well concealed until now.

"You're quite a handful, Bertie."

She couldn't be playful any longer. "I hope I will be. Soon."

Sherard knew he had let himself in for that, and had no answer. At the age of twelve he had looked into Joseph's firelit eyes, eyes he trusted more than he trusted God, on the eve of his first blood stalk for lion. Still learning, but already seasoned enough to understand that the greatest pleasure of the hunt comes before the kill. And Sherard accepted with a pang of regret that one of the joys of living had so far escaped him—seeing the eyes of his firstborn son, eyes with no fear in them while he prepared himself, as Tom Sherard had prepared, for the ceremony of blooding.

"I'm more than twice your age, Bertie. Think about it. And too many of those years are like chains on me."

"No. Only one year. The year just past. Is it that you *can't* love me, or you can't bring yourself to love me?"

After a frowning silence he said, "That's difficult to answer."

"Chains don't make a cage. They can be broken. You only have to try." Her eyes were moist. "Would you try, Tom? For both of us."

He wanted to say no, to put an end to it immediately. He was sure if he did say it Alberta Nkambe would simply get up and walk out, leaving him alone at the newlyweds' table, beneath Buddha's stone weight of disapproval. In a moment of unusual clarity Sherard knew he did not want to spend the rest of his life reliving how that moment had felt.

He took a breath. "Let's see how it goes, Bertie. A day at a time, all right?"

"A day at a time *together*."

"Yes." With a sense of relief he reached across the table and took her hand. Ending, with that gesture, a kind of tyranny he had imposed on her. Bertie Nkambe's heart was in her face. A beguiling, beginning woman, for all her worldliness still defining herself, needing him in the process.

Gao reappeared with ceremonial tea. Bertie poured. They all had a cup, another tradition at the newlyweds' table. The other guests smiled and nodded happily, watching them. There was good luck and good feeling in the air.

Nothing Sherard had drunk or eaten had had much taste for a long time. But the tea was fragrant and delicious, the wine that came next a silvery treasure that restored his palate. There were no menus at the Elegant Forest. Each night Gao's chef prepared a communal feast, and those who were fortunate enough to get a table ate what was brought out to them. Sherard lost count of the courses that arrived sizzling, braised, or chilled. Also he wasn't paying attention to how much wine he consumed. He did remember at one point to ask Bertie about the peep she'd mentioned earlier.

"It was the painter. The ABC girl at the end of this alley. American-born Chinese. I was really engrossed in her work. Had my back to her. She just lifted a corner of my mind, you know, like a tent flap, and looked in. Idle curiosity, I guess. But it was deft. She's had better training than that ice-pick artist on the plane coming out."

"Was she MMF?"

Bertie paused to demolish a lotus flower made from pureed vegetables, then made a judgment call.

"I don't think she's in the Game. Not one of ours, anyway."

"Neither are you in the Game," Tom reminded her. "That's what Gillian wanted, and I insist upon it. And you never take chances, Bertie."

"I didn't do *anything*."

"Could she have peeped you long enough to get some ideas about you?"

"T-blocking leaves a definite signature. Nevertheless, I don't think it's anything to worry about."

"Right. Then I'm not worried."

"Nor am I. Don't know why I brought it up in the first place."

Neither of them paid attention to the Chinese man in a steel-gray silk suit who had come into the Elegant Forest. Midnight shades with Erector-set gold frames complemented the flash suiting. Gao looked up as he was pouring wine into Sherard's glass and turned as stony as Buddha. Then he backed away from their table with a reserved but suppliant bow as the newcomer approached, kicked a vacant lacquered chair ahead of him, turned it around and straddled it, arms across the back of the chair. Sherard glanced at the bead-curtain doorway. Two guys who looked like bodyguards loitered there, looking in. Sherard breathed cologne, took in the expensive tailoring of the man who sat four feet from him, the gold accessories, a thin scar running nearly the full angle of one jaw like a chin strap. In spite of the scar he was a handsome man until he pulled off the dark glasses. His uncovered eyes looked ruined, as if he were suffering from a permanent hangover, or arctic snow blindness. There was no focus in them. The lids trembled.

"Hi. Welcome to San Francisco. My hometown. Great place to eat, isn't it? Gao's the best, kid you not. Don't worry about the bill, it's taken care of. Entirely my pleasure." He finished out of breath, stroked his lips a few times with his fingertips. Some women would find his mouth sensual, some would find it cruel; most would just find it, buzzing with lust like a fly trapped on a windowpane. He slipped the shades back on in mid-blink, snapped his fingers at Gao, pointed to the wineglass in front of Sherard. Gao disappeared into the kitchen. "Name's Danny Cheng." He turned his hard flat head slightly toward Bertie, who looked at him with a level of response she usually reserved for a dirty rest room. "Question is, who the hell are you, Cute Stuff?"

GREENWOOD LAKE, CALIFORNIA · MAY 28

Geoff McTyer drove his Taurus to the vacation house that the Warings had borrowed, the man temporarily known as Phil Haman in the seat beside him. Haman passing the time playing a video game on a Toshiba laptop. That wasn't enough to keep him occupied. He had to make conversation too. Geoff acknowledged the attempts in monosyllables, kept his mind on his driving, tried not to give in to the panic that had resulted from being overtaken by events.

"You're not much for small talk is the impression I get," Haman said, staring at the active matrix screen and the bombast of the video game. His thumb was busy on the controller, lobbing fireballs at digitized goons with broadswords and two-headed wizards. "Or maybe it's just that you haven't warmed up to me yet."

Geoff didn't reply. Another few miles went by, mountainous places cragged and tufted against a softly luminous night sky. The moon floating above the treeline, disappearing at times. Twister of a road. Occasional traffic.

"We got far to go yet?"

"No."

"How far?"

"Up ahead we take a left. Crahss the dam. Then, I don't know. The road follows the north shore of the lake. Look for the name. On a mailbox or something."

"Hassler."

"Yes. Hassler."

"Lot of stress on you. I'm aware of that. I sympathize. She's a honey. You just can't stop thinking about her. How about her shape? Eden have a good shape? Sure she does. You fell hard. I'll bet she fell hard too, good-looking bullnuts like yourself. How did it go, the first time? In your apartment, right? Or, no, maybe it was a camping trip, you're the rugged outdoors type. Wilderness. All that hiking puts whang in your blood. You've built a fire, set up this little tent. Nobody else around for miles. The two of you have known all day that you're going to have sex. Can't go another minute without doing it. The kissing, the touching. The moaning. I love you, I love you. The clothes coming off. But maybe it's too chilly. Or she's too shy to get all the way naked. Just uncover those parts you need to work with, get your hands on. Both of you with your jeans below your knees, back door's the best way to get it in. She's even hotter than you hoped she would be. Hands on her breasts, lips on the back of her neck. Thrusting. I'm not hurting you, am I, Eden? No no don't stop oh its so *big* oh God feels so *good*."

"You son of a bitch."

"This the dam? Pull over when you get across."

Haman turned off the laptop and put it away. On the other side of the small dam they sat in darkness by the side of the road, the lake below them painted by the moon.

"This heartthrob Eden, you lose perspective, you lose your sense of mission," Haman said. "But I'm not here to pass judgment. We all have our work. Mine happens to be wet. I go in, I get out. I work long-range, I work up close. I carry the tools for either eventuality. I'm expressing myself in this manner in order to spare your fucking sensibilities. Purely in terms of job satisfaction, up close is best for me. I like to see their eyes when I'm making delivery. So to speak. Same as show business. There's nothing like feedback from a live audience. But I don't let the promise of visceral reward interfere with my analysis of how to do the job effectively. There's no other factors involved. Politics don't interest me. Don't tell me any of your conspiracy theories. Everything's a conspiracy. I go in, it's done, I get out. My approval rating stays high. I don't know who makes those decisions. I get instructions from so deep inside the Sector it's possible no one actually exists there anymore. That could mean a lot of things. All I want are my instructions. Sometimes it's a blind man, stopping me on the street with a tap of his cane, whispering in my ear. If a month goes by and I haven't made a delivery, I start to feel listless. Apprehensive. Then the Voices begin. Far-off, chanting. A kind of déjà voodoo. I can ignore them for a while. Then it gets so bad they don't let me sleep. 'Bring out your dead,' they cry. 'Bring out your dead!' What do they mean? Are they holding me accountable? I follow instructions. I'm in, I'm out. Sometimes it's a little girl in a Baskin-Robbins, sneaking a crumpled napkin into my pocket."

Geoff's hands gripped the steering wheel. He looked straight ahead. One side of his face was illuminated by the cold sheen from the surface of Greenwood Lake. If he hadn't been certain before, it was clear to him now. A world that would not allow Eden Waring to live in peace was a grim asylum, a lurking hell. He had acquired a new slant on the man temporarily known as Haman. Whoever he was, he had emerged from the rubble of Geoff's former beliefs and misbegotten sense of duty expressly to torment and then to destroy him. Geoff was deeply afraid. But the fear that possessed him, he sensed, also had the power to define him.

After a couple of bleak minutes, the assassin yawned as if he'd been napping, and spoke again.

"What we do now, we locate the house. Stay back until we know if she's there or not. Then I'll take over. You don't have a part in it. When I come out, you drive me back to the burg we came from, I'm history where you're concerned."

Geoff turned his head slowly and looked at Haman. Knew that he was lying, wasn't how Haman had planned it at all. Rather than being horrified, he was almost elated.

"What about the Warings?"

Haman shrugged. "Well, Geoff. You know. What can I do? Unless you have an idea I can use."

Geoff pulled back onto the road, accelerating too abruptly.

"I don't. Let's just get it over with."

A pair of hand-carved *nan* wood doors. Ming-style carved chairs. Eighteenth-century porcelain and ormolu vases. Lacquered gold and black étagère. Tang Dynasty funerary horse, saddled. A green-glazed Han dog. A bronze ritual vessel with water buffalo motifs, three thousand years old. Objects outliving vast buried histories. Things of seductive textures and artistry that begged to be touched, revered.

Danny Cheng was proud of his to-the-trade establishment, on the ground floor of a snowflake-white Italianate house built on Russian Hill in the days of windjammers, the famous China clippers, the Great White Fleet. The original house, Cheng said, had survived the 1906 fire because the roof had been protected with gunny sacks soaked in the wine from its capacious cellar. The fleet was long gone, but the view of the bay west to the Golden Gate Bridge was still as splendid as could be found on many a San Francisco hill.

"So antiques are your business," Sherard said.

"Fine antiques are more of a love affair than a business." Cheng smiled at Bertie Nkambe, who was oblivious to both of them as she drifted among treasures with an expression of near-rapture. "What else do I do? I grow grapes. I raise thoroughbreds on my place across the bay. My father made a little money in his time, and I've had some luck increasing it for him. Danny Cheng's core business is information. Information the CIA or NSA can't get a handle on in spite of their listening devices, the computers faster than whistling piss. I'm after the street stuff. But on a global scale. Words, phrases. A hint here, a whisper there. Morsels and tidbits. A look, a gesture. Pillow talk. Gossip always has that essential element of truth. Danny Cheng's information clock is set two days ahead of Greenwich Mean. I buy, I broker. Who wants my information? The kind of men who are too brilliant to quibble with. Their profession is the exercise of superior intellect. They read summaries. They get briefed. They make instant brilliant decisions about crises and conflicts that decide the fate of the rest of us. Is it possible we know some of the same people? Find yourself in Washington occasionally, Tom?"

"Not if I can help it. I guess I had a different impression of what you do for a living, from the style of the bodyguards you tote around. The ones with the tong tattoos."

"Those old guys? As you say, *style* is what they're all about. Tongs don't mean much anymore. Tongs were little family-run businesses. Big Crime is what it's all about today. Big Crime has intergalactic scope, diplomatic immunity, a line of T-shirts. I need the bodyguards because, would you believe it, my ex-wives like to hassle me. Every last one of them would rejoice to see my head dripping on a sharp-pointed stake."

He was watching Bertie again with a covetous smile, as if he hadn't learned any lessons about women. The air-conditioning was on so low it felt chilly where they were, but Danny Cheng was perspiring. He also seemed to be getting the shakes. Sherard noticed an old man with a freckled yellow head that looked as fragile as papier-mâché. He had come quietly into the display room. He wore red carpet slippers, wrinkled black kung fu pants, a *gi* with a black sash and the emblems of a highly advanced martial artist. He looked serene, unassuming, knowledgeable about death-blows.

Danny Cheng seemed to be aware of the old man's presence before he turned around.

"May I present my father, Chien-Chi?" he said, his hands trembling as he reached for a pocket handkerchief.

Sherard introduced himself. Chien-Chi glanced at Bertie, who came promptly to him. They bowed to each other. Bertie had a black belt of her own. She addressed Chien-Chi as "Master." He made a steeple of fingers that resembled chickens' feet.

"It is an honor to welcome someone so gifted as yourself into our home," Chien-Chi said to Bertie, his voice faint.

Danny Cheng pushed his dark glasses up on his forehead and blotted perspiration from around his weak-looking eyes. Sherard glanced at him.

"This? It's nothing. A bug I picked up in Thailand, comes and goes at inconvenient times. I call it the three-minute ague." He dropped the glasses back onto the wet flat bridge of his nose. Bertie had grasped the prayerful hands of Chien-Chi, whose head remained bowed. They were like that for a few moments. Bertie then said something to him in Mandarin, and slowly, with a thoughtful look in her eyes, released him. Sherard wondered what was going on.

Danny Cheng clenched and unclenched his hands. "What I could use right now is a drink. Tom?"

"Danny, we're both grateful for the hospitality you've shown us tonight, but I think—"

Bertie looked at him. "It's all right, Tom. It isn't late yet. And I'd like to spend more time with Chien-Chi. That's why I'm here. It's important to him."

Danny Cheng's study, in the east wing of the renovated and expanded house, had a view of the Marina district and the bay beyond. It was a large room with minimal furnishings and decoration, a *feng shui* creation that was gracefully impressive. There were two lacquered benches with red saddle leather seats facing each other across a rectangular pearl-gray carpet that took up a third of the flame-finished, dark gray granite floor. A pleasing black oval table lacquered to a mirror finish was at the head of the carpet, eight feet from the unadorned bay windows. Cheng used the table as a desk. There was nothing on it but a laptop computer, a small lamp, and a pale yellow wooden bowl filled with river rocks.

He seated Chien-Chi close to him, with Bertie beside the old man and Sherard on the bench seat opposite. Cheng sat down behind the table. A Chinese girl with a serpentine braid down the middle of her back wheeled in a drinks cart. There were several small carafes filled with pale liqueurs on the cart, a fifth of Glenfiddich, and ginger ale for Bertie. The girl served Chien-Chi from one of the carafes, pouring a few precious drams into a thimble-size glass.

"Snake semen liqueur," Chien-Chi said to Bertie. "It restores the vigor of old men like myself."

Danny Cheng was looking at the screen of his laptop, tapping damp fingers on the table.

"Potent stuff. It's from the five-step snake. Chinese rattler. They call it that because after you're bitten, you take five steps and croak."

"How old are you?" Bertie asked Chien-Chi.

"I don't know. They kept no birth records in the district where I was born. And my mother was too poor to pay an astrologer to draw up my horoscope as soon as I came into this life. But old is old. I know I'm near the end of my last earthly cycle." He took a tiny sip of the snake semen liqueur. "I have had three wives and fourteen children. Danny is the son from my third wife, who was part Hawaiian. She was a doozy."

Danny Cheng looked up. "You shouldn't talk about Mom like that."

"Is that an offensive word? Her unique character is not easily described in any language. No disrespect was intended, even though she left me for a younger man who had a Buick dealership." He turned to Bertie. "I also had a daughter from my third marriage. Did you see her when we touched hands?"

"Yes. She . . . she's lovely. And very much on your mind."

Chien-Chi acknowledged her hesitation with a slight sad nod.

"What did you see about me?" Danny Cheng said with a fretful grin, mopping his face.

"Your father," Bertie said, "finds you trustworthy and dutiful."

"I was wondering," Sherard said, "if there was any bad information on Bertie and me in that file you've been consulting."

"Appears to be straight biography," Danny Cheng said with another glance at the laptop screen. "You were married to Gillian Bellaver. We both know why she was killed, no need to go into that." He paused, tapping a key. "You flew to San Fran today on United listed as G. W. Hunter. Same name on the hotel registry. What does the G. W. stand for, Great White?"

"I make these little jokes."

"Complete with quality fake ID and important credit cards. We do travel in the same circles after all. But if you're here on the q.t., you picked the wrong traveling companion. One of the great beauties of our time. I would have stopped the sweats already if Bertie Nkambe wasn't in the room with me. Wearing motocross leather. A high, high Michael Kors turtleneck that cradles those fantastic cheekbones. I just had to say it. I'm not coming on to you, Bertie."

"What do you know about my aunt Gillian?"

"He doesn't know anything," Sherard said. "Let it lie there."

"I'll take that challenge. There's a certain top cop who is as paranoid about psychics as Hoover was about the NAACP. Did you get that far with it yet?"

Sherard looked at Danny Cheng. Cheng reached for the cut-glass tumbler of scotch that the girl had placed on the table near him, but his hand was trembling and he didn't pick it up.

"No," Sherard said.

"Consider that information part of the hospitality package. In exchange for which—" On a second attempt Cheng was able to get the scotch to his lips without spilling any. He swallowed and put the glass down and joined his hands tightly. "In exchange I want something from Bertie."

Bertie cocked her head and said, mildly amused, "In front of your father?"

Chien-Chi looked at Bertie and they laughed together.

"That sly wink of yours. A megaton turn-on. But Danny Cheng is all business tonight. All I'm asking is for you to put your Gift to work and dish some info. My honorable father and I would then be in your debt for a hundred lifetimes to come."

Sherard said, "Why don't you use that peeper selling watercolors in Chinatown?"

"Lu Ping. My niece. Having your own psychic is more than a status symbol nowadays. Time's coming when you won't be able to conduct business, or protect your business, without one. Computers? What's a machine to minds that can stop a clock? That's what you might call an ironic paradox. I was fortunate to find another psi-active in the family. Lu Ping is definitely a talent, but not an operational talent. Did you actually kill a lion with your bare hands?"

"No, that was Tarzan."

"Apocryphal, huh?"

"Bertie's not an operational talent either," Sherard said. "She's not in the Game, and she's not going to be."

"Just let me delete this information about the lion. Bad information has a way of driving out the good. Usually because it's more colorful."

Sherard wished the bench he was sitting on had a back to it. He stretched his left leg out slowly with a tired wince and sipped his own scotch, looking at Bertie and Chien-Chi. They were conversing quietly, earnestly, in Mandarin. Sherard felt uneasy.

"Let me put your mind at ease about something," Danny Cheng said, tapping on the laptop keys.

"Rather too late for that, Danny."

"I don't have anything to do with MORG. I've never been a joiner. Other than that, I just don't like the bastards. My sister may have been on the plane that crashed today up in Innisfall. It was a MORG paramilitary unit that hit the psi underground's cloister on Maui at one-thirty this morning. They were after Kelane. They got her. My information is good up to that point. Good information is cool and shapely, it breathes on its own. Good information makes my nipples stand up. There's some other stuff I don't quite trust yet. Bits and pieces are still coming in. I'm trusting you all the way here, Great White Hunter. Rona Harvester, code name Zephyr, was on one of those black helicopters, overseeing the entire operation."

"Or it could've been Tarzan."

Danny Cheng went back to his laptop, fingers skimming over the keys.

"No, wait, it fits. Rona Harvester was in Hawaii yesterday and today. Little-known fact: Rona has been guarded by a detail of MORG agents instead of the Secret Service since the President had his stroke."

"They didn't do much of a job guarding her this afternoon."

He smiled in a sensual way. "I have information about that too. The best. It's shapely, it swings its ass, it blows in my ear, it gives me a hand job."

Bertie pursed her lips in a soundless whistle and looked up at the ceiling. Chien-Chi appeared to have dozed off.

"The black helicopter that hit the motorcade belonged to MORG. An HPD helicopter that was in the vicinity pursued it until the pilot was ordered to break off and return to base. Who gave that order? Unknown, but it had plenty of swinging dick behind it. There was no other pursuit. No Air Force or Marine jets were scrambled, although they were only a few miles away. The black helicopter was last seen flying at treetop level toward a supposedly inactive military airfield at Waimanalo Bay, on the north shore of Oahu."

"TV reports had two of the MORG agents in the motorcade detail on the critical list. You're telling me MORG would hit their own people?"

"If that's what Rona Harvester wanted them to do. She came out of it looking like Joan of fuckin' Arc. A hell of a lot more presidential than that baby-faced weenie Dunbar. I think the hit on the motorcade was planned by Harvester and staged by some of the same ops in MORG's Elite Force who raided Maui and took my sister."

"Took her where?"

"The original flight plan of TRANSPAC 1850 had Plenty Coups, Montana, as its destination. You know about Plenty Coups, of course."

Sherard nodded.

"But the plane's course was changed in midflight. They'd have had Kelane doped to the gills, but still she could have done it. Interfered with the controls somehow. I don't know anything about DC-10s. This isn't hard information. It's all speculation. But my father and I believe Kelane is dead."

Chien-Chi opened his eyes. Bertie reached over and took his hand.

"She had psychotronic ability?" Sherard asked.

"Her mind had an affinity for machines, but there was more to Kelane than that. Professionally she was a neurosurgeon, although she hadn't been able to practice for the last couple of years. She spent most of that time on the run. MORG wanted her. They wanted her bad."

"For what?"

"That's what I'd like to know."

"Did Kelane know why they were after her?"

Danny Cheng looked at his father. "I think so. She wouldn't come to us. Too dangerous. We both knew MORG was watching me, watching this house."

"Thanks for bringing us here," Sherard said in exasperation.

"You don't have anything to worry about. MORG broke off its surveillance of Danny Cheng a week ago. I should've realized then that they finally had a lock on her."

"Were you able to tell your sister? Or didn't you know where she was until today?"

"It was best that I didn't know. Kelane communicated with me by E-mail. No return address. I heard from her last two days ago. She said she loved us. By the tone of her letter she was depressed. She said, 'I can't stop thinking about Portland. I never believed they would do it. All because of me. And I'm afraid there will be another Portland soon, if I don't give in to them. I'm afraid. I'm afraid.' "

The mention of Portland invited silence and gloom. Portland was wreckage still faintly glowing from nuclear heat dumped into their midst, disturbing the masterful harmonies of the room. Unthinkable that there could be another Portland in the American landscape. Another medium-sized partly emptied city with a crater of sea-green trianite where the bus station had stood. Ten years from now when the crater had cooled down there would be a memorial park around it. Schoolchildren would raise money to plant dogwoods. Bertie rubbed one side of her face as if something had bitten her. She looked hazily around the room.

" 'They' being MORG?" Sherard said to Danny Cheng.

"What else?"

"MORG would nuke an American city because your sister wouldn't give them what they wanted? Something only *she* could give? Was she sane?"

"I've never doubted it," Danny Cheng said after a few moments. "The insanity is to be found inside Multiphasic Operations and Research Group. 'Out of control' doesn't really describe them. Kelane was on her way to Plenty Coups, but I don't think she intended to show up there, no matter what."

"It's not certain she was on the plane."

"I want to be sure. If she was, I want to know why she was being taken to Plenty Coups."

"Someone of your stature in the information business—"

Cheng shook his head. "I've never been able to get much out of Plenty Coups. It isn't life-enhancing to poke around, even at the fringes. The security is fanatical. An installation the size of the Pentagon, all of it underground. I hear rumors. I appreciate them for their entertainment value. Plenty Coups is a support facility for extraterrestrials visiting the earth. It's the gateway to a subterranean advanced civilization that was here before apes came down from the trees. It's a command post for the New World Order MORG is planning to spring on us one day when there's not much else to watch on TV. It will be the world's largest multiplex, showing nothing but old Schwarzenegger films to an audience of the numbed. Or else it's a new kind of supercult experience, the Disneyland of death trips." He paused. "Now that might turn out to be close to the truth."

"Kelane was a neurosurgeon?" Bertie said, as if she was thinking out loud. "Would that have something to do with MORG's interest in her?"

"The world has a pretty good supply of neurosurgeons," Danny Cheng said.

"Neurosurgeons who are also psychic? With the ability—I'm only guessing here—to work from inside the brain, guiding the laser or the gamma knife or whatever?"

"She has to be beautiful. She has to be tall and part Chinese and have long legs encased in red leather. Above all, she has to have the brains to pick up on what I missed. We would make such a great team. Bertie Nkambe and Danny Cheng. I say this in a purposeful businesslike tone. Keeping it all business here. But you can see, the shirt I have on. It's soaked through."

Bertie said primly, "I'm spoken for."

Sherard said, "Anything else we can do for you, Danny?"

"Coming to that. The plane crash. There was a survivor. Her name is Portia Darkfeather." He turned to his laptop again for verification. "American Indian name, I'd say. She's a contract employee of a MORG proprietary called Accelerated Counter-Insurgency Defense, which provides advanced military training for police and sheriff's departments around the country. Ought to come in handy while they're serving and protecting. ACID is also a cover for MORG's Elite Force. Portia Darkfeather underwent five hours of surgery at the Innisfall Medical Center and has not regained consciousness. Official hospital bulletin." Cheng devoted several moments to stroking his lips before getting to the point. "How close," he said to Bertie, "would you have to be to Darkfeather in order to peep her?"

"Way close. It's in the touch. Sometimes. Other times, I don't see a thing. There are no channels open." She frowned. "And if she's just had surgery, I could cause a lot of trouble by touching her. I might—"

Danny Cheng said, "I've heard about the bleeding thing. That's for real?"

"Forget about it," Sherard said. "I won't—you're not doing this, Alberta."

"But—Tom, Portia Darkfeather might know what it was all about, why MORG has to have a psychic neurosurgeon. After all Danny has told us, aren't you curious?"

"It isn't what we came out here to do. There's more than one huge risk involved. You can be sure she's under heavy guard."

"If I could get my hands on clothing, anything else that belonged to Portia Darkfeather, that would be a safe means of—"

"No."

Danny Cheng looked frustrated. His father turned to Bertie.

"I never thought it was a good idea myself. But Danny can be overbearing at times. So I agreed to this meeting. We thank you for your concern. And I am most grateful to have had this opportunity to become acquainted with you."

Bertie said, "Did any of you feel something, just then?"

As she spoke Sherard was aware of the tremor that seemed to ripple through the house.

Cheng shrugged. "We get those all the time. It's the Ring of Fire. Somewhere around Palo Alto, canned goods are falling off the shelves and everyone having sex just came too soon."

"That's not an earthquake," Bertie said quietly, rising to her feet.

The tremor continued and intensified.

Something rose in the starry night outside the bay window behind Danny Cheng. It was a jet-black helicopter with stub wings and a vectored-thrust propeller. The house vibrated from the nearness of the powerful helicopter, but it made no sound as it hovered fifty feet away in a nose-down attitude. The canopy of the Cobra-style chopper was tinted almost as dark as the fuselage. A twenty- or thirty-millimeter cannon protruded from beneath the nose. Instead of rocket pods there were black boxes with antennalike rods attached to the wings.

Danny Cheng turned slowly to see what everyone else was looking at.

"Which of your ex-wives has one of those?" Sherard asked Cheng.

Bertie wheeled and went to the double doors of the study. She tried to open them.

"Locked," she said. "That girl who brought in the drinks cart? I had a hunch I should have peeped her. *Damn.*"

"I hired Song three weeks ago," Danny Cheng said, adding defensively, "The chick had great references."

Chien-Chi said with a hint of scorn, "Her pussy was her most impressive reference, is it not always so."

"What are you carrying?" Sherard asked Cheng.

"Nine-millimeter Glock."

"Give it to me, and get away from the windows."

"You're going to shoot that chopper down? Before you commence hostilities, let's consider the fact they haven't done anything."

"Yes, they have," Bertie said, coming swiftly back to them. "Don't you feel hot?"

"I run hot and cold."

"I don't. Give Tom the gun and pick up your laptop."

"It *is* hot in here," Chien-Chi said.

Sherard caught the black polymer automatic Cheng pitched to him.

"It isn't the room, it's us. Our body temperatures are going up. They're beaming low-frequency radiation in here."

Danny Cheng picked up his laptop, glancing at it. "Screen's gone black. It was all right a second ago."

"Get out of the way," Bertie said. She threw the table lamp against a wall and the room went dark. She took hold of the oval table and up-ended it.

"Hey, that cost—"

"Take your father over there and hug the floor," Bertie said, her face glistening from perspiration. "We're in a microwave oven here. Tom, we don't have much time."

"Shoot the lock off the door!" Danny Cheng said frantically.

"Your doors are too thick," Bertie told him. "A nine-millimeter won't dent that lock. Get Chien-Chi away from here! *On the floor.* Close to the wall but away from the windows."

"You go too," Sherard said, giving her a push. He picked up a two-pound rock that had spilled from the yellow bowl and sidearmed it through the middle of the bay windows, taking out most of one pane.

"I'm burning up!" Danny Cheng wailed.

Sherard wiped his eyes, crouched behind the table, and took aim at the black box on the right wing of the helicopter. He wondered if they were totally relying on their radar technology to cook everyone in the room from the inside out, or if they would retaliate with the chain gun when they saw muzzle flashes. He hoped they wouldn't want to attract that much attention in one of San Francisco's best neighborhoods. ECM, ELF, Spoofers—he didn't know what was in the boxes. He wanted only to disable the conical antenna, about two feet long and shaped a lot like a circumcised penis, that he was sure was beaming microwave energy into Danny Cheng's study. Another minute of it, and their blood and brains literally would begin to boil. Half a minute, maybe. He already was finding it nearly impossible to breathe, to think clearly.

Roughly twenty yards. He hadn't devoted all that much shooting time to pistols, although he usually carried a Colt Frontier model .45 on safaris. The Glock had a ten-round magazine and fixed sights, probably a four-inch barrel. Adequate at that range, with, fortunately, a moonlit sky behind the soundlessly hovering helicopter.

Through the hole he had made in the bay window he shot the hell out of the antenna and the black box behind it, then rolled out of the way just before the nose cannon erupted, shouting, *"Down down keep down!"*

Then the room lit up, tracers, and the air was filled with flying splinters from the oval table, sharp flecks of granite from the scored floor, plaster dust from the ceiling. It went on for less than ten seconds. At least one hundred rounds had been fired. After that it was quiet, except for someone moaning.

"Bertie!"

"Okay! So is Chien-Chi."

She'd had the presence of mind to pull some of the pearl-gray carpet over the two of them as they huddled against the wall.

"Anybody care about me?" Danny Cheng said petulantly.

"You hit?" Sherard asked. The moaning continued.

"No. It's coming from outside."

The study doors had been shattered by the heavy strafing. One of them was half off the hinges. Cheng kicked the door free of the other hinge and it fell into the hall. The Chinese girl with the long braid was on the stairs nearby, holding on to the railing with one hand, holding herself, blood running through the fingers clutching her abdomen.

Pain and surprise. She looked young enough that dying had never occurred to her.

"You were waiting in the wrong place, weren't you?" Danny Cheng shouted at her. "How were you going to serve us, medium well? Who did it? Who set me up?"

"Don't!" Bertie said. "Help her, she's—"

Blood dripped from the girl's mouth and she died without making another sound, letting go of the railing and tumbling slowly down the stairs.

"Oh, God," Bertie moaned.

"How do we get out of here without being seen?" Sherard said to Danny Cheng. He had to say it twice.

"Wine cellar. There's an iron gate at one end, steps going up into the garden."

"Let's go."

"No, man. Nobody runs Danny Cheng out of his own house."

"He is giving us good advice, Danny. Where are your bodyguards? Why haven't they come to help us?"

"*Nobody!*"

Sherard shook his head angrily, took hold of Bertie and guided her down the stairs. She stumbled near the body of the Chinese girl, almost fell, put down a hand to steady herself. It came away bloody. She stiffened as if rocked by a blow, eyes drifting up in her head.

"Bertie!"

"I'm okay. I'm okay."

Sherard gave her a handkerchief to wipe off the blood. She turned and gave Chien-Chi a pleading look. He smiled sympathetically.

"I cannot leave him. He's foolish sometimes, but he is my son. Turn left at the bottom of the stairs. It's the door all the way back next to the kitchen. Don't worry about me."

"Good-bye, Chien-Chi," Bertie said. There were tears in her eyes.

GREENWOOD LAKE · MAY 29

The Ford Taurus had been up there for quite a while, in the woods off the unpaved road. Three hours and twenty minutes, by Geoff McTyer's Swiss Army watch. It was twenty after one in the morning. Below the Taurus and approximately a quarter of a mile away, Riley and Betts Waring were still up, moving restlessly through the lodge that overlooked the lake. Windows were open. Lights were on in several rooms. There was a small fire on the hearth. Riley had done a lot of snacking in the kitchen. Coffee, chips, sandwiches, fudgsicles. Now he was slumped and snoring in front of the big-screen TV, a heat pad at the small of his back. They could have heard him without the help of the directional microphone Geoff had set up on the hood of his car. Betts had gone through most of a pack of Merits on the unscreened front deck, elbows on the railing, gazing across the alpine lake at mountain peaks still laden with the snows from a recent spring storm.

"Guido Kukierski," Haman said softly. "Solly Lorowitz. D. Hammond Fairchild. Al Farlow. Myron Leets."

It had been immediately clear that Eden wasn't in the redwood lodge overlooking the lake. Not clear if the Warings were expecting her. Sometimes they could hear Riley and Betts okay, but there were problems with reception, frequent breakups due to the stiff wind from the north. The temperature at this elevation had dropped to around forty-five degrees. Geoff longed for some of the coffee Betts had brewed, for innocent good-humored conversation around the kitchen table. His butt was numb. It was cold enough so that their combined breath was fogging the windshield. He and temporary Phil. Of course he'd been temporary too, no denying they were right for each other. Even if it nauseated him to be reminded. He couldn't start the engine and run it for heat. In the silence of the wilderness around them, where an owl's cry carried for a mile, Betts might hear. Nothing for him to do but sit there, Haman droning away.

"Walter Parks. Dixie Bob Del Valle. Jake Glaze. Troy Emmons the Third. Harry. Harry something. *Binks*. Harry Binks."

"What are you doing?" Geoff said irritably.

"No, there were two Harrys." Haman seemed agitated. "Who was the other one?"

"I don't know what you're talking about."

"I need to remember them, all of their names."

"Whose names?"

"Because they're who I've been. They deserve my loyalty. The girls, TinaDollyLizaRona, that's just my feminine half, honey, my bombshell superstar creative self. I talk it, walk it, strut the stuff. I'm a Vegas-style, gettin'-it-on glitzaholic. I don't know if I could do a job as a woman. There's such a thing as too much panache. While the girls are taking stage, the Face just waits. The Face knows it'll come. The next delivery. The little package with the new name. Another death, his rebirth. Face would do them for nothing if they asked him, just keep the new names coming. Harry Ludlow! That's the other Harry. Ludlow. Düsseldorf. Six years ago. He uses a single-edged razor blade. One swipe, clean through the carotid artery. Walk right on by, disappear into the crowd while the subject sits there on the park bench spouting his newspaper red, he can't believe it, his throat's been cut. The average healthy human heart will empty the body of blood through a severed artery in just under five minutes."

Geoff didn't let Haman see him shudder. "Don't you wear disguises? No offense, but as far as looks go you're one of a kind."

"The Face is an asset. The Face doesn't invite casual inspection. It's a great blob of deadness. It isn't remembered because no one wants to remember. The Face was born to be shunned."

"Who are you, really?"

Geoff got a look in return for his question. A bolt of a look shot from the depths of a collapsed mind. A look, a grin—no mere nightmare could have done the moment justice.

"Someone who's hurtin' for a little fun. Surveillance is not Phil Haman's game. Haman is not the quiet surreptitious type like Ludlow or Belzoni. Face has already grasped that. Haman wants action. Those folks down there, waiting on Eden. They'll have to go, sooner or later. Might as well be sooner. After the fun part."

Tom Sherard and Bertie Nkambe had just emerged into the garden of the double-size lot on Russian Hill when Danny Cheng's house blew up.

Part of it, anyway. The side facing east, where the black helicopter had appeared framed in the bay window of Danny Cheng's study. They were jarred by the concussion, but nothing came flying their way. Sherard looked around but didn't see the helicopter. Bertie was in shock. She wanted to go back.

"Chien-Chi!"

Sherard grabbed her by the arm and pushed her through an arbor of climbing roses toward a wooden gate in the seven-foot stone wall.

"We can't afford to be found here."

There was a padlock on the gate. He opened an unlocked toolshed a few feet away, picked up a nine-pound sledge, and with a couple of overhand swings knocked the rusty hasp from the wood.

He looked back again. The house from their perspective was dark. There was a suggestion of smoke in the air. A persistent flicker in one upstairs window, as if a streamer of flame were unrolling across the ceiling.

They went out through the gate to the street behind Cheng's house. Cars were closely parked along the curb on their side. There were two men with dogs on leashes under a streetlamp down at the corner, looking at the side of Danny Cheng's house where the explosion had occurred. A cloud of smoke boiled slowly above the treetops. They heard a siren. They walked the other way, toward the top of the hill.

A curbside door of a tan Lexus opened eight feet away. A man came up out of the backseat, turning toward them. Sherard saw distant light reflected from the thick lenses of the man's glasses. He wore a brown corduroy jacket that hung badly on him. He raised a hand in their direction, palm out, demonstrating, perhaps, peaceable intent. But that was as far as he got.

Bertie reacted before Sherard could close to within striking distance with his lion's-head cane. The hand that the man had partly raised flew up into his face, knocking his glasses askew. He fell back against the door of the Lexus, writhing. Bertie, who was no closer to the man than Tom was, kept him pinned to the door. Conscious but in pain, an acute state of help-lessness.

"No! Oh, God, *please* don't do that! I work for Hannafin! I work for Sen—"

"Ease up, Bertie," Sherard said, glancing at her. Controlled savagery in her face. Her eyes were scary, on a level of imminent apocalypse. He put a hand on her arm. She released the man with a shrug of contempt.

"He was on the plane with us. Told you then I should have fixed him."

"Whetstone! Name's Whetstone. Just call me Rory." Rory Whetstone was finding it difficult to straighten up from an invalid's brittle slump. He tried to adjust his glasses, doing little shuffling dance steps while maintaining his balance. He discovered that his nose was trickling blood, and unthinkingly wiped it on a sleeve of his jacket. "Is *that* what it's like, getting brain-locked?"

"You don't know the half of it," Bertie told him. "I let you off. Complete polarity reversal of the brain, recovery time can be three to six weeks. For those who recover at all." She looked around at the smoke hazing the streetlights. The sirens were wailing closer. The neighborhood had come uneasily awake. And everybody had a dog.

"You've been following us. Did you see it, Whetstone? Who did this to Danny Cheng?"

"Better get in the Lex," Whetstone gasped. "We should whisk ourselves away from here. Senator Hannafin's waiting. Urgently needs to speak to you, Mr. Sherard."

"What the hell," Sherard said with an amazed smile. "Why didn't we just arrange for a black tie reception at Moscone Center? Meet all the interesting locals."

There were flashing blue lights down Russian Hill, prowl cars coming on the fly.

"But not the cops. Tom, I'm nervous."

"Yeah, okay. Let's get out of here."

"Tell Whetstone not to mess with my *chi*."

"He knows, Bertie."

MOBY BAY · MAY 29 · 2:46 A.M. PDT

Eden Waring woke up in Chauncey's bedroom at a quarter to three. Someone was sitting on the edge of the bed watching her, but it wasn't her new friend Chauncey.

"Not *again*."

"If you're going to be hateful."

"I didn't send for you. How could I? I was sound asleep."

"Here I am anyway. So something's bothering you. I can't just switch universes willy-nilly when all is peaceful in your psyche."

The only illumination in the bedroom came from the surface of the sea, bright as steel plate scoured with a grinding wheel, and from the screen of Chauncey's laptop computer. Chauncey was deeply dreaming in her sleeping bag on an inflatable camp mattress, sibilance from her parted lips as she breathed contentedly.

Eden studied her doppelganger, who was wearing a Mighty Ducks hockey jersey, part of the wardrobe Chauncey had loaned to Eden. The dpg was picking at one of her toenails that needed trimming. Eden had split a nail walking in open-toed sandals on the beach. Usually she took great care of her feet, but tonight she'd been too tired.

Eden yawned, still tired. "Where are you, when you're not here?"

"I'm right beside you. Just a smidge beyond the sense barrier. Faithfully mimicking your every move."

"Do *you* have a doppelganger?"

"What would be the point of that?"

"None, I suppose. I'm just making conversation."

"Well, that's something. We're having a conversation." The dpg glanced at Chauncey's laptop. "Nothing new from the folks?"

"They're up at Greenwood Lake. Dad's back is out, but he's okay. I'll go in the morning."

"You haven't told them where you are."

Eden said after a long hesitation, "No. I'm not all that sure of where I am."

"But that's not the only reason."

"Well—"

"Who sent the E-mail?"

"Betts."

"What else did she say, was she chatty as usual?"

"Not so much. I mean, all through college we E-mailed each other a dozen times a day. Back and forth. I was thinking about you. Remember to stop by Circle K on your way home. Gossip and jokes. Did you hear the one about the door-to-door Bible salesman and the housewife who liked to vacuum in the nude?"

"No jokes tonight?"

"It wasn't that."

"What was it, then?"

"A billion E-mails, Betts always signed off the same way. Every time. 'Cheerio, dear one.' "

"Bible salesman, housewife with a vacuum cleaner."

"It's a limerick."

"Oh. What does 'vacuum' rhyme with?"

"Try 'Hoover.' Salesman's name was 'Coover.' Otherwise I don't remember how the damn thing goes, but the punch line's filthy."

"So tonight Betts didn't conclude with 'Cheerio, dear one.'"

"No."

"Bothers you."

"A lot."

Chauncey, in the sleeping bag, turned over on her side. The dpg studied her, picking at the damaged toenail.

"You trust her?"

"Yes. Sure. Chauncey's been real sweet to me. She's driving me up to the lake tomorrow. Better leave that toe alone, it'll get infected."

"Not if yours doesn't."

"What happens to me, happens to you."

"That's the big picture."

"But—I sprained my foot in the first half of the San Jose State game. Swelled up like a toad. Huff wrapped it, but there was no way. Couldn't put my heel down. Without me at point they'd have killed us in the second half. I was all by myself in the training room crying my eyes out when I realized, how strange, my navel's buzzing like there's a tiny bee inside. It tickled. Same as tonight. Buzz, buzz, woke me up."

"If we remember our physics correctly, at the subatomic level it's called a 'Kondo resonance.'"

"I hated physics."

"But it's quantum physics that makes our—your—duplication possible. You're the reflector, and I'm the—"

"Girl from my dreams."

"Quick off the dribble, deadly with the left-handed jumper. Twenty points in the second half. Destroyed San Jose."

"What happens to me happens to you. *Your* foot must've been sprained too. I've always wondered, how did you—"

"I could have explained a lot of things, if you'd devoted a little time to developing the relationship."

"It isn't as if we're actually related," Eden said with a slight shudder. "You're a—"

"Doppelganger, I know. What difference does it make how many times I come to the rescue? Cotton pickers on de old plantation got more respects than does de lowly dpg."

"Sorry. It's still a learning situation for me."

"*De nada.* To answer your question about the sprained foot: I am who you are, but I can't feel what you feel. Doesn't work quite that way in reverse. If *I* get a whack on the head, you get a headache. Paradox. I can mimic your emotions, but what good is that? I'd like to try sex myself sometime. But it might not be much more than a helluva pelvic girdle work-out if the emotional content is missing. Unless—until you give me a name and set me free, old massa."

"Back to that?"

"Blame me for asking?"

"I guess not, I just get the creeps. If you're 'free,' as you put it, some-one else with my face and body and DNA, what do I do for a doppel-ganger?"

Chauncey spoke unintelligibly in her sleep, as if the question had been addressed to her. Eden looked at Eden. Only one of them had a worried face.

SAN FRANCISCO · MAY 29

A tall man with silver hair aglow in the moonlight was walking a marblecake Great Dane across the Golden Gate Bridge at three in the morning. Off-shore in the Pacific there was a fogbank nearly as high as the bridge towers.

Rory Whetstone drove the Lexus past the man with the dog and stopped. Tom Sherard and Bertie Nkambe got out of the backseat and waited for Buck Hannafin. The Great Dane's ears quivered, and she looked up at the senior Senator from California.

"Friends," Hannafin said to the dog. He was smoking a cigar and carry-ing a revolver butt-forward in a western-style holster beneath his Burberry. A walnut grip of the wheelgun showed some dark old notches.

"Hello, Buck," Sherard said.

"Hello, Tom. Haven't seen you since, what, the service for Gillian at St. Bartholomew's?"

"I think so."

"Brings you to San Francisco?"

"Passing through."

"Can't place *you,* young lady, although a little tingle of recognition tells me we've met somewhere."

"Bertie Nkambe." The Great Dane was licking the back of her hand.

"Pleasure. The bitch is champion Roskilde's Pardon My Fancy. They all have names like that on the dog show circuit. She answers to Fanny when she's not putting on airs. My age, all a man needs is his mistress once a week, and a good dog the rest of the time. Fine-looking walking stick, Tom. Pedestrians are banned from the bridge this time of night, but I've earned a few privileges in my life of service. Mind if we press on? I stiffen up if I stand around too long."

"So do I," Sherard said. They continued on the walkway toward the Marin side of the bridge.

"What's on your mind, Senator?"

"You had some business with Danny Cheng tonight, or so I'm told."

"Social occasion. We met Cheng at the Elegant Forest, he invited us up to his place on Russian Hill for a nightcap. Entertainment was provided by a black helicopter that gave us a microwave sunburn, then I think they tossed a package into the house before slipping silently away. What do you know about black stealth helicopters, Buck?"

"No buzz numbers. Radar signature is virtually nil. Some of them are quieter than a ticking clock. Therefore they don't exist. A citizen who says he saw one, and is too vocal about the sighting, gets a visit from some tough-talking birds who convince him otherwise. That's when he learns he's not a citizen anymore, he's an inmate. Razor wire is still optional, but it won't be for much longer. I saw a couple of those choppers up close, touring MORG's facility in Montana."

"They conduct tours?"

"For members of the Senate Appropriations Committee. Still we had to squeeze some balls real hard. Research facility, they call it. Scientific, political, military. Advanced think tanks devoted to new geopolitical strategies and alliances. Plenty Coups. That's ironic. You couldn't miss the paramilitary arrogance. I'd say we were shown about a tenth of what MORG has underground. We had to be satisfied with that much."

"Who's running this country anyway?"

"Name your poison. For sure it's not the duly elected lawmakers on the Hill. Most of us abdicated our responsibilities long ago. Congress hasn't accomplished anything of significance in at least a decade. Into a governmental vacuum Fascism seeps like a gas nobody notices at first. But Congress did its part in creating that vacuum. How do you subvert a republic? No guns required. Only paper. Every session of Congress since I was a wide-eyed freshman, it's going on forty years now, there's been tens of thousands of pages of legislation introduced. All of it self-serving in some way. The bad laws and questionable appropriations get passed with the good, because there's too damn much of it to read, let alone debate. Don't get me started on debate. Doesn't exist anymore. Good honest adversarial relationships, thing of the past. Hell, most of us had good intentions, walking in. A few still do. But C-SPAN and *Crossfire* and thirty-second sound bites have turned us all into entertainers instead of serious legislators. Can anyone tell the difference between Hollywood and Washington anymore? Too many congresspersons lose their souls entirely. Drunks, womanizers, greedheads, sell-outs, even a few traitors in the pack. The rest just get mired and fed up and rationalize the incompetence forced on them by a government that's far too big to accomplish anything useful for the people it supposedly represents. All big government can do anymore is reinforce its own existence."

A highway patrol car passed, slowly, heading toward San Francisco. Buck waved. The CHP officer at the wheel touched off the roof lights in greeting.

"They're good boys. Look after me on my rambles, although I expect I can still take care of myself okay."

"Lot of notches on that gun, Senator," Bertie said.

"I was a light colonel on Hondo Hobbie's staff in Korea. This was Hondo's forty-four. Bought it off his widow after the war. I never shot anybody with it, but there's times when some lobbyist on the other side of my desk is crackin' me foxy, I pull it out of the drawer and lay it on the blotter. Famous for that little gesture, I hear. No other comment necessary. Tom, want to tell me what you and Danny Cheng had on the front burner tonight?"

"We were just getting acquainted. Never saw him before. Danny wouldn't be much to look at now, I reckon."

"Tom," Bertie said, wincing.

"Don't count Danny out just yet. He's been valuable to me in the past, and the chink has more rebound than a new squash ball. Hold your flowers until they're done sifting through the ashes. Occurs to me maybe I ought to share a couple things with you, Tom."

"Sure, why not?"

"Had a long conversation with Katharine Bellaver earlier. You know that Katharine and I go way back, we're like-minded on a number of topics."

"I know."

"You asked who's running the country nowadays. Well, until recently I thought we had a good shot at taking it back from the gang with the black helicopters and the counter-insurgency teams and the detention camps they have staffed and ready way out in the deserts and off in the deep piney woods down south. Our hopes, mine and Katharine's and those of a few more of us who believe the republic is still salvageable with some decisive leadership, our hopes were on the rise when Clint Harvester took his oath of office. Clint knew what was necessary to shut down MORG, and with the help of key people in the FBI and inside the Pentagon he was determined to see it done. The one thing in life Clint Harvester wasn't smart about was his wife. Nothing more dangerous to a man than a two-bit whore with ambition and a scosh more brains than average, but that's what he married. How and why she got involved with Victor Wilding is something of a mystery. The fact remains. Clint was bound to get on to the relationship eventually, take the appropriate steps to return Wilding to private life, or a federal pen most likely. That is, as soon as Clint managed to wriggle himself off of the finger Rona had up his ass—pardon me, Miss Nkambe, but there's no other way to say it. Anyway, Clint's out of commission, probably for good, that was all seen to by Miss Rona and her—"

"How do you mean? The President had a stroke."

"Stroke? I'm not convinced that's what it was. Two weeks before he went down Clint had his checkup at Walter Reed, and he was the picture of health. Yeah, I know. He was fifty-five and it could have been an embolism, some weakness that was there in the brain from when he was a kid and fell off his birthday pony. There are hidden fault lines in every system of the body. But the timing was suspiciously convenient. I know Clint was, let's say, disenchanted with Rona. And she knew he was after MORG. My well-honed paranoia tells me that the so-called stroke he suffered was somehow induced. Something in his food or water, maybe."

Bertie looked at him. "Have you seen the President since he—"

"Yes, I was able to arrange it, without Miss Rona knowing."

"What was he like? How did he act?"

"Childlike. I'm told he had to be taught to feed himself. We've known each other twenty years. There was no recognition in Clint's eyes. He wasn't paralyzed. He obeyed simple instructions okay. But it was like most of his vocabulary and all of his memories had been ripped out of his head."

"Could he speak?"

"He had a few words. None of them I would repeat to a lady."

Sherard said, "What did the brain scans show? A blood clot? Intercranial bleeding?"

"No clots, no bleeding."

Bertie glanced at Rory Whetstone, who was keeping pace with them in the Lexus. They were beneath the north tower, close to the Marin headland. The highway patrol black-and-white drove slowly by again. Bertie stopped and with her hands on the walkway railing looked back at the lights of the city, a close-packed sparkle like the core of a split geode. More distant was a tented amber strand of the Bay Bridge, seemingly adrift in the night like spider's silk. The dark tide surged beneath them. The Pacific fog bank had moved closer. The lights and cables on their bridge were indistinct.

"You feeling okay, Miss Nkambe?" Hannafin asked her.

"Yes, sir. I think—to be sure I would have to see him, but it is possible that you're right and it wasn't a stroke."

"See the President? He's been surrounded by specialists for the last six weeks. You seem young to have yourself a medical degree."

"Medicine's not what I have a degree in."

"Bertie," Sherard said, warningly.

"Tom, it's the *President*. They must have brain-locked him. From what the Senator is telling us."

"Come again?" said Hannafin.

"When you reverse the polarities of the brain's electrical field, the result is instant loss of consciousness. Severe amnesia, confusion, the gestures and habits of childhood or infancy are symptomatic during the recovery period. Provided the victim does recover."

"Lord, where did you learn all that?"

"She still reads comic books," Sherard said. "Buck, it's been rather a dicey night for both of us, and I think—"

"Tom! Black helicopter!"

There was enough fear in Bertie's voice to raise goose bumps. Sherard put an arm around her. He needed a few moments to locate the helicopter she'd seen. The chopper was a couple of hundred yards away, more or less, on the Sausalito side of the bridge, at roadway level and parked in the air side-on to them.

"Yeah, that's one of them I saw up there in Montana," Hannafin said, taking the half-smoked cigar from his mouth and spitting on the pavement behind him.

A car door opened and closed. Rory Whetstone joined them, binoculars in his hand. He gave them to his boss.

"How do they *know*?" Bertie said, holding fast to Sherard. She glanced at Rory Whetstone. He caught the look and shied from it. In her presence he had the demeanor of a spooked child.

Buck Hannafin studied the helicopter through the binoculars, lowered them. The helicopter remained on station, unthreatening in attitude.

"I suppose," he said, thoughtful but hard-eyed, "nobody here needs reminding that if something happens to Allen Dunbar, yours truly is on deck."

Behind the watchers on the bridge one of the highway patrol cars stopped, roof lights flashing. A patrolman joined them. They heard a foghorn lowing.

"Everything okay here, Senator?"

Hannafin turned and gave him the binoculars. "Over there, by Sausalito. Have a look."

The patrolman was a big kid with a power-lifter's body and pyramidal neck. His nameplate said Hawkins. He focused the binoculars.

"Ever seen anything like that helicopter before?"

The other highway patrol car pulled up. A lot of blue lights now, diffused by fog like shades of the shipwrecked stealthily taking over the bridge.

The driver got out but stayed with his vehicle, an arm resting on the top of the open door as he watched them.

After a few moments Hawkins took the binoculars from his eyes. His lips compressed as if in reaction to gastric distress, or a less specific internal turmoil.

"I don't see anything, sir."

"That helicopter? Plain sight. Don't need binoculars. My old eyes probably can't compare to yours, son, and I'm looking right at it. We all are."

"Sorry, sir," Hawkins said, glancing around at the other cop.

"What you're saying then, you don't see that chopper out there without lights or appropriate identification because otherwise you might be obliged to fill out some kind of report. And that's a report none of your superiors want to see come across their desk."

"Sir," Hawkins said with a touch of desperation in his voice, "it isn't for me to say what I can say or can't say."

Hannafin's Great Dane nudged him. He rubbed the dog behind an ear.

"But as far as you and him over there and maybe the rest of the California Highway Patrol, there's no black helicopter out there and never could be any such thing."

Footsteps. The other cop approached them.

"What's *your* name, son?"

"Westernew, Senator Hannafin. Sergeant Jack Westernew. Fog's coming in thick and fast here, Senator, so what we need to do now is escort you and your party off the bridge. We'll be glad to see that you get wherever it is you'd like to go."

Hannafin took the cigar from a corner of his mouth, looked it over, threw it into the bay.

"That's very accommodating of you, Sergeant Westernew," he said with a wry look directed at Tom Sherard.

"All part of our job, Senator. And let me add that it is a personal pleasure to be of service to you."

Betts looked steadily at Geoff McTyer and said, "I knew it had to be something like this. Sooner or later. You rat."

Riley, roused from sleep, complained, "I don't understand this. What's going on? Betts, my *back*."

The man temporarily known as Phil Haman, who was holding a submachine gun, the Heckler and Koch MP5 model, looked around the first floor of the lodge on the lake and saw an ebony grand piano. The sight of it jogged Face, his show-biz persona, to the head of the line.

"Cool. Anybody here play?"

"Eden isn't here," Betts said to Geoff. Her unforgiving stare had enough steel in it to drill out his molars. "I don't know where she is. In hiding. So you're wasting your time, Geoff, or whatever your name is."

"It's Geoff. But not McTyer. I'm sorry."

"A sorry piece of *shit*. Why didn't I kick you out of the house before you got your hands on my daughter? God, but you make my blood boil."

Haman laughed and wandered off to look at the piano and plink the keys. The piano seemed to be in tune. Meanwhile Riley went down slowly on one knee, groaning, then eased lower until he was on his hands and knees.

"Let's lift him up on the sofa," Geoff suggested.

He slid the Glock into his belt holster, helped Betts carry Riley to the wicker sofa with chintz-covered cushions. One huge sunflower on each cushion. Riley was pasty from pain. Betts tried to push Geoff away.

"Let him be. Bulging disk. Fourth lumbar vertebra. Takes a shot of cortisone to get the swelling down."

"How about you, Mama?" Haman called to Betts across the room, which took up most of the first floor of the lodge. "You play the piano?"

Birds were waking up outside the lodge, although there was no sign of dawn yet.

"Where did you get the midway attraction?" Betts murmured to Geoff, rearranging the big pillows, trying to make her husband comfortable.

Riley said anxiously, rolling his eyes to Geoff, "Guns. Why?"

Haman slammed a fist on the piano keys. Betts flinched, mouth gaping as if the wind had been knocked out of her.

"Get over here, Mama Frizz. I do mean now."

Geoff anticipated the return of her outrage, Betts yelling at Haman to fuck himself. He clamped a hand on her wrist, caught her eye. Betts yelled at him instead, stomping, kicking, landing some kicks on his shins.

Geoff hauled her in close, clinching. Hot blood in her cheeks. "Play the piano for him. Do requests. Give me time to try to get us out of this."

"Out . . . of what?" Betts gasped in his ear.

"He'll kill us all. Me included. Then wait around for Eden, kill her too. Now scream at me. Fight."

"Oh oh you bastard! What have you done? What did we ever do to deserve *you*?"

"Maybe someday I can expl—"

Betts slapped him on the side of his neck, hard enough to leave an imprint. Geoff winced, shook it off, and saw Haman's grin over her shoulder. He lowered his head, roughhousing Betts around, allowing her to shove back. Betts screaming her fuckyou's until she ran short of breath. Riley lying on his stomach on the sofa, helpless, eyes like a mad bull's, saying, "Hey hey son of a bitch hands to yourself leave her alone goddamn you!"

Geoff saying grimly to Betts, "Keep fighting. Haman thinks it's funny. We want him amused."

Betts went for his groin with her knee.

WASHINGTON, D.C. · MAY 29

After a massage and catnap Rona Harvester slipped out of the White House at four A.M., using the tunnel that extended from a subbasement beneath the east wing to the basement of the Treasury Department. Four MORG agents accompanied her, making sure that the surveillance cameras were blacked out before Zephyr's passage.

Three black limos were waiting at the Treasury Building. Rona was driven to a small but elegant European-style hotel with its entrance on Ninth Street, just north of Mount Vernon Square. The hotel was called the Chassériau. Brick with a copper mansard roof, many chimneys. There were only six fully-staffed four-thousand-square-foot suites available in the hotel, one suite per floor, with a private elevator for each. The suites were free; the platinum elevator key rented for twelve thousand dollars a night. It was the sort of cachet that billionaire business types from the world's capitals found irresistible. They were accustomed to a lot of pampering and they got that too. Multiphasic Operations and Research Group owned the

Chassériau, so everything the guests said or did within the walls was scrutinized, analyzed, and filed while they were in residence. Most of the counter-surveillance devices that the businessmen counted on for their security had been developed and were sold to them by one of MORG's companies.

The seventh and top floor of the hotel was reserved for Victor Wilding's use. A suite-within-a-suite had been created for the total privacy that was not available to the guests below.

"Victor, God. So *good* to see you."

The kiss was a long one. To Rona it seemed that her ardor overmatched his. She took a step back, studying his face, the fading boyishness. Circles of woe beneath his blue eyes. A haggard, pinched look about the mouth. And fear. Rona dug her fingers into his arm below the shoulder.

"You're blaming me."

"No."

"It happened. We're disappointed. We move on. There's another Avatar, somewhere."

"With Kelane Cheng's experience and ability? I don't think so. The news from Plenty Coups isn't good. He's failing more rapidly. It could be a matter of weeks, a few months at the most. Then I'll be recalled. Victor Wilding won't exist anymore."

"Why is he failing? His body, his heart, they're still strong. The worst violence in his brain, the temporal lobe epilepsy, was fixed years ago. Robin Sandza is only thirty-five years old. *Why?*"

"I don't understand all the terminology. Something to do with the neuropeptides that enable the immune and brain cells to communicate. Chinese medicine teaches that the brain is under the control of the body through energy channels. It's the basis of acupuncture."

"Sure. Cheng used acupuncture as well as traditional invasive procedures. And she had the touch, the instinct, to locate the site of the injury that was keeping Robin in a coma. Damn her for dying on us."

"I've been doing a lot of reading lately. The Bible."

"You're reading the Bible?"

" 'A broken spirit drieth the bones.' Proverbs."

"And?"

"What did Whitman call the life force? The thin red jellies within us, the marrow, the bones? 'Not the parts and poems of the body only, but of the soul.' "

"Who is Whitman?"

"Don't you see what I'm getting at? The reason why he's dying now, after all these years, could be spiritual, not mechanistic. Maybe Kelane

Cheng had the answer, and the power to heal him. That's why we had to have her. The world is swarming with telepaths, latents, or psi-actives, but her power was unique."

"That's enough. We went after Cheng because of this obsession of yours. You *don't* have to die because Robin Sandza dies. You're talking yourself into dying. It's worse than being the drunk my daddy was. You're soaking up the Bible and giving yourself the religious d.t.'s."

"It's the fate of all doppelgangers."

"Robin released you before they drove him insane at Psi Faculty. He named you. That in itself is proof you're not a doppelganger. But if you were. Naked, you'd be invisible. The sight of a dog would have you crapping your pants. Black light would put you on your knees, gasping for breath. Dpg my ass. You are Victor Wilding. Your name is who you are. The name is stronger than death. Get over this, lover."

Wilding smiled dispiritedly. "He gave me a name. But he couldn't give me a soul. That's the difference, the important difference you can't seem to grasp. Because I have no soul I'm still bound to Robin. Maybe in the same way both of us were bound to Gillian Bellaver. Is it a coincidence that he had a seizure a year ago that nearly killed him? On the same day—my research shows it was *the exact moment*—that Gillian was murdered?"

Rona didn't want to be reminded of Gillian Bellaver. She still wasn't sure he believed that she'd had nothing to do with it, the assassination, although Rona had welcomed the funeral of her rival and nemesis as a gift from the demon gods she had been keeping company with all of her life.

"If there's a connection it doesn't interest me. You don't have a soul? Fine. Neither do I. What I care about is that together we are one. One dick, one pussy, one heart, one mind. I me you we us. Afraid of nothing. Stronger than death. One."

"Yes."

"Good. You're listening to me."

"Yes."

"You look better already."

"You were gone three days. I hate it when you're gone that long."

"Oh, how much I love you. I need a drink but first I want you to fuck me silly. Rough, I like it rough. But you know that. Your pounding cock. I don't have anything on under these jogging shorts. Here it is. Forget God. Pussy is God. Put your hands on it. On your knees before Rona's pussy. Pray to Pussy. Here. Now. Lover/lover. I me you we us."

Tom Sherard was aware of Bertie's voice. In the bedroom of the suite. Talking to someone, but not on the phone. She spoke three or four sentences that weren't clear to him. But she seemed to be doing more listening than talking.

He had made a bed for himself on the floor of the sitting room with plush pillows from the sofas. Bertie uttered terrible whimpering sounds of distress. He got up and went inside, found her sitting on the bed trembling. The nightshirt she was wearing was soaked with her perspiration, as if she'd been in the shower. Her eyes were closed.

"Murder," she said. "Murder!"

He knew better than to disturb her when she was like this. He waited. Maybe he'd had an hour's sleep. San Francisco was waking up at the same pace he was. He heard a cable car's bell in the saffron fog outside.

Bertie slumped suddenly, as if she'd been released from the grip of an electric current. She breathed deeply for almost a minute, then fell over against him, sound asleep.

Sherard worked the drenched nightshirt off Bertie. Her sweat was pure as dew, odorless. Her flesh had sheen. Breasts as firm as boiled eggs. Her pubes had been fashionably depilated. Holding Bertie was giving him an erection. If it hadn't, might have been something to worry about. He sighed, left the bed, and got a bath towel six feet long from the heated rack beside the shower and wrapped her in it. She was peaceful, but he wasn't going to sleep anymore. He left her in the bedroom and ordered room service.

He had eaten his melon and English muffin and was on a second cup of coffee while going through the *Chronicle* when the bedroom doors opened and sleepyhead Bertie came out slowly, blinking, still wearing the towel wrap, collarbones to mid-thigh. Thick hair a-tumble. She sat primly on a sofa opposite him.

"I have such a headache. I never get headaches unless I've been Visiting. Is there more coffee?"

He poured a cup for her. "Don't you remember?"

"Some of it," Bertie said, adding sugar cubes to the black coffee.

"Where were you?"

"In the Astral."

"Who did you see? Talk to?"

Bertie sipped coffee, bowed her head. Rubbed it, grimacing.

"What happened to my nightshirt?"

"You soaked it through. I was afraid you'd catch a cold."

"Is that where the towel came from?"

"Yes."

"But you didn't—stay with me?"

"You were dead asleep. You'd been through an ordeal. How about something to eat?"

"I'm not hungry yet." She lifted her head, smiled at him. "You're a lovely man. The only man I ever want to wake up to."

"Right now I feel like a dope. Getting us into difficulty last night. I'm afraid you've been tagged by some extremely nasty people."

"Wouldn't be your fault. Or Danny Cheng's."

"How did MORG get on to us, then?"

"You're not thinking."

"You mean Rory Whetstone, Hannafin's guy?"

Bertie nodded. "First he's on the plane with us, then he's lurking around Cheng's house while we're inside."

"It was on telly this morning. Gas main explosion. So goes the official explanation. Historic old Russian Hill home. Nothing about black helicopters, of course. One body found in the wreckage, presumed to be an employee."

"Song Li. That means Danny and Chien-Chi got out somehow." She sighed in relief. "I'm hungry now. Could I have a ripe mango and, um, let's see, a steak sandwich? New York cut, medium rare, whole wheat. Cucumber relish on the side."

Sherard alerted room service. Bertie helped herself to more coffee, staring out the windows.

When he was off the phone Bertie said, "But Whetstone isn't MMF. I peeped him. He's totally dedicated to Senator Hannafin. If he's tipping off MORG, then it must be an implant of some kind. I think it's a chip with a transponder, not much bigger than an eighth of a carat diamond, embedded behind his left ear."

"I didn't know you also had X-ray vision."

"I don't. And that remark makes me feel like a freak."

"Sorry. Things you take for granted are a bit much for me to swallow whole. Why do you think he's carrying a transponder around in his bean?"

"Because those things effect the aura in the area of the implant."

"Oh. You read his aura too."

"I read everyone's aura. I can't avoid it. Yours is telling me a few things this morning."

"I don't want to hear it."

"I'm not talking," Bertie said with a hint of smugness. "Not now, anyway. Whetstone's aura doesn't betray evil intent. If he's being used by MORG, that's how they're doing it. To keep track of the Senator, of course. Last night when I spotted the black helicopter I thought, maybe they've come for him. Which would mean it was on."

"What was on?"

"What MORG has planned for the immediate future of my adopted country."

"Spell that out?"

"I don't know yet. The other girl knows, I think. Eden Waring. The one we came out here to find. I've found her, by the way."

Sherard gave her a look. Her eyes opening wide, Bertie dared him to scoff. He shrugged instead.

"If it's true, all to the good. I want to cut this thing short and get us well away from here."

"The problem is getting to Eden. That won't be easy."

"Why not? Where is she?"

"A place called Moby Bay, which is about six hours from here."

"How did you come by this piece of news?"

"Tom—I was on the Astral plane last night, where there are no secrets, but beyond that I'm really not prepared to tell you more."

"I'm not privileged to understand, something like that?"

"Because I, I just don't think you can handle it. I want you to trust me. Eden, she's in a kind of prison. Hard to explain what that means, but until she realizes what is going on she ought to be safe there. Before we go to Eden—Danny Cheng said it. We must see the woman in the hospital. The one who survived yesterday's plane crash. Barely survived, she may not live much longer."

"I like this less and less. However inadvert, I've exposed you."

"Oh, if only I'd been awake to enjoy—"

"Bertie."

"I'm sitting here in this towel, and you ought to see your aura. You don't have to say anything, Tom. Oh, maybe just—'Take off your towel, Bertie.' "

"We could hope for a more leisurely and less distracting time. There's a rightness that just isn't ours yet. To put it another way."

Bertie rubbed the back of her neck. "But we might have been blown to pieces a few hours ago. So. There are pros and cons. I *am* still kind of jumpy. Astral Visits take it out of me, and you've got so much on your mind you probably wouldn't—"

"Only the events of the past few hours. Only the death of my wife. If I couldn't protect Gillian, how—what am I supposed to do when you're knocking around the Astral by yourself?"

"No problem, I'm safe there. I have a wonderful guide. Tom, listen. Gillian never told you, but her powers were only half of what they were when she was my age or younger. It just happens. Otherwise she would have seen it coming, and that gunman on Madison Avenue would have been meat loaf. But I've got everything Gillian had at her best, and more. Remember what I almost did to poor Mr. Whetstone?"

"Vividly."

"Nobody's going to hurt me. Or you."

"So you're protecting *me* now?"

"Just like a man. You do come riding in on a very high horse sometimes. I need you, Tom. We're on a hunt. I need your skills if I'm going to be successful."

"A hunt, is it?"

"I know how you feel, but I have my Gift for a reason. I'm called to do this. I can't refuse."

"Do what, Bertie?"

"Eden has to tell me that."

"Didn't you say there were no secrets in the Astral?"

"I haven't met her yet. She can't get there, not from Moby Bay."

"Sounds like a fascinating place." He ran out of words and stared unhappily at the carpet. After a minute of that Bertie got up, holding the towel with one hand. She put her other hand on his shoulder, then moved it to cup the side of his neck in her palm. He looked up.

"You see, it's, the fact is, you are—"

"I know, a bit much at times."

"And did you have to be so damned beautiful? An abundance of gifts I can't be convinced I deserve."

She touched her forehead with her index finger.

"Whatever's going on in here, Tom—"

Her hand moved to the center of her breastbone.

"It's just an ordinary workaday heart. Like yours. Everybody's. Same old moonshine and tears. But my brain was touched by lightning before I was born. Should have killed us both, my mother and me. Glad it didn't. The lightning, or what it left behind, is still there. In a certain state, just this side of sleep, I see it sometimes. A mind within my mind. A separate consciousness. Quiet. Glowing. Powerful. I see by its light things you'll never see. Don't think about the lightning, Tom. I swear it will never hurt you. Just think about me."

"I do. I always will."

With a smile she wiped a leaking eye, bent down to kiss him lightly.

"You shaved already? I'm going to take a shower and get dressed before I eat."

"I should make a couple of phone calls. Old friend and client of my father's who I think is still living in the Bay Area. If I'm going on a hunt, I want the right equipment to do the job."

WASHINGTON, D.C. • MAY 29 • 6:45 A.M. EDT

They had breakfast and then it was lights down and the DVD player on in the room beneath the hotel, a room that floated cagily inside a concrete bunker, furnished in angles of steel and suede, nothing remotely decorative, no personal touches. Soundproof, shockproof, impervious to ESP, it was the den of a man with a hush-hush empire to run in a city of mazes and cross-purposes founded on a swamp. Victor Wilding inserted the disk in the DVD player. Rona waited, yawning. Crackle of grit in her jaws. She'd put in a strenuous twenty-four hours, with only two short intervals of sleep since Hawaii.

During lulls she still saw Frank Romanzo's head disintegrating in a bloodstorm, which was hard on her nerves. Fit of temper, no practical resistance to her trigger finger. But Kelane Cheng had refused to be broken. It was a lesson Rona had to consider once again. There were absolutes in the human spirit.

Then Rona's husband was right there in the darkened room, speaking again in full sentences. For a few moments her mind refused to assimilate this. She pressed back into the low curve of her chair on an outgoing tide of blood and was forced to shut her eyes, feeling coldly depleted, syncopal. She uttered sounds that might have been laughter.

"What's wrong?"

"I'm okay." Still in a fragile state of mind, Rona had another look at the tube. She had grown accustomed during the past few weeks to the Clint Harvester sequestered at Camp David, his mind as potted as a mummy's. Now he was speaking in his familiar westerner's cadences of acts of terror in formerly untouchable American venues, innocent cities of the heartland. Speaking, in the past tense, of events still on the drawing board as far as Rona knew. And Rona knew everything. Speaking of the nation's resolve to end its ordeal at the hands of faceless extremists taking advantage of too-liberal immigration laws. Speaking of the need for strong countermeasures that would begin with the reinstitution of a military draft for eighteen-year-olds of both sexes and the nationalization of police and sheriff's departments. Speaking of a massive purge of all criminal elements, known and suspected.

"Whose voice?"

"His."

"How?"

"All the words are there, in the old speeches. We've prepared new speeches, like the one you're listening to. We can write as many as we need, for whatever occasion."

The explanation, and the paste-up speech, pleased her. It had been the sound of his voice that had attracted Rona to Harvester, before she knew who he was. She'd first heard him boldly amplified across the fairgrounds on a Fourth of July in Great Falls, Montana. Running for governor. No previous political experience. They were celebrating one of those old-fashioned Fourths. There was a PRCA-sanctioned row-day-o. Bunting, bands, politicians, and good-looking college girls on horseback.

Rona was twenty-five. She had flown up to Montana with her second husband Travis and three of his buddies to fly-fish. She'd been married two months and four days and had already made up her mind that three months with Travis would be her limit. He'd been sober less than half the time since she'd met him. A pre-nup existed, but Rona had had the opportunity after the whirlwind romance and Vegas hitching to dig into his irresponsible past and get, on tape from one of his close friends whom she'd fucked for the purpose, details of a hit-and-run with Trav at the wheel, two left for dead and a young girl now confined to a wheelchair, elements that wouldn't play to Travis's advantage on *Hard Copy*. And his daddy was still sufficiently competent to make massive changes in the will.

"The mouth movements. His expressions."

"Morphing software any kid can buy. It's a fun thing."

"He looks, God, what a thrill. I'm shivering. The return of Clint Harvester. How long can we get away with it?"

"Limited exposure. Getting into and out of the helicopter on the south lawn. A motorcade or two. Clint at Burning Tree. Waving, smiling. He hasn't lost that smile. Of course no one gets close enough to ask him any questions. Dunbar can carry on with the grunt work, cabinet meetings, state dinners, Clint will always be indisposed. All speeches, like this one, will be canned. All we need is the face. The setting, his suit, the pattern of his tie, those elements are interchangeable and undetectable under normal scrutiny.

How long? We don't want to string it out. First, the good news of Clint's return. Then the second nuclear event on U.S. soil occurs. While the nation is still in shock, give it a week I'm thinking, comes the assassination. Clint Harvester dies in your arms. You take it from there."

(Rona had been a serial adventuress from puberty, thumbing her way along many roads in several countries. Sniffing out the humanity that remained in the used-up places, the hardscrabble byways of a continent. Getting wise to herself. Good footwork when trouble loomed. Carried a sharpened screwdriver in her boot. Also a little bottle of knockout drops for the would-be hustlers during those times when she needed to appropriate some cash. *I knew how smart I was the day I was born.* After a year among her sainted surfers she'd been located by Mom and Dad, Henry on the wagon for the fifth or sixth time during their long-suffering saga, back to the block and cleaver. In the keeping of her parents once again she'd finished high school and actually enjoyed it this time. Elected prom queen in spite of the Black Widow tattoo just below her right shoulder. The day after her eighteenth birthday she left home for good, landed in the Haight. Still the epicenter of the flower-power culture and a heavy drug scene. A dovecote of the charmed, the futile, the precociously wasted. On weekends no room to move but in the street. Rona had tried a lot of substances, walked the edges a few times, but lack of control over herself dished up fears she couldn't handle. At eighteen she had the innate selfishness of the driven but undirected. Restless in pursuit of a destiny that was hard to divine. She only knew, instinctively, that it had to do with the acquisition of power.

(Nixon had fled the White House with one last mawkish grin for the cameras, pausing beneath the blades of Marine One, unaccompanied by his near-catatonic wife. In Frisco Rona tumbled to activist politics. The entertainment and social values appealed to her more than causes. But she got herself arrested several times on behalf of the farmworkers and dissident Cal Berkeley students and Huey's Panthers over there in Oakland. Charges were routinely dismissed. Involuntarily hanging around courthouses and the OPD, Rona met a young attorney named Bill Frederics, who was on a fast track with the Organized Crime and Criminal Intelligence Branch of the California Department of Justice. She moved in with him after the second date.

(Through Frederics Rona had access to classified information, including her own FBI and CIA files. She learned a great deal more about power, and who really had it in a democratic society. The solution to extinguishing the ideologies and uncivil strife of minority groups that the government found bothersome was to establish a rationale for treating those groups as criminal organizations. New strike forces, such as the Office of Drug Abuse Law Enforcement, could be created by presidential decree, immediately becoming autonomous monsters with no congressional oversight possible. ODALE, which soon became the Drug Enforcement Administration, was empowered to draw support for its operations from other government agencies such as the FBI, the IRS, and Customs.

(Only MORG declined to cooperate. The White House, with Gerald Ford completing Nixon's term, failed to make an issue of MORG's refusal.

(Rona had never heard of Multiphasic Operations and Research Group. Frederics didn't know much about them, either. Other agencies, state and federal, had a certain muted fear of MORG agents.

(Interesting, Rona thought.

(She began to read about the White House, then to visit regularly in her dreams. Uninvited. She opened impressive doors and walked down corridors lined with portraits of former heads of state and the occasional bucolic painting. In the way of dreams, people came suddenly from doorways, menacing at times, asking her questions. *Oh yes I belong here.* Her heart thumping badly. Up a flight of stairs. A glimpse of a man in a bedroom who might have been the President. Buttoning his shirt. Shooting a look her way. She recognized LBJ, a sulky hound dog with terse mean eyes. Giving him a big wave. *It's okay, I belong here, Mr. President.*

(Rona flew to Washington and did the tour. She was twenty-one. Much of the White House was unavailable to tourists, but the effluence of power was everywhere. It gave Rona a permanent low-grade fever. That night, alone in her cheap hotel room miles from monuments with the antique glow of lanterns and that famous address where all of the hard-traveled roads converged in her imagination, she wept bitterly, certain that she did, as the dreams had foretold, belong there. No idea of how to make it happen. So many loose ends in her life.

(With a little thought she hit upon politics as the nexus. Money begat power, but politics sustained it. Rona made some assessments. Bill Frederics was ambitious, to a point. He wanted to be California's attorney general, a modest pinnacle but probably the best he could hope for. But that lay well in the future. He didn't have a legacy, and there was [as Rona had discovered six months into her first pregnancy] Bill's craving to swing both ways. A stronger desire than either ambition or money. San Francisco gays were beginning to come down with a puzzling and fatal wasting illness doctors couldn't name.

(Rona handed her two-year-old son Joshua over to her mother to raise, packed up her new college degree in political science, and moved to

L.A. This time she was after a gold-rush grubstake. A couple of million would do.)

"I've seen enough," Rona said to Victor Wilding. "It's great. Just what we need. Turn it off."

Wilding removed the disk from the DVD player.

"The girl we talked about. She's on my mind."

"Oh, yes. Eden, isn't it?"

"I've got Homefolks all over the place." "Homefolks" was MORG's domestic operations division. "Innisfall. She hasn't showed up yet. She didn't go home. Staying with a friend, we believe. Family's not at home either. There were people camped in front of the house all night, it's taken on the nature of a religious vigil is what I hear. Sixty-eight Deep Creek Road is becoming a shrine for the nebulous, the credulous, and the half-bright."

"Eden will turn up. Casey left a message on her answering machine. I invited Eden to call me. Who could refuse an opportunity like that?"

"I've been looking into Eden Waring's background. She's adopted. Illegitimate. Born in a Provençal village in the hills above St. Raphael. Mother was a French adolescent, fifteen years old, confined to a sanitarium of considerable reputation: for a hundred and fifty years they've catered to the needs of royal nutcases and addicts. Eden's birth date was November 7, 1979."

"Should I be interested in where she came from?"

"Yes. The mother's name was listed on the birth document as Beaulieu. One of the more common names in the L'Esterel region, the other being—Bellaver."

Rona nodded slowly, waking up to his pitch.

"Expensive place, you said. So the mother came from wealth. I thought the Bellavers were English."

"Anglicized French."

"You believe that Eden's mother could have been Gillian Bellaver?"

"I know that Robin Visited Gillian in a Connecticut village called Mt. Carmel the night before he went completely crazy. Destroyed poor Gwyneth, climbed out on that icy roof in the storm. By then he thought he was immortal. Wouldn't listen to anything *I* said."

"I know, you've told me a hundred—How do you mean, 'visited'? Teleported himself?"

"Not even Robin Sandza could do that. Only dpg's have the ability. Visualize a place, the next instant we're there. It isn't one of the talents you get to keep, once you're set free. The rest of it just fades away as we get older. All I have of Robin anymore are his memories. *All* of his memories, which are now my nightmares. He made me a man, but left too much of himself in me."

"Don't go there. Look at Rona, darling. Think about who *we* are, what we've become. I me you we us."

"All right. I'm sorry. You know I haven't slept since you left."

"That night in Connecticut. What happened? How could Robin—"

"Conceive a child? He couldn't, not in the Astral. He needed a surrogate to accomplish that. His own father. Peter Sandra was right there, asleep beside Gillian. Robin took possession of his father. While Robin made love to Gillian in the Astral, Peter did the same to Gillian on the earthly plane. And remembered none of it when he woke up in the morning. This was in early February, 1979. Almost exactly nine months later Eden was born. Who knows what this girl is really like, what she's capable of."

(So she heard this resonant voice unmarred by the slightly tinny amplification of the fairgrounds sound system and was drawn to it through the dust and flies and pods of horseshit, walking around family groups all dressed in rangewear down to the toddlers in their sunshaded strollers, dodging sweet pink clouds of cotton candy, and came to the bunting-draped bandstand populated by a western swing band, local politicians, rivals for bigger and better state jobs sitting in a row of wooden folding chairs.

(Clint Harvester was a tall man in tight-fitting twill trousers and a tan jacket with western-style leather darts on the pockets. He was blond with a widow's peak. He had blue eyes that could only be described as winsome and a sharply angled jawline. He stood out against the clouds. Other men behind him seemed dull and muddied in his brilliant wake. Rona had only to listen for a couple of minutes to understand that Clint Harvester had vision. She loved visionaries. They flew to the heights. They dealt in grand concepts. They tended to be vague or stupid about everything else. He spoke without a text during his allotted ten minutes, rambling, his humor wry and dry, winning laughter and cheers from his twenty-odd supporters in patriotic sashes and buttons with Clint's face on them. More than half of Clint's claque were young women.

(Rona insinuated herself among them and stood, taller than most, beaming up at the country-squire spellbinder on the platform. He couldn't avoid seeing her. Her smile was constant, encouraging, approving. He looked at her more and more often, ran over his time, and had to be cut off. Rona was offered a *Clint When It Counts* button. She put it on, then walked around to the back of the platform where Clint Harvester was leaning against a pickup truck, a white-faced calf tethered in the bed. Clint wearing a tan Stetson now, having a beer with campaign workers and a dark-haired woman. Pretty, diamonds flashing as she drank from a tall paper cup, but her skin had been sunwrecked in a country of stark weathers. Rona took her to be his wife. Rona stood ten feet away from the group with the unnerving self-possession of the inspired and righteous until Harvester, sensing an irresistible force, looked her way again.

(Looked Rona's way, and never looked back.)

GREENWOOD LAKE · MAY 29 · 10 A.M. PDT

The sun came up. The man temporarily known as Phil Haman expressed interest in getting some breakfast.

Betts was hobbled, her mouth sealed with duct tape, but he'd left her hands free to play show tunes, sight-reading from sheet music he took from one of two custom-designed titanium suitcases that traveled everywhere with him. The other contained components of various weapons socketed in dark gray foam rubber. Airport security never troubled the assassin. He traveled by corporate jet or, if there was no time constraint, in his own star bus, a thirty-six-foot motor home.

Haman had taken Geoff's Glock from him and used more duct tape, twisted like rope, to hog-tie him on the floor next to the sofa on which Riley lay facedown with his own hands taped behind his back. They could watch television by raising their heads, but neither man chose to. Riley's mouth also was taped shut.

Having secured everyone to his satisfaction, the assassin yielded to Face, who passed the time until dawn working up a likeness of Rona Harvester, using the breakfast bar as a makeup table and many photographs of the First Lady to guide him. He talked exclusively to Betts, praising her for her deft piano work, explaining as he went along what he was doing to transform Face into Rona.

"Complete Concealer hides the little imperfections. Then I use foundation, of course, and after that a light powder. Now we dust the lid and brow with ivory, umm-hmm! There. I'm going to use a number four brush with cocoa shadow and draw a *big* curve along the lashes, then fill in the crease. After that I think we'll go with a creamy pink shimmer, but I'm open to suggestions. It's possible with theatrical lighting that 'wild white' might be the thing. Just jump right in and nod or shake your head, doll. I can see you in my mirrors."

When Betts required a break from rippling the ivories Face turned on his micro tape recorder and listened to Rona Harvester's voice. The First Lady had taken elocution lessons and knew how to make the most of a clear pleasant soprano, but she had toned down or eliminated vocal tics, space fillers, and the like, and there was no strong regionalism in her voice for a mimic to exploit. She did have some pet expressions. "End of story, no tears." "Change the tune and we'll tango." And, "Don't try to sell me *that*," usually spoken with an exasperated leer and the Rona *look*.

Face demonstrated *the look*. If Betts hadn't been in a state of terror, her blood pressure maintaining in the mid two hundreds, she might have laughed. *The look* was an arms-folded, head-cocky, sideways glance of utter disbelief. Face had Rona Harvester cold.

By the time his cheese omelette was crisp at the edges the First Lady, with the addition of false eyelashes, had come alive, slightly caricatured but full of sass in the house overlooking the lake. He hadn't brought an appropriate wardrobe with him, but Face had scrounged a pair of heels in a bedroom closet that didn't cramp his feet. He'd found a bra in a dresser drawer that he wore, stuffed with wadded tissues, over his sleeveless undershirt. That, and Jockey shorts, were all he was wearing. Pale hairless hide from the neck down, a carnival head complete with ash-blond wig floating above the vaguely feminine body.

Face made Betts sit on the floor where he could keep an eye on all three of them while he buttered toast and ate his omelette. He watched TV. In one of the world's fleapits with unpronounceable names ancient grudges had flared again. Unshaved paramilitaries in a ruined square fired automatic rifles into the air with a lot of snaggle-toothed grinning and gusto. It was something to do. There was a plague of locusts somewhere else. Seething miles of insects. In only a few moments they covered the lens of the cameraman sent to record their devastation. Five boys who attended an exclusive prep school in Connecticut admitted bringing down a 747 with a surface-to-air missile crafted in a basement workshop. It had been something to do. Four women held for a year and a half as love slaves in a remote Ontario farmhouse had been rescued by provincial police. The black-bearded slavemaster had shot himself as the doors were battered down. Face helped himself to a second cup of coffee. The women taken from the farmhouse wrapped in blankets had the look most often seen on the faces of death-camp survivors. Wincing in the wan northern light. Not believing in their freedom. Not sure they wanted it. Life owed them an explanation.

On a breezy Washington morning Rona Harvester crossed the south lawn of the White House toward a waiting helicopter. Pard, the Harvesters'

Border collie, walked beside her on a leash. There was a white patch the size of a playing card on Rona's forehead, souvenir of the ruckus on Ala Moana Boulevard. But there she was, in a pink churchgoing suit, on her way to visit and pray with her husband at Camp David. She acknowledged remote cheers from passersby outside the iron gates. Face got down from the breakfast bar stool and wandered closer to the TV, watching as Rona handed the collie over to a Marine at the foot of the helicopter steps and turned, smiling, with the exuberant, fists-in-the-air gesture that she had quickly made her signature. Face set his coffee mug down and mimed the smile, the gesture. Reminded himself to buy a pair of white gloves like those Rona was wearing.

Geoff McTyer thrashed violently and made incoherent sounds, trying to get his attention. With the First Lady off the screen Face finally looked at Geoff in annoyance, squatted in the high heels beside him, and ripped two layers of duct tape half off, uncovering Geoff's mouth.

Geoff gasped. "Told you . . . my father . . . FBI Director . . . let me go, or—"

"Still trying to sell me *that*?" Face said in Rona Harvester's voice, with a sideways twist of his torso, accentuating the lift of the falsies, pointed like the noses of bird dogs. His long eyelashes fluttered mockingly. "Anyway, I don't have anything to do with it. Talk to *him*. Phil, you know. What's-his-name."

"Haman you goddamn moronic bastard I'm trying to—"

"End of story, no tears." Face replaced the metallic gray tape, then slapped Geoff hard in the mouth to make sure the tape stuck. He looked up at Betts, whose eyes, reddened and frantic, were fixed on something else. Outside a motorboat was gunned across the wisping surface of the lake. They all heard another sound, inside the house, the cocking of the H and K machine gun as it was readied to fire.

"Is that all there is to it?" Eden Waring's voice shocked them all. "Pull back this little lever? Then what? Start shooting, I guess."

Face rose slowly to his feet, looking toward the breakfast bar where he had carelessly left the gun, entrusted to him by the man temporarily known as Phil Haman, beside his plate.

"Well, hel*lo*."

"Hello yourself," the girl said, aiming the gun at him. "Why don't you get away from them?"

"You're even prettier than your picture. Where did you come from?"

"You'd be amazed. I *said* get away from them. *Now*."

"Well, the truth is, I feel *much* safer where I am. Knowing you probably won't try to shoot me. Because I just don't think you're the warrior type.

Oh no no no no. And I think, being a sensible young thing and not all that proficient with a weapon like the one you have in your hands, that you're just a teeny bit worried about cutting loose and oh my, I can assure you there will be a *hail* of bullets the instant your finger squeezes the trigger. It doesn't take much pressure. I won't tell you how much. I *would* advise you not to hold the stock against your shoulder. And I'm not shitting you. Someone near and dear could also be shot. It's very likely, in fact. You might even shoot yourself. Being unfamiliar with that weapon."

"Untie Geoff and Riley."

"I'm *not* unwilling, if it would pacify you. But *he* used duct tape. You know what that's like. Yards and yards of duct tape. Once it's twisted and knotted, there's no way. I'd need a sharp knife or scissors to cut through the tape. You must have slipped in by the back door. Yes? But I didn't hear a car. Did you ride in on your mountain bike?"

"Betts, you have your hands free. Find some scissors."

Betts looked from Eden's face to her hands, as if she'd forgotten about them. She glanced at Face, reached up, and tried to pull off the tape covering her mouth. Face slipped in behind her, locking an arm straight up, placing one hand on the side of her head. The other hand cupped Betts's chin, forcing her head up and sideways.

"Push-push-*snap*," he said. "If you don't put the gun down, Eden. Really, you'd be amazed how little force is needed to separate the spine from the head. We've never involved the girls in bloodletting, but that doesn't mean—" His voice changed suddenly, and Haman took over, all business in spite of the getup. "—I *won't* do it, you little asshole. Now let's just move over there, Mama Frizz, so Eden can hear it nice and loud when your neck breaks."

"Here," the girl said. "You want it, just take the fuckin' thing."

She pitched the stubby machine gun as if she were letting fly with a set shot from thirty feet. A lot of arc to the toss, the gun almost hitting a rough-hewn redwood beam overhead before coming down. As soon as the gun left her hands she turned and was running toward the door of the deck at the back of the house.

Haman's reflexes were almost as good as hers. He released Betts, giving her a sideways shove, caught the machine gun in one hand, leveled it, and shot off half a magazine at the fleeing girl.

Bullets stippled the screen wire as she was going out the door. She was hit at least twice, high on her back, and went down on all fours on the deck outside, her only sound a strangled gasp as the door slapped shut behind her.

Haman kicked off the heels and started after her. Betts reached up from the floor where she'd fallen and grappled, trying to stop him. He turned and struck her in the side of the head with the butt of the H and K, delivered a side-kick to her chin, dropping her unconscious across Geoff as he struggled on his stomach with his hands tied close to his ankles. Haman turned the machine gun on Geoff, muzzle four feet from the back of his head, then decided it could wait until he finished off the girl. He should have been able to see her, lying out there on the deck, but apparently she'd dragged herself away from the door.

So walk out there, flip her over, look her in the eyes. Smart-mouth little bitch. Had the drop on Face. Wasn't *his* approval rating at stake. Hit Eden again, a quick burst, walk away. Or, no, she owed him a few minutes of play time. Carving knife, not the H and K. Beginning an inch below the navel, left-right, back again, all the way to the trachea, see if it could be done in a single smooth cut, finishing ear-to-ear. Then drag her by the heels inside to complete the family diorama. Torch the place. And home to Glitter Gulch before dark.

CAMP DAVID · MAY 29 · 10:40 A.M. EDT

His appetite is good," Clint Harvester's personal physician told Rona. "Physically I'd say he's in the best shape of his life. He runs and swims at least two hours a day. His resting pulse is fifty-eight. His blood pressure—"

"Is this supposed to be the good news? So he's not in a wheelchair. I'd take that anytime if I knew that one day soon Clint would be able to put enough words together to make a sentence I could understand."

"His mind is quite active," R. Traynor Daufuskie said encouragingly. We've done PET scans while he watches TV or is subjected to various other stimuli. He appears to be listening when we speak to him. He hears words, but his ability to generate them is nearly gone. He can obey simple directions accompanied by demonstrations. Of course we have no definition of what consciousness—language, visualization, self-awareness—is. The concept is not measurable by means currently at our disposal. Clint's language skills have mysteriously vanished. I say 'mysteriously' because the cognitive areas of the brain show no abnormalities, such as would occur from a burst blood vessel. The seizures—electrical misfires—are occurring randomly throughout the brain, but they are greatly diminished. No more than one

or two a day. Neurons have been destroyed, obviously. Dead neurons probably can't be replaced, although there is some evidence now to the contrary.
The plenum temporale in the right hemisphere appears normal. The failure
may be in the neurotransmitters, which could improve greatly with the
monoamine oxidase A protocol we have him on."

"I don't have a clue as to what you're telling me. Tray, does he know
who I am when I walk into the room?"

"Yes. But for now his memories are all post-trauma. That's how retro-
grade amnesia works."

"He doesn't know when or where we were married. He can't recall how
we first met." Rona's head was down. She bit her lip until tears came. "He
doesn't know he's President of the United States." She used a handkerchief,
dabbing at her cheeks, then looked up with a forlorn smile. "There's no
chance he'll simply snap out of it?"

"Please don't give up hope. The human brain exhibits remarkable plas-
ticity. The President can and probably will relearn a good deal of what has
been erased. But we must be patient."

"I'd like to take Clint home. I mean, to the White House, not the ranch.
Sit him down behind his desk in the Oval Office. Who knows? Familiar
sights, people he's been around for the last three years, something might
go clickety-click."

"Well—I don't know how he would respond to that much stimulation.
And his attention span is, unfortunately, quite short. Then there's the problem of primitive, aggressive behavior, immediate gratification of his urges."

"Have I missed something?"

"On two occasions the President has attempted to have sexual relations
with women who have come into his, uh, orbit at inopportune moments.
A Secret Service agent assigned to the POTUS detail, whom he followed
into a bathroom, and a Marine Corps nurse who entered the suite to take
his blood pressure when he happened to be—"

"Rubbing one off? I'm sure you can give the President a shot of something that will help him keep his mitts off his pump handle. For my sake,
if you wouldn't mind. Traynor, my wifely instinct tells me the change from
Camp David to Washington will be wonderful for him. I want you to bring
Clint down tonight. Late tonight, please."

Cardinals had flocked to a bird feeder in a tree outside the President's suite.
Clint Harvester was standing idly at the windows watching them when
Rona walked in. Two Secret Service agents were keeping an eye on Clint.

He was wearing denim, his comfortable old ranching duds. He had a
good tan. He saw Rona reflected in the window and turned slowly, eyes

without the velocity of coherent thought. She hurried across the room. Her lips met his cheek as if she were kissing a soap bubble. Clint smiled.

"Caw," he said.

"I've talked to Tray Daufuskie. He's very pleased with your progress. We're all praying very hard, Clint."

She turned to the Secret Service agents and let two tears fall.

"I'd like some quality time with my husband."

"Yes, ma'am."

When they had gone Rona took off the jacket of her pink suit and sat down, watching her husband.

"I know you can't understand what I say."

There was a quirk to his lips that couldn't be called a smile. He said something that sounded like "voogle."

"It was never anything personal. I always liked you, Clint. You were just what I wanted, and needed, at the time. Media appeal. A prince from the far country. You never failed at anything you tried. Didn't know shit about politics. Thought there was room for civility. A little spilled blood but never any gore. You needed me to run your show. I could handle the rats. And they're all man-eating rats, aren't they?"

He was looking at the bird feeder again, as if Rona weren't in the room.

"If you turned around you would see me crying. But you won't turn around. There's nothing to see behind you anymore."

Clint was now watching a fly that had found its way to the window-panes.

"By the way, I had nothing to do with Linda's untimely death. You don't just slink away from competition like me and sulk. That hurt little smile, heavy with tooth. She should have come at me with fists flying. Had me tied up and thrown into a stall with a crazed stallion. A woman who won't take a man's dick in her mouth doesn't deserve to keep him. End of story. A few tears. That's my human side. The rest of me requires no explanation. A rabid genius boils the marrow of my bones. A cock-eyed soothsayer/poet/surfer told that to me. I was just fourteen. How could he have known? Probably it was just a line he came up with so he could fuck me. Boy did it work. I'd like for you to look at me now, but you won't. If we could go back just one time. Montana. Sky red as sunburn, a hawk drifting home. Your old fleabag asleep by the fire. Horses in shadow wood. Your eyes sliding in and out of me like rapiers and then we do it. Ah. Do it. The peace at our beginning. There are ways of living that are far more unpleasant than dying. I see that. You standing there. I understand. A broken spirit drieth the bones. Someone quoted me that today. I think he's in a little bit of trouble about the soul thing.

I never would have expected that. I'm uneasy. Too much is coming up. All the chips are in the middle of the table. Speaking of poker. You'd have been a far better politician if you had let me teach you how to deal seconds. But that would have diminished you. The American People would have caught on the minute you started dealing seconds. I've never underestimated the AP. The Anointed Media shovels a lot of crap at the AP, as we direct it to do. But there's a knowingness deep in the collective gut of the AP. We keep the lights low and the music soft but eventually you just can't feed the AP any more crap. I know this and it's the one thing I'm afraid of. Dream about too often. Always the smoke and the dead and the blood red skies and the guillotine, waiting at the end of screaming streets. There's never time to do my nails."

Clint murmured something.

"Seriously. I wonder what history will make of us. Rona and Clint in the ambers of time. Myths dressed in mythy black. I'm preparing a gift for you. A martyrdom that will live a thousand years. Magnificent. I feel it's the least I can do, repayment for the ride you've given me."

Clint Harvester watched the fly crawl up the windowpane, crawl down again.

Rona got up, feeling greatly refreshed, put on her jacket, and left the room. Hum-drum, he watched her pink reflection flash good-bye.

The two Secret Service men returned, sat down, and resumed watching Clint. Eight-hour shifts. They didn't play chess. They didn't look at TV.

After a while the fly came unstuck from the glass and rambled away. A word, too, floated in the air.

"Cunt."

The Secret Service men looked at each other.

Clint Harvester stared at the bird feeder as if he were counting seeds in the glass hopper.

GREENWOOD LAKE · MAY 29 · 7:55 A.M. PDT

The assassin went outside to find that the girl he'd shot wasn't where he'd expected her to be. There was nothing on the redwood deck at the rear of the house except a pile of firewood under a tarp next to a stone chimney.

And a wide smear of blood, what he took to be blood, not as dark as the color of the sealant protecting the wood deck.

The blood had begun to bubble, producing a mist. That was a new one. He'd spilled a lot of blood, but he'd never seen it act like that.

He looked around. No hiding places. There were steps, and a flagstone path through beds of low-growing juniper and redwood mulch to the front of the house. The conifers on the hillside behind the house grew too far apart to provide concealment, and there wasn't much understory rooted in the acid soil. He saw another vacation home sixty or seventy yards away, lower on the hill and closer to the water. Only a part of the roof and chimney were visible from where he stood in broad daylight wearing a designer wig, a padded bra, and Jockey shorts. Holding an assault weapon.

This wasn't going well. He had the low suspicion that Eden Waring was playing him tricky somehow. On the other hand there was the blood, proof that she'd been wounded. She had to have burrowed in somewhere attempting to hide. Beneath the deck or house was one possibility. Losing more blood, going into shock.

He looked under the deck. No. So where. Then he saw a sandal beside the path near a corner of the house. Running, headlong. Panic. Wounded. Obvious then where she'd gone. The boathouse.

He went down the slope to the edge of the lake, the dock that enclosed three sides of a metal boathouse painted a faded blue. There was a deck above the boathouse. Voices floated in the calm air from a distant part of the lake. Fishermen. Birds sang cheerily, squirrels played frisky games from tree to tree. He found another lost sandal a few feet from the dock. Padlock on the boathouse door. There was blood on the padlock. Eden couldn't get in. She hadn't been that far ahead of him, so if she'd jumped into the lake there would still be ripples. The water was calm, shading from bottle-glass green to black in the periphery of the boathouse.

Calm. A calm morning.

Nothing showing on the deck above the boathouse but some stacked canvas chairs and a couple of marine storage lockers, one with a coil of bleached rope on the lid. That made it easy. She was in the other locker, trying to make herself small, listening for him. Terrified.

Should have gone into the lake, he thought. More of a chance. But probably she couldn't swim with at least two bullets in her back and shoulder.

He let her hear him coming, but took his time. The dock floated on barrels. The mild slap-slosh of water as the dock dipped slightly from his weight. Up the metal ladder to the deck. It was surfaced with some kind of rubberized nonskid stuff. There was a diving board. Maybe Eden hadn't realized she'd left another bloody handprint scrambling into the vinyl locker. Blood fizzing in the sun. Just fizzing away. If that wasn't the damnedest thing he'd ever—

Grinning, he flipped up the lid using the gunsight on the muzzle of his H and K.

The locker was empty, except for a discarded Mighty Ducks hockey jersey and a pair of running shorts.

His head jerked around in astonishment and annoyance. Toy-size speed-boat bounding full-throttle near the far shore. He turned and looked at the house on the sparsely wooded slope. There was a long slant of morning sun across the front deck. And silence.

He looked again into the nearly empty locker. Reached down with his free hand and lifted out the hockey jersey. Three rather neat holes in the material from the high-velocity slugs, a diagonal going from left to right inches below the collar and shoulder seams. Nailed her, all right. From the placement of the holes he could tell he'd missed the spinal cord, but bones in both shoulders would have been splintered. Leaving her—theoretically—helpless to do much with her hands or arms. There were two exit holes in the front of the jersey. One slug had stayed inside Eden.

Then where was all the blood? Should have been more blood.

What little of the girl's blood remained was fading away as he stared at the holes in the woven material.

Something dropped on the deck behind him, making a small thud.

The assassin whipped around ready to fire, adrenaline lighting up the stress center of his brain like an arcade game. The entire boat dock rocked slightly from his momentum.

He saw nothing but mountains and spacious skies. Sun dazzle on the wide lake. He was alone on the deck. No movement except for the .223 caliber slug rolling in a tight semicircle with the motion of the deck a couple of feet from where he stood.

"You can have this back." Eden Waring's voice, the rest of her nowhere to be seen in the electric blue.

A stream of brass issued from the SP5 machine gun as the assassin sowed the air and the deck all around him with lethal lead. He stopped after four seconds, caught his breath. Then he fired a few more rounds into the other marine locker, the one where there had been a coil of rope on the lid.

The implication of the missing rope didn't occur to him until he felt it around his neck, digging in savagely as he was yanked off his feet and dragged backward toward the ladder.

Geoff was staring into Riley's pain-clouded eyes when they heard the gun-fire.

"He's killing Eden!" Riley screamed. Then his eyes disappeared into his head as the color of his face faded from red to ghastly gray and he slumped,

head down and half off the sofa with the sunflower cushions. Geoff helpless, horrified. Riley was inert. Not so much as a last wrenching breath.
Over that fast. Heart.

Geoff's heartbeats were a series of explosions. He squirmed against the
hog-tie job, going nowhere. Found himself up against Betts. She was lying
on her back. Breathing. One ear was swollen and red and there was a mouse
on the cheekbone where Haman had gunbutted her. The rest of her color
was not so good. He bumped against Betts frantically, trying to bring her
around. Make it to the kitchen on hands and knees if she had to. Bring a
knife to cut him free.

Betts opened her eyes partway, blinked, looked at him uncomprehend-
ingly.

"Go away."

Geoff made frantic noises in his throat.

Betts moaned softly, closed her eyes.

"I don't feel good. Numb. Hands are numb."

Voiceless, trying to make her understand.

Betts, love of God he's comin' back for sure. Not much time. Get me
loose.

"I feel sick. My head hurts."

Get up get up get up.

"Hands numb. Can't feel my hands. *Stop* it."

Talking to her with his eyes. Pleading.

Comin' back. Kill us all. Get up.

Betts rolled away from him and vomited instead.

The front door was opened.

From where Geoff was lying on the floor he couldn't see the door. Only
a swift morning shadow on a paneled wall. Unidentifiable except for the
jut of breasts. All he could think of was Haman made up to resemble Rona
Harvester. Wearing that ridiculous stuffed bra. Haman was here. Geoff felt
crushed, defeated.

One hand free. If he just had one hand—

He saw bare feet coming toward him. Long athletic legs, tanned. Jogging
shorts, hockey jersey covering her to her hips. He saw two small holes in
the jersey at the level of her collarbones. Sunlight was adding flame to her
hair this morning. Her eye had turned in, as it was apt to do when Eden
was stressed. But it was her right eye.

She glanced at Geoff but went to Betts first, helping her to sit up, cleaned
vomit from inside her mouth with a finger so she wouldn't aspirate it. Betts
was breathing okay, not laboring, but her eyes were unfocused. The girl
put her down again with a pillow beneath her head. Then, on hands and

knees, she lifted Riley's head, placed two fingers against the carotid artery in his neck. After a dozen seconds had passed she sighed and moved his body so it was lying faceup on the sofa.

Then she came to Geoff, tugged at the tape across his mouth with fingers that reeked of Betts's vomit, and removed his gag. Geoff coughed violently, his own gorge rising. She stepped back out of the way, looking coolly at him.

"Are you okay?"

"Yes. Can't believe. Eden, he shot you. *Saw it*. How bad?"

She shrugged. "It's nothing."

"Where is he?"

She turned and walked to the kitchen. With her back to him he counted three more round holes in the Mighty Ducks jersey. Only holes. There was no blood.

"Down at the dock. Tied up. I threw his gun in the lake."

"How did you—? Should have shot him, he's too dangerous!"

"Can't do that. I can't kill a human being."

"He shot *you*."

"I told you, it's no big deal."

She opened drawers in the kitchen, came up with a pair of scissors, and walked back to him.

"What do you mean, 'no big deal'?"

"I'm not hurt. Okay?"

"I'm looking at holes in that shirt. *Bullet holes*."

"You're getting a little shrill. Why don't you just shut up, big guy. Everything's under control. Too bad about Riley, though."

"What is this? What's goin' on?" Geoff looked around, eyes flashing fear. "I'm dreamin' this. He's dead, and you go, 'Too bad about Riley.' What? What? That's not the Eden Waring I know! Eden would be grief-stricken. Loved her daddy. Okay, then this ain't real. You can't be Eden, so, fuck, I don't know. I must be trippin'. How? Haven't had a controlled substance since I was sixteen. Wish I *was* stoned. Otherwise means I lost it. Breakin' point. All I wanted was to be a SEAL but couldn't handle the cold, wet all the time, they didn't let you sleep, I just cracked. Washed out. My old man could've spit on me. I must've washed out again when the front door opened. Just wait till he hears the news. Ha ha HAH! Geoff bought the whole fuckin' nut farm this time."

"You're not so bad. Stop breathing that hard, you'll hyperventilate."

She knelt beside him and snipped away at the duct tape with the scissors. Geoff sat up rubbing his wrists. He put a finger into one of the holes in the hockey jersey. Firm flesh underneath. No trace of a wound. She didn't flinch, just smiled in a humoring way.

"Satisfied?"

He withdrew his finger. He was trembling, electrified, as if he'd stuck the finger into a light socket.

She slowly raised the jersey, gathering it above her bare breasts. She took a deep breath, expanding her chest until her rosy nipples peaked.

"Any of this look familiar? Ought to."

Geoff got to his feet, staring down at her. He was wobbly. He put a hand against the back of a wicker chair, stumbled into a table, and knocked a lamp to the floor. Made it to the front door and outside.

She had the feeling he might pass out and hurt himself. Probably could have handled this a little better. She sighed again and followed Geoff.

WASHINGTON, D.C./QUANTICO, VA. • MAY 29 • 11:24 A.M. EDT

Rona Harvester and Pard, the family's Border collie, left the Marine helicopter that had returned her to the White House and were met by Rona's communications director.

"How was the President this morning?" Melissa asked.

"Robust. That's the word I'd like for you to use in all future releases."

"Wonderful. Such good news."

"He's still having a few difficulties with the King's English. But he's dying to come home."

"To the White House?"

"Yes. For a few days. Not too strenuous a schedule. But I want him to be seen in familiar surroundings. The world has been wondering and waiting. Clint's return should be a real tonic for the stock market. I'll talk to Rumsill and Pearce, have them load up on futures for the blind trust."

"Wouldn't that be a violation of—"

Rona scowled. "Melissa, there's a wide gulf between opportunism and fraud."

"I didn't mean—"

"Buy some S and P June calls for your own account. The offshore account, of course. Next. Alert Clint's staff, I'll meet with them at two this afternoon. Some strict guidelines must and will be observed. We don't want

Clint to feel pressured. Next. I want TV time tonight. Eight o'clock, all the networks. Tell them Rona needs ten minutes."

"That may be—"

"Giving me all kinds of shit this morning! I ask you to do something, I get this face. Are you having cramps? Your boyfriend losing erections again? Is your moon square my sun in a bad sign? Rona Harvester is going to address the nation at eight o'clock. Who's going to object? I need Couric or Walters to boost my ratings? I'm hot. Right now I'm walking up to the South Portico and there are twenty cameras trained on me. My well-wishers are legion. Calls of love and support are coming in from everywhere. I'm the most talked-about woman on the fucking planet. It requires no explanation. *Next.* Effective immediately, we are moving our entire operation from our space to the southwest corner of the west wing."

"The Oval Office?!"

"Yes, Melissa. Now get that incredulous grin off your face while I take a bow," Rona concluded, turning for a last fists-in-the-air flourish to acknowledge distant cheers before disappearing inside the White House.

Bob Hyde was halfway through a three-mile run along a back road of the FBI's turf on the Quantico Marine Reservation, where he had a weekend house. A member of Hyde's security detail, jogging a dozen feet behind him, took a cell phone call. After a few words he stepped up his pace to move abreast of the Director. Hyde glanced at the bodyguard and at the phone in his hand, looking annoyed. It was a warm morning and he had drunk too much the night before, while with the President pro tem and after, when he had entertained the loan-out mistress of a New York Congressman. Hyde never had had much of a sex drive, but as he got older he developed a perversion that occasionally he was driven to indulge. Otherwise he became morose to the point of depression. The act both thrilled and disgusted him. But his curiosity had been rewarded. The Congressman was right. For a mere slip of a girl, she owned an incredible bladder.

"What is it, Stahlnut?"

"Urgent call, sir."

"I don't care how urgent. When I'm running."

"Says he's your son."

After a few moments the Director broke stride and stood panting in the shade of a hickory tree by a winding brook. In the distance a squad of Bureau recruits was hoorawing through an obstacle course.

"This is Hyde."

"Dad."

"*Geoff.* Wondering when I'd hear from you."

"I know this isn't a secure line."

"Save it, then."

"Can't, sir. I have to tell you. I can't do it. Carry out my assignment. I've already done too much to hurt her. She'll never f-forgive me. Riley's dead. Huh-huh-heart attack. She'll never, in her life, ever. But I have to protect her! Can't let you do this. I'm s-sorry. I love her, sir."

"Are you crying? What's going on? Have you lost your—"

"No, no! I know what I'm doing. I almost lost it, but I understand now. *She* explained. How there can be t-two of them. I can deal with it. This isn't like when I washed out of the SEALs, Dad! I'm not having a break-down. I'm in, in, I've got 'plete control of myself, sir."

"Where are you, Geoff?"

"Place called Greenwood Lake. Northern California. People named Hassler own this house. You see, what happened was—"

"Is she there? Is the subj—the Waring girl's with you right now?"

"Well uh yes. But that's the hard part to expl—"

"Geoff. Listen to me, son. Stay right where you are. You need my help, I can tell."

"Complete control. I'm not messed up!"

"Wasn't implying you were. You've been under a lot of strain, I appreciate that. I'm going to help you. Are you listening? Now there's someone else, from Impact Sector—"

"Shit, I know about him! Crazy son of a bitch. He was gonna whack me too." There was a silence. Hyde mopped his brow. Geoff's voice changed. "Wasn't your idea, was it?"

"Geoff, no, of course not!"

Geoff's voice growing colder. "So that wasn't your plan all along? Because, because you hated me for washing out of SEALs?"

"I've never hated—"

"Never loved me either. God damn you! And all I ever wanted, you bastard, *wanted*. How could you do this to me! Put me in this position? Well you'll never find me, I promise. Me or Eden. I'm protectin' her now. You won't get your hands on her. I'm firmly resolved. God is my witness and I will kill you first!"

"Don't say that. You're overwrought. Exhausted, from the sound of your voice. What happened to the covert from Impact?"

"Neutralized. He failed. Like you think *I* failed, but I haven't because Eden is the only one who matters to me anymore. Now this is what I want you to do."

"You want—yes, all right. Talk to me."

"Get a medevac chopper up here, right now. Betts needs medical attention. And Riley, poor Riley! I never wanted anything like this. But I'll make amends. I swear."

"I'm coming out there. Stay where you are. That's not an order. I'm asking as a concerned male parent."

"Fat chance," Geoff said, choking out the words. "I never . . . want to see you again."

"Don't you understand? Has she warped your mind? This girl can be extremely dangerous—hello?"

Hyde lowered the phone, looked down, looked up, a face full of storm signals. He pitched the cell phone to the nearest bodyguard.

"Stahlnut. Chopper on the ball field over there, secure communications, I'll be waiting."

"Sir!"

"Then notify TAC at headquarters. I want Mach two transportation to Innisfall, California. On the line and smoking, forty minutes. National Security Directive authorization, X-Ray Niner Six Six Delta Rover. McDurfee, have my valet pack an overnighter. Tell him not to forget my military-issue Glock and two extra thirteen-round mags. Then alert Impact Sector to an incoming Code Red. Raise some dust, son."

GREENWOOD LAKE • MAY 29 • 9:05 A.M. PDT

Geoff McTyer rubbed his face carefully, as if he were afraid it had begun to soften and was about to assume a strange shape in the sun.

"You can take me to Eden, can't you?"

"Not the way *I* got here," the dpg said. They were sitting on the dock. She had removed her sandals and was splashing her feet idly in the water.

"How did you get here?"

"Visualization travel. Easy for me, impossible for youse."

"What?" Geoff said. He bent over, scooped some water in one hand, and dashed it across his face.

"Just poking a little fun at your accent. You don't look good."

"Visual what?"

"It's a doppelganger thing. But you've had enough input already for one day. Sensory overload. Frazzles your dendrites."

"I want to know everything," Geoff said gamely. "You're sayin' I can't handle it? You won't freak me out. I've already been there and back."

"It's just that you keep throwing up. Your eyes are rolling around in your head. Sensory overload. Give yourself a raincheck. Lie down in the shade for a while."

"I'll sleep later. Time to go. I'll drive. Tell me where."

"What about Betts?"

"Help is on the way. I don't want to be here when."

"Frankly I'm in no hurry to get back," Eden's doppelganger said.

"Why not?"

"What happens if I pull off this jersey and drop my shorts?"

"Oh, Jesus! Don't do that again."

"It *was* a little cold turkey. For you. Well, one disappearing picture is worth, and so on. Reason why I did it. Anyway, we go back and I resume my inferior status, I mean, I'm purely a doppelganger again. Until and if Eden needs me. Pardon me if I'm enjoying what little freedom I'm allowed, okay? And I have to say I enjoy hanging out with you, Geoff. I think you need me more than you need Eden right now. So there it is."

"I'm responsible. You don't know what could happen to Eden!"

"Eden's a cautious soul, since all of the commotion began. That's why, when Betts didn't sign off her E-mail with the usual 'Cheerio, dear one,' Eden decided I should put in an appearance instead. Get the full skinny and report back to her."

"She'll be waitin', then. Let's move. Hit the road."

"Eden won't be worried. She knows I can't get into trouble on her behalf. Very much trouble. I've proved to her I'm the dependable sort. Any luck, and I'll make corporal this year."

Geoff shuddered and closed his eyes.

"Coming down with something?"

He shuddered again. "I'm in control. Once in a while, talking to . . . *you*, it's like a cold slap in the face."

"I resent that. Nothing frigid about me. I have body heat. Go ahead, verify that again. Put your hand on my breast. Or anywhere else you want to, I'm not shy. I can have sex. Eden's asleep now, she wouldn't know. The way it works, there's no direct communication between us when I'm traveling, unless it's an emergency. I'm saying—if I need to be more explicit—while we're doing it my homebody probably would enjoy a lovely wet dream." She smiled, a sunny flattering come-on. "Takes a real man to satisfy two women at once."

"I've never felt less like havin' sex."

"Oh," the dpg said. She looked down, then kicked one foot to scatter her reflection on the water. "I thought men always wanted to have sex."

"I haven't slept. My nerves are shot. Doesn't have a thing to do with you."

"Or what I am?" She kicked water in his direction, frowning.

Geoff shrugged uneasily.

"We need to get out of here. I talked to my old man, dropped the fat in the fire, how long ago?" He looked at his watch. "Twenty minutes we've been sittin' here? It's not safe to hang around. Wheels are in motion. Events are turning. Where's Eden?"

"Spoil sport."

"Do you have to do what I tell you?"

"No. You don't get three wishes either. Jeez."

"Then what can I do for you, is there somethin', I mean besides have sex, which I guarantee I cannot manage right now?"

"Well . . . no point in talking about it. Humans don't keep their bargains. And you're a lying rat."

"A man can change. What do you mean, 'bargain'? So there *is* somethin'."

"Could be." She stood up suddenly, wet legs gleaming in the sunlight, and stretched, her navel popping into view. She reached down and gave his earlobe a playful tweak. "We can discuss it on the way to Moby Bay. By the way, Geoff, what do you want to do with that stale twinkie we have tied up?" She raised her eyes to the deck above them, then looked meaningfully at the compact Glock automatic he'd stuffed inside his belt.

Geoff looked uncertain.

"Do I get a vote?" the dpg asked. "I say kill him. You'll be doing him a favor. Another hour and his makeup will melt in the sun. Then you won't be able to tell if you're looking at his face or his ass."

Geoff went up the ladder with Eden's dpg following.

The assassin was hog-tied and silenced, his baroque evil undiminished in bonds of gray tape. The Rona Harvester wig was askew. The hatred in his eyes, when he looked at Geoff, was as indestructible as brimstone.

Geoff drew the gun. Stood there, not aiming. The assassin smirked and yawned, then closed his curly lashed eyes. The eyelids shimmered prettily. Geoff grimaced and put the Glock away. Turned to find the dpg looking at him with faint disapproval. Geoff trembled.

"His own people will take care of him. Let's go."

"Why didn't you shoot him?" the dpg asked as they left the boat dock.

"We are reduced to monsters not by our aims, but by our appetites," Geoff said. "I read that somewhere. Let's say I don't want to acquire the appetite."

She smiled. Eden's smile, a dimpled girl of quiet humors.

"You may not be such a loser after all. I'll put that in my report."

Geoff and Eden's dpg took a few minutes to look in on Betts. They made her as comfortable as they could, gave her water and a prescription painkiller Geoff found in her purse. Betts's face was swollen. She gripped the doppelganger's hand, muttered but didn't talk. She seemed not to know where she was.

On the way down the porch steps to Geoff's Taurus they heard a helicopter.

WESTBOUND: ANDREWS AIR FORCE BASE/INNISFALL · MAY 29 · 1905 HOURS ZULU

An F-16B with two 150-gallon drop tanks for extended range flew FBI Director Robert Hyde to California. At thirty-nine thousand feet over western Kansas, two miles above a storm building in front of the Rockies, Hyde was on a secure sat channel with Special Agent in Charge Dolph Hackett of the FBI field office in Sacramento.

"What did you find at the lake?"

"The covert from Impact Sector," Hackett replied.

"Status?"

"He's on the way here now by helicopter."

"What has he had to say?"

"Word is he seems a bit off-base. Disoriented. When we asked about the girl he, uh, had a fit of giggles. I'm told. Says he'll talk only to someone from Impact Sector."

"Chill the covert until the IS team arrives to debrief him. The foster parents?"

"We found her in a battered condition. She was choppered to the medical center in Innisfall. Her husband was deceased, apparently from natural causes, although that remains to be determined."

"Location of Runaway?"

"He's taking back roads, traveling south by southwest. Don't know how much longer we can track him because of LoJack's limited range. We have two stealth helos en route from Travis with FLIR and photo recon capability. But Runaway is traveling through some heavily wooded country, which makes surveillance more difficult."

"I don't want to hear difficult. I'll personally alert Shepherd at NSA. We need a dedicated satellite. I don't want to hear that we've lost Runaway."

"No, sir. We won't lose him."

"And I want a confirm on the girl."

"ETA for the helos is less than ten minutes. We'll know then if she's with Runaway."

"Good job, Hackett. I had the greatest respect for your father. You're a credit to him."

"Thank you, sir."

MOBY BAY · MAY 29

By noon on Sunday Eden was caught up on sleep. When she got out of bed her upper back was sore and felt bruised in three places across the shoulders, as if she had been jabbed sharply with the rounded end of a broomstick.

She had yogurt in the kitchen with Chauncey, who cautioned her not to eat much more. Her father was hosting a Memorial weekend barbecue and everyone who lived in Moby Bay was coming. Wick McLain was one of several local painters who shared a gallery on Main Street. He was an affable man with a narrow face, distinguished by a cascading mustache and prickly stubble. He was already at work on the patio fussing over his three-thousand-dollar stainless-steel propane-fired grill, only a little smaller than a restaurant's range. A couple of neighbors were setting tables on the lawn that sloped fifty yards to the bluff overlooking the blue Pacific.

Because Eden was their guest, Chauncey dug up some old Django Reinhardt seventy-eights from the family's music library and put them on the Bose changer.

"Did I hear you talking in your sleep last night?" she asked Eden.

"Might've. I was restless." Eden couldn't stop yawning.

Chauncey's brother Roald trooped into the kitchen with a raiding party of his buddies, all of them carrying Toys "R" Us battle gear.

"Don't touch a thing," Chauncey warned them as they circled a large table filled with cooling pies. Mia McLain had been up since dawn to do the baking.

"We're starving."

"You can have the rest of this box of Ritz crackers. Eat them outside."

"What happened to all the Kool-Aid?" Roald complained, head inside the refrigerator.

A couple of the boys were staring at Eden.

"You're the one's been on TV."

"Yeah, I guess so."

"How did you know it was gonna crash?"

"She had a preshun, stupid."

"A what?"

"Premonition, Stevie," Chauncey said.

"Oh, yeah. I have those all the time."

"Oh, that's BS, Stevie," the other boy said.

"Put the milk back," Chauncey said to her brother. "We have barely enough for the cookout, and I don't feel like driving to the co-op to buy more."

"I'm thirsty!"

"It's not BS. *You're* BS and a ay aitch too."

"You don't even know what a prema, m-meshun is."

"It's like seeing stuff that didn't happen yet."

"Yeah? Tell me something that didn't happen yet."

Stevie screwed up his face, biting his lip. Nothing occurred to him.

The other boy had shaggy red hair and was missing his two front teeth. He smiled broadly at Eden.

"He thinks he's a Jedi Knight and can put people to sleep with the power of his mind."

"I put my *dog* to sleep just by staring at him!"

"Oh, wow. Your dog sleeps all the time anyway."

Chauncey said to the redhead, who looked to be a year away from puberty, "Just knock it off, Sterling. Your mouth is way too big sometimes. Roald, there's sodas in the cooler on the patio, if I make myself clear."

Ignoring Chauncey, the redhead, eager to nail down bragging rights, said to Eden, "I can already do something none of the other guys can."

Chauncey rapped him smartly on the side of his head with her knuckles. He pretended to sag into a stupor, then grinned impudently at her.

"What did I say about the big mouth? You're under oath. Save it for Tuesday nights. Eden's not interested anyway. She has more Talent than the rest of you put together."

Mia McLain came into the kitchen. She looked very much like her daughter, except her hips were bigger and her complexion rosier.

"Stop cluttering up the kitchen, boys."

"Sterling's angling for a reprimand," Chauncey said sternly.

"I am *not,*" Sterling said with a sulky glare. "Besides, she's one of us, isn't she?" He glanced at Eden. "Or didn't you tell her nothing?"

"*Anything.* Eden knows all about Moby Bay," Chauncey said. "Bye-bye, Sterling."

When the boys had cleared the kitchen Chauncey looked at her mother. "He can be such a little shit."

"Well, when you're that Gifted at an early age, you hardly know how to behave." She smiled fondly at Chauncey. "Or do you need reminding?"

"Come on! I was an *angel* compared to Sterling."

"Whoa, Nellie. Not my recollection." Mia McLain looked at Eden, who was fitful, picking at the flecks of polish left on her fingernails. "How are you today, Eden? Sleep well?"

"I don't remember much," Eden said evasively. "Thanks for letting me stay over."

"Our pleasure. You gals have time for a nice swim before everybody gets here."

"How about it, Eden?"

Eden looked at the kitchen clock, wondering what had happened to her doppelganger, who had been gone for almost ten hours. "Sure."

"Gotta warn you," Chauncey said. "No suits. We're nature lovers here. If you're okay with that."

"No problem, long as the kids aren't hanging around getting an eyeful. What is it Sterling does that he's so proud of?"

Chauncey and her mother exchanged the fleetest of glances.

"Oh," Mia McLain said airily, "conjuration is probably the word that describes his Gift best. Chauncey can explain in more detail, if you're really interested. We're all conjurors in Moby Bay to some extent. It goes with the territory."

"Magic?"

"Call it that. White magic, of course."

"As opposed to black magic."

"That's a no-no around here."

"White magic is like making a playing card float in the air around the table? Stuff like that?"

"There you go," Chauncey said cheerfully. "Stuff like that. Come on, let's hit the beach."

"Don't forget your sunscreen," Mia reminded. "And take plenty of beach towels to bundle up in. That water's *cold.*"

Tom Sherard and Bertie Nkambe ate lunch at a Denny's on the outskirts of Innisfall. Sherard had rented a Ford Expedition in San Francisco for their trip to northern California.

"The less time we spend here, the better," he said.

"I know. Aren't you going to eat the rest of your BLT?"

"No, you can have it." Bertie had already put away a fruit plate and a Denver omelet. She was having a chocolate shake for dessert. She owned a metabolism as efficient as a blast furnace. But she needed to run thirty miles a week to keep the calories from ganging up on her. She was dressed for roadwork now.

"The stadium area will be sealed off," Sherard said. "I don't think you'll get very close to the crash site. Within a couple of hundred yards, possibly. Don't know why you think it's worth the risk."

"I'll be just another Sunday jogger on campus. After last night at Danny Cheng's the two of us are probably an item, but alone I won't be recognized."

"Those two-way radios we bought at Wal-Mart have a limited range."

"Worry, worry, worry," she said, chewing confidently and dabbing her lips with a paper napkin.

"What do you hope to gain by going there?"

Bertie glanced at the sports watch on her wrist. "The crash happened, let's see, about twenty-five hours ago. The imprint is still strong. The ether is swarming with impressions. Can't say what I'll visualize or feel. It could be scary. Overwhelming. But I might learn something important. The fact is—"

Bertie looked up with a smile as the teenage waitress brought her chocolate shake to the table.

"Excuse me, but aren't you Whitney Houston? We've been sort of wondering, back in the kitchen."

"If only. Must be the hair and the cheekbones. I can whistle but I can't sing for sour apples."

"Miss, may I have the check now, please?" Sherard asked. He looked at Bertie again. "What were you saying?"

"Fact is, Kelane Cheng might still be around."

"Portia Darkfeather was the only survivor."

"Some of those who die unexpected or violent deaths don't pass on to the next plane that easily. They have a tendency to remain on our level.

For decades, or centuries, of earthly time. Remember the photo shoot I did at Gettysburg last August? You'd be amazed how many Union and Confederate soldiers there were, killed in battle but unwilling to accept their fate. Unable to leave. I saw a line of them on horseback, way off against the sky on the windy edge of nowhere. There was this boy, one-legged on a makeshift crutch, one of many ghosts rising like willows from a blood crevasse. He came closer than the others. He couldn't have been more than eighteen. We talked. His name was Hannibal Raines. From Ohio, I think he said. Wanted to know where his regiment was. So sad. I didn't give good picture that day. I told Len I had a stomachache, but it was my heart, not my stomach."

Sherard felt a sudden warmth, a flush to the head that momentarily dimmed his vision.

"Gillian is still around, isn't she? Like the souls of those Civil War dead. And you've seen her. Haven't you?" Her lashes flickered, but she didn't look away from him. "Why won't you tell me?"

"I can't, Tom. I can't talk about Gillian now. There are Mysteries I have to honor."

"If I had your power. If I could just see her, one last time!"

Bertie reached across the table, touched his cheek.

"You will, Tom. I promise you."

WESTBOUND/CALIFORNIA HIGHWAY 299 · MAY 29 · 1:40 P.M. PDT

Why are we stopping?" Eden's doppelganger asked Geoff McTyer.

They had pulled off the two-lane road into a riverside campground, most of which lay in shade beneath a canopy of huge trees at the noon hour. This was high green country of near wilderness on the eastern slope of the Coast Range. Fly-fishermen in waders were walking the knee-deep river, casting their lines through long shafts of sunlight. Those children immune to nature played video games beneath camper awnings. An old couple swayed gently together in a double hammock. Hamburgers and hot dogs sizzled on grills, smoke like a faint blue fog drifting above the campground.

"Thirsty," Geoff said.

"Me too, come to think of it."

Geoff looked at her. They'd been driving back roads with the top up, but her face had taken on a glow, as if she'd been exposed to the sun for an hour or more.

"You're turnin' red."

"I feel red."

"You haven't been in the sun."

"Still don't get it, do you?"

"Get what?"

"Eden must have gone swimming, or else she's sunbathing. She hasn't had much of a chance to be outdoors this spring."

Geoff looked at her thighs, then pressed down with his thumb, leaving a white mark. The dpg smiled at him.

"I am who Eden is. I know what she knows. The only difference between us is, she's left-handed and I'm right-handed. Mirror images. We each have our purpose but she runs the show, so to speak. How does that work? It's a dichotomy common in organic compounds, like stereo isomers. Did you take O-chem? No? Let me see if I can explain. I'll use calcium eleonate as an example, just to prove doppelgangers occur as naturally as sunflowers or olive trees. Calcium eleonate is composed of two stereo isomers with identical chemical composition, and because of the way they're strung together one is the image of the other. Nature also gives us left- and right-handed molecules in amino acids. But it's the left-handed amino acids that make DNA, RNA, and other life proteins. What does the other guy do? Watches out for the health of the organism. There, now you have a perfect example of the doppelganger's role. Because I'm not needed all the time, it isn't necessary to be visible all the time. Now we get into mirage effects, and the optical properties of ellipses occurring naturally in the atomic substrate—"

"Don't staht that again."

"You're being a weenie. Nothing to be scared of. I thought I explained, dpg's are here to serve. Like the R-molecule, we're very helpful in ways you never know anything about. The religious types call us 'Guardian Angels.' Isn't it beautiful here? Why don't we just stay awhile, maybe spend the night? Remember the general store a couple miles back, where you stopped for gas? I noticed camping equipment, canoes to rent. What do you say, Geoff, give your nerves a rest. You need to learn to kick back."

"My nerves are okay."

"Ha ha. If you say so. What are you looking at now?"

"I thought I saw a helicoptah."

"Another one? You still believe we're being followed?"

"I don't know. I don't see how." Geoff looked at the part of the sky visible through the canopy and suddenly smacked himself on the side of his head with his palm. "Oh, shit!"

"That must have hurt. What's the matter with you?"

"LoJack. I didn't think about it. I'm so stupid."

"Aside from that, what's LoJack?"

"Antitheft trackin' device for my cah. They could've gotten the frequency from Cal HP in Innisfall. But the range is limited, and I don't know if it works at all up here in the mountains."

Eden's dpg looked uninterested.

"Well, if they do have an idea of our location, and they've brought in helicoptahs, I don't think they can find us beneath these trees. I'll get rid of the LoJack, just in case."

"How long will that take?"

"Maybe half an hour. Gettin' to it is the difficult part."

She smiled. "Half an hour? Good. I'll just stroll around, if you don't need me for anything."

"Don't get lost."

"I can't get lost. I mean, I can return to my homebody in a flash, whenever she wills it. You're the one who would be lost."

Geoff stared at the dpg.

"Right now I'm the only one who can help Eden. Keep her alive. You don't know what my fathah is capable of. And without Eden, what are you?"

THE WHITE HOUSE · MAY 29 · 4:25 P.M. EDT

Before meeting with her own staff, Rona Harvester had a chat with four of her husband's key people: Chief of Staff "Pep" Slingbury, National Security Advisor Bayard "Beau" Chanson the Fourth, Cody Vollers, White House Communications Director, and Val Domingues, the press secretary.

"As you know, I was at Camp David this morning. After visiting with Clint and Tray Daufuskie, I made the decision to bring Clint home."

They were on the terrace below the solarium on the south side of the executive mansion. Pink geraniums and purple petunias were in bloom. Rona's favorite colors. She was dressed casually, in size-eight Wranglers and a calico shirt, with a kerchief knotted casually at her throat. They were drinking sodas. Rona didn't allow boozing in the White House except for wine or champagne on state occasions. She had cleaned up too much of her father's vomit in her youth, and liquor had never passed her own lips.

The men looked uneasy, but none of them wanted to speak up.

Rona smiled. "Clint and I had a nice talk. Of course I did most of the talking, he does have this little impediment, still. But I know his mind. I know it will do him a world of good to be back at his desk. And I'm confident that the American people—"

"Mrs. Harvester," Beau Chanson interrupted with a nervous twitching of his shoulders, "the President certainly is looking fit—he was when I saw him toward the end of last week—but I'm wondering if we're not perhaps being overly optimistic in assuming that he is ready for the, the level of exposure that you're contemplating while he, in all fairness, seems less than a hundred percent mentally."

"I'm never overly optimistic about anything except my next lay, Beau. But I'm quite confident that the rapport my husband and I have enjoyed for twenty-two years, the extraordinary like-mindedness we share, will be more than enough to overcome any small difficulties Clint may encounter while resuming his duties. I will be there for him, every moment. At his side. Getting back to the American People, and what they want—" She turned her smile on Cody Vollers. "It has been made abundantly clear that they want to feel good about their country again. The shock of Portland hasn't begun to wear off. The American People want the man they elected by a fifty-six percent popular vote three years ago *here,* at his desk, leading them in difficult times."

"Mrs. Harvester—"

"Yes, Pep?"

"I know—we all know—where your heart, and your loyalty is, and it's—inspirational to all of us—"

"You break into a sweat when you're shoveling heavy shit, Pep."

"Then may I speak as frankly as I feel I must, given the circumstances?"

"You know me and I know you, Pep. Wouldn't have it any other way."

"Thank you. Our President, Clint, probably my dearest friend—" His lips trembled. "A man whom I admired without reservation is . . . he's hopelessly—the stroke has left him with the mind of a very young child. God knows I would give my own life to change that. But it *is* a medical fact."

"While that is factually correct, it is also a gross misrepresentation. Just how damaged is his mind? We don't know. All I know is what was in his head before the stroke, and what I believe is in his heart even now. Together, Clint and I can do this. His appointed task. Together we will reassure the American People that there *is* hope in a world turned against us. Belief is better than dread. Hope is the balm for grieving hearts. We are giving back to the country our beloved leader."

Again Rona endured their silence, while she drank from a wineglass filled with Orange Crush and watched them coolly, wondering who would challenge her. Beau Chanson was her odds-on favorite, and he didn't let her down.

"Well, if this isn't a masterpiece of badly used inspiration," Beau Chanson said in his famous going-to-battle growl. She'd been waiting for this. Beau was old Birmingham money, a wing shooter and a horse-and-hounds fancier. They'd ridden together in the Virgina hunt country. She'd once walked in on Beau in his hunt club suite when he was wearing nothing but an unbuttoned shirt and had given him a friendly feel, saying, "Now I know why they call you 'Mr. Beau-dangles.'" While he looked down at her with smiling disdain. Should have let it go at that, but then he said, "You can get it hard if you want to, Rona. But I'd sooner stick it in a beehive than give *you* a hump."

"Qualms, Beau?"

"Qualms? For the love of God! How do you have the effrontery to believe you can pull off this *charade*—no, I'll name it what it is, an outright farce—and not destroy the very soul of our republic? You do Clint Harvester neither credit nor honor with your scheme! We must accept that his time is done. You have always been astute in your depredations, but you must reconsider this course of action and not diminish what was pure gold in Clint Harvester to pennyweight."

"I'll bet you swiped that one from the old Confederate spellbinder, your great-grandfather. Glory be, they sure could spiel in those days."

"You would be well advised to accept my advice," Beau Chanson said with a hard glower.

"I was wondering if you still have that old beehive I mailed you, once upon a time."

Slingbury and Vollers looked puzzled and wary. Chanson set his glass down.

"I believe I have overstayed our little get-together. I intend to fax my resignation to Allen Dunbar before rejoining my wife and children in Nantucket for what is left of our Memorial Day weekend."

Rona was smiling. Within her smile a serpent lay coiled.

"Nonsense, Beau. You're not resigning. And if the thought crossed *your* mind, Slingbury, dump it. No one is stepping down from Clint's staff or his cabinet. No excuses will be permitted. We *will* have a unified show of strength and support for his return. So now you all look as if you've lost your zeal for public service! Pity. As us kids used to say, way back in the peaceful and prosperous Eisenhower era, 'like it or lump it."

"If you think you can intimidate me." Beau Chanson was furious to the point of an arterial blowout.

"I'm giving you a chance to leave gracefully after our inspirational heads-up. Otherwise it's time for hard knocks, and you won't be neglected."

Chanson said through gritted teeth, "Just where do you think you can go with that threat?"

"Where should we go? How far?" Rona stood musing, an eye to the sky as if cloud nine had appeared. "All the way back to Auburn University in '63? The preemie in the toilet in the Chi O house? A *black* man's baby, delivered in the middle of the night by one of the sisters of an all-white sorority? Very effectively hushed up. But do you think that the mother who was also a murderess wonders, even now in comfortable estate in her late middle age, does she still have images of that expelled six-month fetus, red and dripping until she flushed, and flushed again, and drowned it? Does she see, on those nights when the wind dies and frost first appears and she is sleepless and looking back into a past she can never repair, see her first-born clinging to a windowpane like an unfinished ghost?"

"Monstrous," Beau Chanson said, staring at Rona with a frayed desperation, the expression of a man undergoing a debacle of the senses. The other men looked elsewhere, shamefaced and with a touch of terror in their own eyes.

"The old sins endure," Rona said, and she sighed as if she genuinely regretted it was so.

"The files. All the files were expunged," Chanson said in the tone of a man uttering last words to a hanging judge.

"But not all the voices were stilled. That's always how it is, I suppose. Anyone else tired of his job? Peppy? No? *Wonderful!* I'll look forward to seeing all of you in the Oval Office Tuesday morning, eight sharp. Sorry about Nantucket, Beau. Give my best to Mimsy and her five surviving children when you speak to her again."

Rona had kept her own staff waiting in the solarium with the bulletproof glass, part of the First Family's residence on the third floor. She apologized and then took up her first order of business.

"Where is the girl?"

Peach Boondecker, the holder of the slings-and-arrows durability award among long-time Rona staffers, broke the news that they didn't know.

"She's probably lying low until the spotlight is off. Who could blame the poor kid?"

"I can't put too much emphasis on this. I want her. I want Eden what's-her-name *here*, in Washington, and it had better not be later than teatime tomorrow."

"We know she has a steady boyfriend. Not live-in. He's a cop. Sunday is his day off, so we haven't been able to locate—"

"I can't believe how badly you're handling this, Peach. Never mind. Melissa, get me Katharine Bellaver. Holiday weekend, she'll probably be at the farm in Westchester." Rona turned to her appointments secretary. "Ingrid, adjust my schedule with Countess Von Alstine and Women Against Female Circumcision, at the Watergate. Dinner's out, but I'll still do the keynoter at nine-thirty."

Another staff member came into the solarium and handed Rona a note. There was a call for her on the secure line in her bedroom.

"Rona?" Victor Wilding said. "Thought we should share this. Robert Hyde is on his way to Innisfall by Air Force jet. ETA in twenty minutes."

"Why?"

"Bureau's after the girl, obviously. Just as obvious, they have a good lead on her whereabouts. And Hyde is taking a personal interest. Hyde doesn't want us to have her. She must be hot. More impressive than we imagined."

"Do you know what their lead is?"

"We had a report from our sources at Cal HP. The FBI accessed the frequency of a LoJack belonging to a young Innisfall cop named Geoff McTyer. We also know they've put an Air Force Special Weapons unit on alert at Travis. Helicopters. Frisco FBI's SWAT team left the Bay Area a few minutes ago, headed north."

"She's with her boyfriend, and they're on the road somewhere."

"More about him. We have his file. McTyer was his mother's maiden name. He's Robert Hyde's son, undercover for the Bureau."

"So they've known about Eden Waring for a long time! But if Hyde's kid has been cozy with her, what's all the urgency? Hyde flying Mach two to the Coast, and Bureau's ordered up the SWATsters—oh, yeah, *wait* a goddamn minute."

"Right."

"This kid, McTyer, he turned on them? On his old man? He fell hard for Eden Waring. Now he's protecting her. Which means she's on the Impact list. Just as her mother was. That's why they're running."

"You got it."

"Victor, we must find them first! Who do you have there in Innisfall?"

"A big crew. We're monitoring the Bureau, of course, but that doesn't give us much of a jump. Right now we can only hope we get a break."

"The Bureau. Those sons of bitches. Nothing but trouble for us."

"We go head-to-head on this one, if we have to. MORG and the Bureau. I don't care about the consequences."

"Just find Eden Waring," Rona pleaded. "Congress is recessed and Justice is a shell. We can handle the fallout. Victor, I'm going to have a meet with Katharine Bellaver. Today. Eden may be in touch with her already."

"Be careful. She has important allies. Don't give them cause to unite against you."

"*We're* taking over, Victor. The sooner Katharine Bellaver has that message, the better we'll get along."

INNISFALL · MAY 29 · 1:50 P.M. PDT

The National Transportation Safety Board and FAA investigators had secured most of the south campus of Cal Shasta University with the help of a platoon of National Guardsmen. Bertie Nkambe and other Sunday joggers couldn't come within two hundred yards of the crash site. There were some picnickers on a hill overlooking the stadium, a few curiosity seekers watching through binoculars the activity around the wreckage of the DC-10. The air was fresher on the wooded hill than it had been close to the site, but Bertie thought she probably couldn't enjoy a picnic lunch while any trace of burnt bodies lingered.

She paused to have a drink from the water bottle she was toting and reported back to Tom Sherard, who was waiting for her on the other side of the airport in the Ford Expedition. She used the limited-range walkies they had picked up at Wal-Mart.

"I can't get close enough to do any good."

"Let's be on our way, then. According to the map I have, Moby Bay is a good two hours from here. There's no direct route. Secondary roads across the mountain range."

"I'll just catch my breath and do my tai chi workout. Be there in twenty minutes."

Bertie put the walkie in a fanny pack and began her exercises.

Three girls, eight to ten years old, came out of the trees on the jogging path and crossed the sunny open space where Bertie was concentrating on her tai chi forms. The girls were having an earnest discussion about something, interrupting each other but not quarreling.

"Well, I can't take it home with *me*."

"We can't just let it die."

"Maybe it isn't dying."

"Sure looked that way. Poor kitty."

"Maybe I could ask my mom."

"You've got three cats already, Jana."

"It belongs to *some*body. It's wearing a collar."

Bertie relaxed, breathed deeply, and said, "What's up, guys?"

The girls stopped and looked her over. Decided she was okay. One of them pointed back along the jogging path.

"There's this cat in a tree. A white cat. Looks like a dog got after it or something. One ear's torn and bloody. And its fur is dirty."

Another girl said, "I smelled smoke."

"I'm Bertie. What's your name?"

She was the smallest and youngest. "Jana."

The others introduced themselves.

"Grace."

"Danielle."

"Sisters?"

"Cousins," Danielle said. "We're all cousins."

"Where's this cat you're talking about?"

"We could show you."

"I've gotta go," Jana said.

"No, you don't," Grace, the oldest, said. "Mom said two-thirty and it's only twenty after."

"I mean peepee!"

"Oh. Why didn't you do it in the woods? Okay, tell Mom we'll be right there." She looked up at Bertie. "You wanta see?"

"Sure. I like cats. We had a couple on the farm when I was growing up."

"What kind were they? Siamese?"

"African lions," Bertie said. Grace and Danielle looked at each other, confirming that they were too sharp to put up with this. Bertie shrugged. "I grew up in Africa."

She answered a dozen questions about her childhood and the coffee plantation in Kenya on the short walk to where the girls had discovered the injured cat.

It wasn't easy to see, crouched a dozen feet off the ground where two leafy limbs of the oak joined the trunk. A young Persian with a crusty cut on one ear. Only a small part of its fur, on and around the face and breast where it had been able to clean itself, was white or grayish. The rest of the fur was blackly streaked or singed. The cat had lost most of its whiskers, apparently to the fire it had barely escaped. The cat's eyes were closed, as if it was too exhausted to pay attention to them.

"Do you think kitty was in the plane that crashed?" Danielle asked.

The older girl said, "Everything on board burned up. Except the one they have in the hospital. She was thrown out but she's not going to live. That's what Rich's mother told him, and she's a surgical nurse."

"Let's have a look," Bertie said, moving closer to the tree. The cat's eyes opened partway at her approach. Bertie stood very still, gazing up, a hand raised high above her head. She remained that way, relaxed and motionless, long enough for the girls to become restless.

"What are you going to do?" Grace asked.

"Figure out a way to get him down. Take him to a vet for shots and stitches. He was on the plane, for sure. Traumatized, but I'm sure he'll be okay."

Grace said, "What's traumatized?"

"He's scared. In shock."

"How do you know it's a boy cat?" Danielle asked.

"Oh—just something about him. I can't explain."

"Danielle. Gracie!"

"That's Jana. We better go. Thanks for taking care of him, Bertie. You gonna adopt him?"

Bertie smiled but didn't look around at them. Nearly all of her attention was focused on the cat. Her right hand remained in the air, fingers spread, moving slightly, as if she were reading something written there in spectral braille. The Persian cat had lifted its head and was staring at her.

"I'll just leave that up to Warhol," she said. "When he's feeling better, and we've had a chance to talk."

WESTBOUND/CALIFORNIA HIGHWAY 299 · MAY 29 · 2:25 P.M. PDT

They were waiting for Geoff and Eden Waring's doppelganger at the bridge over the Burnt Oak River in the mountain town of Valleyheart, sixty miles east of Moby Bay. Two SUVs from the sheriff's department and a unit of the California Highway Patrol. Geoff spotted them from half a mile away as he was driving down the narrow switchback road into town.

He came to a skidding stop. The convertible top was down. He looked at the bridge in the valley, saw the glint of sunlight on binocular lenses. They were expecting him.

"Oh, my God."

"You must've been right about the helicopter," the dpg said. "Can you go back?"

Geoff appraised his chances. Cliff wall on the right side of the road, steep forested slope on his left, with a steel guardrail nearly flush with the road.

"By the time I get turned around, they'll be up here. If they've done this right, there'll be another car comin' up behind us, any minute."

"Back up. Just out of sight of those deputies at the bridge."

"Why?"

"You're getting out."

"What for?"

"Who do they really want, you or me? Eden, I mean."

"Eden."

"Back up, get out, climb over the guardrail. Find something to hang on to for a few minutes. Just don't let them see you."

"What are you gonna do?"

She grinned at him.

"You'll find out. When it's all over, if you don't see me around, retrieve your car and go to Moby Bay. The family's name is McLain. Eden's staying with them."

"Every law enforcement agency in northern California has my vehicle description and plate number by now. If they're usin' helicoptahs—"

"That's a good point. Maybe you ought to borrow one of their cars, tune in on the radio traffic. Come on, let's get moving."

Geoff put the Taurus in reverse and screeched uphill around a sharp curve in the road, stopped. They heard a siren on the road behind them.

"Leave the engine running," she said.

Geoff vaulted out of the car, cleared the guardrail, slid on his heels a dozen feet down the slope that ended at a precipice, and grabbed a flowering purple rhododendron well rooted in the feldspar. Looking up, he couldn't see the road. Then Eden's face appeared above the guardrail.

"Give me about twenty minutes," she said. "That should be long enough for them to call in that pesky helicopter. Lay low, then head for the bridge. I've got your car. Don't worry, I'll take good care of it."

Eden's dpg was halfway to the Burnt Oak River in the Taurus when the other CHP car came flying up behind her, blue lights flashing.

She continued downhill at twenty-five miles per hour, swerving to keep the highway patrol from passing and cutting in front of her.

Fifty feet from the police-model Ford Explorers blocking the bridge, she stopped, pushed the cheap sunglasses Geoff had bought her above her hairline, and sat with hands high on the wheel of the Taurus as law dogs of various jurisdictions converged on the car. Guns drawn. One of them was even pointing a shotgun at her, as if she butchered small children and drank their blood.

The driver's door was yanked open.

"Step out of the car! Step out of the car *now*. Hands where we can see them!"

"Yes, sir. Please don't shoot me."

One of the deputies, a woman, pulled her away from the car. Not too gently. She had a sweaty forehead and a glum nearly lipless mouth. Nameplate read R. HUMBARD. Another dep was reaching for handcuffs. That wouldn't do, the doppelganger decided.

"Are you Eden Waring?"

"Who?"

"Is your name Eden Waring!"

"No."

"Where's the man who was in the car with you?"

"He's hiding in the trunk. He has a shotgun. I'd be careful."

That distracted all of them. Long enough for her to slip out of the grasp of Deputy Humbard, run furiously the dozen yards to the river's edge, and jump.

The Burnt Oak River was about six feet deep from spring runoff, clear and swift, dashing over and around a bed full of boulders. Near the bridge where she went in the rocks were fewer. She popped up in a flume and was swept beneath the bridge. Deputy Humbard had just a glimpse of the dpg's soaked red head before she disappeared again.

"Help!" Eden's doppelganger yelled to enhance the effect, her voice producing an echo in the gloom below the single arched concrete span.

"She's in the river!" Humbard advised, scrambling down the bank herself but staying clear of the rushing water. She flipped up her sunglasses but couldn't see anything beneath the bridge. She climbed the nearly vertical bank and ran to the other side. Meanwhile four deputies and highway patrol cops were trying to flush what they thought was a man with a shotgun— as dangerous as a spitting cobra—from the trunk of the car without putting themselves in harm's way. They stood well back with their own shotguns leveled while the sheriff unlocked the trunk lid, using the lid release inside the Taurus.

Deputy Humbard looked downriver to a bend where the tree-heavy banks were lower and the river broadened into a series of shallow rapids. The dpg was nowhere to be seen.

The deputy ran to one of the SUVs and grabbed a flashlight from the front seat.

The trunk of the Taurus was open, but the lid remained down. There was a lot of shouting going on.

Deputy Humbard climbed down to the river's edge again and disappeared with her flashlight beneath the bridge.

None of the other deputies and officers could figure out how to raise the trunk lid without risking their lives.

A military helicopter had appeared five hundred feet overhead, casting a shadow over the scene but making only about as much noise as a bass boat outboard. They had to look up to be sure it was there. Only one of the deputies, who had been an Army reservist until he joined the sheriff's department, had seen a stealth helicopter before. It was an eerie sight in this remote part of the country, like a UFO appearing in broad daylight, and it added to the tension.

Another deputy had an idea. He pulled rescue equipment from his SUV, extracted dacron rope with a hook on one end, eased himself into the backseat of the convertible, threw the rope and hook over the trunk, and yanked the lid up.

Deputy Humbard climbed up to the roadway with some soaked wadded clothing and a pair of wet leather sandals in one hand. She stared at the hovering nearly silent helicopter for a few seconds, then joined the guys, who were unloading the trunk of Geoff's Taurus. Tool kit, fire extinguisher, gym bag, a metal suitcase, locked.

"Sheriff?" Humbard said. "This is what she had on when she jumped in the river. No sign of her now."

She wrung out and spread a Mighty Ducks hockey jersey on the hood of the Taurus, added a pair of nylon running shorts and the sandals.

"You think she drowned down there under the bridge?"

"No, sir. She had to've pulled herself out of the current to take her clothes off. Sayin' if this is all she had on. Didn't find underwear. But I guarantee she's not down there. There's just no place to hide."

"Maybe dived in again, swum naked underwater downstream."

"I suppose she could've, little ways, but I never caught sight of her. Then the river gets too shallow at the bend for anything but wadin' and rafting."

The sheriff pondered the athletic jersey on the hood of the Taurus, stroking his short salt-and-pepper beard. He wore sunglasses with yellow reflective lenses. He took them off and looked closer, then picked up the jersey. Deputy Humbard was in the front seat of the Taurus, searching.

"I don't see a purse, or a wallet even."

"Here's a name tag," the sheriff said. "See if you can make it out, Rache."

She took the jersey from him. "Yes, sir. Looks like Chan—, no, that's a *u* there, so it's *Chauncey*, McLain."

The helicopter moved on, across the river and the heads of townfolk gathered at the other end of the bridge, and settled in for a landing opposite the Chevron station a block away. Sideways, blocking Valleyheart's main drag.

The sheriff turned and looked at it. A blue light was blinking inside the cockpit. He couldn't see anyone inside. But the booger was big enough, he thought, to hold eight men, not including the pilot.

"Sheriff," one of his deputies said, "you better come look at what's in this metal suitcase."

"If it's a severed head, just close it up again. I only ate my lunch a half hour ago."

"No, sir, it's weapons. High-grade stuff. A broke-down fifty-caliber with a humongous damn scope. And a MP-5."

The sheriff looked at the helicopter again. A door had opened.

"Close it up anyway. I have a hunch we're about to go out of business here. This whole deal may be something we don't want to know too much about."

They were dropping down from the helicopter now, men in dark blue windbreakers or ballistics vests and baseball caps with FBI stenciled on them in bold white letters. Six men. Three of them carried automatic weapons.

Another helicopter, twin of the first one, had arrived on the scene. In the front seat of the Taurus Deputy Humbard looked up, shielding her eyes with one hand, then looked at the sheriff.

"McLain," he said, shrugging. "There's some McLains in Moby Bay. One's a painter, I think. I remember admiring his seascapes when we were there a few months back. But his price was a little too steep for me and the woman."

The red-haired man had been waiting in the shadowed study of the rectory of Immaculate Conception Church in suburban Washington for about fifteen minutes when the priest, Father Giles Ducannon, walked in with an apologetic smile.

"Sorry to keep you waiting, Mr. . . . Barnes, is it?"

"Joe Barnes," Victor Wilding said, rising from his seat but not offering his hand. He was holding his Bible, an expensively bound new standard version. "It's very good of you to see me on a Sunday afternoon. Sundays must be your busiest time."

"Actually, no. Apart from saying early Mass and confessionals before the ten-thirty Mass, I don't have much else to do. Catch up on my reading, work on my short game on the putting green out back. I'll be umpiring girls' softball at five. But I'm always available for home or hospital visits or to hear confession."

He looked expectantly at Wilding. Ducannon was a burly man of middle age, built like a medieval siege machine. He was going bald. The hair he had left was like rust around his ears and down his jawline, spurred side-burns. He wore wire-rim glasses with round tinted lenses the color of a harvest moon.

"I'm not Catholic."

"I see." Ducannon glanced at the Bible. "But perhaps you have some questions for me?"

"Yes, I do."

"I hope I can help you. Would you like tea, or coffee?"

The focal point of the study was an alabaster statue of the Virgin, life-size, Mary looking not much older than fifteen. In her soft amaze, she glowed like the depths of a diamond. Wilding's eyes were drawn to the Virgin again. He declined refreshment. The priest suggested with a gesture and a smile that they sit down.

"Was she the perfect woman?" Wilding asked.

"For us, yes. I'm a Marist father. The Society of Mary."

"Could there have been a virgin birth?"

"Once, and only once."

"I'm not doubting it. Doesn't seem strange at all to me."

Ducannon nodded encouragingly.

"I think I ought to tell you. Barnes isn't my name. There are reasons why I can't tell you who I am."

Ducannon nodded, cautiously considering his next question.

"Have you committed a crime?"

"I'm not charged with any crime. I'm not a fugitive."

"All right," the priest said, after a few moments. "Why don't we go on, then? To be charged with a crime means that a crime has become known to certain authorities."

"Yes." Wilding's eyes skipped around, came to rest, inevitably, on the polar whiteness of the Virgin. "I am, let's say, a man of authority myself. The ordinary laws don't apply to me."

"But there is only one Final Authority. God the Almighty."

"I'm willing to believe that."

"Have you committed a crime that you want to confess to God, and ease the burden on your soul?"

"There are two problems with that. Saying that I've committed a crime is like saying Pol Pot had lapses of taste. And this business of souls. I don't have one."

"All of God's children have souls."

"I told you. The ordinary laws don't apply."

"God's laws are immutable. Nothing has changed on this earth since He made it. We all have a history of sin and guilt, suffering and redemption through His grace. Our streams and oceans are salted with the tears of the common misery and a longing for peace; the air is filled with cries and prayers, the dialogue of unbearable solitude. These are the sounds and wounds that time repeats, endlessly, while playing no favorites. Are you dying?"

"I don't know. I think I am."

"And you're afraid."

"The light's too bright in here. Can you do something?"

"The only light is the light of the most holy Virgin. Her light has never dimmed; nor will it ever go out. I've observed that you haven't been able to take your eyes off Her."

"I didn't have a mother."

"You were an orphan?"

"Not in any sense you can understand. Can we talk about the soul?"

"Of course."

"According to natural or, I suppose, spiritual law, if a woman gives birth to you, you are born with a soul."

"That's true."

"There are good souls and bad souls."

"Debatable. And I admit that I have problems with the actuality of theological hell. No matter, God cherishes all souls. As does our beloved Mary.

And salvation is easily within the grasp of all men." Wilding was perspiring heavily, rubbing his hand across his mouth. Ducannon looked concerned. "Are you sick?"

"No. *He* is. Failing badly. He might die any day."

"Who are you talking about?"

"My fa-fa-fa-therrr. In a manner of speaking. The one who created me."

"God the Father? But God is Eternal."

"*No.* Robin Sandza had the powers of a god, but he was only fifteen when he—when I—I *became.* Was made. From nothing, from his left-handed art. Not so much as a borrowed rib bone. Or a shadow."

"Your Bible will tell you—"

A look of strident anxiety came and went in Wilding's eyes.

"Hebrews 11:3. 'The universe was formed at God's command, so that what is seen was not made out of what is visible.' *I* was a thought that took on flesh, made in his image, and consigned to my appointed sins. Are you a drinking man, Father? I've always appreciated a shot of Irish for calming the nerves."

"Why, yes. That might be—if you would excuse me for just a—"

Wilding reacted with a violent start, not overtly menacing but scary just the same.

"Never mind! Stay put. Don't try to call anyone. I'm *not* insane. I only want—not to die. To go on. I want to be in the company of the undying."

Ducannon eased back into his seat, focused intently on Wilding, biting his underlip with gold-reinforced teeth.

"Then you must confess your sins to God. Set yourself free."

"Am I a man? Or do I only look like a man?"

"You are a man. One greatly in need of relief from suffering, whatever the nature of—"

Wilding put his Bible on his knees, picked up a letter opener from a table beside his chair, and plunged the point into the palm of his left hand, hard enough to cause blood to squirt. Ducannon looked appalled.

"No, don't!"

Wilding let the letter opener fall to the floor and clenched his wounded hand tightly. "Do I bleed like a man? I bleed, I feel pain. I get wet when it rains. I have my highs and lows. I love sex. In case you were wondering. I might even be able to conceive a child. I'm not just a neutered replica, a damn donkey!" Wilding hunched forward to the edge of his chair. "But I don't have a soul. Robin couldn't give me that! Without a soul there's no connection—not to man, God, Eternity. You don't believe in hell? The fire ever after? I'll take hell! I'll take it, because at least it's *there*. Hell is not nothing. Hell is *something*. Hell would be a blessing for me, because I won't just disappear when *my* creator takes his last breath." He glanced at his outthrust fist. His French cuff was turning red. "Oh, am I dripping on the carpet? Sorry."

Ducannon had his handkerchief out. "Let me take care of that for you, Mr. . . . are you still unwilling to tell me your name?"

"Call me Vic," Wilding said wearily. His eyes went around to the Virgin as the priest bound his wound and tied a knot in the handkerchief.

"You should have this looked at—Vic. When you leave. Why don't you let me drive you to a hospital?"

"St. Elizabeth's, maybe? The nuthatch? I'm not falling for that one, Father."

"I'm only concerned about the severity of—"

"The bleeding's almost stopped. I'm too impulsive, sometimes. But I've done worse to myself. That's our little secret. In an hour there won't be a trace of the wound. I heal fast. Don't worry about the carpet. It's not ruined. My blood just goes away." Wilding stood. Ducannon stared up at him. Wilding said, "There'll be a check in the mail, couple of days. A nice little contribution. Church can always use an extra five or ten, I guess. Listen, I'm better now. Really. A man in my position doesn't have anyone he can confide in. Maybe we could meet again. Maybe if I—I don't know. Took some vows, or something. While there's still time."

"God is always listening."

"I need—need a way out, Father."

"You have made that very clear to me, Vic."

VALLEYHEART, CALIFORNIA · MAY 29 · 2:44 P.M. PDT

Eden Waring's doppelganger, drying off in the sun, stood with hands on her invisible hips watching the FBI guys jog across the bridge toward the roadblock. The other stealth helicopter was banking for a landing on a Little League ball field a couple of hundred yards downriver.

If anyone had been looking her way, they would have seen only drops of water hovering in the air. A few of the drops were moving slowly downward, sliding as if on a sheet of glass, occasionally splashing to the ground. But this phenomenon went as unnoticed as a swarm of gnats against a background of trees of different hues like a mixed-green salad.

She was trying to decide what to do next, mindful that she had left Geoff

McTyer hanging—literally—below the mountain road three-quarters of a mile uphill. It might not be too long before the sheriff, or whoever was going to be in charge, sent a search team back up the road. Another distraction was called for.

Both of the SUV units that formed the roadblock were parked facing the town. The sheriff and his deputies stood behind the Explorers, watching the FBI team approach them, watching the second helicopter above the treetops.

Five vehicles in all, counting Geoff's Taurus and the two highway patrol units. And two helicopters. There were also a couple of cars and a van waiting on the town side of the bridge to get across, and the roadblock had stopped, so far, a camper, a pickup truck, and a church bus filled with raucous kids, most of them hanging out the windows. There was some traffic on the river too, canoes passing beneath the bridge.

The man who seemed to be boss of the FBI team took the sheriff aside. Two agents looked over Geoff's Taurus. Another one got behind the wheel of one of the SUVs and drove back across the bridge, apparently on his way to the ball field to meet the incoming chopper. The sheriff looked a little miffed. Eden Waring's doppelganger moved closer to eavesdrop.

"James Brooker, Special Agent in Charge of the San Francisco field office. You're Sheriff Udale?"

"Jones. Udall's my first name, that's with two ls."

"Right. Do you have the girl and her boyfriend in custody, Sheriff?"

"No. She was alone in the car when we stopped her. She said he was in the trunk with a shotgun, but that turned out not to be true. It was just a diversionary tactic on her part. But it got our attention. She slipped out of my deputy's grasp before she could be handcuffed, ran to the river, and jumped in with no hesitation. We haven't seen her since."

"Could she have drowned?"

"Not likely. Water's clear and not deep. Plenty of people saw her jump in. Then she climbed out of the river under the bridge and took her wet clothes off. That's her jersey lying there on the hood of the Taurus."

"Took her clothes off? You mean stripped naked?"

"That is how it appears to us. She wasn't wearing all that much to begin with."

"A young woman in her birthday suit, and still she got away with all these townfolk hanging around gawking? That doesn't make sense to me, Sheriff Udall."

"Jones. It's Jones. I'm only telling you what we've observed and what we believe to be true."

"But you don't know where the young man is either, since he didn't pop up from the trunk of that car?"

"Probably got out up the mountain a ways."

"You send some deputies back along the road to look for him?"

"No, sir. We thought he was in the—"

"Want to do that for me now, Sheriff? Since there seems to be no immediate danger in this area."

"All right. What if we find him, and he does have a shotgun?"

"Sheriff U—Jones. That young man is very valuable to us. If any harm comes to him, I promise we will render your ass and turn your testicles into blue-ribbon nut butter. Inform your deputies, Sheriff Jones."

The sheriff shrugged and dispatched two deputies in the other SUV, sent Rachael Humbard and a highway patrolman down to the river again to see what might have been overlooked. Special Agent Brooker pressed the send key on his walkie and ordered the helicopter parked in front of the Chevron station back into the air. Eden Waring's dpg walked behind him to the bridge and started across. Now that the helicopter was no longer blocking the way, it was time for the merry chase she'd been cooking up.

FBI Director Robert Hyde was the first man out of the helicopter after it landed on the Little League field. Four boys and a girl with gloves and bats were standing near the backstop.

"Sorry about your game," Hyde said. "You children go home now."

The boldest boy among them spoke up. "Who are you?"

"I'm the Director of the Federal Bureau of Investigation. From Washington. This is a matter of national security. Please disperse at once."

Hyde never had known how to talk to kids. They stayed right where they were. Another boy said, "*My* dad's a park ranger."

The sheriff's department SUV pulled up. Another agent from Hyde's helicopter handed him a walkie. "It's Mr. Brooker, sir. I'll handle the Little Leaguers."

"Yes, Brooker. Where's my son?" Hyde listened. He didn't like what he heard and cut Brooker off. "What about the girl?" This explanation was more involved. Hyde studied some buttermilk cloud formations. He went for a walk, to the first base side of the diamond. The other FBI agent, whose name was Wellford, huddled with the gang near the backstop.

"None of what you're telling me makes any sense," Hyde complained angrily. He didn't feel well. The mad dash through time zones had left him with a headache his usual remedy couldn't handle. He'd been unable to cope with food all day. And something about the news of the girl shedding her clothes and vanishing impacted him at an even deeper, visceral level. For several weeks Hyde had steeped himself in the accomplishments of psychics. Because of the extensive evidence compiled by his predecessor Carsten Burrows, he had become a reluctant believer in supernormal powers, at least the power demonstrated by Robin Sandza. Belief, he had found, was better than dread. But dread had returned, with a sting like death. What if Eden Waring possessed even more astonishing Gifts?

He gave Brooker a tongue-lashing, even though he wasn't sure his Frisco SAC deserved it. Hyde had the shudders. The Little Leaguers were racing each other toward the village center. Wellford approached Hyde with a smile he modified upon seeing the Director's face.

"They're good kids. I told them I spent four years in the high minors with the Orioles organization, until my arm gave out. Then I pulled my favorite weapon on them."

"You pulled your weapon, Agent Wellford?"

"I gave them some money for ice cream. Raymond Chandler used to say, 'My favorite weapon is a twenty-dollar bill.' "

"I don't think I know him."

"He wrote hard-boiled detective novels. My father collects them. And old radio shows. *Boston Blackie. Sam Spade, Detective.* Are you feeling okay, sir?" Robert Hyde had passed a hand over his face as if he were wiping away thick cobwebs.

"I've felt better. I'm going to take a walk, have a look around town on my own."

"Yes, sir. Do you want me to—"

"No, stay here and monitor all communications." Hyde took a couple of steps, hesitated, looked around at Wellford.

"Old radio shows. I don't make a habit of remembering my childhood, but there was a program I listened to with my father. It always came on during the hour I visited once a week. He was hospitalized for, they called it battle fatigue in those days. Now it's post-trauma stress disorder or something. He never recovered. I never heard him say my name. That's not what I was thinking about. There was this radio program, was it called *The Whistler*? He had the power to cloud men's minds."

"I believe that was Lamont Cranston. *The Shadow.* 'Who knows what evil lurks—' "

"The Shadow! You're right. It was The Shadow who clouded men's minds, so they couldn't see him. What foolishness. I only listened to the radio when I was with my father. I'm sure it was all he did. All day long. Stare at the wall in his little room at the VA hospital. Listen to the radio. Feeling—I don't know that he felt anything. My mother wouldn't let me

hear those programs at home or go to the picture show. She said my imagination would be overstimulated, and I would wet the bed even worse. Her
scorn. Worse than any whipping could have been, but she never laid a hand
on me. So I learned that imagination is a bad thing. But that's not what I
was thinking about, either. Why should I? I'm not a child anymore. I didn't
enjoy being a child. Did you?"

"Yes, sir. I played a lot of ball."

"That's right. You played baseball. The Orioles organization. Good for
you, Wellford. I think I'll take that walk now."

Nearly everyone in Valleyheart was at the bridge, or outside the ice cream
shop half a block from the bridge, their attention focused on the comings
and goings of law enforcement officers. Kids were scampering around. Another unit from the sheriff's department was now blocking access for in-
bound traffic on the west side of Valleyheart, which, except for some raft
and canoe traffic on the river, had been effectively sealed off from the rest
of the world.

The dpg's idea was to borrow something sturdy, a big pickup truck or
a full-sized SUV, one with extra lights mounted over the windshield, and
drive through the roadblock on the other side of town, lights flashing and
horn blowing. Attract a lot of pursuit, draw them all away from Geoff's
precarious hiding place. Then he would have to get to Moby Bay on his
own. She was calling it quits for the day. Eden had become impatient, the
dpg could feel her impatience although they had no direct line of communication. It was sort of an etheric wake-up call.

Valleyheart was a small place, the few side streets ending abruptly after
a couple of blocks, or continuing as unpaved residential lanes with A-frames
or log homes set on deep lots.

Beside a frame church in need of a fresh coat of white paint there was a
parking lot where asphalt turned to gravel, and in the lot stood a lone
Toyota Land Cruiser, shocked-up for hard mountain terrain. The LC probably hadn't been washed in six months; side windows were streaky with
dried mud. It had an abandoned look. Just what she wanted, if the owner
had left the Toyota unlocked and the keys handy. Valleyheart seemed to
be the sort of place where people didn't bother to lock up their homes or
vehicles.

The door on the driver's side wasn't tightly closed. The tinted dirty
window was halfway down. Eden's dpg stepped up on the running board
and looked in. A handful of keys lay on the driver's seat. She opened the
door and scooped up the keys, settled herself.

The pit bull that had been left behind made only a grunting sound as it lunged toward her between the seats. She smelled it before she saw it, and with a yelp of terror she threw herself against the door and tumbled to the graveled ground outside. The pit bull, wearing a choke collar, leaped on top of her as she rolled over, clamping jaws with the grip of a bear trap on her right forearm below the elbow. Terrified, hurting so horribly she couldn't scream, the doppelganger was pinned flat on her back by the dog's paws. His ugly blunt head, jaws apart, jerked side to side as his teeth sank deeper into her paralyzed arm.

Eden Waring was carrying a wooden bowl of potato chips from the kitchen to the patio of the house that overlooked the Pacific when the shocking pain in her right forearm caused her to drop the bowl. She went down on one knee, holding the arm tightly with her other hand.

"Eden, you okay?" Chauncey McLain asked her.

"Cramp in my arm. Don't know where it came from. Look at the mess, I'm sorry."

"No problem, I'll pick up. Why don't you put a cold pack on your arm, there's a couple of them in the freezer."

"I'll get it for you," Roald McLain volunteered. He had developed a crush on Eden, and had been following her around worshipfully since the girls returned from the beach.

"Thanks," Eden said. She gritted her teeth, slumped on a redwood bench. Way too much pain. What was happening? Then she felt a jolt in the mind, a bumper-cars sort of collision with another mind, and the next instant it was as if she were falling, a thousand miles a second, out of the sky and through a grove of trees cool and darkly green, then shooting into unbearable light where the pain had its origin. All this while sitting on the redwood bench beneath the mesh sunshade of the patio, feeling the rough flagstones beneath her bare feet. Roald kneeling beside her to apply the cold pack where it hurt.

Get the dog off me, he's breaking my arm! I'm afraid of dogs! Pull me back, Eden!

"Thanks, Roald," Eden murmured, holding the cold pack in place. "It feels good. I need to go to the, uh, the bathroom. Be right back, guys."

In the bathroom she locked the door, then lifted the cold pack gingerly. Eden looked at her swelling forearm. Black and blue, the flesh torn by savage teeth.

Someone's coming! Pull me back!

Eden raised her eyes to the cabinet mirror over the sink, saw her own frantically twisting, naked body and a pit bull with her arm in its jaws.

She recoiled from this vision, shook her head angrily, looked again.

New perspective. She saw a man's face this time. In his middle to late fifties. Gray hair, crew cut. The hard-nosed, adversarial look of a man whose mind has long been closed to laughter. She had never seen him before. She would have remembered. Religious zealot, a destroyer of some kind. Egotist in a stark stone mask. But there was a childlike horror in his eyes belying the stonework when he stared back at Eden, as if his emotional surge protector was failing. His tan looked tarnished.

"All right," Eden said. She gritted her teeth against the pain in her arm and continued, "Just what the hell is going on here?"

He trembled; or it might have been the instability, the thin dimension of his image disturbed by mountain wind.

"This can't be. You can't—you don't exist."

"Not within the bounds of your reality," Eden said indifferently. "Now would you do something about this pit bull?"

"What?"

"Are you dense? He'll chew my arm off. Do you have a gun?" It was just a hunch on her part, but he nodded, slowly.

"Then take out your gun, mister, and *shoot* the goddamn dog!"

He looked down. His hand went beneath his coat. But he didn't pull his piece. He looked into her eyes again.

"Where is he? What have you done with my son?"

"I don't know what you're talking about. I don't know you."

He was beginning to look like living proof that there is life after death. "But where are you? I can't *see* you! I might hit you."

Enough of this, Eden decided. She was far away from him, but somehow she understood that she could do it. Put his panicky resistance on hold. Take control of his thoughts, his actions. Her exhilaration had the power of a celestial storm, a great Pacific wave reaching the shore. She rode this wave, surfing into his mind . . .

You killed my dog! Son of a bitch, what did you go and shoot my dog for?"

Robert Hyde discovered what it was like to almost jump out of your skin.

He felt something stir in his mind, creepily, like a deathwatch beetle. He was looking at the body of the pit bull, shot between the eyes with the Glock 21C he was holding, half of its head in bloody fragments. He turned. There were two men converging on him, backwoods dwellers with unkempt shoulder-length hair, outrage in their eyes. Behind them FBI agents running full tilt to the scene. But he could handle this.

"Your dog attacked me. I had to shoot him."

"Buster never attacked nobody, and that's God's own truth, mister! I ought to kick your ass from here to—"

"Let's don't do anything rash, boys."

The dog owner's buddy, looking around, blanched at the sight of automatic weapons aimed their way, dug in his heels, and pulled at the other man's arm.

"Harris—"

Hyde was able to holster his weapon after two tries. There was no expression on his face. His brain felt like the moon lying empty in black space, a husk of something once fruitful.

"Not within the bounds of your reality," he heard Eden Waring say once again.

The dog owner was down on one knee, picking up the remains of his pit bull.

"Aww, Buster." He began to sob. "Goddamn guvmint assholes. Shoot a man's dog and walk away. Just like Ruby Ridge, ain't it? Well piss on you, bastard. Piss on all a you!"

Agent Wellford holstered his own gun and looked at the Director. "Gave us a scare, sir."

"Have you found my son yet?"

"No, sir. Sheriff may have something. He says."

"Let's talk to him."

Eden felt very tired. The swelling had disappeared from her arm. She sat crying softly on the edge of the bathtub.

"Is that all of it?"

"Yes."

"Riley . . . Betts. I've got to get home. *Now.*"

"In my opinion," her doppelganger said, "that's not a very good idea."

Knock on the door. It was Chauncey McLain.

"You okay in there?"

"Yes. Sure, Chauncey."

"Party's started. You must be starved, girl."

"Be right with you."

Eden reached for a washcloth, ran cold water in the tub, bathed her face and cooled her throbbing eyes, then balled the cloth and hurled it wrathfully.

"Geoff," she moaned. "How *could* he? I owe him. Oh, God, do I ever owe that bastard, and he *will* get what's coming to him."

"Maybe you shouldn't judge him too harshly."

"Will you shut up?"

"Just trying to be the voice of reason here. I know how upset you are."

"Shut up now. I mean it. I don't want to talk anymore. I have to think. It's so horrible. Yesterday. I just want to go back to yesterday, wake up in my bed, iron my graduation gown again, go over my speech. I want my diploma, damn it, I earned it! If I have such great powers, then why don't I have the power to do *that*?"

"There are some physical laws we can't transcend. You need to brush your hair."

Eden brushed without looking at herself in the mirror. Unable to endure herself any longer. Or her doppelganger.

"Leave me alone now."

"Here's an idea. I could put on your clothes and join the party, give you a chance to rest and collect your thoughts."

"Like hell you will," Eden said, yanking the brush bristles through her unruly hair.

As soon as the first helicopter flew over and landed in front of Valleyheart's Chevron station, Geoff decided that he should forget about whatever Eden's doppelganger had in mind and get moving. She had told him where to find Eden. That was all he needed from her, or *it*. He was still in a state of high confusion—weirded-out probably better described his emotional level—whenever he thought about the dpg. It was useful to think about nothing else except the urgency of getting to Moby Bay. The state cops had made him, and the roads were tied up. Reacquiring his car wasn't an option. But there was a river below, swift and bright in the sun. He had seen canoeists, kayakers, and rafters on the river. And the Burnt Oak, he was sure, ran to the sea on its northerly course down from the mountains. With luck, the mouth of the river would be near Moby Bay.

No way down but the hard way. It wasn't a sheer drop, but the angle of descent was steep. Mossy ledges and ravines crisscrossed with deadfalls, sparse sunlight beneath the tall trees. There was no clear path to follow.

Getting down to the river was one thing. Then he would need a canoe.

The Ford Expedition Tom Sherard had rented in San Francisco came equipped with a telephone. They were a half hour out of Innisfall after an emergency visit to a veterinarian's when the phone rang. Sherard glanced at Bertie Nkambe, who seemed as startled as he was. Warhol, the cleaned-up Persian cat, was wrapped in a soft baby blanket on her lap, dozing after a hefty shot of antibiotic.

"Who knows where we are?" Sherard said.

"Nobody. Oh, wait. I did order a large thin-crust with anchovies and three kinds of cheese from the Flying Pizza delivery service. 'Pies from the Sky'? It's big country up here. Oh, smile, damn you."

Sherard smiled. "I don't like anchovies."

"They're for Warhol. Maybe you should answer the stupid phone, Tom."

"I know I'll bloody well regret this," he grumbled, putting the caller on speakerphone.

"Am I talking to Jungle Jim, the man with the gold lion's-head cane?"

Danny Cheng. Sherard shook his head in amazement and annoyance.

Bertie said delightedly, "Is this the man with the bad gas leak?"

Cheng's voice was raw and strained, as if he'd eaten a lot of smoke.

"The leaks have been stopped for now. We won't go into names, places, or past regrets on this broadcast. I'm all business today. You're really not too tall for me, you know. I can deal with six feet of long legs, bold haughty buttocks, breasts that blush like ripened pears in their warm dish of cinnamon brûlée."

"I'm six-one in flats. Is your father okay?"

After a coughing fit Cheng said, "And sends his best."

"How did you find us?" Sherard asked.

"Please. I'm the Infomaniac. Being burned out of my house hasn't cramped my style. I thought you might have had a change of heart and acted on the nudge I gave you. Then you'd need wheels to get around."

"I wish I had better news for you," Bertie said. "But all I have is a cat."

"A cat?"

"A survivor everyone else overlooked. Boy kitty. Name's Warhol, according to the tag on his collar. There's a definite resemblance. Anyway, I get along well with cats. This one belonged to someone we talked about last night. American Indian name. That's about all I've been able to get so far. Warhol's been through hell, and right now he just wants to sleep. Later I may have information you can use. Where are you?"

Cheng cleared his throat and coughed deeply. "Safe place. The country hacienda of a great American. There are a few left who can't be bought or intimidated. You might remember meeting him last night. He was very impressed with you, tall girl. He'd like to continue the conversation you were having about another valuable public servant whose luck has been running ugly. I'm talking about rearry rotten ruck, like there's a fix in by someone near and dear to the public servant under discussion."

Sherard said, "Can't do it. There's too much risk. We've reason to believe your host is bugged but doesn't have a clue."

After a few seconds Cheng said cautiously, "Some leading experts from a well-known private firm can negative that."

Sherard glanced at Bertie, who nodded.

"Put it this way. Tall Girl thinks a trusted and loyal aide of our friend may have had outpatient surgery recently, perhaps to remove a suspicious mole behind his left ear. Check his medical history. If there *was* a mole or even an ordinary wen and it was taken, something else quite unobtrusive might have replaced it. This could be confirmed at a good private clinic, say in Switzerland or Buenos Aires."

"Tall Girl?" Danny Cheng said, requesting an opinion.

"He seemed overworked to me, poor guy. He could use a vacation while having that checkup. I'd see that he was on a plane tonight."

"So those are *his* travel plans. What about yours? Not hanging around the hot zone, are you?"

"Waiting on a pizza," Sherard said. "And you're fading out."

"I got messed with pretty good last night. Somebody's going to suffer." He coughed hard again. "Need to go hawk up some more black stuff and catch a nap. We'll talk later. Like the melancholy hooker, I'm just too blue to blow right now."

Geoff McTyer reached the river bottom after twenty minutes of laborious descent, his toes bruised from being jammed to the front of his inappropriate running shoes while he braked his way downhill. The river was running briskly and loud beyond the thinning trees. He badly wanted water but even this far from civilization giardia was a hazard, no matter how pure the streams looked. He licked his dry swollen lips, tasted blood where the underlip had cracked open again, and stood within a dozen feet of the riverbank for a minute or so, catching his breath, getting used to the light. He had been traveling in deep shade most of the way down. Here the sunlight was stronger but subdued, as if it were filtered through greenhouse glass.

He heard voices, then a canoe suddenly went past him. If either of the occupants had looked up they would have seen him, but they were both busy navigating a shoal close to the bank. Laughing. Then the bottom of the battered aluminum canoe scraped rocks fifty feet downriver and slowed, listing slightly, swinging around sideways in a secondary current away from the main channel. The college kids, a girl and a boy, jumped out and dragged their canoe to shore. They wore flotation vests over long-sleeved athletic warmups, and hiking shorts with low-topped boots. They were both wet; soaked, in her case. But having a great time. Watching them, Geoff felt as if he were looking back from the end of his life at the happiness he had known with Eden in similar circumstances. The girl grabbed a rucksack out of the canoe and said she was going to change. The look she gave the guy was an invitation to follow her, back into the trees where they wouldn't be disturbed.

Geoff figured they were giving him at least fifteen minutes, maybe longer, to steal their canoe. Depending on whether they were going to have stand-up sex or just fool around while getting into dry clothes. Then it might take them the rest of the afternoon to walk out of the wilderness and report the theft. If there was anything else in the canoe—food, bedrolls—he'd leave it for them.

Ten minutes later he was moving swiftly downstream toward the Valleyheart bridge. There were a couple of canoes and several kayaks beached near the bridge, where the roadblock was still in effect. But now they were letting vehicles pass through town after the deputies looked them over. He saw a helicopter on a baseball field, and FBI field agents everywhere. A tactical force, but not one he was familiar with. Probably from Impact Sector, the deep-cover group his father had begun as a partial answer to MORG. Geoff had never seen anything like the helicopter. It was a stealth fighter with rotors, huge and menacing.

For a few bad moments he thought the cops were stopping traffic on the river as they broadened their search for him. Then he realized the boats belonged to a church group on an outing. They'd paused for sandwiches and ice cream. None of the law enforcement personnel were paying attention to them.

The river was running rough and a little tricky above the bridge. He had to concentrate to maneuver the old canoe through some good-sized boulders. He was wearing a pair of taped-together sunglasses he'd found on the floor of the canoe and a spare yellow flotation vest. And he was wet, hair flattened and clinging to his forehead. They'd have photos of him by now, up on the bridge, but his official FBI ID picture was almost three years out-of-date. The more recent photo from Innisfall PD had never flattered him much anyway.

He'd reached the bridge, keeping his head down as much as possible. There could be another helicopter in the air, covering a wide area with its cameras. He was wary of technological marvels, the one-in-a million chance he could be nailed by a computer programmed to compare his facial bone structure, scanned from a quick snapshot, with measurements on file in his medical history.

But it wasn't lightning-fast technology that did Geoff in; it was pure chance. That, and a pair of borrowed, loose-fitting sunglasses.

The FBI building in Sacramento, the state capital, was ordinarily a somnolent place on a Sunday, particularly a Sunday before a national holiday,
but Special Agent in Charge Dolph Hackett had canceled everyone's day
or weekend off. Before the day was over the Director might be there, and
Hackett, just thirty-two and on a fast track with the Review Board, was
acting unusually tight-assed with those agents who had not been dispatched
to Innisfall and the clerical staff as well. Not knowing precisely what was
going down both annoyed Hackett and made him uneasy. He knew who
Eden Waring was, but he didn't know why she was, unofficially, a fugitive,
a subject of intense interest to Hyde himself. All of the Bureau's activities
so far in tracking her down were, to Hackett's mind, extralegal. Or if they
were not, he had yet to see the appropriate authorizations. They were acting
at a level of wartime emergency. And what was so important about Geoff
McTyer, Waring's boyfriend and a small-town police officer, that had
earned him the designation "Runaway"?

Then there was this character from Impact Sector, this cross-dressing
covert temporarily known as Phil Haman, sitting nearly mute in the interrogation room. Going on five and a half hours now. Drinking a lot of black
coffee, making frequent trips to the bathroom, but refusing to scrub the
disgusting makeup off his face, remove the wig and padded bra, put on a
man's clothes. What was with the goddamn Rona Harvester impersonation,
Hackett wondered, the mannerisms and dead-on voice?

Hackett was tempted to see if he could pry some useful information out
of Haman (to use his current handle). But assassins bothered him, as they
did most of the straight-edge, ambitious young agents the Bureau still managed to recruit and keep. All of them knew about Impact Sector, but
avoided talking about it. There was occasional, very quiet speculation about
who might be in charge there. Wherever *there* was. Impact Sector, some of
the agents believed, was allied with the unit of the Special Operations
Group exclusively devoted to MORG surveillance. Everyone with the Bureau accepted, as an article of faith, that MORG was relentless in its efforts
to choke off funding to the Bureau, eventually bulldoze the J. Edgar Hoover Building to rubble and push the entire pile into the tidal basin. Only
the efforts of Allen Dunbar, until very recently the dual chair of the Senate
Select Committee on Intelligence *and* the Senate Judiciary Committee, had
so far kept the powers of the rival intelligence agencies somewhat in balance.

Hackett's father had been Executive Assistant Director over investigations in the last years of Hoover's reign. He had known almost all there was to know about the founder's personal peculiarities and official derelictions. But "Hardball" Hackett had never uttered a disparaging word about either his boss or the Bureau while raising two of his sons to join him at the FBI. Charles had defected to the Blackwelder organization early on, but Dolph had his father's code of loyalty. He respected Robert Hyde, and could tolerate the covert stuff because everybody did it; you adopted the enemy's tactics in order to survive. Still he didn't relish close contact with a stone killer like the cross-dressing Haman. And he'd been directed to leave Haman in isolation until further notice. A visit, possibly from the head of Impact Sector—whoever he was—could be in the works.

Hackett indulged his curiosity by dropping around to the viewing room where Haman, in the adjoining room, was under constant watch through one-way glass.

"What has he been doing?" Hackett asked the agent who was one of two men assigned in half-hour shifts to keep an eye on their covert.

"Crossword puzzles. About every fifteen minutes he gets up and pours another cup of coffee. Drinks it, goes to take a pee. Standing up, I might add. He doesn't close the door is how we know that. Comes back, does another crossword puzzle. Hasn't touched the sandwiches we provided. Oh, and watch this."

Haman had put down his pencil and book of puzzles. Something had come over him, a lurking fear. He raised a hand to his throat, where there was evidence of a rope burn. He looked left slowly, then right. Then he turned in his chair and studied the room in its entirety. Table, three wooden chairs, a freestanding bookcase with nothing on it but the Mr. Coffee machine and plastic bowls containing packets of artificial sweeteners and a nondairy creamer. There was a water cooler in one corner with a blue-tinted five-gallon bottle upside down on it. Blinds on the east-facing windows. The door to the small bathroom stood open. Haman continued to massage his throat. Then he suddenly bent over and looked under the table. He straightened immediately and looked around again, moving his head and upper body instead of just his eyes.

Finally he was still. His gaze became fixed on the mirror behind which Hackett and the other FBI agent were watching. He seemed to know someone was there. A strange chilling smile appeared. Then he picked up his pencil and crossword puzzle magazine and settled back into his routine, sipping coffee while he worked a puzzle.

"What do you make of him?" the subordinate asked Hackett.

"Bit of a fidget, as my English nanny used to say."

"Yeah. Wonder what he looks like under all that makeup? Are you going to talk to him?"

"No. He's not our deal. Leave him be until IS takes him off our hands."

The water cooler in the interrogation room belched. The pencil in Haman's hand snapped in two. He looked at the cooler and then at the pieces, reached out and placed them on the table along with the puzzle book. He appeared to be making up his mind about something. Then he stood and began deliberately to undress, beginning with the Rona Harvester wig. The padded bra and Jockey shorts came off. Then the false eyelashes. He walked into the bathroom and began to remove the makeup with a damp towel. When he returned bare-assed and bare-faced to the interrogation room the agent watching with Hackett gasped.

"Jesus, look at that! He's all bone and scar tissue."

Hackett said with a grimace of disgust, "Tell Leona to go out and get him something to wear at Target. A pair of overalls, anything. One of those Stetsons with a bulldogger crease that'll hide some of his face."

The assassin temporarily known as Phil Haman sat down and folded his arms across his bony chest. His eyes closed almost immediately. He took three deep breaths by mouth and his head nodded forward. Just that quickly he was asleep. His mouth remained open. Some drool ran down from one corner and dripped from his chin. They heard a raspy snore.

Dolph Hackett shook his head and went back to the conference room in use as a command center while the Director was personally conducting an operation close to the Sacramento FO. The next time he had occasion to think about Haman, one of his agents had a separated shoulder and a concussion, another had a crushed larynx, and Haman was nowhere to be found.

MOBY BAY · MAY 29 · 4:28 P.M. PDT

Chauncey had come to the door of her bedroom a couple of times to check on Eden while she was sobbing her heart out. On her third trip all was quiet inside. She knocked, and Eden answered in muffled tones that Chauncey interpreted as an invitation to come in. She shut the door behind her because the house was getting noisy, particularly in the kitchen. Nearly everyone in Moby Bay seemed to be arriving at the same time for the barbecue and, after dark, a patriotic fireworks display at the edge of the Pacific. The music on the outdoor speakers was loud and rocking: Linda Ronstadt's cover of Chuck Berry's *Back in the USA*.

Eden had curled up on Chauncey's bed. The shutters were closed. Chauncey slipped down beside Eden, dabbed under her eyes with a tissue, held her hand.

"What did you find out?" Eden asked.

"You know hospitals. They don't get specific. The computer has Betts listed as serious but stable. No visitors, no phone calls."

"I can't call her? Why *not*?"

"That's all the information I have."

Eden sat up. "But what about Dad?"

"I phoned all three funeral homes. He's at Brickalow's."

"Oh GodohGodmyGod, *Riley*. I can't, I just—I've got to go *home*, Chauncey! I want to see Betts, there're arrangements to be made. People to call, Riley's brothers and sister—"

Chauncey gripped her hand more tightly. "Eden, listen to me. I don't know how you found out something had happened to your mom and dad. I'm sure it's not my place to know because you're the Avatar and your powers are beyond my—"

"Will you *stop*? All I'm asking is for you to drive me to Innisfall, or if you don't want to, then loan me your wheels and I'll—"

"Something's going on, I get that much, and I think you may be in danger. The man I spoke to at the funeral home, he . . . sounded surprised when I asked about Riley. Surprised, cautious. Then he had too many questions. Wanted to know who I was, asked me if I knew where you were. Asked three times, was I *sure* I didn't know how to contact you, and there was something about his tone, as if he thought I was lying."

"So what? It's a funeral home. They have my father. There are procedures to follow, I guess."

"He wanted to know how I knew Riley was, uh, deceased. Like it was privileged information. And why no visitors for Betts? If she were in critical care I could understand. I just have a creepy feeling about all this. What you might be walking into."

"Innisfall is my home. I was raised there. I have friends who will help me!"

"They were your friends yesterday. Before the plane crash. Are they your friends today?"

"That is an awful—what do you *mean*?"

"I think you know what I mean. The last time I looked at the news on TV, there was still a mob scene outside your house. I'll bet there are some interesting messages on your answering machine. You're an instant celebrity, Eden. But there's a kind of religious hysteria building around your celebrity. You've attracted followers already. You're a source of inspiration to the gullible or the devout. And you could be prey for the wrong kind of people, the Bad Souls. Some of them work for governments."

"Thanks, I needed the shit scared out of me." Eden fell silent, breathing slowly. Her eyes were red from crying, but alert. Chauncey studied her, concerned. Eden resumed in a subdued voice, "I know, Chauncey. A lot of what you've said is true. There's a guy I loved and made love to, he— he was spying on me all the time. I don't know what that's about. Who sent him to—to *study* and humiliate and betray me? But I will find out. And I swear *none* of them will get off easy." She looked up at Chauncey. "You're right. I need to be careful. I don't feel special but I know I'm different. Always have been. I've had dreams all of my life. Prophetic dreams. I dreamed about Portland. Three times. Then it happened. I couldn't *do* anything. Last night I dreamed about another city. For the third time. It's becoming clearer to me, but I still don't know where it is. There's a big university, close to downtown. A wide, wide river just outside of the city. Maybe it's a lake. Beautiful. The city is hilly and green, lots of churches. I think a bomb is on the way, right now, to this city. Thousands more will die. I can't allow that. I have to stop them, whoever they are. I'm so sick about Riley. Sad for Betts. But I know she'll be okay without me for a little while. And I have things to do. Things to do. Please help me, Chauncey. I feel so alone."

WESTBOUND/VALLEYHEART TO MOBY BAY · MAY 29 · 4:57 P.M. PDT

Two big, and largely unknown (to the general public), dark gray "Conan" helicopters traveled seaward over the Humboldt redwoods southeast of Cape Mendocino, destination Moby Bay, California: specifically latitude 40° 28'19" N, longitude 124° 24'46" W, the precise location of a one-story, four-bedroom, two-and-a-half-bath home of redwood siding with a shake-shingle roof, one and three-quarter miles from the center of town, on a long, gently sloping, nearly treeless headland with an eye-filling vista of the ocean. The home of Wick and Mia McLain and their two children. Chauncey, twenty-one, and Roald, who has just turned thirteen.

The FBI did not have dossiers on either of the adult McLains. Routine stuff had turned up from the credit bureau computers. Wick, a self-employed artist, got behind on the Visa card occasionally, but he was punctual about his car and mortgage payments, so he maintained a fairly decent credit rating. The McLains appeared to be unremarkable small-town churchgoing Americans—except, oddly enough, Moby Bay had no church of any denomination.

The photo recon pictures generated by NSA's digital cameras aboard a K-234 satellite nicknamed "Jack Flash" and currently in geocentric orbit far above this two-acre plot of California coastline, showed a Memorial weekend cookout in progress at the McLains'. Sixty guests, with more arriving as the helos moved in: most of them were outside. Robert Hyde counted another dozen people circulating inside the spacious house; all of the bathrooms were occupied.

Hyde hadn't counted on a party. Too many people to sort through once they were on the ground, with Bravo chopper circling the LZ, checking for breakaways. They could have used some backup, but there wasn't time. And he had been forced to leave an agent behind in Valleyheart to make room for his son in Alpha chopper.

The Director didn't look at Geoff again, who was seated forward behind the pilot, his back to the com station where the relayed satellite photos appeared on two computer screens. Knowing how close he had come to killing his son was a torment. Hyde had a bad headache, brought on partly by his efforts to ignore the memory of an angry pit bull, seemingly levitated, and a bodiless female voice demanding that he pull his Glock and *kill* the brute. This momentary departure from reality he had rationalized as a whisper of psychosis, a fleeting mental incapacity brought on by stress and disorientation, the demands of flying at nearly Mach two for two thousand miles with, perhaps, a subtle defect in the delivery system depriving him of all the oxygen his brain required for optimum functionality.

That part of the paranormal experience he had coped with adequately. Explained it away. The rest of it still haunted him, like the voice from the radio in the stillness of his father's tiny cheerless room on visiting days. The mocking, nerve-prickling laughter. *The Shadow knows . . .*

When he had failed to act in the face of the pit bull's aggression, someone had acted for him. Someone had . . . no, some *thing* . . . No. It was a *presence,* neither hellish nor quite human, a dark cloudlike but *feminine* presence with the strength of a fist pushing into his mind, pushing *him* aside. His persona, his ego, his will. Neutralizing him. Taking operational control.

"You killed my dog! Son of a bitch, what did you go and shoot my dog for?"

The next thing he was aware of, the next thing he heard.

Standing there in sunlight with the bloody dog at his feet, his Glock in his hand. His mind all there once again. Casually vacated, or perhaps *abandoned* was the word, once her purpose had been done.

The power to cloud men's minds . . .

Hyde thinking, with a tremor of anguish: *You can't—you don't exist.*

Smelling the blood of the dog. His own perspiration popping out cold as winter rain. Seeing the sway of trees on a windy bright afternoon.

Hearing her again, the uninsistent note of contempt in her voice.

Not within the bounds of your reality.

"Give me an ETA," Hyde said to the pilot of Alpha chopper. They were cruising at 170 mph at four thousand feet, easily clearing the modest peaks on this side of the Coast Range.

"ETA nine minutes and twenty seconds, sir."

"Roger that." The Director returned to the high res satellite cameras' meticulous scan of the people at the Memorial weekend cookout. Searching for the face of Eden Waring, which also was displayed, in the senior portrait from her college yearbook, in a window at the upper-right quadrant of one screen for instant matching purposes. Geoff should have been assisting him with the identification process. But Hyde didn't know what to do about his wayward, hostile son. Obviously Eden Waring had clouded the boy's mind as easily as she had clouded Hyde's. Turned his own blood against him. Deprogramming eventually might restore Geoff's mental equilibrium and his loyalty. For now he was just a nuisance and a potential hazard.

It would have been better, Hyde thought, if the canoe carrying Geoff beneath the Valleyheart bridge had come along just a few pulsebeats later. His own pulse rate was in the hammering hundreds at the moment he looked up and recognized the eyes of his son, appearing in the gloom like blue comets as the badly fitting sunglasses he wore slipped to the end of his snub nose. Hyde had just vomited at the edge of the river; he had gone there to get out of the sun and have a look for himself at the site where Deputy Rachael Humbard reported finding the girl's hockey jersey, shorts, and sandals. Where she had vanished. Not appearing again except in voice, in the Director's invaded, violated mind. That recent memory had brought up deep bile flavored with fear, set him to retching so strongly his stomach muscles cramped and he thought he might faint.

The recognition:

A lone young man in a canoe, square face, Geoff's eyes, unforgettable even to a neglectful father. Hyde had lunged from the shore and tumbled into the canoe as it passed him, drawn his gun again and jammed the muzzle of the double-action pistol against the back of the boy's head. Only a millimeter, a slight increase of the tension in his trigger finger, from slaying him.

Angry at Geoff's betrayal, but more afraid of what might be controlling him.

Some clear-air turbulence over cloud-shadowed mountainside, recently burned over, had the helicopter bouncing. Hyde stared at the back of his son's head. Geoff had been uncommunicative since getting over the shock of seeing his father in a remote area of northern California. Another magical appearance to be reckoned with. His mood was more apathetic than chastened. He wouldn't say anything about the girl who had been with him in his car, except that it wasn't Eden Waring. He didn't know her name. He'd given her a ride, sure; that was all. Where was she now? Shrug. No idea. Looking level and sullen into his father's eyes. No giveaways: nervous blinking, eye movements, surreptitious body language. Hyde was experienced at detecting liars. So far he didn't think Geoff was lying.

Hyde's fear lay dense and deep. Because he knew Eden Waring *had* been there, not twenty minutes ago. Less. She had compelled him to kill a pit bull. It had been Eden's voice he'd heard in his mind. He was familiar with the way she sounded from listening to a tape of her botched valedictory address at Cal Shasta.

A last shouted question for Geoff: *Where was Eden?* Another shrug, a disconsolate twist to Geoff's taut mouth. Maybe he knew. But Geoff would say no more. Standing in sunlight on the riverbank beside the beached canoe, Geoff was shaking and looked exhausted. Possessed, Hyde might have thought, his skin prickling. But he willed himself not to. He needed to get that behind him: his own slippage, his momentary disconnect, not a blackout but a whiteout. The subsequent helplessness, loss of self and memory lapse.

Discount the evidence of his senses, concentrate on what was known.

There had been a girl with Geoff, who, the sheriff said, resembled Eden Waring. Waring's fingerprints were all over Geoff's car, but she'd been his girlfriend for almost two years. Move on. The girl, whoever she was, had managed to elude the roadblockers. All right. What was left—all they had to go on—was a name tag in the hockey jersey. Chauncey McLain of Moby Bay, California. Geoff had not reacted to the name. But very likely he had been headed toward Moby Bay. There wasn't much else west of Valleyheart on the road he had taken. All right. Move on. In force. Turn the fucking town inside out if necessary. But find Eden Waring.

"Sir, do you want to have a look at this?"

The Air Force computer tech at the communications station indicated one of three screens in front of him. The relayed digital image from Jack Flash. Lawn party at the McLains'. The tech had singled out two young women who were walking slowly side by side toward the edge of the bluff. Turning their heads toward each other, apparently deep in conversation. The taller of the two women used a lot of hand gestures. She was barefoot. They both wore sleeveless tops and cargo shorts.

"They came out of the house maybe thirty seconds ago. I hadn't seen them before."

"Isolate and enhance," Hyde said.

The tech tapped at his keyboard. Cameras aboard Jack Flash afforded only a high-angle view a few degrees from the perpendicular. It wasn't possible to see the women's faces. Hyde looked again at the yearbook portrait of Eden Waring. He was a student of faces, although he had long ignored his own. It had been years since he had even looked into a barbershop or medicine cabinet mirror, and he had no idea of when his hair had begun to gray. Eden wasn't a raving beauty. But she had allure, a different thing altogether, and rare. A slightly fierce look—the boldness of her eyebrows, the direct, discerning competitor's gaze. The faint curve of her wide smile seemed to mock the process of being fixed in time by the photographer's lens. From her expression she might have been at the point of joyous laughter or merely satisfied with herself, savoring a sensual capacity that had overwhelmed Geoff McTyer. Most human beings revealed their lives, past and future, in their faces; routine faces for the most part, lacking intellectual heat or danger. Hers was a face of guardian prowess. It guarded an unnamable border that the traveler approached at his own risk.

The helicopter bounced again. Hyde saw Geoff McTyer's dark uncombed head loll as if he had fallen deeply asleep harnessed to the seat.

"Sir, I think we may be able to ID one of the women."

The tech had retrieved six seconds' worth of the enhanced image from Jack Flash and further enlarged it. The taller of the pair seemed to be reacting to something, flinching perhaps, as a gull flew at them from below the bluff. One click at a time her head turned in a sideways tilt, her face was slowly revealed as she looked at something above her head and off to her left. Sun flare on each dark oval of the glasses she wore.

"Freeze," Hyde ordered.

The tech was busy at his keyboard. His software took the yearbook portrait of Eden Waring, copied it, and gave them three-dimensional views in several different planes. The tech selected the plane he thought was closest to the angle of the face on the satellite image and transferred both to a third computer screen. He was humming to himself, pleased with his work. Three more key taps and the three-dimensional, computer-drawn re-creation of the yearbook portrait slid into place over the image of the upturned face captured by Jack Flash.

"Yowzer," he said. "Maybe a five percent error factor, but I'd say this puts us in the championship round."

"Can you get rid of the sunglasses?"

"Coming up. Presto. No sunglasses. Yowzer, yowzer, yowzer. Let's do the comparative math now."

"Doesn't matter," Hyde said. "That's Eden Waring." He looked at his watch. Six minutes to go. "Return to tracking mode. We've got her."

When he stretched in his seat and glanced back over his shoulder he saw that Geoff was wide awake and staring at him as if there were a terrible pressure behind his eyes.

As if he knew something that even now he wasn't willing to tell.

MOBY BAY · MAY 29 · 5:01 P.M. PDT

Trust me," Bertie Nkambe, her face filled with wonder and dismay, said to Tom Sherard. "Moby Bay isn't real. None of it. Look at Warhol, he knows it too. *Mbeya sana*. He doesn't like this place."

The injured cat had opened his eyes, looking somewhat dopey from the antibiotic and a painkiller; but Warhol's ears were on alert and he was trying to stand up in Bertie's lap. She petted him, but in spite of the sedation he refused to be still. "Good boy, good boy," Bertie soothed in a nursing croon.

They were driving slowly down Main Street with the ocean in full view, immense but tranquil in quilted gold at the horizon. Main Street was four blocks long. All of the business establishments were on the east side of the street, two- and three-story buildings of cypress and redwood clapboard or dark ivied brick. Every business displayed patriotic bunting or Old Glory, large flags flapping in a good breeze. Old-growth oaks in a strip of parkland lined the ocean side of the bluff. A red-and-gray-frame city hall and volunteer fire department anchored one end of Main Street, and a squat stone lighthouse, scrubbed white and pitted by a century and a half of rugged storm blast, stood at the other end on a promontory surrounded by gardens, sunlit clouds of fuchsia, and flowering shrubs.

"Not real? Moby Bay is on the map, Bertie, that's how we found it. And the town is in the guidebook. 'One of northern California's oldest and loveliest coastal villages, founded in 1847' if I'm quoting correctly."

"Is that all?" Bertie commented, looking around, her mouth slightly ajar. "Maybe the town is only a hundred and fifty years old, but the site is older, *way* older. Five thousand, ten thousand years, I couldn't say. I don't know how long they've been living here."

"Who? Obviously no one is around right now. Town is locked up tight. Sunday afternoon." Bertie only shook her head, perplexed, biting her underlip in agitation. Something welling up in her. "Or did you imply that the people who live here aren't real either? Then what use would they have for a volunteer fire department, a funeral home? What do they lunch on at the Gray Whale pub?"

She shrugged off his attempt at humor. "They're real enough, I'm sure. Probably too real to deal with sometimes. That happens when the Fallen of Terra and Malterra establish a neutral zone to resolve their differences. Neutral, but not serene. Funeral home? There are no immortals. Both the Fallen and the gods-elect have finite life spans. Their lives are much longer than ours . . . of course."

Sherard could see the pulse in her throat. It was coming. One of the rare doom moods, a dark rapture. A Seeing. Bertie flinched slightly, staring straight ahead, holding Warhol close. She suddenly pressed back into the leather seat, eyelids tripping, eyes drifting up in her head.

"Bertie!"

She had begun to tremble. Sherard touched her; Warhol lifted his head and snarled possessively. Bertie was cold to his touch, unresponsive. Sherard glared at the cat and said in a soft tone, "Bertie? I wish you wouldn't do this." *As if she has a choice,* he thought. "Where are you, Bertie?"

A windy sigh came from her throat. He wanted to do something for her but knew he was helpless. When the seizure, or psychic trance, or whatever name was applicable to the spells that came over Bertie had run its course, she would be none the worse for the experience. Sometimes, if an ordeal was involved, she would wet herself. He couldn't bear to witness her distress, although this time, compared to others, it seemed mild.

He parked near the lighthouse, left the engine running and Bertie to her visions, pausing only to touch the tips of three fingers to his mouth and press the kiss gently onto Bertie's lips. She was still sighing, but the muscles of her arms and shoulders appeared loose. Warhol, hunched in her lap, spat at him again but was too weak to get his tail up.

He walked up a path to the base of the lighthouse, glancing back at the dark blue Expedition, Bertie unseeable behind the tinted windows, and at the closed silent town. He felt an eerie prickling across his shoulders. There had been a shift in the tone of the balmy afternoon. The breeze had strengthened to gusts with a suggestive nip to them and was blowing southwest across the headland. No clouds out there on the rim of the earth, but bad weather was brewing along the Coast Range, towers of cloud illuminated by stormlight.

Nearby someone began to play an accordion. Sherard was jolted from his thoughts. He circled the lighthouse and saw an old woman on a park bench. She stopped in midtune and beamed at him.

"Hello!"

"Hello," Tom said. It was a definite relief to see someone, after Bertie's assertions and current behavior. "I was beginning to think no one was at home."

"Oh, we shutter early, at one P.M., on Sundays before a holiday. Tomorrow will be exhausting, you can bet, *mobs* of tourists. So we do our own celebrating a day early. Everyone else is at the barbecue. But one of us always stays in town till sundown, when Moby Bay becomes officially closed. We had a motorcycle gang visit once, and there are occasional vandals, even though Moby Bay is hard to find. It's not too lonely, being the closer, and I have my accordion."

"So this is a real place," Tom said, with a smile that felt a little odd on his face.

"Certainly! Who informed you otherwise?" She put her accordion on the bench beside her and looked keenly at him, then smiled a merry smile. "Oh, I see. It's that lovely young woman you're traveling with. So she's prescient, is she? Well, well."

Sherard looked over his shoulder. He couldn't see the Expedition where he had parked it, and seated, there was no way the woman could have seen it either. He looked back at her, curiosity in his face.

"I'm Wardella. Wardella Tinch."

"Tom Sherard."

"So pleased to make your acquaintance, Tom. What part of England do you hail from?"

"East Africa. I've spent very little time in England, actually. How did you know there was someone with me?"

Wardella rummaged in a crocheted bag at her feet and pulled out a pair of binoculars. "From up here I command all of the road into town. I saw your splendid SUV coming a mile away. I thought, no, we're closed, turn them away. Then something came over me and I realized you should be allowed to come this far."

"That may have been a mistake," Bertie said from behind Sherard, and he heard the racking of the pump on the Benelli M3 tactical shotgun, one of three guns he had borrowed from a former client of his father's who lived in San Francisco. She walked by Sherard without a glance, the stock of the shotgun going to her shoulder. He had a glimpse of her eyes, which looked a little feverish. The Benelli was aimed at Wardella Tinch, whose face may have turned a half shade redder than it was when Sherard first saw her. But she never stopped smiling.

"There you are," she said. "Alberta, isn't it? That was my mother's sister's name, I've always liked it as well as my own. I'm Wardella, by the way."

"Am I going to have to shoot you, Wardella?" Bertie said coolly.

"Oh, no, I don't think that will be necessary at all."

"Then don't try shifting on me."

"I couldn't. I mean, I'm not one of *those*."

"We can always find out the hard way."

Staring at her with that amiable smile, Wardella said, "I get that you are very advanced."

"Yes."

"And it's obvious what—I should say *who*—you are here for."

"That's right."

"I can't help you. Once I brought her to Moby Bay, to a safe harbor, our relationship ended."

"What's safe about this place?" Bertie asked, still looking down the black twenty-inch barrel of the shotgun at Wardella.

"Bertie, what are you—"

"Not now, Tom. You have to let me handle this."

"I'm sorry for all the trouble you're going to," Wardella said. "But we intend to keep the Avatar right here in Moby Bay. Whatever you may think of *us*, we're better than the alternative that Eden faces."

"Where is she now?" Bertie asked, scowling.

"At the barbecue, with her new friend and protectress Chaunccy Mc-Lain, whom she met last night." Wardella turned and gestured to the north rim of Moby Bay, less than a mile away, and turned back to them. She said to Bertie, "Aren't you tired of pointing that shotgun at me?"

"No. Did you lie to keep Eden here?"

"I should think you'd be better informed. I'm not permitted to lie."

"But you went into her mind and then you deceived her."

Wardella drew back slightly and contemplated the allegation.

"How would you know about that?"

"I know Eden's Good Lady. I know who she really is."

"Oh." Wardella nodded respectfully. "Well, you *are* exceptional. As for my little—deception, I have the option to, um, *pose,* should the occasion warrant it. Eden needed to be separated, ever so gently, from the world in which she was raised, so that she could be prepared for the world as it really is. Everything is being done for her well-being and eventual better-ment. We all know, don't we, that she no longer has a place in *your* world. I scryed her fate the moment I saw her face on the television news. She was to be hunted down like a poor helpless fawn, then destroyed by Mordaunt's Malterrans. Needless to say, Eden represents an enormous threat to the hold they've managed to secure on this planet."

Sherard said impatiently, "I've heard quite enough. Bertie, time to get Eden away from here."

"I'm afraid I can't allow that," Wardella said. "Now, it really is closing time. For both of you."

Wardella shifted her gaze to Sherard as Bertie cried out, "Tom! Look away!"

She wasn't in time. Sherard suddenly found himself blinking in full exhaust-hazy daylight on a New York street, the brazen popping of an automatic weapon lingering in his head with the blare of traffic and, dread-fully, screams. He stared at the body of Gillian Bellaver, flung down like a cramped dancer. Fifteen, twenty feet away. Bloodied hands coming away from her body.

"Tom! Help! Come to me, I'm hurt!"

He had not been fired upon. His legs were okay. This time he would get there. Gilly would be saved.

An upwelling of pure joy erased any sense of caution. Her death, then, had been a cruel dream. In moments he would lift Gillian in his arms. She would no longer lie there in a tide of sidewalk blood with that dead gone stare.

Gillian.

The New York street, the punchwork bullet holes in a liquid shop win-dow reflecting that stalled moment of crowd terror, the levels of toned glass and pure burning light falling from high blue; the hubbub ceased in his head, all sensation faded in favor of the light in his wife's eyes as he went to her. He heard a voice, a cry for him to *Stop—don't touch her!* but it was too distant to be reckoned with. All he cared about was embracing his wife, finding his life again in her healthy pulse.

Gillllliannnn!

Sherard was yanked backward by the collar of his bush jacket. His bad leg caved; he sprawled in pain as Bertie fired the Benelli much too close to his ear, stepped around him racking the pump again, and finished scattering

Wardella Tinch's head all over the park bench and the wildflowers that flourished behind the bench.

"Good God!"

Bertie turned to him, lowering the shotgun. Her face was congested with loathing, her breast heaved. She couldn't keep her gorge down and went to her knees vomiting as she flung the Benelli aside.

"Why? Why did you shoot her?"

"Tom. Get me . . . some water. That fountain over there."

"Do you realize what you've *done*?"

"Yes." She heaved again. "Blew the shit . . . out of a little old lady. She was in your *mind*, Tom. Don't you know what she was up to? Once you touched her she would have eaten your brain for a snack before she toddled off to their tribal barbecue. Take a look in all that . . . mess if you have the stomach for it. Tell me what you see. But don't get too close. And don't touch anything, some of it is still alive."

He got the water first, soaking a handkerchief and taking it to her. Bertie lay back on clean grass, eyes opening and closing, while he bathed her overheated face.

"This is major trouble for us, Bertie, I don't care what your motive was."

"Not trouble like you think. It *is* a social error to kill one of them in their own habitat. The others will come after you."

"Who? What others?"

"Just go and look, Tom. At what's left of Wardella Tinch. Then we need to get moving. I'll be okay. Let me rest a minute longer."

He stared at Bertie for a few moments, feeling both awe and fear. She smiled as if his expression had cut her to the quick. Then he approached the park bench.

Fortunately the wind was at his back. Bertie had been a wonderful shot since her childhood. What remained of Wardella's head after a hurricane handful of double-aught buckshot passed through could have been collected with a large damp sponge. But, incredibly, she seemed to be breathing. Beneath a peasant blouse her blood-soaked bosom moved, as if something inside the material was trying to fight its way out.

The cotton began to tear. Sherard saw teeth, heard a snarl, then a snout and a small striped head ripped free, turning bloody as it continued to fight the drenched clinging cloth. Then there were two heads where breasts should have been, dark noses for nipples. Doglike heads dripping heartsblood, bodiless, sharp angular eyes smarting from hatred of him.

"Now are you sorry?" he heard Bertie say. "Those things, in their world, are *fisi*." She used the Swahili word for hyena. "Worse, I think."

Sherard backed off gagging. Bertie sat up suddenly on the grass. She pointed at the sky, where the lowering sun had tinted a sprawl of thundercloud the deep wine shade of a terrifying birthmark.

"Tom!"

He saw them. About two klicks away and high, twin helicopters resembling the gunship that had risen like a ghost outside Danny Cheng's windows the night before. These helicopters also might have been silenced; no sound came to their ears on the wind. But they were larger, big enough to carry eight or ten men, assault forces perhaps. And they were coming at astonishing speed right to Moby Bay.

When Sherard looked away from the sky Moby Bay, the town, wasn't there anymore. He and Bertie were standing on a rocky promontory with the wind hissing through gaunt trees; gulls soared above the long waves. The lighthouse was gone. Wardella Tinch and her breastwork of sharp-toothed creatures had vanished too. The tough wind-shaped oak trees along the bluff remained, but there were no homely buildings with big flags flourishing in the stiffened wind and nothing was on the road but his rented Ford Expedition.

Bertie had picked up the shotgun and was tugging at his hand. "Tom, come on!"

It occurred to Sherard as they ran that he should load the other major weapon he had brought along, an old but well-cared-for Holland and Holland .50 caliber, like the rifle that his father, one of the last of the elephant hunters, had willed to him in the early sixties.

One of his early memories was the sight of an elephant's skull in his father's study at Shungwaya. The skull had been halved with a two-handed bandsaw to reveal nature's cunning honeycomb of bone that protected a brain the size of a bread loaf. The skull astonishingly light for its size— even at the age of six he could lift it—but strong enough to support tusks weighing up to 150 pounds each.

The same principle of cellular construction, Sherard knew, had been adapted for use in modern aircraft design where the bearing of weight was of critical importance.

Each .50 caliber cartridge for the twin barrels of the H and H, 477 grains of powder, generated a full two tons of impact from each long barrel. There wasn't a more powerful rifle to be found anywhere.

And after the events at Danny Cheng's Russian Hill house, Sherard was curious to discover which might be the supreme challenge to a hunter: a bull elephant capable of charging at thirty miles an hour through thornbush that would rip a man apart, or another damned helicopter up to no good.

———

Hungry?" Chauncey McLain asked Eden.

"I don't think I could eat anything."

They had walked back to the house and the guests who were lining up to serve themselves from steaming platters of ribs and a dozen side dishes. The big screen of the projection TV on the patio held the image of Rona Harvester and the legend *Live from the White House*. The First Lady was seated on a sofa in the Blue Room, her head still bandaged, but the bandage was smaller. From her pleasant expression Eden assumed it wasn't bad news that she had for the country.

The two young women paused to watch.

"What's this about?" Chauncey asked one of her relatives. It was hard to hear because of all the backyard chatter around them.

"The President's going back to work."

"Why aren't they together then? Where is he?"

"On his way to the White House from Camp David."

"It's another one of Rona's pep talks," someone else said.

"Oh, you leave her alone, Jim. She's been through such an ordeal."

"I don't know why she doesn't wear a flesh-colored patch instead of that bandage," Eden commented.

"I was thinking the same thing," Chauncey said with a hint of disdain. "You don't have to beg for my sympathy. If I want you to have it, I'll gladly give it to you."

" 'She has the eyes of a door-to-door Bible salesman. But they're deluxe Bibles.' Betts used to say that. She's—Betts is very sharp about people."

Chauncey held Eden's hand. "Tomorrow we'll go to see her. Promise."

The wind was up and Eden felt chilled. Some paper plates and napkins were blowing around. Chauncey shuddered and Eden put an arm around her.

As she did so, she thought she heard Geoff McTyer.

Eden can't stop them love of God run get away!

"Sweater time," Chauncey said, smiling. "Let's go inside." She raised a hand to brush strands of blond hair back from her eyes. "What's wrong?" Chauncey asked as Eden's gaze jumped from Chauncey's face to the sky. Seeing the sniper's bullet coming from two thousand feet away, seeing it whole as if it was momentarily stopped in her mind; but the voice—yes, Geoff's voice—and the flash of warning didn't give her time to act. She could only witness the rest of it, seeing the sharp-nosed bullet rip through Chauncey's upraised hand and head, her bones no defense against it, flesh nothing before such speed and power, soft as green banana; Eden hearing the implosion of the TV screen behind them, glass was nothing either as the bullet sped on through it and through the redwood wall behind the set, finally shattering the ankle bones of a seven-year-old girl standing on tiptoe to place deviled eggs on a tray in the McLains' kitchen.

Chauncey's falling weight jerked Eden's arm taut as she slumped to the floor of the patio. Bone fragments gleamed like fish scale in the welling-out of blood and cerebrospinal fluid near the middle of the dead girl's forehead. Eden's head moved downward with the slumping of Chauncey's body, which was galvanized by the shock wave that blew out her heart valves. The second shot from the sniper's rifle missed Eden, instead flattening one of Wardella Tinch's poker-night friends who was turning to stare at the downed girl.

As Eden leaned over Chauncey and began to spiral into shock, hopelessly trying to wipe clean her friend's forehead with the edge of her palm, Chauncey's open eyes, which had been fixed and expressionless, suddenly came to life and focused on Eden. Her small breasts swelled as she took a breath. The trembling ceased. Chauncey reached up and touched the hole in her forehead, whistled softly.

"Jeez, that'll give you a headache," she said, and smiled sympathetically at Eden. "They're after *you*, aren't they?"

Mia McLain came out of the kitchen carrying the child with the shattered ankle. The girl was eating a cookie, and except for a couple of tears on her cheeks, she seemed unconcerned about the injury.

"Melanie got a boo-boo," Mia said. She looked at her daughter. "You should see yourself! Can't you get up?"

"Yes, Ma, just give me a sec. I mean it's not the most fun thing that's ever happened to me." She reached out to Eden, who drew back with a sharp intake of breath, as if the kindly gesture had scorched her skin. Behind her the elderly gent who had been hit in the breastbone by the rifleman's second shot was getting to his feet, wheezing and laughing. Eden whipped her head around at the sound of his laughter, whipped it back to Chauncey. Eden's mouth was open as if her jaws had locked.

Some of the cookout guests were casually watching the helicopters that hovered in the sky north of them. Others had gathered around Eden and Chauncey, forming a human barrier between Eden and the sniper.

"Whoever he is, he can shoot," Wick McLain said ruefully. "Hell, I hope this doesn't spoil the party for everyone."

All within earshot assured Wick that they were having a great time.

Chauncey sat up, stretched. Someone handed her a napkin to mop her forehead. She tried to touch Eden again. Eden scrambled back on all fours. The little girl in Mia's arms laughed, spitting cookie crumbs.

"She's *scared*."

"Looks like they're comin' in," one of the chopper watchers observed. "Wonder how many of them there'll be?"

"Does it matter?" The elderly man who had been drilled through the breastbone chuckled as he poked a finger into the hole in his necktie. "Those ribs'll keep, won't they, Wick?"

"But if there's enough of *them*," Wick said, jerking a thumb in the direction of the helicopters, "nobody's gonna have any appetite left."

Mia gave him a stern look and made a side motion of her head in Eden's direction. Eden was still crouched on the patio floor, eyes jerking around in her head; Eden was already far gone into a limbo of silent hysteria.

"Poor thing," someone said.

"Part of her education. But she doesn't need to see this," Chauncey said, getting to her feet. "Unless she wants to. I can tell she doesn't. Isn't that right, Eden? Better go in the house for a little while. Lie down. You're part of us now. Nobody's going to bother you, ever again. Promise, kiddie."

Take us down! Take us down now!" Robert Hyde shouted to the pilot of Alpha helo.

The chopper descended to the headland in tactical attitude, a gut-clenching ride.

"They're taking her into the house!" an observer on Bravo helicopter reported.

"Get over there, over there, sit on the house! Nobody else goes in or out! There are children down there! Use flash bangs, tasers, and pepper spray where necessary! We already have a drag coefficient of two!"

"Sir—" the sniper in Alpha helo said, "sir, I know I couldn't have missed, but the other girl, the one I hit in the head, I don't believe this—she's up on her feet!"

"Drag coefficient of one," Hyde corrected with a tight smile. "And shut the fuck up."

Geoff said in a voice that only a couple of the men and women aboard either helicopter heard on their headsets, "Don't go down there. I'm warning you, *don't go.*"

He had one hand cuffed to the frame beneath the seat he was in. For several minutes he had not taken his eyes off his father.

As Alpha helo circled and went in a small crowd of cookout guests was walking toward the anticipated LZ not far from the edge of the bluff. Lightning flashed in the east. They were not a welcoming committee. None of them were smiling. The tall figure of Wick McLain was out front, like a patriarch, his full handlebar mustaches luffing in the wind.

"Does anyone see weapons! Are they in resistance mode?"

"Negative, negative!"

"For the love of God," Geoff said miserably, and closed his eyes at the jolt of the hard landing.

Six FBI agents from the San Francisco SWAT team, in full protective gear, exited Alpha helicopter twenty yards from the deliberately oncoming men, women, and teenage children. The agents wore no identification. Robert Hyde was mindful of the static he knew he was going to hear from the Justice Department. Until he set the AG straight about the importance of this mission.

"We're here for Eden Waring!" the team leader used a bullhorn, although the helicopter was making very little noise; standing directly beneath the rotors it would have been possible to have a whispered conversation.

Wick McLain, still in the lead, said in a reasonable voice, "You are on private property. It also happens to be sacred ground. You now have the chance to return to your helicopter and leave without further incident."

The agents fanned out in a semicircle and began to advance.

"Step aside, please!" roared the bullhorn. "We only want Eden Waring! We know she is in the house! Bring her out! No one will be hurt if you cooperate."

Wick McLain turned to the others, one of whom was his son Roald, and said in a tone of quiet amazement, "Now they tell us they don't want to hurt anyone! What say you?"

They shook their heads in unison. There were a couple of low-pitched ominous growls. Wick gestured for restraint, smiled, and turned to his son, who looked back at him eagerly.

"Me first?"

Wick considered the precocious boy's request, fingered his extravagant handlebars. The others murmured their approval.

"*Eat,*" his father said to Roald.

Fierce yelpings, shrieks of greed, and liquid moans of pleasure. A noise like the dry hiss of 'hoppers in a plague year. Screams from the SWATsters outside the helicopter as flash bangs, tasers, and jets of pepper spray failed to protect them from an onslaught they were totally unprepared for, from horrors that had no reference to anything they'd ever seen. Their minds broke before their bodies were sundered.

Twisting in his seat, Geoff McTyer shouted to the pilot, "Get us out of here!"

His father was calling for Bravo chopper, for firepower and ground reinforcements.

"No!" Geoff said. "You damn fool, we'll all be killed! Don't go near them! Fall back!"

The five men remaining in the helicopter saw nearly unidentifiable lumps of human beings flying from the midst of the carnivores' picnic to pelt the fuselage and windows. Something hurtled through the open doorway and lay twitching on the deck. It had the head of a man with his lower jaw and an ear neatly removed. The tongue stood out from the depths of the throat like a dog's pink erection. The sniper who had taken two shots at Eden Waring attempted to slam the door shut. Something dark and shrill came at him, gliding beneath the helicopter blades. He was snatched from the doorway by the six-inch talons of a young but beautiful gryphon.

The feathered goddess, another of the wonders in this whirligig of the unearthly, had a blemish on her forehead, puckered like the navel of an orange. Her long blond hair flowed in flight between the great spread of wings. She gripped the sniper by his shoulders, sucked out his eyes, then flung him to the rocks at the edge of the sea and turned toward the house, soaring with a cry of transcendence past Bravo helicopter. The sky was low and brawling, suffused with lightning.

Chauncey's father, doomsday in his eyes and hands outflung as carnage stained the ground around him, cried out, "*Condemned* are the intruders and despoilers of our peaceful community!"

A fusillade of tracers from the .50 millimeter cannon aboard Bravo lit Wick McLain up, but he absorbed twenty rounds and stayed on his feet. He raised his hands again. A dust devil swirled in front of him, turned dark and grew with tornadic force. Bolts of electricity illuminated the faces of terrified men in Bravo.

Alpha helicopter began to lift off but was pulled back to the ground by gleeful youths with the strength and appearance of yearling grizzlies.

"Cut me loose!" Geoff McTyer pleaded with his father as the giant chopper strained and trembled, the rotors a smoky blur while the pilot tried to get them airborne.

The largest of the were-bears leaped straight up, almost ten feet from the ground, and into the helicopter through the doorway. It landed light on its toes and looked around with an intimidating roar, lunged and removed the pilot's helmeted head with a single blow, sending it like a cannonball through the wind screen. The helo dropped straight down. Geoff's face smashed into the pilot's seat. Two front teeth snapped in half. The were-bear turned to Geoff, who was crouched behind the pilot's seat with blood on his mouth. Scintillant fur stood out in a ruff around the bear's head. It drew back a paw for another swipe. Geoff closed his eyes, dropping his head wearily. What a hell of a day.

But the decapitating blow he expected didn't come.

"Yo. What's this?"

Geoff looked up again.

"What? Did you—?"

The were-bear said in a teenager's voice, breaking at every third or fourth word, "Why are you handcuffed to the seat? You one of them or not? What's your name?"

"Geoff. I'm . . . no. I used to be. FBI, I mean. None of this is my fault! I didn't want them to come. I told them not to. What in God's name *are* you?"

"*His* name? God's forgotten about us," the bear said, voice slipping again, falsetto to basso. It reached down, grasped the cuff that held Geoff to the seat, and broke it open with an easy twist.

"Where's Eden?" Geoff asked, his own voice shrill.

The were-bear looked cautiously down its long nose at him.

Behind them Robert Hyde came off the deck where he had been lying stunned since the helo's hard landing and shot the beast five times in the face and head. It fell backward out of the chopper. Hyde lunged after it and slammed the door shut.

There was a stunning flash in the sky as Bravo helicopter was destroyed by a bolt from the twister. Father and son flinched as their copter was buffeted by the shock wave and bombarded with debris. Glass that could not be armored because of weight considerations was chipped and spider-webbed.

"CAN YOU FLY THIS?" Hyde demanded.

"I don't know! I've only logged ten hours in our police helicopter! This thing is like the space shuttle!"

"Fly it, or we'll die here! Get us off the deck!"

Geoff unsnapped the harness of the headless pilot and wrestled the body out of the left-hand seat.

"Blood," he moaned. "So much blood!"

"Don't quit on me AGAIN!"

"Shut up, God damn you! My hands. Slippery." The odor of gore all over the seat turned him away, gagging.

"GO!"

His father was pointing the Glock at him, as if the threat had any substance. Geoff made no move to assume the controls. "Not without Eden!"

"We'll figure that out later. Do what I tell you!"

"You son of a bitch," Geoff said, and with his left hand raising the collective he sent the madly vibrating, smoky helicopter flapping out over blue water like another panicked gull, leaving storm and slaughter and the *noli me tangere* of Moby Bay behind.

"Eden, get up! Come on, snap out of it, we're getting you out of here!" Eden lifted clouded eyes. She was crouched in a darkened corner of Chauncey's bedroom. Her mouth fumbled with the effort of producing speech.

"Who . . .'re you?"

"I'm Bertie. The big guy in the doorway is Tom." Subvocally she added, *We're friends. You can trust us.* But Eden held back.

"The screams. *Oh.* What's happening?"

"A lot of bad stuff. You don't want to see it. I think you've seen enough already." Bertie, holding Eden up, glanced at Tom.

"We're okay," he said. "No telling for how long. Let's move."

"Where are you taking me?"

"To see your mother."

"Betts?" Eden said, her eyes wandering in confusion. But Bertie, who was bigger and much stronger at this point, succeeded in half carrying her toward the front of the house.

"Your real mother."

"You're lying. Where's Chauncey? I saw Chauncey get shot! Then she— Huh. She just . . . got up, like it didn't happen. But it *did* happen!"

"Sounds like a neat trick. Tell us about it later. Tom?"

There was an explosion that shook the house, the black sky flushing orange. Debris peppered the roof. Sherard, holding the Holland and Holland rifle in one hand, pushed the screen door open and glanced outside. Thick oily smoke rolled past the house from the ocean side.

"One of the helicopters," Sherard said. "Let's get our girl to the SUV."

"I don't want to go!" Eden wailed.

"She's getting windy again." Bertie smiled gently at Eden. "You'll like us better when you get to know us." She let go of Eden with her right hand, propped her chin up gently with the left, and knocked her cold with a solid uppercut.

Sherard tossed his rifle to Bertie and gathered Eden up, throwing her over one shoulder, wincing as his game leg shuddered.

"Can you make it?" Bertie asked anxiously.

"What do you think I am, obsolete? And where the devil did you learn the haymaker?"

"Muhammad Ali taught my brother, and Kieti showed me. He never could knock me out when we traded punches, but I floored *him* twice."

"Follow me and shoot anything that looks the least bit unfriendly."

"You mean like *that*?" Bertie said as the gryphon with Chauncey's small neat head rose from concealment behind the Ford Expedition, unfurling a seven-foot spread of wings in the stifling murk around them.

"An excellent example. What is it?"

"Put her down," Chauncey said. "And I'll let you live."

"Body of a lion, wings of an eagle, the face of an angel," Bertie said admiringly. "A one-woman menagerie. I forgot to mention, you smell worse than jackal shit." Bertie shouldered the rifle and said to Tom, "Where do I shoot this whatcha-call-it?"

"I've changed my mind about letting you live," Chauncey said, and launched herself at Bertie with outflung claws.

Bertie fired the first of two rounds from the double-barreled hunting rifle, breaking a wing. The gryphon's flight plan was canceled and it smashed facedown into a flowerbed ten feet from where Bertie was standing. Glared at Bertie through a loose garland of uprooted red and white petunias.

"Oh, you bitch," Chauncey said, trying to move the smashed wing, digging up more of the garden with her lion's claws as she crept forward, gathering herself for a leap. "But you only have one bullet left."

"Eat it," Bertie said, firing again. The heavy bullet tore through Chauncey's small neat mouth and exited in a sprayed mash of hindbrain. The gryphon collapsed.

"Let's go!"

Sherard, limping badly, carried Eden the rest of the way to the SUV. Bertie sprinted past him, got in behind the wheel. The engine was running. As soon as Sherard had Eden tucked inside they took off.

"Nice shooting," he commended her when he'd caught his breath. "Too bad we can't have it mounted, a gryphon would make a nice conversation piece at the old homestead." His hands were shaking. He looked back once, at the pall of smoke, and had a glimpse of creatures he couldn't identify gathering around the fallen gryphon. Lightning flashed over the bay as they drove around it. Rain beat down on the SUV. It was a dirt road, fast turning slippery, but they were in four-wheel drive.

"Will they come after us?" he asked Bertie.

"They probably stick close to home. We can only hope. What next?" Bertie asked, intent on her driving.

"Just put Moby Bay behind us. Do you know who or what they were?"

"Shape-shifters. Other than that, I'd have to get hold of one and delve into their genealogy. I'm not that interested. Tell me something. Is it normal to feel this horny after you've been in a bad scrape?"

Sherard laughed. "Is there any thought you're not willing to express?"

"To you, no."

"It's quite normal. First the adrenaline of fear, then the marvelous realization you haven't been killed. Then you want a smoke and a drink and above all you're driven by the survival instinct to—"

"Propagate the species. *Yes.*"

"We're three now," Sherard reminded her.

"But Tom. I've waxed an old lady and a gryphon already today, my adrenaline is spouting through my ears, and—" she concluded in a querulous lisping voice, "Bertie wanth to get *laid.*"

"We aren't out of this yet. Our priority is to locate a decent airport, lease a jet."

"Yes, sir." Bertie kept her eyes on the narrow empty road in the booming thunderstorm, sniffed a couple of times. Tears drained from her wide-open eyes. "I was just being smart-ass. Trying to keep my mind off . . . certain things. Actually I'm exhausted and ready to scream."

"I know."

"And you keep making fists."

"I know."

"You shouldn't have given up tobacco. I don't really care, as long as you don't smoke in our house once . . . we're . . . married." She cried harder, loosing big gusty sobs in response to thunder above them and thunder in her heart. "If we live that long."

"We'll be okay. Maybe I should drive."

"I'm doing just fine, damn it!"

In the seat behind them Eden groaned softly, awakened by the rocking of the SUV on the twisty, unpaved road.

The mobile phone rang.

Sherard and Bertie glanced at each other. She wiped at one soggy eye, shuddered, and almost drove off the road.

"Shit!"

The phone continued to ring. Sherard rubbed his jaw, then shrugged and answered cryptically. He listened for a few moments.

"Yes. I know your voice. Yes. I understand." He glanced back at Eden. "We've bagged our limit on the license, and now we're on our way." Bertie looked worriedly at him. Sherard shook his head slightly, continued to listen. "I see. Very well. I'll want to confirm this, of course. Yes, there's a number I can call. Once I have verification you may expect us later tonight."

He put the digital phone back in its slot on the dashboard.

"Who was that?" Bertie asked.

"Senate Majority Leader Buck Hannafin. Forget about the airport. Looks as if we're staying in California. We'll head south, sticking to back roads for a while. When it's safe to do so we should stop. I have to find a pay phone to call Katharine."

WASHINGTON, D.C. • MAY 28 • 10:42 P.M. EDT

Interesting news," Rona Harvester said over the secure phone in her executive mansion study, which was decorated with Plains Indian artifacts and a painting of Rona mounted on the Appaloosa gelding Clint had given her for their fifth wedding anniversary. She had just returned from the Watergate hotel and hadn't kicked her shoes off yet. She had a fiery corn between two toes of her left foot. It had been giving her pure misery for the last hour and a half. "But what can we do with it?" she persisted.

"Probably nothing yet," Victor Wilding said cautiously.

"You gave me the impression we had Hyde by the balls."

"Only if some Air Force property was jeopardized today. Hyde committed serious breaches of procedure by grabbing those Conan stealth helos off their pads at Travis. They haven't been certified for active duty by the Pentagon. You know what those fucking helicopters cost; they'll be howling at High Command. But AG's on her third or fourth honeymoon with Hyde since he covered her ass before Judiciary on the Alfiero matter."

"Then it would be Clint's call, wouldn't it? I mean, of course, *my* call. And you know how I love squeezing big-time *cojones.*"

"Careful, Rona. I'd like to be rid of him too, but he holds a lot of chits in this town. The Bureau's black files are as deep as our own."

Rona changed the subject but didn't abandon it. "So we know from the intercepted NSA satellite photos that Eden Waring is definitely in Moby Bay, California."

"Is, or was just a few hours ago. Positive ID. The Conans were last heard from en route to Moby Bay. They're long overdue back at Travis. According to the senior crew chief of the stealth wing, there were no provisions for a midflight refueling. The choppers would have been at bingo fuel no later than 1930 hours PDT. For the last couple of hours there's been a violent spring storm thrashing around that neck of the woods. No further coverage from the satellite has been received."

"What are the possibilities?"

"The helos are on the deck somewhere, sitting out the blow. Or else they got to Moby Bay, picked up the girl, made a run for it down the coast. An effective search can't be conducted before daybreak."

"I'm thinking about what happened to TRANSPAC 1850. I mean, what do we believe *really* happened?"

"According to the black box, something or someone was seriously fucking with the avionics. It seemed almost deliberate."

"Kelane Cheng. Her brain waves against a mere machine. No contest. What if Eden Waring has the power of Kelane? Aren't there psychics who can make it rain just by staring at some clouds?"

He didn't reply immediately. He was drinking something.

"Yes. A standard exercise in our training program."

"If Cheng could change the course of a DC-10, maybe Eden Waring could brew up a helluva storm to meet some incoming choppers. Maybe, nothing! I *love* this girl! I've got to meet her."

"She could be dead too, by now," he said, with a yawn that she took to be resignation.

"I don't think so. We're going to find her. Victor, if Bob Hyde is dead, *c'est la guerre*. But in case he pops up again, and empty-handed, I think we should have the ceremonial sword ready for him."

"Other than todaysh—*day's*—activities, the best thing we have on Hyde is that he likes an occasional golden shower from a teenager."

"And if a couple of dead stealth pilots turn up in the wreckage of those Conans?"

Wilding didn't answer immediately. Rona heard ice cubes chinking together in a glass as he swallowed.

"Then the Joint Chiefs will drag out the old rugged cross. Not even Allen Dunbar will be able to help Bob Hyde then."

"And Clint, I think, should do a brief TV appearance accepting with great sorrow the Director's resignation. How much time will you need to prepare that? Better make it a dark suit and subdued tie deal; you know, like for a funeral."

"Twenty-four hoursh"—he cleared his throat—"*hours*, give or take." Rona didn't miss the drag in his voice, the slurring.

"You don't sound too cheerful, lover." She was going to ask him what he was drinking, thought better of it.

"Tired is all."

"Damn, I wish we could be together tonight! But I've still got rows to hoe, probably won't catch more than twenty winks with Clint next door. I have to admit, having him back so close gives me the skin crawls. As if I'm about to be haunted."

"Not you. Nothing gets to you, Rona."

She didn't like that. Not that she felt insulted. It was the inference that *he* was down, way down, tonight. Focused on every waning heartbeat of Robin Sandza out there in Plenty Coups. Wilding himself was a young man in sound physical condition. All of his doctors agreed on that. But cases of otherwise healthy people dying from dread were documented in medical annals. No denying that Victor was, if not in a state of dread, sliding in that direction. Now what was she supposed to do? Any medication he took other than aspirin had debilitating side effects. The antidepressants unleashed extreme mania and violent paranoia, which during previous episodes had resulted in the purging of formerly trusted deputies at MORG. Right now Rona needed him stable and sane, strong in her purposes.

"Why don't you turn in, Victor? Tomorrow's a holiday, my schedule's light. We'll spend quality time together."

"Good. I'm going to read a little more, until I'm sleepy."

"What are you reading?" she asked carelessly.

"*Revelation.*"

BASKING ROCK WILDERNESS AREA, CALIFORNIA · MAY 29-30 · 6:43 P.M.-12:20 A.M. PDT

Geoff had flown sixty miles down the northern California coast from Moby Bay when problems with the Conan helo's avionics forced him down. A finger cove afforded the only level strip of beach he could locate along this wild stretch of shoreline. The shadowed beach was part sand, part rock. He underestimated the length of the combat helicopter. The shrouded tail rotor struck a large boulder just before touchdown, and the helo tipped violently to port. The body of the headless pilot, which had been draped over the right-hand cockpit seat, was flung against him. Sparks from the rotors striking the rocks showered in through the hole in the window beside him.

Geoff cut the ignition, but within a few seconds there was a haze of smoke in the cockpit. He heaved the body off him, unbuckled, and tried the radio. It didn't work. He hoped that the emergency beacon, reporting the helo's location, was operating, but much of the cockpit instrumentation was unfamiliar. A small miracle he'd made it this far.

Robert Hyde, strapped down in the cabin, was bleeding from an ear and appeared semiconscious. Geoff got him out of the helicopter, went back to look for a medical kit and survival gear.

The ocean was alight but the cove, with steep forested walls on three sides, had begun to darken. The tide was coming in. He judged from the high pile of driftwood and flotsam at the end of the cove that almost all of the beach would be underwater at high tide.

He returned with the supplies to where he'd left his father sitting with his back against a wave-polished chunk of driftwood. Robert Hyde looked up at him, although holding his head erect seemed to give him vertigo.

"Where are we?"

"I don't know, Dad."

"Are you hurt?"

"I'm okay. Broke a couple of teeth. How about you?"

"Headache. My head is . . . feels mushy on this side."

Geoff looked at him. His father's hair was matted with blood above the trickling ear. "Better not touch it. They'll find us before long. We'll get you to a hospital. That may only be a scalp wound."

"I'm going to need your help."

Geoff looked around the cove, then at the tumbling surf half a mile away.

"We can't walk out of here, Dad. Don't worry. We'll be found."

His father was shuddering. "Not what I meant. We need to . . . get our story straight. I don't think any of the others are still alive. I never knew such terrors could exist on this earth. But we didn't see them. We did *not* see those things. We were on a . . . training mission. A sudden storm separated us from Bravo copter. We turned south. Back to Travis. But we—"

"Dad."

"We cannot say what happened. Because the truth is sheer insanity. They will, uh . . . they'll lock you, they'll lock *me* away in a little room for the rest of my life. A room like my father was in." Hyde moved closer to Geoff with an expression of deep anguish and gripped him hard by the shoulder. "He just sat there. I didn't want to go to see him because, because he never said my name! *The Shadow knows.*"

"What? Dad, how are we going to account for what's in that helo I flew down here? Look, *look* at me, I've got blood everywhere. And there's a headless Air Force pilot inside! Eight other men are missing. What plausible explanation is there? That little room you're talkin' about is the gas chamber!"

"B-but we—"

Geoff touched his father's face. His skin was cold.

"It'll be dark soon. There's a thermal blanket in the medical kit. You need to stay warm. Should be plenty of driftwood above the high tide line. I'll make a fire."

"Are you t-telling me I'm finished? My career? All because of that girl?"

"Eden had nothing to do with this! It's you, *your* obsession, don't you understand? Eden could never hurt anyone. She was no threat to you. *Why?* Why couldn't we just leave her alone? Instead you send a monster like Phil Haman after her. Don't tell me about the terrors of this earth! Some of them are your doing!"

His father's eyes shifted, to something far beyond Geoff. His body stiffened, and he screamed.

"They're back! God help us!"

Geoff turned, pulling from his belt the Glock automatic he'd found on the floor of the helicopter's cabin. He turned and saw nothing except a few lenticular clouds, shadowy shapes low on the horizon. The cloud closest to the mouth of the bay had a wraithlike shape, with wings and a body and a tail. And after the horrors they'd experienced, Geoff thought he could distinguish a face in the cloud, a clawlike tentacle reaching out to them. He shifted his body, blocking his father's view, pressed him back against the barkless log.

"It's nothing. Clouds."

His father breathed through his mouth. His eyes closed momentarily.

"I'm thirsty."

Geoff gave him water from one of the 4.5-ounce packages stored with a case of MREs, then wrapped him in the blanket from a survival kit he had found aboard the helicopter.

"You'd better take it easy. I'm gonna build a fire. The temperature will start droppin' soon. No tellin' how long we might have to wait for . . . for a search team to find us."

"That's my pistol, isn't it?"

"Yeah." Geoff took the Glock from inside his belt, withdrew the magazine, and counted the remaining rounds. Eight .45 caliber cartridges. No reason to anticipate that he would need them, although probably there were some California brown bears in the neighborhood. Most likely they would show up around dawn to fish in the tidal pools.

The thought prompted a shudder as he remembered the bear-thing with the kid's voice that had leaped, so effortlessly, into the helicopter as they were lifting off from the scene of the catastrophe at Moby Bay.

What in God's name are *you?*

His *name? God's forgotten about us.*

Small foaming waves were coming farther up the spit of beach, washing across the floor of the helicopter. If there'd been an electrical fire aboard, an automatic suppression system had smothered it. Geoff moved his father to a dry ledge twenty feet wide and a few feet above the high tide line, gathered wood, and built a fire inside a ring of stones. There was no liquor in the survival kit. He made strong tea and scrambled eggs from an MRE pouch. His father drank some of the sweetened tea but wouldn't eat. Geoff choked down a high-energy bar. He was wearing a flight jacket they had given him back in Valleyheart. That and the other blanket should get him comfortably through the night, he thought, if the air temp didn't fall below forty degrees.

He gathered more wood to feed the fire. By then it was past nine o'clock and a few stars had come out above the darkening sea. Closer to shore the sky was hazy. His father needed to relieve himself but couldn't stand without help. He complained of pain in his kidneys. With the flashlight Geoff looked for blood in the fitful stream of urine. It was darker than it should have been. After making his father somewhat comfortable again Geoff also examined the head wound. No further external bleeding. There was no way to tell what was going on inside his skull. Some men could absorb hard blows with no significant damage to the brain. For others survival could just be a matter of luck. His father was conscious and restless, hot but not sweating. Unresponsive when Geoff tried to talk to him.

Then Geoff lay down exhausted on the mossy ledge, using one of the survival kits for a pillow. He had a flare gun in a pocket of the flight jacket. He resolved not to close his eyes. He hoped the caffeine from the tea would keep him awake.

An hour and a half later he was awakened from uneasy sleep by his father's scream.

A moment before he had been sitting in his car with the assassin, who was wrapping gauze around his head, hiding what there was of his face. The assassin claimed the gauze made him invisible.

Now one of Geoff's feet kicked out toward the low fire and he got a cramp in his thigh. He sat up cursing and kneading the quadriceps with both hands and looked for his father, He wasn't there.

"Dad!"

Sounds of fearful weeping froze his heart, and the next thing he saw as he looked frantically around almost shattered it.

The narrow bay, filling with the tide that had nearly submerged the helicopter, was misted over. The forest rising steeply on three sides of the bay was shrouded, as if by the gauze of the assassin in Geoff's dream. The moon was directly overhead, its light giving some definition to the tall straight trees, like Christmas cutouts in black paper, through which the sea mist flowed. Here and there rocky ravines cut back into the mountains away from the creeping water. There were some huge boulders at the mouth of the largest ravine. Atop one of them, as if it were a rounded stage, stood several still figures unrelated to humanity (that much was clear in spite of the mist) and, at their feet, another figure all too human and recognizable, writhing slowly, an arm held above his head to ward off whatever violence or terror the silent watchers threatened.

Geoff reached for the Glock automatic he had put beneath his flight jacket, but it wasn't there.

His father, sobbing. Pleading.

He couldn't find the pistol. All he had was the flare gun with a single load, and a flashlight.

"Dad!"

Still hobbled by the cramp in his thigh he splashed down off the ledge into ankle-deep water and started toward the ravine, aiming the beam of his flashlight at the creatures on the rock.

"Get away from him! Leave him alone!"

Instead they changed positions, coming closer together with their backs to Geoff, blocking Geoff's view of his father. They kneeled slowly around him. Then the sobbing stopped abruptly.

Geoff slipped and fell on the slick rocks of the beach, losing his grip on the flashlight, which flickered out as it rolled away down a sloping shelf underwater. Screaming in frustration, he lunged to try to retrieve it, getting a faceful of water that stung his sore eyes.

Groping beneath the surface, he touched a bare foot and an ankle; his hand slid higher, to a slender but supple calf before he snatched it away and scrambled back, opening his smarting eyes.

Girl, blond, pretty, early twenties, standing in a slosh of seawater that came nearly to her bare knees. Standing where no one had been moments ago, hands at her side, looking calmly down at him. She had a very small face that made her eyes seem as large as the plummy eyes of children in a Keene painting.

"Oh, *shit!*"

"Scare you?"

"Where'd you come from? Fall out of the sky?" No idea why he had said that, but it made her laugh.

"Yes. But not like you did," she replied, glancing around at the swamped Conan helicopter. She turned her face back to him. She would have been pretty, but there was something wrong with her mouth; it had an ugly twist to it. And there was a mark of some kind, a round scar on her forehead that gleamed like the moon that was in and out of clouds above their heads.

As if she knew what he was staring at, she covered her mouth with one hand.

"I know. It's not pretty to look at. Can't seem to get the lips right, but I will. Takes practice. I need a mirror, but I haven't had time to just sit and work at it. Try to imagine what *you'd* look like if you'd been shot twice in the face today. Oh-oh. Sorry. That scared you, didn't it?"

Geoff's lungs felt like sacks of cement in his chest. He made strangled noises trying to breathe.

"Don't worry, bud. I wasn't implying you were going to get hurt. What happens to you from now on is your choice. I'm Chauncey. What's your name?" Behind the hand held loosely to her mouth it looked as if she were chewing.

"Geoff," he said, a winded sigh. He tried to get up. He was only in about two feet of water, but his knees had washed out. He couldn't stand. This frightened him more than her supernatural appearance.

Chauncey showed him her small mouth again. "This look any better to you?" She smiled. It was a terrible-looking smile, but he nodded. "Okay. Like I said, I'll work on it. That's the thing about suffering trauma when you're in an alter shape. I don't think I'll be able to do anything about my left foot for a while."

She lifted her leg slowly out of the water. It was as shapely as the right leg down to her ankle. But she had, instead of a petite foot, the paw of a lion, beads of water dripping from the ebony claws.

"Like walking with a bucket on my foot," she complained. Her grimace of a smile shot halfway up one cheek as if her face had suddenly become highly plastic, unmanageable. A shattered front tooth gleamed wetly in the long gap of her mouth. Chauncey felt the anomaly and with her thumb smoothed her mouth back to approximately where it belonged. But now it was too big, grotesquely wide. She softly patted her lower lip, reducing an ugly lump. "Oh, damn," she fretted, licking and patting. "But I don't want to bother you with my little problems, it's all cosmetic. We should be talking about your future. Your father has already made his decision, as you can see."

Geoff had forgotten about his father and the shadow-creatures surrounding him. But when he looked he saw that his father was alone on the boulder at the mouth of the ravine, sitting up cross-legged. His face, white by moonlight, was turned toward Geoff. Were his eyes open? Geoff was too far away to tell.

"Dad? Are you okay?" He made another attempt to get to his feet.

"Better than okay," Chauncey said. "He's recovered his honor."

Geoff tried to wade through the water, but it felt thick and heavy, dragging at his legs, holding him back. He paused, trying to catch his breath, and in those few seconds he saw his father raise the Glock automatic, muzzle first, beneath his chin. Holding it in both hands, he pulled the trigger, and the mist flushed red around him as what remained of his head pitched forward.

"Dad . . . ddddyyy!"

Chauncey's hand was on his shoulder.

"It's all right. I told you. Our honor has been satisfied, and your father has redeemed himself in the most honorable way left to him."

"No! Get away from me! You're a fuckin' freak show, all of you! You *made* him kill himself!"

"Not true. We don't have that kind of power. We can't make anyone act against his will. We can't seek revenge, or kill in cold blood."

"You did a good job of it today!"

"That's where you're wrong. We can defend ourselves on our ground, in our home place, by whatever means we find necessary. That dispensation ends at the boundaries of the home place. You're angry and you're frightened, but I can't hurt you, Geoff. All any of us can do is reason with you. Explain your choices."

"What are you talkin' about! What have you done to Eden?"

"We gave her sanctuary. Which you violated today. I don't know where Eden is. While we were . . . busy, the others took her away, by force."

"What othahs? You don't make sense. None of this. Why did he have to die?"

"Don't you know who they were?" Chauncey persisted.

"No!"

"Or where they've gone?"

"Oh, God!"

There was no sound accompanying the appearance of flames. He noticed them first reflected in Chauncey's large dark eyes. He felt the heat, then the mist of the bay was tinted orange. He looked around and saw the body of his father engulfed, Hyde still seated on the boulder like a holy immolator at an Asian protest rally. Standing well away, almost into the trees, were small groups of watchers, dark except for the vivid amber of their slanted eyes. The flames leaped and whirled. The heat was intense. The heat and the burning father, corpse though he was, made Geoff dizzy from nausea and despair.

"So you have nothing to tell me."

Geoff stared at the pyre, swallowing, weeping.

"Just leave me alone."

"You haven't heard your choices."

"There'll be search teams. They'll find us in the morning. I have to get through the night, that's all."

She nodded. "That's one choice. To be rescued."

"Yes."

"Geoff, you see the Auditors waiting over there, don't you?"

"The what?"

"If you choose rescue, then we'll go away and leave you here. All of us but one, whom the Auditors will choose from their number to be your companion for the rest of your life. Give yourself a few moments now, look the Auditors over, and try to imagine what that life will be like. You'll be constantly watched, by eyes that never blink. Never close. The Auditor won't speak to you. He'll have nothing to say. He will only watch, and wait."

"Wait for what?"

"For you to go balls-up, dungeon-style paddycrackers. Forty-eight hours to fracture time is about average, I'm told. That's when you'll begin to talk to your Auditor. Talk, talk, talk. Plead, moan, and whimper for him to forgive you. But forgiveness is the Pardoner's game. He's only an Auditor. *Your* Auditor, until the end of your days."

Geoff ran his tongue over his broken front teeth. His lips twitched into a frozen position, a kind of snarl.

"Or—" Chauncey had been working on her smile. She almost got it right this time. "You can go back to Moby Bay, and live there. A few mortals—Wardella's husband Mychal was one of them—made that choice, and many of them adjusted nicely in time. You will be . . . tolerated, and we're not so hard to take, really, in our everyday appearances. You might even marry one of us. It's a simple, undemanding life in Moby Bay, except for occasional disturbances like today's. There are always problems with the Bad Souls, the Fallen of Malterra. Those who have no hope of God's forgiveness. I'm telling you, it makes them *mean*."

Geoff was trembling. He couldn't look at Chauncey any longer. He looked instead at the flames, at the diminished wisping remains of his father.

"The third choice, of course, is the best one," Chauncey said. "It satisfies—"

"Your honor? What sort of honor do monsters have?"

"There you go, confusing appearance with evil. Not all of the Fallen were evil. The Bad Souls are permanently locked into human form. All except Mordaunt, who is *Deus inversus,* the Darkness of God. All of you mortals can consider yourself lucky that this is so. Gives you a fighting chance, at least, although evil has had the edge for the last hundred millennia. Maybe because it's never boring. Why *we* are shifters is part of the

whole Redemption package. Unlike the Malterrans, eventually we may return to a state of Grace. First we do our lessons. In order to understand
the nature of all creatures that swim, fly, walk, or crawl, we assume their
identities." Her smile was okay now, somewhat rueful in tone. "But damn
it can be tricky! Learning how to shift, I mean. My brother's only thirteen,
but he's already better at it than I am."

"Thirteen? How . . . old are you?"

"Try Antediluvian. Earth years, I'm twenty-two. Life, death, rebirth, we
go through cycles of renewal like everything else that is vital in nature.
Refreshes our outlook, keeps us sharp mentally. I was born July 28, last
time. That makes me a Leo. Want to see my paw again? I guess not. I've
been working on this damn gryphon for the last year and a half. Mom says
I've always been too ambitious. She's probably right. Combining different
body parts from the avian and animal worlds and getting them to work
together, kind of a hoot but it's exhausting. Roald says I should've started
with a chicken, the little jerk. What did you think of his were-bear? He
took first prize in the eighteen-and-under competition at our winter solstice
revel."

"Were-bear? Is that . . . what it was?"

"But anyway. Getting back to you. That third choice. If you're buying
the total redemption package. It's really a bargain. Spare yourself in this
life, you wrestle a lot of heavy baggage into the next. You go with scabs,
murk, and mildew. The soul deserves a clean delivery, Geoff."

"I . . . don't know w-what to do."

She nodded. "Sure. You need a little time. You're lost, you're cold.
Throw some more wood on your fire, heat up some of the instant coffee
that came with your survival gear. Wrap yourself in a blanket. I'll be around
if you want to talk."

"No. W-what time is it?"

"Time doesn't mean anything to you anymore, Geoff."

His eyes were smarting. He rubbed his throat, trying to ease the choking
tension there. He turned away from Chauncey, seeing the flames on the
rock again like radiant branches of a tree nourished by the consumed heart
of his father.

"Oh, Geoff?"

He turned back to her. Chauncey's right hand was out. He saw a compact Glock automatic lying in her palm.

"This is yours, isn't it?"

He stared at the pistol for a few seconds, then waded three steps toward
Chauncey. The surf beyond the misted bay was like the blood rushing
through his heart. His fingers closed over the dull black slide of the Glock,

fingertips grazing Chauncey's wrist. It was unexpected, that touch, comforting in a way. Imagining himself blind and finding a flower in the dark. A single beat of his heart said *courage*.

Geoff looked up and into her eyes.

"Thought I'd lost it," he told her. He lifted the Glock from her hand. Held it as he might've held a key poised at the threshold of a lock on a mysterious door. "Thanks."

"What you think is the end is only another place to go to."

"I wanted to see Eden again." There was no strain in his voice, no sorrowing notes. His mind felt clear, open to possibilities, raised remotely above the ruck and misery of self-pity and other merely human perceptions, immaculate as an observatory. The reality was clear as well, like the gleam of new stars; his purpose now etched plainly in firmament but only large enough to accommodate the humble event.

"I know," Chauncey said. "I can promise you this. If she ever needs our help, she'll have it."

TWO

AND HAD I NOT THE FLAME RESERVED . . .
THERE'S NOTHING SPECIAL OF MY OWN TO SHOW.

—MEPHISTOPHELES, IN *FAUST,* PART I, SCENE 3

WASHINGTON, DC · MAY 30 · 12:50 A.M. EDT

After talking to Victor Wilding, Rona toned up in the White House gym. Then she had a massage, a B-12 shot given to her by a protégé of Clint Harvester's personal physician, and enjoyed a light supper just before midnight in her second-floor suite. The music on her Bose stereo system was up-tempo bluegrass: Ricky Skaggs, Alison Krauss. Various R-Team staffers came up to the residence from the First Lady's east wing offices, bringing files, departing with instructions. Some of them were a little bleary-eyed or had coffee nerves. They all were impressed and as usual slightly intimidated by Rona's crispness and energy level. Only one small tantrum resulted from the visits, when Rona found out she couldn't view the covers of three news magazines that had inserted coverage of Rona's Hawaiian dust-up at the eleventh hour.

Katharine Bellaver arrived at the White House at twelve-fifteen. Rona kept her waiting while she finished off a round of phone calls. Two minutes for the new young wife of a global media mogul whom she wanted to cultivate. Three and a half minutes for the President of France (Rona had been taking twice-a-week French lessons for five years, and she managed to pull off a mildly dirty joke in the language that he hadn't heard before). A minute and a half for Allen Dunbar, who seemed a little depressed by India's heat and the news that Clint was returning to the White House. And ten minutes for Barbara Walters.

The butler on duty in the executive mansion had parked Katharine in the solarium. Rona breezed in. She had deliberately dressed down for this meeting: off-the-rack Wrangler Riatas, huaraches, a loose-fitting linen shirt, and two ropes of Cheyenne Indian beads. She also wore, on a shirt pocket, her lucky *Clint When It Counts* button from his tailgate campaigning days for governor of Montana. Katharine had once remarked to someone who had told someone else, etc., that Rona seemed to have gone a little hog-wild after she moved into the White House, willingly making herself a victim of fashion overload. Titter, titter. Rona had established blood feuds over lesser slights. But she'd never needed a reason to dislike Katharine Bellaver. Her dislike was instinctive, a reaction against privilege and pedigree. And there was the fact that she'd been such a good friend of Clint's.

"Katharine, I am *so* sorry to keep you waiting!"

Katharine looked up from the book of Ansel Adams photographs she'd been slowly leafing through. "Not at all, Mrs. Harvester."

"Can I have Thomas bring you something? Coffee?"

"Thomas already asked. But I'm fine." She looked at Rona's bandaged head and bit her lower lip delicately. "How are *you* feeling, after that ordeal?"

"A little headache, still."

"Was it a bullet fragment? I didn't think those limos could be penetrated."

"We're not sure." It had been a small nail file Rona had ready for the occasion. In the slam-bang uproar none of the other occupants of her limousine had seen her gouging her forehead as she pressed both hands to Clint face. "It's really good of you to interrupt your holiday. I know you have so little time to relax these days, those endless dialogues over human rights violations. Which of course is a matter of deep concern to us all."

"Peach Boondecker suggested that it was urgent." Katharine regarded Rona with a half smile and the porcelain poker face that had been a part of Jackie Kennedy's superb defenses. Katharine made "urgent" sound a little ridiculous, but she was a professional diplomat. "Peach said that she couldn't tell me more. I assume she didn't know." Katharine's smile said, *Up the ante or fold your hand.*

"It's more in the nature of a personal matter," Rona said.

"Having to do with Clint? Is he here?"

"No. I expect him back soon. About two A.M."

"So late?"

"We wanted to avoid a fuss."

"Well, of course," Katharine said with a hint of derision in her eyes. "There's quite a crowd on Pennsylvania Avenue, for this hour. The WELCOME HOME CLINT signs." She didn't mention the WE LOVE RONA signs, outnumbering those addressed to the President.

"Nothing warms the heart like a spontaneous outpouring of affection," Rona observed.

"That couldn't be more true. But . . . is Clint ready to go back to work?"

"As ready as he'll ever be."

"The pressure. I worry, Mrs. Harvester."

"No one could be more concerned about his health than I am. I can take quite a load off my husband's shoulders, and I'm prepared to do so. By the way, since you've been calling the President of the United States 'Clint,' just as if he were still one of your confidants and bedfellows—which I certainly don't begrudge anymore—would it break your patrician jaw to call me 'Rona'?"

"Well, no. I don't think so." Katharine paused significantly, and smiled. "Rona." She folded her hands comfortably in her lap, cocked her head slightly. "Your information—by the way—is both rancid and wrong. Clint and I always have respected each other too much to roll in the hay together. Now, what's up? Shall we?"

"I want you to tell me where your granddaughter is, and when you expect to see her."

Katharine glanced down, head dropping slightly as if she'd been rapped smartly on the back of her skull. When she looked up again she was okay, no fault lines showing in the porcelain, her smile correctly quizzical.

Rona yawned rudely. "Please spare us both the bullshit denials. I know everything about the circumstances of her birth, who Eden's father probably was. I'm sure you were present when she was born. Why did you give the kid away? Was Gillian too crazy at the time to take care of her own daughter? Or were you afraid of what she had brought into this world?"

"You asked me if I'd care for some . . . refreshment. I believe I would now."

"Glass of sherry? Oh, that's right, you don't drink sherry. Neither do I. Let's see, this time of the night don't you favor Stoly over ice, once you've brushed and flossed and settled down to do some reading, usually about twenty minutes' worth, before tucking yourself in? I've never been able to read in bed. Gives me a stiff neck every time. Thom-*as!*"

Katharine was thoughtfully silent, her eyes focused past Rona's head, until the butler had served the requested drinks, lowered the lights at Rona's suggestion to a shadowless twilight luster, and departed.

"Drink up," Rona said cheerfully, rising to click her glass, filled with citrus punch, against Katharine's. She kicked off the huaraches before settling down again, small feet tucked under her on the love seat. Katharine was now gazing at nighttime Washington through the solarium windows, rolling the crystal tumbler between her hands.

"Secret Service didn't like us being up here at night," Rona told her. "Possibility of snipers, they said."

"Neither of us seems to be afforded much privacy by our circumstance."

"What a world," Rona said, drinking. "But I learned a long time ago to study all the pug marks around my waterhole, learn the habits of the . . . creatures who make them."

"Until thirty-six hours ago, my granddaughter had led exactly the sort of life I wanted and hoped for her. It may be possible for Eden to find that life again."

"Oh, I don't think so."

"With difficulty. With the help of those who love her."

"Let's be realists, Katharine."

"Your view of 'reality' is appalling."

"Eden has *come out,* don't you understand? With her bloodlines she's

one of a kind. You know Bob Hyde; he thinks psychics are potential enemies of the state. The Bureau screwed up badly on psi research and instead
of going with the trend he snuffs all the psi-actives he comes across. Today
Bob had his SWATs hunting Eden, probably with orders to shoot her on
sight."

Katharine reacted as if Rona had dropped a burning match in her lap.
Rona said soothingly, "From the information I have, Bob may have seriously underestimated our girl. The Air Force helos he co-opted for the
hunt are long overdue at their base in California. Now let's get back to the
point. *Have you heard from Eden today?*"

"No."

"Do you know where she is?"

"If I did—"

"You wouldn't tell me? Don't you understand how *wrong* you are? I
thought I'd detected some concern for Eden. But with all of your money,
your resources, you can't protect her. Hyde and the Bureau are relentless.
So are the agents for a hundred nations eager to see this country fall. They
would find Eden very useful to their purposes. There is only one place on
this earth where the girl will be safe from now on. *Here,* Katharine. The
White House. Under *our* sovereign protection."

Katharine sipped from her glass, eyes closing briefly.

"Turn Eden over to you?"

"Why not? You did it before. How do you think she'll feel about you
once she knows this?"

"Eden has always known she was adopted."

"I call it abandonment," Rona said ruthlessly. "No justification. Cold-
blooded. You didn't want her. That's how Eden will see it. Call me anything you like, but never say I don't know what makes human beings work.
I've taken plenty of them apart in my time."

"Leaving the ruins where they fell," Katharine said. She shook her head
grimly. "What matters . . . is how we make amends for our mistakes. How
we say we're truly sorry. Tom—"

Rona caught the misstep. Katharine looked into her glass, wincing
slightly.

"You were going to say?"

"Nothing."

"Tom? Tom Sherard? Gillian's husband, yes? *And* another of your ex-
lovers. That's what life is all about; interesting situations." Rona had a glow
on; she was nearly vibrating, like a plucked cello string. "Oh. I get it. You
sent *him,* didn't you? To fetch Eden home. See? There's another mistake.

You should have gone to her right away, instead of sitting back, waiting for the girl to be brought to you. She's going to resent that, Kath."

"I think it's time we said good night."

"So soon? I was hoping you'd stay over. We have a vacant bed or two. Historical significance. Important people have bled and died in them."

"That's very gracious of you . . . Rona. But I will be going."

"Clint'll be here in an hour. I thought you'd want to say hello." Rona paused to savor a moment of yearning in Katharine's eyes. "There is a slight possibility that he might remember you."

Katharine stood, setting her glass down. She stared at Rona until Rona's whimsical grin crept beneath her skin.

"It's beyond my comprehension how you can abuse him as you so obviously plan to do. And run the risk of . . . turning Clint into a humiliated, pathetic figure before the eyes of the world."

"Believe me. There's no risk."

"What can you hope to gain?"

"Here at the White House we're all just doing our damnedest to get the ship of state back on an even keel. Protecting your vital interests, as well as mine. By the way, the polls tell me a majority of true-blue Americans think that the United Nations is obsolete, as well as a threat to our internal security and sovereignty. All of these half-assed little dictatorships with the GDP of a sidewalk hot-dog cart voting against the most powerful nation in the world on matters crucial to our economic development—I want to puke all over my *Post* when I read about it. You and I need to sit down soon and rap about the job you're doing up there. Good night, Katharine. I'll look forward to meeting Eden in the very near future. We'll get along great. I relate well to kids her age; my polls show they're my biggest support group."

"Your polls? It almost sounds as if you're running for office," Katharine said, pausing on her way out.

Rona had not bothered to uncurl from the love seat to walk Katharine to the door. She returned Katharine's looking-back stare with a blunt look of her own.

"Run for President? Why should I? I'm already there."

The eight California Air National Guard search and rescue helicopters, older-model Hueys with exterior tanks for extended-range flying, appeared shortly after sunrise in the vicinity of Moby Bay. Observers saw a town already preparing for a heavy influx of tourists. Delivery truck drivers were unloading cases of food and drink for the ice cream and doughnut shoppes and Moby Bay's two cafés, the Gray Whale and the Keg 'n' Burger. Merchants were hosing down the sidewalks in front of their establishments or replacing red, white, and blue bunting that had been damaged in the late-afternoon storm of the previous day.

A convoy of government motor pool sedans and eight-passenger vans that had left Sacramento at two-thirty A.M. drove into town a short while later, escorted by highway patrol cars. Twenty-six FBI agents from the San Francisco and Sacramento field offices. They bought six dozen doughnuts and coffee and ate their breakfasts while they canvassed the town with photos of Eden Waring.

Chauncey McLain and her brother Roald were helping their father set up a sidewalk exhibition of paintings by local artists. Three FBI agents, led by Dolph Hackett from Sacramento, called on her. One of them was carrying an evidence bag. Hackett told Wick McLain they needed to ask Chauncey some questions, was there a place they could talk to her off the street? Wick blustered some, saying, What's this about? and, My daughter hasn't done anything, and Chauncey smiled reassuringly at him, Of course not, it'll be okay, Dad, and Wick said, Well all right why don't you use my office in the back but leave the door open please where I can see my daughter while you're talking to her.

They showed Chauncey a photo of Eden Waring. Chauncey studied it thoughtfully, then allowed the light to dawn. "Oh! Didn't I see her on TV? She's the girl who had a premonition about the plane crash over there in Innisfall, saved just a whole bunch of people, right?"

"But you don't know her personally?" Hackett asked.

"No. If I'd ever met her, I think I would remember. But, you know, when I'm on tour I meet so many people."

Hackett glanced at the agent with the evidence bag, who took out the wrinkled Mighty Ducks hockey jersey with Chauncey's name sewed in it. "Does this belong to you, Miss McLain?"

"I did have one like that. Number 12. I wore it sometimes on tour last fall."

"What tour are you talking about?"

"I'm with *Pussy Whip*. Do you guys listen to metal?" The youngest of the agents smiled but didn't commit himself in front of the boss. Chauncey liked his curly hair and forthright jaw. She addressed herself exclusively to him. "We've cut three albums. I don't think there's any around the gallery, but I could send you one. *Feeding the Sharks* is our latest." She turned the jersey inside out and peered closely at the name tag. "It's my shirt, all right, here's my name! Isn't that crazy? I don't have *any* idea where I might have left it, we played thirty-nine venues in forty-six days."

Dolph Hackett grilled her for another ten minutes concerning Eden. Chauncey remained charming, chatty, and uninformative. They wouldn't let her keep the hockey jersey. Hackett said it might be returned to her, eventually. As the G-men were leaving the young agent spoke for the first time.

"How did you get hurt?"

She was wearing a soft bulky cast from the ankle down on her left foot. Chauncey gave him her brightest smile of the morning.

"Oh, just horsing around. Bye, nice meeting all of you. And hey, good luck."

Chauncey watched them go, gathered up the used coffee cups and dumped them in a wastebasket. She yawned. No sleep at all last night. No sleep for any of the citizens of Moby Bay. There had been just a heck of a lot of tidying up to do. But her wrapped foot was one of two reminders of yesterday's encounter with attack helicopters and government men with hostile attitudes who would forever be unaccounted for no matter how long the search went on. Lost perhaps in a sparsely inhabited wilderness area, or deep down in the graveyard sea.

The other reminder, of course, was Eden herself. Not lost, just missing for now. Chauncey comforted herself with the thought. They would meet again.

FLAMING RIVER RANCH, IVANHOE, CALIFORNIA · MAY 30 · 8:50 A.M. PDT

Eden heard voices outside and a good distance away; more distant than the voices were the sounds of sheep. She opened shuttered doors of her cavernous room and walked out onto a dark-floored veranda polished to a gleam. There was a sloping roof overhead with old-fashioned ceiling fans, red metal lanterns on the whitewashed walls, some rugged-looking, eighteeth-century mission-style furniture. Her eyes watered from the brilliance of a cloudless sky over low forested mountains. She saw a stable with a Mexican red tile roof, two windmills, sheepcotes, a small orchard, a few cottonwood trees along a river split by low sandbars into many streams like spilled molten silver, and a marshy pond with ducks coasting amid the cattails. Beyond the river cattle grazed on open foothill range. She saw a horseman and a pack of motley ranch dogs, led by a Great Dane, trotting beside the horse.

Voices.

Eden shook her foggy head and cleared a dry throat. She had a case of nerves. And she was very hungry. She smelled woodsmoke and meat on a grill, followed the shady veranda to a courtyard that was almost the size of a football field. It was partly enclosed by four ranch buildings, including the hacienda she'd come out of, crossed at random by wide graveled paths that led variously to a small chapel with a bronze bell in a cupola; a swimming pool filled by a fountain made from an old half-stuccoed adobe brick chimney that stood tall at one end; garden plots with rock and sand and pieces of gray driftwood accenting green cactus, scarlet paintbrush, and softball-size tomatoes on the vine; outdoor ovens in a loaflike construct of plastered adobe; a smokehouse and a three-tiered fountain covered in ceramic tiles the size of postage stamps. Near the kitchen a breezy pergola stood between two centuries-old California oaks.

Three Hispanics were at work, one of them with a long-handled iron fry pan the size of a manhole cover. Four people were seated around a plain wooden table in the pergola, apparently in the early stages of breakfast. Two of them, both Oriental, were strangers to Eden. The other two were virtual strangers. They had brought her to this ranch, wherever she was, from Moby Bay, arriving in the middle of the night. Eden with sickening memories and a monumental headache, nerves like prowling spiders beneath the skin. A woman named Luisa had taken her directly to a cool candlelit room and a palatial four-poster bed with diaphanous curtains hung all around. Luisa gave her a tablespoon of dark liquid for her headache and nerves, talking almost nonstop but in a low voice, comforting words in Spanish as Eden moaned. Then she applied cold cloths, dipped in something pleasantly astringent, to Eden's head. Between the third and fourth cloths she had fallen deeply asleep.

"Would someone please tell me where I am?"

They hadn't seen her coming. The tall Englishman got up right away and walked toward her. He had a limp. She remembered that his name was

Tom. The African beauty, turning now, smiling at Eden, was Alberta. She had dim memories of being socked by "Bertie," which was what the Englishman had called her during the long drive. Other than that Eden didn't know a damn thing about either of them. Where they'd come from, what they wanted from her. They'd been pleasant but not all that talkative. Not about to drop her at the nearest bus stop. At pee breaks Bertie went into the john with her, as if Eden had the energy to attempt a getaway. Eden was by turns afraid of and indifferent to them; then, as it grew dark and late, she was apathetic about everything, half conscious, wanting only not to be tortured by the sight of Chauncey McLain rising up from the patio floor of her house with a large ugly bullet hole in her forehead.

Moby Bay is a special place. Protected.

Like a wildlife refuge?

That's a good one. It's a refuge, all right. But the wildest thing about Moby Bay is Wardella's poker night.

Oh, yeah.

"Good morning. You didn't sleep as long as we thought you might. Would you care for breakfast, Eden?"

Eden stood fast, staring at him.

"Do you mind answering my question?"

"This *shamba* is called the Flaming River Ranch. Sheep, dairy cows, some horses. You're in central California, or so I was told. I'm new here myself. Kenya is my home, much of the time. The Flaming River comes by its name from the colors the setting sun paints the waters on lovely days like this one. A man named Buck Hannafin owns it. The ranch has belonged to his family for a hundred and forty years. Buck is also the United States Senate's Majority Leader." Eden nodded tersely; everyone in California knew that. "Buck is out riding, but he should be back soon." Sherard smiled sympathetically at her still-angry expression. "Come on, now. I know you must be hungry. We couldn't get you to eat a thing on the way down last night."

"Why am I here?" Eden asked, not budging.

"Have you enjoyed the attention you've received for most of the past two days?"

"*No.*"

"You're here to rest up and try to put all that behind you."

"Why should I trust any of you?" Eden said, shooting a look past him at Bertie and the Oriental men. They were Chinese, she decided.

"For one thing, we're entirely sympathetic to the . . . difficulty you find yourself in."

"Yes? What is that?"

"There are people who have an almost psychotic fear of you, of what you represent."

"Me!"

"One or more of them probably were responsible for the murder of your mother."

"Oh, Jesus! Betts . . . is *dead*?"

"No. I'm sorry, I didn't think before I—I'm happy to say that your Betts is on the mend and safe now, thanks to Buck Hannafin. She's not far from here, in a private hospital where security is of the utmost concern. It will also be quite safe for you to visit her today. I was talking, not about Betts, but about your natural mother, who also was my wife for twelve years. Her name was Gillian. You look very much like her, Eden. In a little while I'll show you some photos of my wife. You and I should have a lot to talk about. But try to eat something first, get some sun, recover your strength."

His voice was kind; his compassion, she hoped, was genuine. She responded with a rush of tears. Sherard put an arm around her.

"I'm sorry," Eden sobbed. "It has just been so goddamned *hellish*."

"I can assure you things will be a great deal better for you from now on."

She tensed in his embrace.

"You think so? Well, you don't know the dreams I have! And I had another, last night. The third in the series. After the third dream, it *happens*."

Buck Hannafin rode his big bay gelding to the gazebo with his dogs—two Border collies and a tawny Rhodesian Ridgeback in addition to the black-and-tan Great Dane—all gliding around him and clamoring for treats after their outing. He handed out Milk-Bones from a saddlebag. Two stable hands came running frantically to take his horse from him. Buck wore a white shirt unbuttoned over his tanned chest and white jeans with a pair of canary-yellow leather riding boots. Cut quite a figure, in or out of the saddle. He walked up to Eden, swept off his rancher's straw hat, and greeted the startled girl with a grandee's bow. Then Buck straightened up a little creakily, saying, "For a minute there I thought I was seeing Miss Audrey Hepburn herself, just the way she looked when she paid the ranch a visit back in '58, maybe '59 it was."

"Audrey Hepburn?" Eden said, the name but not the face familiar. But obviously Buck Hannafin believed he had paid her a great compliment, so she smiled back at him. "Thank you." Hannafin himself was totally familiar;

she'd seen him on television and in the newspapers often while she was growing up. Riley and Betts had been scornful of most politicians, but Betts had done volunteer work for two of Hannafin's campaigns. If he was okay with Betts, then—Eden put out her hand, and Buck Hannafin took it tenderly, looking into her eyes. "And thanks for . . . looking after Betts."

"She's in the care of some excellent people. We got a Northern District judge out of bed at three in the morning to contravene the FBI's protected witness writ, put Betts aboard a chartered flying ambulance to Nevada, then switched aircraft for the trip down from Tahoe. Single engine, no flight plan, pilot's one of my nephews. She's resting comfortable right now where nobody could get to her even if they knew where she was. Easier to crawl naked through a storm drain full of barb wire. And you have the same guarantee, with Buck Hannafin's seal on it." He took Eden gently by the elbow, walked her up to the gazebo. "Here come the T-bones and easy-over eggs. Let's sit. I assume you know everybody by now."

"No, I don't."

"My old friend Chien-Chi from San Francisco, and his son Danny. They had a little misfortune at their place two nights ago."

Danny Cheng was wearing his blindman's shades. Their fingers barely touched; Eden withdrew her hand quickly.

"Oh, my God. *Your* house?"

"Well, they saved most of it," Danny said with a curious smile. "You barely touched me. What else did you see?"

Eden gave her head a quick shake, but her eyes had glazed. Danny sought to grip her hand again. Bertie reached up and blocked his hand away from Eden.

"Hey, Danny," she said. "You want news, watch TV and give us poor psi-actives a break. It's work, and it can be hard on a girl."

Eden looked at Bertie, her vision clearing. Questions in her eyes.

Bertie shrugged, smiling.

"Yeah, me too," she said. "But we'll have a chance to compare notes later."

Eden was still claiming a big share of media attention on this Memorial Day. So was the disappearance of FBI Director Robert Hyde, who, the Bureau reported, had accompanied an elite but unnamed task force on a "training mission" in northern California. A huge search and rescue operation was under way. No further details.

And President Clint Harvester had returned to the White House from Camp David after a lengthy period of recuperation following his stroke. The President's personal physician, R. Traynor Daufuskie, read a brief statement for the press proclaiming Clint to be "champing at the bit" and "one hundred percent" in his desire to get back to work. It was breezy in the Rose Garden where Daufuskie made his appearance. Sunlight sparkled on the lenses of his reading glasses. He had to hold his tie down to keep it from whipping him across the nose. When he finished reading he looked up unsmilingly, somewhat like a man watching his firing squad line up ten paces away, and abruptly turned the podium over to White House Press Secretary Val Domingues, who announced that the President would address the nation and the world at nine o'clock Tuesday night from the Oval Office. It would be a major address. Meanwhile the President and Mrs. Harvester were enjoying a quiet holiday, relaxing together in the residence. Steven Spielberg had sent a print of his latest, as yet unreleased movie to the White House, and they planned to watch the film after dinner with a few close friends. That was all. No questions.

The network they were watching in the shade of the gazebo switched to a correspondent outside the White House grounds, who pitched in to fill the time by selecting well-wishers from the crowd assembled on Pennsylvania Avenue hoping for a glimpse of the First Couple. Everybody was in an upbeat mood, cheering for the panning camera. Their President was back, and now the Bad Things that had the country jittery would soon stop. Clint would have the answers.

"Lying sonsabitches," Buck Hannafin commented, rubbing the ears of ch. Roskilde's Pardon My Fancy, his Great Dane. "I can't imagine how they hope to pull this off. Address the nation? Clint couldn't tie his shoelaces the last time I saw him, and that was barely five weeks ago."

"If he was brain-locked," Bertie Nkambe volunteered, "he could have recovered spontaneously."

"So you've told me. Would you bet those odds?"

"No, sir."

Hannafin shifted uneasily in his cane chair, staring at the TV screen. The satellite picture was sharp. "Something's up," he said. "Some scheme of Rona's. Being as how she's never demonstrated scruples or restraint in her life, it may have extremely tragic consequences for us all."

Eden sipped from a second glass of orange juice. "What do you mean by 'brain-locked'?" she asked Bertie.

"Reversal of the polarities of the brain's electrical field. Screws up the mind something awful. Like a jolt of lightning, only more precise in its aim. But I don't believe what happened to the President was a naturally occurring phenomenon."

Chien-Chi said, "It is a discipline that can be mastered, but only by a very small number of the adept. A matter of directing the Life Force in precise focus. Somewhat akin to the discipline of giving form to one's mirror image. But this is only possible if the adept is left-handed." He smiled at Eden. "As I have observed you to be."

Eden winced as if she had left her own mind carelessly open to the wry and reserved old man, and was silent. She wasn't sure that she wanted to be friends. With any of them.

"How can they risk putting Harvester on TV if he's not competent?" Sherard asked Hannafin, who shook his head in bemusement.

Danny Cheng said, "It can be done. Undetectable, which means no risk at all. I have friends in the computer business. All they need is the President's voice, some tapes of past speeches, and a camera in his empty office. They can give him any look they want, have him say anything, and it will be seamless, like a live feed."

"Maybe the American people can be fooled by camera tricks for a little while," Hannafin said. "But the President's business revolves around meetings and phone calls; otherwise he can't do business at all. Right now there's a conspiracy of silence about the condition he's in, but that conspiracy *will* be broken. Rona can only go so far with this. Question is, has she totally lost her own mind? Or does she believe with Victor Wilding's complicity and resources that she can get away with anything? What are the limits? Where are we headed? The day Rona Harvester set foot in the White House, I had real fear for our country. And I'm not the only one on the Hill who feels—"

Eden scraped her chair back, muttered "Excuse me," and walked swiftly away from the table, her head down. Bertie started to go after her. Tom Sherard gestured for her to stay put. Bertie thought about it, shook her head at him, and followed Eden.

When she caught up the two young women walked silently the half mile to the river. They took turns throwing sticks into the water for two of the ranch's Border collies to retrieve. After about ten minutes of this Eden sighed and glanced at Bertie.

"I'm sorry. That was rude, leaving like I did. I couldn't listen to any more of it."

Bertie shrugged. "Sensory overload. I've had some bad moments myself the last few hours."

"Right now I don't . . . I can't care about everyone else's problems. I'm all raw inside. I just want to see Betts. Put my arms around her. Hold her. Be held."

"I'll drive you," Bertie offered.

While Eden had slept and dreamed, the planes arrived, as they did every day at this time. Because it was a National holiday the work force at MORG's Plenty Coups facility, nine miles east of the ramshackle town and twenty-two miles southwest of Billings, Montana, was reduced by one-third. Only four of the 216-passenger planes from the Airbus fleet landed at three-minute intervals on one of the two long runways. There was a control tower at Plenty Coups, a maintenance center with fire trucks and snow-removal equipment, six big hangars, and a cargo terminal. MORG also had its own cargo fleet, consisting of 747s and a couple of Russian-built air freighters. Everything used or discarded at the facility came and went by air, including the garbage. U.S. military and civilian aircraft seldom landed there; they needed high-security clearances to enter a rigidly enforced no-fly zone. The planes were painted a light gray and had no markings except for FAA buzz numbers. In the beginning, during construction of the facility, the windows of each Airbus were blacked out. This caused anxiety for many passengers and cases of vertigo, so the practice was discontinued.

Two of the planes came from their maintenance base at the little-used municipal airport in Billings. Another flight originated in Denver, a daily round trip of two and a half hours. The fourth came from Silicon Valley. Everyone at Plenty Coups worked a thirteen-hour day, three days a week, which made the longer commutes, from California, Colorado, or Washington State, tolerable. The pay scale, even for maintenance personnel, was very high, well above Civil Service levels. The pay compensated for minor inconveniences such as being grounded by weather for an extra shift or two. Multiphasic Operations and Research Group paid extremely well in return for absolute silence from its forty-one hundred Plenty Coups employees.

Buses fueled by natural gas met each plane. The buses had an escort of Humvees with watchful armed security personnel. Arriving employees were logged on to the buses electronically. Then the buses drove in a convoy, spaced one hundred feet apart, through flat treeless grassland for one and three-quarter miles on a four-lane divided highway with snow fences on both sides. In all but the worst weather two helicopters were in the air over the facility around the clock.

The convoys' destination was an above-ground terminal whimsically done up as a frontier fort, but the stockade fence was constructed from steel-reinforced concrete posts and each half of the twelve-foot-high entrance gates was the thickness of a bank vault door. The security guards carried automatic weapons but wore the uniforms of General Custer's 7th Cavalry, a conceit of Victor Wilding's, who was a collector of Western Americana. No one had ever pointed out to him the implicit irony.

Inside the gates the road divided and slanted underground for a third of a mile through an in-bound tunnel to another portal with a blast-proof door that eighteen-wheelers could drive through. Beyond this door was a staging area the size of a city block where supplies were unloaded and routed and employees, after clearing a checkpoint, caught the trams that departed every two minutes. The Plenty Coups facility was in the shape of a wheel one mile in diameter. Three trams of five cars each made the rounds on the outside of the wheel, stopping at each of the twelve spokes where more security doors admitted employees to their specific work zones. Moving sidewalks the length of each spoke completed the cycle of transport from their homes to their offices, plants, or laboratories.

Every foot of the way was scrutinized and recorded by surveillance cameras. The most sensitive areas, including the Psi Training and Neurological Engineering divisions, at the hub of the wheel, had the best and most advanced security. No one without proper authorization and identification, which in some instances included full-body scans that revealed every possible physical anomaly, had ever managed to get inside Plenty Coups. The best way in was to join the work force. But MORG's standards were high, their background checks paranoiac.

On the other hand, the Neurological Engineering people actively recruited subjects with useful skills who had no cognitive impairments but were not psychologically adaptable to ordinary communal life. Many of them were recent parolees from civilian and military prisons.

MAY 30 • 5:46 P.M. MDT

Victor Wilding had acquired the Director of Neurological, Marcus Woolwine, from the CIA by giving him vastly more money and latitude in his research, and by promising there would be no oversight committee to meddle in the doctor's business. Woolwine reported directly to Wilding, when he felt like it.

Wilding disliked traveling far from his headquarters at the Chassériau Hotel in Washington, but at least three times a year he found it necessary to visit Plenty Coups. Marcus Woolwine met his plane. They were driven to the facility under armed escort.

Woolwine was a small, tanned, hairless man approaching eighty years of age. He still played a lot of tennis, and in spite of the fact that they were long out of style, he wore mirror sunglasses in and out of doors.

"I've studied all of the videotapes your agents obtained at the crash site of TRANSPAC 1850. The graduation exercise in the stadium. Eden Waring is on many of the tapes, of course. Is it true that she has no siblings?"

"None that we know of."

"Then she may be capable of a remarkable feat. On one of the tapes, where the clarity of image is excellent, there are two Eden Warings. They appear simultaneously, but fifty yards apart."

"Someone in her graduating class might resemble her."

"We did the usual enhancements and measurements. The likenesses are too close to be coincidental."

"Proving what?"

"That Eden Waring can produce her doppelganger. We know that Kelane Cheng could do the same. On a tape of not particularly good quality, shot from a distance, a figure that may have been Cheng's dpg is momentarily visible, walking away from the flaming wreckage of the DC-10."

"*May* have been."

"One could speculate that in her dying moments Cheng released her doppelganger to make contact with Eden Waring. The implications intrigue me. When can I meet her?"

"We don't know where she is. The Bureau was sitting on Eden's adoptive mother, Betts Waring, at the Innisfall Medical Center. But someone with a lot of clout, Katharine Bellaver probably, had her removed to a private hospital, where she would have been admitted under another name. All of the law enforcement agencies we control in California are checking the admissions records of institutions in their jurisdictions. Also, the body of Riley Waring was transferred yesterday to a funeral home in Riley's hometown. Burial's Tuesday morning. We'll be covering it, but we don't look for Eden to risk showing up."

"Too bad. The girl may be immensely valuable. The godlike interface between our world and all levels of extrasensory perception. Not to mention the possibility that she is key to Robin Sandza's continuing survival."

Victor Wilding quelled the familiar dreadful sensation of hanging by a thread over a void. "We'll find Eden Waring. There's other business."

Woolwine said after a few moments, "So you're proceeding with *Babycakes.*"

"There's never been any doubt of that."

"But you're no longer willing to entrust the . . . the project to a team from your so-called Elite Force."

"No."

Woolwine smiled slightly, a tidy satisfied smile.

"I did warn you, sir. No matter how intensively they are trained, how well motivated with quasi-religious or political fantasies—programmed, if you will—all terrorists, our own or those of another nation, attract attention to themselves. They leave a distinctive spoor in the air. The World Trade Center, the Federal Building in Oklahoma City, the Convention Center in Portland—those perpetrators subconsciously gave themselves away. They *wanted* to be caught and revealed to the world in all of their holy infamy. So they made deliberately careless mistakes that subsequently led to arrests and the publicity they craved. *Briar Rose* might have ended in the same way. There were some highly accurate sketches of the *Briar Rose* team in all the media within days following the event."

"Yes, I know."

"This happened because the horrible nature of nuclear destruction was weighing on the subconscious minds of those men before they reached Portland to plant and activate the device. Thus when they needed to be anonymous, just faces in the crowd, they imparted a telemagical warning to the more prescient who happened to notice their presence near ground zero on the day before the blast. You were wise to take my advice and have the team . . . professionally neutralized and their ashes scattered to the four winds soon after they completed their assignment. But I can't help wondering, Victor, why—"

"*Babycakes* will be the last one, let me assure you of that."

"Gracious, I hope so. Of course it's not my business, forgive my little indiscretion. Obviously there are those political matters that can best be resolved by boldly seizing an initiative, however pointless it may seem in the beginning. I'm not political. You have asked me to provide a team of utmost reliability. Expert, efficient, psychologically up to the task of incinerating several thousand of their fellow human beings without a qualm."

"Sounds as if you're describing homicidal maniacs."

"Oh, no. No no no. You might as well have one of *those* walking around wearing a sign. 'I'm here to nuke Paducah.' Even the best of nature's psychopaths, nicer people you never hope to meet, have their flaws and lethal idiosyncrasies. Randy and Herb, on the other hand, are without a single human flaw."

"Then they aren't actually human."

Woolwine said with his neat inoffensive smile, "Well, that could be a matter for debate."

The Plenty Coups facility had three workout complexes, two for employees, one for executives. Randy and Herb were playing racquetball in the executives' gym.

The two men appeared to be in their middle twenties. They had a sweaty glow of good health. Randy was dark and compact, with the speed and pounce of a hunting cat; Herb was blond and lean, with long arms and deceptive quickness, effortlessly rifling back shots that had seemed out of his reach. Randy had dimpled round scars on his upper torso and on one calf inches below the knee; Herb had tattoos: a sailing ship on one shoulder, the popular ghettoish barbed wire around a bicep. They played with relentless but good-humored competitiveness.

Woolwine and Wilding watched them from the gallery above the courts.

"What makes them an ideal team?" Wilding asked the head of Neurological Engineering and Research.

"For one thing, they have complete physiological empathy while carrying out complex tasks in which the performance of one team member is dependent on the performance of the other. Neither Randy nor Herb is burdened with the human emotions that detract from efficient tasking. Love, hate, anger, fear, and, in particular, anxiety: all of these are detrimental to the working memory. By manipulation of various naturally occurring brain chemicals such as the catecholamines and the opioids, we have programmed these emotions out of their limbic circuitry, while heightening the motivators such as self-confidence and enthusiasm. These motivators, in turn, expedite access to that ecstatic state which my esteemed colleague Mihaly Csikszentmihalyi named 'flow.' Athletes call it 'The Zone.' Peak performance effortlessly achieved. In such a state nothing detracts from achieving the goal. Potential distractors are . . . dealt with lethally but dispassionately."

"Bioengineered psychopaths."

"If you insist on the term. But your naturally occurring psychopaths, while they exist without empathy for other human beings, have their perverse fantasies and are, inevitably, inspired by the fear they arouse in others to commit atrocities. Randy and Herb have no capacity for fantasizing. Their infrequent dreams are colorless, mundane. They are, to simplify, the first of their kind: bioengineered solely for games and tasks, which are one and the same to them. They are intelligent, resourceful, and loyal. Competitive, but always controlled."

"Do they have their implants?"

"Oh, yes. They're ready. Randy and Herb will be monitored every step of the way by the Watchbird communications team assigned to *Babycakes*."

"What about their sex drives?"

"Normal and healthy."

"That could be a problem. They get the urge for nookie, they want to pick up women. Call attention to themselves."

Woolwine nodded. "But rather than tamper with the sexual urge, which could affect their gamesmanship, it seemed a better solution to provide them with comely women agents from the *Babycakes* support team during their stay in—But of course I don't know the intended target. Would you like to meet Randy and Herb?"

"No."

"When will they be needed for—"

"The device is ready. They can leave tomorrow. I have a few minutes. I want to visit RS while I'm here."

"Certainly."

"Any change for the better?"

"I'm afraid not."

"If you can do all that you've done with Randy and Herb, why can't you at least stabilize Robin Sandza? His body is physically sound. Brain-damaged or not, he should live to be fifty, sixty years old at the least."

Woolwine, who was oblivious of the circumstances behind Wilding's anxiety, said, "There are intangibles in his case. And we have yet to isolate the chemicals, or the mechanism, that supports the will to live in the primitive brain. It may be a matter of 'affective blindness.' Or, if one gives credence to the existence of a 'soul,' which simply may be an etheric 'second self' like the doppelganger—"

Wilding flinched, then shook his head in annoyance.

"Just don't let him slip away from us. His daughter may be the answer. I'll get her here. Whatever it takes."

FLAMING RIVER RANCH · JUNE 1 · 9:30 P.M. PDT

Bertie Nkambe flew Kirk and Wendell in from New York, at her expense, to do the makeover. Kirk was the hairstylist, Wendell the makeup artist she used on most of her photo shoots. They each earned three thousand dollars a day.

"Worth it," Bertie had said cheerfully when she approached Eden with the idea. "Believe me, I can wake up looking like old fish some mornings, with a cover for *Elle* overdue. I depend on Kirk and Wendell to make me lethal again."

"Why do I need a new me?" Eden said skeptically, quoting Bertie.

"Because the old you is on the cover of *People* this week. Front page of yesterday's *USA Today* above the fold. You're hotter than a rock star. Extrasensory perception is the big media buzz."

"Bertie's right," Tom Sherard said. "A different look is a sensible precaution."

"Well—then I could go to the funeral, and not be hassled, right? Betts still isn't strong enough to be there. He's—Riley's the only father I've ever known."

"Let's think about that," Sherard hedged.

"Meaning no?" Eden flared. "Sorry, Tom. I've known you for two days and I understand where you're coming from. My mother died an awful death, but that has nothing to do with who I am. I'm almost twenty-two and *nobody* runs my life for me."

"I'm only asking that you not make an emotional decision that could put your life at risk."

Eden stared speculatively at Bertie. "So that's you in all the head shots you showed me? Kirk and Wendell, they did those different looks with scissors and paint?"

"They're geniuses. You won't know yourself."

For a few moments the strain she'd been under returned to dull Eden's eyes. Then she smiled. "I don't anyway. So what the hell. We go for it."

Buck Hannafin, newly barbered and well shod, arrived back at the ranch at nine-thirty from the office in Ivanhoe where he'd spent much of his day on the phone or video-conferencing, preparing for committee meetings, his return to Washington imminent. The others, except for Bertie, had gathered in Hannafin's game room, where there were tables for billiards, backgammon, and poker. Tiffany lampshades. Racked sporting guns, some of them more than a hundred years old but well cared for. Trophy heads—grizzly, stag, Dall sheep—lined the knotty paneled walls with their mellow luster. There was whiskey and plenty of it in bold decanters. That air of yesteryear, strong booted men with impressive whiskers establishing dominion, creating empires out of range and timberland. Women seemed an impertinence in a room like this one. The lights were low.

As Bertie had requested, a large cut-crystal bowl had been placed in the center of the pool table, which was covered in rust-red baize. The bowl measured two feet in diameter. In the bottom of the bowl there was a white votive candle.

Buck looked twice at Eden when he came in, the second time with a perplexed smile. Only when she smiled back and he recognized a telltale dimple did he realize whom he was looking at.

"Scrape me off the sidewalk and call me sticky! With your poker face on, don't think I ever would've known you, Eden."

Eden had to laugh. Buck put his arm around her, looked at the crystal bowl on his pool table, looked at the other faces.

"So what are we up to here? Where's Miss Bertie?"

She came in with Portia Darkfeather's Persian cat cradled in her arms. Warhol, in spite of some patches where the vet had shaved away singed hair and treated burns, was looking fit. He was wearing a new rhinestone collar Bertie had bought for him.

"Sorry I'm late. Had to be sure Warhol was up for this."

"What do you have in mind? Some kind of psychic stuff, all of us gathered around the table here? Like a, what do you call it, a see-ance? I don't think I'll be much good at it, because I don't believe—"

"It's just an experiment," Bertie said blithely. "Because Warhol may not be at his best, I thought we could use a boost in the mental energy in the room. Okay, Danny and Chien-Chi, why don't you stand about at the middle of the table on my left, Tom and Buck on my right, and Eden, you'll be opposite me at that end. Can we lower the lights a little more? Good. Don't you just love the drama?" She looked at Danny Cheng. "Not to worry. Nothing spooky is going to jump out at you. We hope. Why don't you take your shades off, Danny? They inhibit the empathy we're aiming for. Tom, light the candle please."

"What do you want me to do?" Eden asked with a game smile.

"You and I will concentrate on Warhol. And Warhol—well, he just may go to sleep, who knows? End of experiment, we'll play poker instead." She touched Warhol lightly on the top of his head with two fingers. Warhol's eyes narrowed peaceably. The candle flame in the crystal bowl was steady. The others watched it without having been told to watch. Above their heads the artificial eyes of bodiless animals acquired an interior glint of flame and menace.

They breathed. They watched. They were silent. Warhol's eyes widened. In the silence his purring had a motorized monotony, a sound of journey. Eyes widening, narrowing. Danny Cheng's weak eyes watered, and he rubbed them. Chien-Chi's face was a mask of noble serenity. Tom Sherard felt a certain weightlessness, a sense of transport. He saw through the candle flame to other fires, lonely, in places where he had been to hunt as a boy and would never return to. Buck Hannafin's stomach growled. His eyelids were heavy, as if he had gone to sleep on his feet.

Looking at the placid cat, Eden felt a mild wind in her face and smelled prairie on the wind, a scent of sage and sun-warmed grassland. The small flame rose between her and Warhol, growing in the shape of a pillar, but a twister of a pillar filling her conscious mind like a firestorm. Fascinated, Eden lost awareness of everyone around her. The cunning blue eyes of the Persian cat were like a magnetic center of the whirling, unearthly beautiful pillar. She felt as if she could fall headlong into the melding pupils of those attractive eyes, fall unscathed through surrounding fire, fall like a hawk with folded wings, wind rushing in a torrent around her, into bottomless blue. Her body was jolted. Her lungs emptied, a long sigh ending in plummeting weightless tranquility, an abiding sense of peace. Then there was another slight jolt. Eden looked up, startled, as if she had been given a poke in the midst of forty winks.

Hot where she now is. Very hot. The racy wind tugging at her newly-styled moussed hair. A scent of horses on the wind. She looks out from a modest hilltop at limitless prairie, sun-crisped razory graze. No roads up here, to this place. Some small dusted-over trees, not enough of them to be called a grove. Hot fly-specked horses whipping their tails across twitching flanks in scarce shade. In the distance, old mountains, creased and pale as faded denim, with a single heavenly dark cloud above.

Stones like a dry riverbed surround the burial plot, gleam of mica in newly shoveled earth. The open grave, sun striking deeply into the ground where the new, varnished coffin rests, hardware glinting, too hot to touch. There is no shade for this funeral. The shovel standing up with a westerner's tattered black hat hanging jaunty from the handle, a mock-mourner.

Eden hears someone singing: a high-pitched, staccato Indian death chant.

Portia Darkfeather is there, half hidden behind one of the horses, her stallion Dark Valiant. Having taken off her blouse, she is wringing out her sweat in streams as she continues her mourning song.

She drapes the wrung-out blouse across the saddle, reaches up to unpin her hair, letting it down like a dark river falls. The wind whips strands here and there, across her face. Hawklike nose, heavy brows, reddish-bronze skin tone, unmistakably the face of a Plains Indian woman. Her lonely lament ends abruptly. Eden has claimed her attention.

Darkfeather comes out from behind Dark Valiant, who gives her a nudge with his nose. Long-waisted, nude down to the silver-and-tooled-leather belt of her leggy Wranglers, she walks straight to Eden, giving her head a couple of flourishing aftershakes to facilitate the drying of that raven's wing of shimmering hair. Her gaze dense with the wild life, eyes as white as diamonds. She smiles.

"Hello. I'm Portia. I wasn't expecting anyone else. Sorry, but I don't have another shirt to put on."

"That's okay. I'm Eden. It's hot, isn't it?"

"Yeah. Hot. I'm used to it. Grew up out thisaway. But we may have rain once the Pardoner gets here."

Eden looks around at the burial plot.

"Do you want me to help?"

"Thanks. But there's only one shovel. And dying is, in the end, it's just down to your ownself, right? I mean, nobody else can do it for you."

"I guess not. How did it happen?"

"Plane crash. But you know about that."

In a flash, but without distress, Eden relives the events of her graduation day. She nods.

"Yeah. I do. Who else did you say was coming?"

"The Pardoner."

"Oh. Sure. Then you'll be on your way."

"Right. We have a little more time, though. Come on, let's hunker down in the shade a while. There's stuff you probably want to know. Tell me, how's Warhol?"

"Doing great. He misses you."

"Miss my kitty too," Portia Darkfeather says, with the suspicion of a tear in her eye. "Sorry I can't offer you refreshments. But as I was saying, didn't count on company today. Doesn't mean that I'm not happy to see you, Eden." Darkfeather looks around with a slight shrug of uneasiness as a cloud, or a shadow, momentarily dims the sun. She won't look up. "I only have a few minutes. What do you need to know?"

"Portland. Why, and who, and all that. And the next time. That's more important. It's soon, isn't it?"

" 'Fraid so."

"Do you know where?"

"Madison, Wisconsin."

"Is there time to stop it?"

"That I don't know. Rona didn't—"

"Rona *Harvester*?"

"A very bad person. But not a Bad Soul. Neither am I." She blinks a teardrop. "The Pardoner won't see Bad Souls. They're pure evil, no hope for them." More tears fall, and she sobs. "I don't know what he'll say to me."

"It's okay, Portia. But what does Mrs. Harvester want?"

Darkfeather wipes her eyes and after a last tremulous sob recovers her voice.

"One word, five letters. *Power.* She's taking over from Clint after the next nuking. She'll have him assassinated, not that it wouldn't be a blessing, he's totally brain-locked. I don't know how they did it. There's a place called Plenty Coups, west of here. Put your forehead against mine, I'll show it to you. And everything else that's going on there."

Their foreheads touch. Temple to temple, and Eden slips inside Darkfeather's receptive mind. Eden swallows hard, her senses amuck. Then flashings, mind-numbing images. *Flash, flash.* She withdraws in dismay.

"Oh, no. Oh . . . no!"

And she closes her eyes momentarily. The wind is stronger beneath the trees, buffeting her. Eden feels the heat of the day like a weight on her lungs. But the sky has darkened. There is a fist of thunder in her brain. The stallion and packhorse mutter and shy nervously. When Eden looks up Portia Darkfeather is gone.

"Portia!"

Oh . . . she's just over there. At the burial ground. Kneeling penitently at the feet of the Pardoner, hair down over her naked breasts. He places his hand briefly on the crown of her head. She lifts her eyes, speaks to him. Eden can't hear what she is saying. The Pardoner smiles, but his smile is fierce. His blond hair is a little straggly on his shoulders. But his snakeskin suit is immaculate, so too the gold tooth in his smile. The spurs of his boots are made of silver, and sharp as talons.

Darkfeather trembles.

Eden gets to her feet to go to Darkfeathar's defense, even though they have just met. A hand gently pulls her back.

Eden looks around, at the face of the Good Lady.

"I thought I'd lost you!"

"Of course you haven't," Gillian Bellaver says to her daughter.

"Don't hold me like that. Why can't I help Darkfeather? I saw her life. I know everything that was done to her. *Somebody* has to speak up for her!"

"No, Eden. It's too late. There's nothing to be said for her now."

The cloud is furious, dark and low over the burial ground, like multiplying wasps brutal with buzz-tone.

"I don't want to see this," Eden moans, but she watches anyway with Gillian's arm comfortingly around her. The Pardoner's horses are black and neatly trimmed and have small silver hooves; the silver hooves and the patient cunning heads of the black horses make Eden feel giddy. The chariot behind the horses glows as if it is made of moonlight.

"You'll never get *me* up in that thing," she says as the Pardoner takes Darkfeather by the hand, raises her from her knees, and leads her away.

"Now you're being foolish. And forgetful. There's no eternal reward and there's no eternal punishment. There are just lessons to be learned. Or relearned."

"What about the Bad Souls?"

"Slow learners," Gillian says with a wry smile. "Very slow."

"There's a couple I have to deal with. Quickly. Help me."

"Can't do it, Eden. That's just not the way things happen. Here, there. Wherever."

"I hate the way things happen! I've *missed* you. Always. They deliberately kept me from you. How fair is that?"

"Life doesn't have to be fair. Or understandable. Only useful. Lessons, Eden. And now you've overstayed. Kick some butt, darling."

Eden blinks away tears, feeling Gillian's grip loosen. There is a trail of fire out there beyond the burial ground, rim-wrinkles on the dry land, a meadowlark-yellow wake in the darkened air, ascending, somewhere. Or perhaps descending—the dark is closing in and Eden has vertigo, can't tell which end is up, her right hand from her left. Strong winds try to lift her off her feet. Eden feels fragile, incomplete. Abandoned.

"*Mother!*"

Silence.

WASHINGTON, D.C. · JUNE 2 · 8:20 A.M. EDT

"Good morning, Mr. President."

"Good morning, Mr. President."

Clint Harvester appeared fit and chipper as he walked, discreetly guided by his wife, through the outer office to the Oval Office in the White House. Tan two-button suit, size forty-six, a subtle window pane check that the President had the height and heft to wear without seeming clownish, a light blue shirt with French cuffs, dark brown Peal shoes. Clint had had a workout and a rubdown and a good breakfast with his plastic tablespoon and a bib to absorb spillage. He was all smiles, although if anyone had been afforded the opportunity to observe him closely, the smile was just a touch gaga.

There were new faces at the secretaries' desks, two of them from the R

Team, but he wouldn't have recognized the old faces. Mary Ellen Connaught, who had been Clint's personal secretary since his statehouse days in Montana, had been removed to the President's private study. Rona still needed Mary Ellen, and she was less of a potential problem in isolation. Rona had paid a high price for Mary Ellen's cooperation; even so she didn't trust the fiftyish spinster, who was a secret drinker.

Washington's insiders and, particularly, the media establishment, led by a diligent hack with investigative best-sellers to his credit and the sanctimonious nature of a castrated monk, had been trying to fan embers of rumor into publishable flame since the President's return. All of them clamoring for a few minutes with the President to check out his alleged fitness for themselves. The White House correspondents were likewise grumbling and prying away at their sources, although Rona had banned them from all but their little corner of the White House. The press corps could be persuasive with long-time White House functionaries, but Rona had terror on her side and everyone working there knew how effectively she could use it.

The senior staff meeting in the Oval Office featured Clint's six and two of Rona's, plus National Security Advisor Beau Chanson at Rona's request. The President's staff murmured "good morning" as if they had loose bridgework to protect as well as their reputations. Clint beamed at them. He was humming a simple tune that had stuck to a batch of memory cells in his disordered brain, a commercial jingle he'd heard on TV.

Rona smilingly sat Clint down in a leather armchair placed to one side of his desk. From her purse she took out a Rubik's Cube and handed it to her husband to play with. For some reason he was fascinated by Rubik's Cube, the bright colors probably. Rona took Clint's chair behind his desk. The blue suit she had chosen to wear today exactly matched the indigo field for the fifty stars on the flag behind her.

Beau Chanson was staring at a spot of egg yolk on Clint Harvester's tie. No one else in the Oval Office wanted to look at him. Rona put on her reading glasses and glanced at the two-page summary of current and upcoming White House events for which Clint would be, at the last minute, indisposed. She cleared her throat. Beau Chanson looked over at her, rising to some sort of challenge. Obviously Clint's loyalists had elected Beau their spokesman.

Rona offered him a relaxed smile and said, "Out with it, Beau."

"The question is, Madam—Mrs. Harvester, how long can murderers get away with the crime if there is blood on their hands that won't wash off."

Rona cocked her head with a certain combative fervor. "That's a movie, isn't it? No, wait. A play. What was her name? Help me out here, Beau."

"Lady Macbeth," Chanson said dourly, inspecting his own hands. "But of course I wasn't drawing a parallel strictly between you and—"

"Now I remember! Read it in high school. Loved him, hated her. She had big ideas but lost her nerve at crunch time."

Beau nodded tensely.

"Not a good analogy," Rona said. "We haven't murdered anyone. Clint's speech the other night was a barn-burner. It raised patriotic temperatures across this land. My land. Your land. The most prosperous nation on earth. Clint socked it to us. Get your chin up, America! What does it matter where the speech actually came from? They were *his words.* All speeches are a form of manipulation. Does that equate to guilt-ridden stares and bloody hands? I've lost my husband. Yes, it's true. God bless him, I may never get him back. Whole and hearty and loving. My strength and my inspiration." Rona paused briefly, trying to remember if she was taping this. Yes, the recorder was voice-activated. "The man I love so deeply is all but gone. That is the tragedy we must all bear. Yet we cannot lose sight of what we've gained since he was elected president. Clint Harvester is nothing less than the Abraham Lincoln of his era! A symbol of what is right about America and will always be right. *Clint When It Counts* has become more than just a slogan. It echoes in the mind of the American people like the words of 'America the Beautiful.' Our man from Montana, those spacious skies. Riding out of the frontier with our nation's standard held high. Thank God we're a country that respects image even more than idealism. How can we afford to lose Clint Harvester now? So there's an element of deception involved in continuing the new spirit of optimism which the polls are going to show this week. What of it? Clint looks buff, doesn't he?" She gave her husband a fond glance, and noticed with a tingle of surprise that he had solved Rubik's Cube and was just sitting there playing with an earlobe and studying her amiably. "A hell of a lot more presentable than Boris Yeltsin, trying to keep his mouth out of his eye while he stumbled through official duties." Rona paused to catch her breath. "Now let's get over our little guilt spasms, shall we, our metaphorically bloody hands. As the Aussies say, it's crap bananas. We have got ourselves a fucking country to run."

The Shipp and Proffit Funeral Home and Crematory ("Family owned and operated since 1926") was located on West Sutter, an area of turn-of-the-century homes, most of them large frame Victorians restored and occupied by lawyers and antique dealers. The home was conveniently located a block from the small city's hospital. There were two acres of grounds with radiant willow trees, a meandering creek, and a prayer garden, nondenominational.

Both of Riley Waring's parents were deceased, but his brother Carl was mayor of Holbrook, so the turnout for Riley's funeral was a civic event. Carl and his wife also had nine children, three of whom had children of their own. Betts couldn't attend and Eden's whereabouts was unknown. Even so the funeral was covered by both local TV stations and three syndicated junk-journalism gossip shows, each with its own satellite uplink truck parked on Sutter. The weather was fair and all of the media attention, including a circling helicopter with a cameraman standing boldly outside on one of the skids, attracted a crowd of local people hoping for a glimpse of Eden. And Eden was just about the only topic of conversation among the arriving mourners. Carl had anticipated something of a melee. Reserve police officers were on hand. Four California Highway Patrol motorcycle cops had showed up for escort duty. Big guys on their police-model Harleys. Carl hadn't requested them, but he was touched by someone else's thoughtfulness. A note to the Commissioner would be his first order of business when Carl returned to the office.

Shipp and Proffit could accommodate very large funerals if necessary, by turning the three viewing parlors on the first floor into one big chapellike room. Riley Waring's mourners numbered close to two hundred by the time brother Carl rose to deliver his eulogy.

There were two late arrivals, escorted upstairs from the basement by Sandy Proffit III and in through a side door. Most of the mourners were looking at Carl, a big man with the sort of homely face women often found endearing, hair dyed too dark for his age, and a weight problem that was always threatening to get out of control. Carl gave the latecomers only a flicker of a glance, enough to register that he didn't know them.

The man was tall and had a weathered face, an outdoorsman's tracklike wrinkles at the corners of sharp, somewhat hooded gray eyes. He walked with a limp and carried an interesting-looking cane, dark and knuckly, capped by a gold lion's head. The young woman with him wore a simple black sleeveless dress, a strand of pearls, dark glasses that hid much of her face like the Lone Ranger's mask. Her blond hair was cut short and slicked back in a tight arrowhead. They took seats to one side of the expanded viewing room. The young woman placed both hands on the Bible she had brought with her, and sat quietly with her face turned toward Carl and the rosewood coffin behind him, banked with floral tributes. Carl shouldered his burden of sadness and began to talk about his brother.

In the Multiphasic Operations and Research Group's surveillance van, which carried the logo of a florist in a city thirty miles north of Holbrook, technicians from Watchbird Section were running tapes acquired from several cameras that had been trained on the parking lot, all exterior walkways, and every outside door of the Shipp and Proffit Funeral Home. A dozen tapes flashed by on as many screens of a computerized scanner called Face-Up, but faster than a human eye could follow. The technology was the design of a MORG proprietary. A database contained Eden Waring's facial contours, and the computer was searching for a match among the twenty or so young women approximately Eden's age who were attending Riley's funeral.

"We expect her to be disguised," a Watchbird techie explained to one of the MORG agents assigned to the funeral. "But she would have had to put on at least thirty pounds in less than a week to change her facial features enough to fool Face-Up. That's a lot of Häagen-Dazs."

"Face-Up don't fuckup?" the agent murmured.

"Cool. Where did they get you, Comedy Central?" The technician, who had a foot and a half of arrogant bushy mustache and a hairless pate, fingered his keyboard lovingly. The center screen of the display, somewhat larger than the others, was projecting a winner. He froze and enhanced, added Eden's yearbook photo to a box on the screen. Enhanced that. Superimposed. In the other photo her face was lifted toward the surveillance camera over the door of a basement entrance.

"There's your girl. I think I dig her more as a blondie. You guys need printouts? How about something in the style of a wanted poster? If there's a reward, I was there first. Like I always am."

Uncle Carl?"

The other mourners had dispersed. Carl Waring had paused at the head of his brother's casket for a few moments of contemplation and prayer. He turned to see the blond girl who had come in late. The man who had accompanied her was standing some distance away, arms folded, watching them. She took off her sunglasses as she approached him. Now he recognized her. Tears flowed. They embraced.

"You came."

"Of course."

"Have you seen Betts, Eden?"

"Yes. She was hurt, but she'll be okay."

"How—? I don't understand what's happened."

"I hope I can explain it to you."

Two of the funeral home associates had appeared and waited with clasped hands to close Riley Waring's coffin.

Carl glanced at the tall man who had come with his niece, wondering who he might be. He said to Eden, "Would you ride with me to the memorial gardens? We can talk on the way. It'll just be family there, Marge and the kids and the minister, of course."

Eden glanced back at Tom Sherard, who nodded.

"Certainly, Carl. Oh, that's Tom. He's a friend. Tom, do you mind following us in your SUV?"

Sherard nodded, smiled at her, and, leaning on his cane, limped out the door.

With their arms around each other, Carl and Eden turned for a last look at Riley. His face like a cleverly painted wood carving in the immaculate deeply gleaming coffin. He was wearing a double-breasted suit Eden hadn't seen before. Eden clutched her throat as if it were full of nettles and uttered a sound between a sigh and a sob. She appeared to collapse. Carl looked at her in anguish and bewilderment. Sandy Proffit III stepped forward smoothly to take the convulsed girl off Carl's hands. He'd seen it happen many times.

"She just needs a few moments," Proffit said. "I'll take her into my study. Mayor, if you're ready to join your family now—"

Carl nodded dumbly. Eden, grieving, was led away, supported by Proffit and a matronly woman who seemed to be there solely for such crises. They spoke soothingly to Eden. Carl wiped his eyes. The other Shipp and Proffit employees who had been waiting to take Riley's coffin down to the hearse in the rear courtyard drew a curtain between Carl and his brother's earthly remains. Carl stumbled out to the vestibule where his wife and children were somberly gathered.

The family was ushered into waiting limousines on the street. Carl stayed on the sidewalk, looking back at the front entrance, wishing Eden would come out, wishing it was over with. Media people, cameras; a small crowd remained behind police barricades, all of them hanging on like vultures waiting for a prospector's pack mule to die.

He noticed the man who had accompanied Eden behind the wheel of an Expedition that was coming out of the parking lot. Instead of turning left to join the small cortege he went the other way, down Sutter toward the Interstate. Carl felt confused. Why was he leaving? Carl heard a helicopter overhead. Still circling, as it had been when they arrived almost an hour ago. He didn't look up. His brow was sweaty. He ate a couple of Tums.

The helicopter was landing behind Shipp and Proffit's. Coming down near the courtyard and the hearses parked there. One hearse, with the rear door open, had received Riley's coffin and was now being loaded with baskets and small trellises of floral remembrances. Some of the flowers were scattered like chaff in the whirlwind generated by the descending chopper.

Two men wearing dark blue blazers left the funeral home by the front entrance and jogged down the wheelchair ramp toward Carl. Sunglasses. Take-charge types. Like the Secret Service men one saw keeping pace watchfully beside the presidential limousine. These men also had the little radio receivers, ear-buttons with pigtail cords that disappeared beneath their shirt collars.

"Carl Waring?"

"Yes?"

One of the men showed him identification. Photo, thumbprint; the name of an agency Carl didn't catch except for four boldly capitalized letters. M-O-R-G. *What the hell was—*

The spokesman propped his sunglasses on the dome of his head. He had a freckled face like rusting sheet metal and eyes as expressionless as peepholes in doors.

"You can accompany your brother to his resting place now. Our condolences."

"But—I'm waiting for—"

"Eden apologizes. She won't be able to join you and the family at the cemetery."

"She—what are you saying, I don't understand what this is about!"

The other agent, who was lanky and had a sour-grapes expression, said, "There's no problem, really, Mr. Waring. Nothing to concern you. Sir, would you get into the lead limo now? I believe the hearse is on its way."

Carl glanced between the two men. The hearse was headed slowly up the drive to the street. And, in the courtyard below, escorted in lock step by two men not unlike those he was confronting, Eden had crossed the bricks to the black helicopter, a helicopter with a decided wasplike appearance.

"There's Eden! Where is she—my God! You've *handcuffed* her?"

Neither man bothered to look. Mr. Freckles said, "I don't think you saw handcuffs, sir. Probably sunlight was reflecting off one of her bracelets. There were no handcuffs."

Carl hesitated, stood a little straighter, and said, "Gentlemen, I don't know who you are, but I am the mayor of this city and I *demand* to know where you are taking my niece. Is she under arrest? Permit me to have a look at your warrant."

One of the city cops came off the street where he was directing traffic to see what was up.

"Mayor, anything I can do?"

The sourball MORG agent glanced at the cop's nameplate and said, "Government business. You're out of your depth here, peace officer Pat."

Carl didn't like the way his heart was reacting, and he was suddenly short of breath. Eden had disappeared into the back of the helicopter. He watched with a growing chill of dismay as it lifted off, hovered, banked east, and poured on the speed. He hadn't known helicopters could move that fast.

"This is outrageous! By whose authority! You have no right! I demand!"

"Go easy, Your Honor. Your niece is taking a little trip. Some people want to talk to her. She'll be okay. VIP treatment, we guarantee."

"Free country! Constitutional right! Due process of law!"

"I think he's about to come in his shorts," the lanky one said to his partner. "Seriously."

"Let's break this up," Mr. Freckles suggested. "Please get in the car, sir. Or do you need our assistance?"

"You better not touch him," the cop named Pat warned. And then to the sourball agent: "Who do you think you're looking at?"

"Am I looking at something? I don't see anything. A pile of day-old dog crap, maybe."

Mr. Freckles said, "Learn to use a little psychology, Kyle."

The lanky one lifted his face disgustedly to the sky. "Jesus, I hate it down here in the minor leagues."

Nobody said anything else for a dozen seconds. Carl couldn't talk at all. He had choked to the chinline and was seeing red. Feeling inadequate. Intimidated, as the silence wore on. He'd always been first in his class, captain on the field. In his third term as mayor of Holbrook, California. Intimidated? Carl Waring? It was emotional sacrilege.

His nine-year-old daughter GayLee poked her head out of the lead limo of the cortege and clamored, "Come *on*, Daddy! My dress is making me itchy. I *hate* new dresses!"

Carl looked at her, then looked to see if the black helicopter was still visible against the summery buttermilk clouds. No trace of it. He looked again at the MORG agents. He found his voice. But it was shockingly weak to his ears.

"We'll sue."

"Free country," Mr. Freckles said with a slight smirk.

WASHINGTON, D.C. • JUNE 2 • 2:45 P.M. EDT

Rona Harvester interrupted a tour of the White House she was conducting for the Senegalese president and his wife to take a call on a secure phone.

"Got her!" Victor Wilding said, sounding almost jubilant, a welcome contrast to his recent mood and tone.

"Wonderful, Victor! Any problems?"

"No. Just as a precaution she's been sedated."

"That may be wise. Where are you taking her?"

"Plenty Coups. I'm already here and I thought, since you're planning a trip to the western White House next week, it would be convenient for you to meet her where we can guarantee security."

"Good idea. I assume everything else is going well?"

"The cake is out of the oven. Delivery date is the sixth. By the way, if you haven't been watching the news—"

"I don't watch the news; I'm all the news I care about," Rona said, half jokingly. "But AG called me. Search and Rescue located one of the Conan helicopters?"

"It had crashed in an isolated cove where, apparently, some cultists have been practicing ritual sacrifice. They discovered fragments of what may be human bones on a rock that served as an altarpiece."

"Doesn't that give you the creeps?"

"The remains of the pilot were in the chopper, but there's no trace of Robert Hyde yet."

"Now, do you suppose—"

"The Bureau's forensics people may be able to tell something from the bits of bone that weren't consumed. But only if Hyde's DNA is on file someplace. Maybe he kept frozen sperm in the office fridge, along with a bowl of boogers and a ball of belly-button lint."

"You're in *such* a good mood today. Love you with all of my heart."

"Can't wait to see you—Madame President."

"Oh, Victor. We don't want to uncork the champagne just yet."

The girl was tucked away in the bedroom of the apartment reserved for Victor Wilding when he was in residence at the facility. She was sleeping off the narcotics combo she had been injected with prior to the flight from Metro Oakland airport to Plenty Coups, which had kept her numb and dumb all the way. Marcus Woolwine had already paid a visit to her bedside to withdraw blood and supervise an IV drip with a chemical mix designed to repress fear and unwelcome memories and elevate her mood to the level of, say, a newly crowned Miss Universe. She was wearing a headband of Woolwine's invention that provided electromagnetic stimuli to several different areas of her brain, interspersed with taped instructions and information she would find useful upon awakening. She had two registered nurses from the facility's medical staff watching over her, but they wore mufti. Dr. Woolwine had specified sandals, shorts, and Polynesian print shirts. Soothing colors and fragrances had been chosen to take the edge off the apartment's rather austere, masculine look and further refresh her spirits when she woke from a sleep deepened by pharmacology. As soon as they learned her preferences she would have her own apartment, anything else she wanted. But she would never spend another moment alone, nor set foot on the surface of the world again.

Not that she would miss her other life, Woolwine assured Victor Wilding. Her foster mother and college friends. What was left of that life would exist in her memory like a rosy dream of childhood.

"She now will be entirely focused on pleasing the most important person in her life—her guardian, mentor, friend. Lover, if you'd like. She's at the peak of her beauty and vulnerability at this age. So tempting. But I advise against taking full advantage of the affections we are going to create for your benefit."

"Whatever you say. But how long will it take before she trusts me completely?"

"I'd like three days. If it's a rush job, I suppose I can cut the time to under fifty hours, but—"

"Three days! Aren't we taking a hell of a risk with all this brain engineering? Destroying what makes her unique?"

Woolwine held up a cautionary finger. "Remember, what we are doing with this girl is positive conditioning. Reinforcement of basic emotional needs. Enhancing her pleasure drive through hypnotic hyperesthesia. We are making her *very* happy, even as she slumbers. Now, if you'll recall the case of Peter Sandza—"

"It's because of his father that Robin has been on a ventilator for twenty-some years. He deliberately dropped Robin from the roof of Psi Faculty. Not that I blame *you*, of course. You were on another team then. You had your orders."

"Just so. Peter Sandza was both a challenge of rehabilitation—he was in miserable physical condition when I got him—and a feat of *negative* emotional conditioning. We researched the subconscious dynamics at our disposal—Peter was engaged in a life-and-death pursuit, which took the form of an archetypal quest in the paleomammalian brain—and strengthened his will to find his son at all costs. We did nothing to disturb the cutting edge of his high purpose. We didn't want him to lose a jot of his animal cunning. Remember this. When Peter Sandza was on a hunting trip at the age of ten, he accidentally shot his father to death. A classic archetype that horrifyingly came to life. From that moment his life was shaped by an act of accidental violence. Peter slew the godhead; thereafter he sought to atone for his error by undertaking a painful quest against what are commonly held to be the evils of the world. But the quest was largely a delusion proposed by the archetypal Black Magician: Childermass, our founder. In the beginning Peter's quest served as a time of rigorous preparation and testing. Peter compensated for what might have become a pathological monomania by marrying and fathering a son of his own. Thus he led a, quote, 'normal' life at those times when he needed to lay down the banner and quit the arena for a while."

"But how did you condition him to—"

"Peter had been a lieutenant commander in the Navy. He often referred to young Robin as 'Skipper,' and when he did so the boy invariably responded with 'Commander.' A term of both affection and respect."

"You got all of this out of Peter through hypnosis?"

"Yes. We assumed that Peter Sandza would overcome the obstacles placed in his way by the Black Magician and eventually be reunited with his son. We reinforced in Peter's mind the usage of Robin's nickname. 'Skipper' would very nearly be the first word from his lips. And Robin surely would respond with a joyous 'Commander.' The single word that would compel Peter to instantly destroy his son, with whatever means were at hand. As it happened, Robin was dangling from the roof in Peter's grip, and when Peter heard him say 'Commander,' he released him to smash on the rocks below. He was simply obeying an instinct more powerful than the one we overrode. Peter loved his son. But don't forget that Robin had acquired mythological status in Peter's unconscious mind. The circle had closed. Peter slew his father; Peter's primal fear was that Robin would grow up to slay *him.* That fear allowed Peter temporarily to assume his own father's role. Peter simply defended himself, as his father could not."

Woolwine did something Victor Wilding had rarely seen; he took off his mirror sunglasses and looked straight at Wilding. His eyes, the yellow of aged ivory, glowed with a chilling rapture.

"I wrote the last act of a grand tragedy that was preordained when man first began to walk upright. Fascinating, don't you think?"

Wilding looked toward the closed door of his bedroom and helped himself to another shot of whiskey. Woolwine waved away the offered bottle and continued to regard Wilding steadily. Wilding wished he would put the glasses back on.

"That girl is Peter Sandza's blood. Gillian Bellaver's prowess. My last hope. Whatever is there in her brain that makes it unique—don't fuck with it, Doctor. There can't be any more tragedies."

Woolwine rose from his chair, no effort for him in spite of his years. He stood five feet seven on bowed but muscular legs.

"If you'll pardon me, I'm running late for my game with Dr. Fries. We wouldn't want to lose our court." He slipped on his reflective glasses again, a businesslike but somewhat dismissive gesture. "By the way. It may reassure you to keep in mind one simple fact. Marcus Woolwine has never failed."

4:40 P.M. MDT

Victor Wilding met with the Director and chief strategist of MORG's Accelerated Counter-Insurgency Defense operations, a man named Willis "Bronc" Skarbeck, in the Situations and Planning Center.

Bronc Skarbeck was a lean man with chili-pepper-red hair, dyed, and fuming blue eyes. While serving as commanding general of the Marine Corps he had been passed over for chairman of the Joint Chiefs. Not long after this crushing disappointment he suffered a psychotic break, paying lewd attention to a sixteen-year-old girl who was the granddaughter of a Supreme Court justice and a patient of his psychologist wife. The two of them set out in a twenty-nine-foot boat intending to sail around the world. They didn't make it out of Chesapeake Bay. Bronc lacked critical seafaring judgment with half a quart of rum under his belt, and after he cut too closely across the bow of a large yacht the Coast Guard put an end to his spree. That night General Willis Skarbeck led off the evening news.

But in spite of the busted career and wrecked marriage and court-ordered psychiatric hospital time Bronc subsequently served, Victor Wilding thought Skarbeck probably still had good mileage left and gave him a job offer. The job description was to plan a military-style takeover of the United States government that would not involve hostilities with the military establishment currently in place, then implement that plan.

Bronc said bullshit, couldn't be done without massive intervention by a major foreign axis like the recovering (from a bout of democracy) Russians and their newfound, slant-eyed buddies to the east.

He was urged to give it more thought. Starting with the premise that if the American People were scared enough of an outside threat to their security (an unnamed supergroup of terrorists supported by a dozen nations that, individually, could not defeat the U.S. in armed conflict), and there was someone they could turn to who seemed to have the power to keep their hopes and dreams alive, they would put up with a shredding of the Constitution and the Bill of Rights to obtain the security they desired. Most of them didn't care all that much for politics anyway. The AP just wanted things to go on working the way they were used to having them work. It was an imperative of human nature.

So Bronc came up with the idea of ACID, which was a kind of Big Daddy for local law enforcement agencies throughout the country. ACID provided money, training, and matériel that was gratefully received. ACID used a tidal wave of profits from MORG's global drug operations to create a unified force of agencies that ranged from state game and fish commissions to major-city police departments. Within forty-eight hours of the national emergency that Bronc postulated, his Accelerated Counter-Insurgency Defense command would be in charge, by Executive Order. Every base commander of every military installation in the U.S., many of whom were clandestine MORG supporters (either through bribery or blackmail), would be relieved or implemented by ACID personnel. The evacuation of official Washington would be conducted quietly. Bunkers had been prepared for the legislators in the Maryland and Virginia countryside, where they could count on a long stay while Clint Harvester ran the country from the western White House. But Rona soon added her contribution, even bolder ideas than Bronc Skarbeck dared to conceive.

The detonation of two or three nuclear devices on American soil was a regrettable part of the master plan. Even Rona had hesitated to use nukes. But only nuclear terror and the threat of more bombs had the power to unite the masses and escalate their approval of the Harvesters to near idolatry.

The American people would pray to Jesus. But only Rona could give them hope, give them back their lives.

On her terms.

The main feature of the Situations and Planning Center was a three-dimensional computer-constructed map of the United States, based on high-resolution satellite photographs, that took up an area the size of a football field on the main floor. A gallery like a running track in a gymnasium afforded a view of the layout. The gallery was honeycombed with virtual-reality booths in which technicians could monitor MORG operations in as many as twenty cities simultaneously by following agents equipped with sophisticated transponders, cameras, and sensors along the streets or through skyscrapers. Ride in elevators with them. Take an advance look at potentially dicey situations as a mission unfolded and advise the team leader. All the super-computers needed were street numbers in order to create a complete virtual-reality environment, including customers sipping coffee at a sidewalk café and a basset hound peeing on a nearby hydrant.

Marcus Woolwine's contributions to virtual reality, Randy and Herb, had departed Plenty Coups at noon with lots of fishing gear in the back of their '97 Jimmy and a Hiroshima-yield nuclear device in what appeared to be a large tackle box. The box had been designed to shield neutron emissions. S and P Center was tracking Randy and Herb eastbound on Interstate 90 through the Wyoming grasslands. They would be stopping for dinner in Rapid City, South Dakota; then Herb would take over behind the wheel. They had a reservation at a Comfort Inn near Sioux Falls where they would sleep with the tackle box in the bathtub and MORG agents occupying the rooms on either side of them, fully alert through the night. A dedicated satellite fifty-five miles above the Comfort Inn also would be watching. The atomic demolitions device, like the one that had been detonated in Portland, was Russian made and had once been a part of a 132-bomb stockpile. At least eighty-four of them could no longer be accounted for by the Twelfth Department's high command. MORG owned six, and knew the whereabouts of twenty more.

Victor Wilding spent little time on this aspect of his briefing. The countdown for the bombing of another midsized American city was under way.

Wilding had made only one change, albeit a crucial change, in the last twenty-four hours, based on weather forecasts for the upper Midwest. It seemed that on the morning the bomb was to be detonated, a cold front out of Canada would be near the original target, which was Madison, Wisconsin, with prevailing winds that would carry what was left of the hot stuff (up to a lethal 800 REM) down to Chicago in a matter of hours. MORG's Homefolks department maintained a large base of operations near Chicago. Also Victor Wilding had had some good times there. He liked that toddlin' town, and didn't wish to contaminate it.

On the other hand, he'd never been to Nashville and hated country music as much as Rona enjoyed it. Nashville was in store for some nice late-spring weather at the zero hour; the anticipated fallout, according to MORG's meteorologists, would be confined to sparsely populated lower Appalachia.

So Randy and Herb were on their way to Nashville. A new site for the *chemodan,* the Russian name for their highly portable nukes, had been selected. Ease of access was guaranteed. Nashville was a done deal.

"Now let's talk about the assassination," Wilding said to Bronc Skarbeck.

PIÑATA HOT SPRINGS, CALIFORNIA • JUNE 2 • 7:45 P.M. PDT

There was a trace of sunset remaining when Tom Sherard saw the Greyhound sign near the southern end of the main drag of Piñata Hot Springs. He pulled off the road onto the gravel parking lot around the adobe-style café that also served as a bus station. His bad leg was hurting fiercely. Too many hours on the road, driving more or less aimlessly, until he was satisfied that he hadn't been followed. Around noon, after leaving the funeral home in Holbrook, he had turned over the Ford Expedition to the rental agency at Fresno's airport and picked up another SUV.

As the name indicated, Piñata Hot Springs was a spa and resort town in a valley between dusty dry mountains about seventy miles northwest of L.A. The café, called Mintoro's, seemed to be a popular spot with locals, most of whom drove pickups. The kind of pickups loaded with options. There were no buses around.

Sherard found a place to leave the SUV and got out with his cane. The coming night held a promise of high-desert chill. Inside the café there was a small crowd waiting for tables, but he saw her as soon as he came in, sitting toward the back of a snug corner booth, head down, a hand to one cheek as she listlessly turned the pages of a fashion magazine. There was an uneaten sandwich on a plate in front of her, a cup of coffee.

She flinched when he eased into the seat opposite her, then smiled wanly. He saw with a slight shock of remembrance that her left eye was turning in, as Gillian's eye had done when she was overly tired and under severe strain. Eden wore a pale yellow shirt and khakis with cargo pockets, clothing that she had taken with her in her shoulder bag to the funeral home in Holbrook.

"Hello, Eden."

"Hi. Thought I was going to be stood up. In the middle of nowhere."

"Just watching my back, in case."

"You must have learned a lot about stalking, or being stalked, in your profession."

"Vanishing profession, I'm afraid. When did you arrive?"

"Seven, seven-fifteen. Bus was late." She stifled a yawn. "Sorry. I've had six cups of coffee since noon, and I still can't keep my eyes open. They must have done something to my dpg." Eden glanced around as she spoke, fearing eavesdroppers. "Doped her, even though she knew we wanted her to be cooperative."

"Yes, they probably would take that precaution." He smiled, but the smile didn't feel right to him. He shrugged uncomfortably, watching her. "I rather imagine it's as if one has a twin. An emotional kinship."

"Not the same. There really isn't a relationship. I don't think about her that much, any more than you think about your own shadow. We get along, although she has a lot of attitude. Suppose I do too. I've always known my dpg existed, and that if I needed her . . . like today . . ."

"How did you pull it off? I left, according to plan, but I spent the rest of the day worrying that something might have gone wrong."

"No big deal. I don't have to meditate. I don't fall into a trance. There has to be a problem I can't solve by myself. A crisis. I get a buzzing sensation, like there's a bee in my navel. Then she's *there,* but not for everyone to see. She has to put some clothes on first." Eden lowered her head, as if she found this embarrassing. "I went into Sandy Proffit's bathroom—black marble and gold fixtures, by the way—and she was waiting. She was a blonde too, that was a shock. I guess I was expecting my old face. I gave her my dress and put on the things I'd brought with me. We talked about what could happen, where she might be taken. Then the MORG guys showed up like we thought they would, you know the rest. I waited an hour and hiked to the bus station. I was careful. I doubt if anyone saw me leave the funeral home. I placed a call to Bertie, that pay phone we chose yesterday, to let her know I was okay."

"Do you know if your doppelganger is at Plenty Coups?"

Eden shook her head. "If I had the mental energy I could locate her, see what she sees when she's conscious. But I'm exhausted. I'm not sure how long I can keep going without a firm sense of reality."

She looked around the café again, slowly, with sad eyes. Sherard held her hand.

"We'll leave in a minute. How long have you been aware that there are two of you?"

"*Two* that I know of," Eden said with a slight shudder. "If there are any more of me, probably I'm schizoid. I don't have the power to guarantee my sanity." She smiled painfully. "When did I find out? It was one of the Dreamtime lessons the Good . . . that my *mother* taught me, when I was a child."

"Gillian," Sherard said, smiling tautly. Then, although he knew it was a bad time he had to ask, "Can you take me to her, Eden?"

"Bertie thinks so. But I have to ask Gillian. *Muth-er.* Don't know why it's so hard for me to say. Not used to thinking of her that way. Tom, won't it just keep the hurt going on forever? Gillian has let go. She'd want you to do the shame. Same. God, I'm tongue-tied. And so tired. Please Tom. No more for now. You said we could get out of here. Anywhere. I don't care where we bed down for the night." Her eyes closed momentarily, her head nodded sleepily. Then she looked up, alarmed. "But we can't . . . you can't . . . Peter Sandza . . . I don't want to do what Gillian did."

"I've had no such thoughts, Eden," he said stiffly.

"I'm not talking about sex. Of course not. I know you and Bertie . . . Tom, Gillian caused Peter to hemorrhage. He had a stroke because he spent that one night next to her, and she dreamed. She killed her best friend while dreaming. The girl was prone to nosebleeds. I was never allowed to have sleepovers when I was growing up. I had to insist on a single room when the basketball team traveled. My room at home couldn't be near Betts and Riley's room, because Betts knew about me. I never let myself fall asleep when I was with my boyfriend. I can make people bleed when I'm dreaming true dreams. Seeing the future. I noticed there were a lot of bloody noses graduation day, and it wasn't the plane crash that caused them; it was *me* seeing the crash before it happened."

"I know about the bleeding. Gillian and I always slept together. But by the time we were married that aspect of her power was much diminished."

"Thank God, then there's some hope for me."

"There's every hope for you, Eden."

They spent the night in the VIP suite of the golf resort near Piñata Hot Springs that was owned by a long-time friend of Buck Hannafin's. Eden must have passed a relatively peaceful night. When Sherard knocked on her door at eight-fifteen she was already up and gone.

Eden had left him a note and an i.o.u. that made him smile. She had borrowed two hundred dollars from his wallet to buy a few things. He found her on one of the tennis courts wearing a new outfit from the pro shop and playing the resort's resident pro. She had a somewhat erratic but ferocious game; apparently basketball was not the only sport at which she excelled. The pro was Hispanic, short and wiry, on the backside of fifty. He still had most of his game but his legs were about gone, so Eden gave him all he could handle. Sherard ate breakfast on the terrace overlooking the courts and glanced through the L.A. *Times* while he kept an eye on Eden.

After the match she stopped by his table, towel around her neck, face damp, a sparkle in her eyes he hadn't seen before.

"Hope you didn't mind about the money."

"Of course not. You looked good out there. Are you ready to eat?"

"I'm starved, but I want to swim first. Do you play golf, Tom?"

"Eight handicap, usually."

She looked in the direction of the first tee. "They rent clubs here. I could reserve us for nine holes around four-thirty, when it's not so hot."

"Good."

She picked up a glass of water from the table and drained it. Sherard smiled. Eden looked around again. "Nice here."

"Yes, it is."

"Can we stay another night, do you think?"

"That's up to you."

Eden lowered her voice. "When is Bertie leaving for Wisconsin?"

"Tomorrow afternoon, by corporate jet. Another good friend of the Senator's. The plane also will be at our disposal, when you're refreshed and ready to go."

Eden nodded, and he saw tension returning to her body until she threw it off with a shrug.

"Don't think about it yet," he cautioned her. "Play hard, sleep well, recharge the batteries."

"Hard not to think. I'm not so sure I can find it, even with Bertie helping. I couldn't locate the one in Portland during Dreamtime. I don't even know what the fuckin' thing looks like. I can't visualize it. If I miss, we could all die."

"You're everything Gillian was, and more. You will succeed."

"You know that you don't have to go with me, Tom."

"Don't be ridiculous. I may be useless on your playing field, but I have my own talents. Did you dream last night?"

"I always dream."

"Bad dreams?"

"No. Peaceful. I was leading Portia Darkfeather's horse home for her. His name is Dark Valiant. I wouldn't mind owning him. I'd like having a horse and living in Montana. What wonderful skies they have there. Days can go by with nothing to listen to but the wind. I wouldn't mind that kind of loneliness. It's a place where I could feel secure."

"Don't forget that something not so wonderful lies beneath the grasslands."

"Plenty Coups. Where Darkfeather worked, and trained. I'm sorry she's gone. She could've showed me one of those devices. If that's where they keep them. Showed me how to disarm the bastard. By the way, it's Russian."

"How do you know that?"

Eden threw up her hands. "I know a lot of things without knowing *how* I know them! I've been thinking about it, so—"

"So now it may be up to what your doppelganger can spy out for us. Do you have confidence in her?"

Eden shrugged again, turned away abruptly.

"Last time I sent her out, I had to get her loose from a pit bull. God only knows what she'll be up to this time. She's me; which means she has all of my, ah, shortcomings. Where she stumbles, there I fall. I'd better go change now." She looked back at him, a quick smile. "See ya later."

Sherard watched Eden jog away and mulled over a useful piece of information. If she was right and the nuclear device was of Russian origin, perhaps stolen from their stockpile of portable bombs, Buck Hannafin might be able to quietly obtain an exact description of what the ad hoc NESTers (for Nuclear Energy Search Team) would be looking for, once they all had assembled in Madison, Wisconsin. Buck had considered, then reluctantly ruled out, alerting the government agencies involved in counterterrorism to the potential threat to America's Dairyland. Because MORG would be one of the agencies so informed. MORG would then either cancel the delivery or move their device somewhere else.

Thinking about what they were up against, the deadly risk not only to themselves but to upward of three million innocent people, ruined Sherard's digestion. He left the terrace to find a pay phone from which to call Hannafin.

SAUSALITO, CALIFORNIA • MAY 30-JUNE 1

The assassin once known as Phil Haman had obtained new identities for himself within a couple of hours of making a violent exit from the interrogation room at the FBI's Sacramento field office. Not the least of his talents was picking pockets. As for disguises, a quick trip through a Kmart provided everything he needed for a radical change in appearance, which he accomplished in the handicapped stall of the men's room in a Burger King down the street. He had every confidence that the Bureau would consider his defection and apprehension an in-house project. He traveled south in a rented car charged to a pharmaceutical salesman from Seattle, abandoned it in Oakland, and took a taxi into Berkeley. There he changed identities once more in a third-rate hotel. BART took him across the bay to San Francisco. A Hyde Street cable car delivered him within two blocks of the Sausalito ferry, and by sunset he was walking the six blocks to Poppa Too Sweets', a barge-based waterfront bistro that he owned through a dummy corporation. He maintained an aerie above the restaurant, small but ultra-secure, where he discarded identity number two, showered, drank half a bottle of the North Coast's finest Pinot Noir, and took a nap that lasted for fourteen hours.

He dreamed about killing Eden Waring. When he woke up in his safe house she was the first thing on his mind. It was early afternoon, mistily overcast. He looked up through a gray oblong of skylight over his narrow bed. He smelled the sea, heard voices on the nearby wharf, heard the moan of the incoming ferry. He felt calm and secure, not inclined to brood about his predicament and potential disgrace. Even though it was clear to him what he was up against. He had killed the girl, that was a fact, because he didn't miss. She was dead, then she'd come back from the dead. He was willing to accept that now. Supernatural intervention. She'd been resurrected. She had wanted her revenge, but the assassin had seen, looking into the kid's eyes, that Geoff McTyer didn't have murder in him. What a pussy.

So it would be up to Eden Waring's ghost, or whatever it was, if it chose to pursue him. For now, the assassin felt sure, he had eluded it. He did not feel its presence in the safe house. Matter of time, he assumed. He knew he would see Eden Waring, or Eden's shade, again. What then? How could he lay a ghost for good?

In the meantime the assassin was more concerned about his professional reputation. His standing with Impact Sector. Given the opportunity, he could explain about Eden Waring's death and subsequent resurrection. But that wasn't going to happen. They never debriefed him. He had no direct contact with them. There was no phone number to call. They would not bring him in. But they already would know about the botched assignment. They had judged him. It would go into his jacket.

The fear of a less than perfect approval rating burned like a branding iron held to his heart.

Would Impact Sector intercede for him, smooth things over with the Sacramento field office? He'd been a little rough on a couple of the agents while taking his leave. So he couldn't return to Vegas anytime soon. Face was upset about that. Face needed the limelight to survive. All the assassin needed was a clean approval rating.

He got up and took another shower. He felt like being young again.

The assassin selected from his own cache of false identities a new face, a name. The appropriate hairpiece with matching eyebrows and mustache came out of the wardrobe and makeup trunk Face had provided for the safe house. He filled in the lunar wasteland he saw in his lighted makeup mirror. Using the old skills soothed him. When he was finished he looked, in the magnifying mirror, no older than thirty-five. Attractive. His name was now Corey. Corey DeSales.

He fed himself and after dark picked up one of the boys who worked the waterfront and took him back to the aerie, where the lights were seductively low. The boy was winsome and experienced, but although the assassin had given himself a new face neither of them in spite of their labors could give him a sustainable hard-on.

Corey paid the boy off and retired with another bottle of wine, candlelight on his new, lugubrious face, thin chest, and flaccid pecker. He didn't need sleep. He needed an opportunity to redeem himself. But Impact Sector might choose to punish him.

The worst punishment he could conceive would be never to hear from them again.

Buck Hannafin met with a select group of people whom he had reason to believe he could trust, i.e., important Washington insiders and members of Congress who had no professional blemishes or personal peccadilloes on their records: illegal campaign contributions, vote fraud, perjury, bribery, misappropriation of funds, drug addiction, ill-advised love affairs, or sex with a minor. Anything Rona Harvester could know about and use to her advantage. The meeting was on neutral ground, at a farm near Middleburg, Virginia. The farm was the weekend retreat of Roswell Fullmer, senior partner of a major East Coast law firm. Fullmer had once served the nation capably as Attorney General. His expertise was important, and Hannafin had invited him to attend.

The remaining nine participants included Wanda Chevrille, head of the CIA, a woman with a nun's peaceful face and a complex mind; Nick Grella, head of the intelligence division of the Secret Service; Admiral Wesley Sobieski, Chairman of the Joint Chiefs; and John Wellford McGarvey, who had been Clint Harvester's Chief of Staff for his first two years in office. McGarvey had resigned after one too many personality clashes with Rona.

Buck Hannafin began the conference in his usual blunt beetle-browed manner.

"To borrow Ronald Reagan's conception—I believe he borrowed it from someone else, but never mind—we have an *evil empire* in our midst. The basis for a fascist dictatorship authorized by Executive Orders has been in place for some time. The architects of this seditious conspiracy are, of course, Rona Harvester and her paramour Victor Wilding."

The representative from the CIA shook her head in silent disgust.

Nick Grella said, "This won't be in the news tomorrow, but while Clint Harvester was posing with his golf clubs at Burning Tree today, the Secret Service was formally booted out of the White House. The 'presidential' signature on the change-over memo has to be a forgery, but a good one. We probably couldn't get a consensus on the forgery from the FBI's handwriting experts to take to the Attorney General. Meanwhile I have twenty-four hours to turn over our files to MORG."

Admiral Sobieski had been looking over copies of the Executive Orders that McGarvey had thoughtfully taken with him after losing his job. The Admiral whistled dismally.

"I knew some of these existed, but my God! Where did *this* one come from? EO 13083 wipes out the Tenth Amendment to the Constitution! All state and local authority is revoked." He looked at Roswell Fullmer. "Can this be challenged legally?"

"There is an avenue for challenge, Wes," Fullmer said. "Public outrage, heavily endorsed by the media, prompting a constitutional amendment supported by men of individual honor, personal character, and absolute independence, as Daniel Webster once described our Senate." He smiled, nostalgia in his peacock-blue eyes. "The good old days, we like to think."

"There's still a handful left in Congress to defend the high ground," Buck said. "But the ablest legislator I know on the Hill is leaving after this term to take over the family banking business."

"We've still got you, Buck," McGarvey said.

"Long as my pacemaker holds up, John. Let us not forget how I've survived. My forebears had a good bit of money laid by, so unlike Lyndon and his ilk I never had to steal an election to get my start in politics. And I never did acquire the stink of ambition."

Admiral Sobieski tossed aside his copy of the Executive Orders.

"Hell, the military complex is relegated to managing public transport, utilities, and food distribution!"

"One critical function of martial law," McGarvey said. "Which of course supports the dictatorship disguised as executive fiat. All power is converted to the presidency, overnight; but indisputably we have a captive President, incapable of making rational decisions."

"Quite a setup," Buck commented. "But as things stand right now, Clint Harvester is both Rona's strength and the fatal flaw in her lofty ambitions. Executive Orders can't be countermanded. Therefore Clint has to be removed, legally, from office as soon as possible. And there's no EO granting Rona the right of succession."

"We hope," Wanda Chevrille said, leaning into the conversation like a chess master about to pounce. In concert with all of Clint's loyal supporters, she thought Rona was trash. "But Mrs. Harvester has long been using Eva Peron's career as a template. She has popular approval. All that appears to be lacking now is an adequate pretext."

Buck stroked his forehead, keeping his eyes down momentarily. He knew what the pretext was, and it gave him heartache to conceal this knowledge from friends.

"If there is such an order," Fullmer said, "it's of recent origin, and Justice would have no difficulty proving the order a fraud, once Clint Harvester's true mental state became public knowledge." He looked around at his guests. "Unless, of course, all members of the judicial and executive branches, and most of us sitting here, are scheduled to become unpersons."

That earned a full minute of uneasy contemplation, the participants moving, emotionally, closer to each other. Admiral Sobieski, the only one there who was drinking hard liquor, poured himself another bourbon.

"EO 1099," Buck said. "With the communications media in the hands of our new government, only Rona Harvester's voice will be heard in the land."

Further silence.

Buck continued, "Unless Clint Harvester recovers his faculties and his own voice. Highly doubtful. Rona will martyr him before that happens."

"What are you saying, Buck?" Wanda asked, eyes narrowing.

"I'm saying that past a certain point in her ambitions, Clint is more useful to Rona dead than he is alive. I do believe the thought has crossed her mind."

"Leapin' Jesus," McGarvey said, not disagreeing. He knew Rona Harvester better than anyone else in the room.

Buck nodded gravely, then looked at the head of Secret Service Intel.

"Nick, what are the chances we could get Clint to ourselves long enough to have him certified incompetent by psychiatrists? Forget about his personal physician, Tray Daufuskie is already compromised."

"How much time are we talking about?"

"I'm no head doctor, but I did some asking around. Four hours maximum."

"With MORG in control of White House security now—no chance."

"What if we kidnap him, then?"

"Get real, Buck," Wanda cautioned.

He smiled. "In a manner of speaking. I figure what we need to do is make Clint available for evaluation without anyone knowing what's going on." He looked at Nick Grella.

"As I told you, we no longer have responsibility for the President. End of story, as FLOTUS likes to say."

"You don't have access to him at the White House. When is the President most vulnerable, if you don't mind giving up a few trade secrets?"

"No secret. 'Rawhide' is vulnerable to unplanned access when he's anywhere but inside the White House. On the campaign trail. Official state visits. Vacations. I hated those trips to the western White House."

"Yeah, why? It's a ranch. Four people per square mile out that way."

"The Big Country Ranch covers about twenty thousand acres. The President and Mrs. Harvester don't like having company when they're out riding, which they do every day at Big Country, weather permitting. They ride hard and fast—that's a nightmare in itself, trying to maintain a visual without the aid of a helicopter or light plane. And there's always the chance, although they're both accomplished equestrians, that 'Rawhide' might take a fall and break his neck. They can easily shake off our guys riding security. The Harvesters enjoy getting all lathered up, hot and bothered you might say, then hopping off their mounts in a secret place and, uh, having sexual relations."

Wanda Chevrille, whose nickname at the CIA was the Virgin Queen, winced slightly. "In spite of his condition, do you suppose they are still . . . having relations?"

"From what we hear," Nick said, "it's just about all he wants to do these days."

"Did Rona ever ride by herself?" Buck asked.

"Now and then, when the President had business to take care of."

"I mean, totally alone."

"I believe so."

Buck Hannafin and Nick Grella looked at each other for a time. Nick was uneasy; Buck shifted his weight in his leather club chair and bore down on him, a flash in his eyes like sharp sabers rising.

"Let's hear it, Nick. What do you know?"

Grella said, "It won't be announced for a day or two, but before we got booted off the POTUS detail Zephyr penciled in a week at Big Country for some R and R. They're scheduled to leave on Sunday."

"That figures. Rona has the brass balls of a Minoan bull, but she's kept Clint on display at the White House as long as she dares. We have some time. A few days, week at the most. No doubt in *my* mind that while the President is relaxing out west he'll meet with an unfortunate accident. Around the stables, or when he's at full gallop across the prairie."

Wanda Chevrille looked as if she might be wanting to ask Buck to "get real" again, but she reconsidered. Except for two or three nervous coughs there was silence in the room. Buck Hannafin scanned concerned faces and faces with the sickly expressions of long-time public servants with nowhere left to scramble.

"Do we do this?" Buck demanded. Menacing, outraged. "Do we try to save Clint Harvester and put Rona behind bars where she belongs? She's got conquest on her mind and an exit planned for the rest of us, an exit as swift as strychnine in the throat of a rat."

PLENTY COUPS, MONTANA · JUNE 6 · 1:20 P.M. MDT

After a morning of wind surfing and shell collecting, Eden Waring's doppelganger met her best friend Victor Wilding for lunch on the terrace of the Muronga Reef Club, of which he was a part owner. The stone-paved terrace was shaded by several gazebolike structures with thatched roofs. A few yards away the white sand beach sloped into the shallow lagoon, turquoise near the shore, deep blue beyond the coral reef where gulls, frigate birds, and a few boobies soared. The dpg looked around contentedly. Away from the beach she had slipped on a lime-yellow shantung lounger split up one side to the waist. Behind the terrace and the firewalkers' pit were luxury log-and-thatch *bures* grouped around patios and small saltwater swimming pools. Looming over the resort, an ancient eroded volcano overgrown with jungle blocked a third of the still-unclouded sky. She had been there long enough to know that by midafternoon clouds would gather, the short driving rains would come. Time then to curl up for a nap in her hammock. She wasn't quite aware of just how she passed the time each day. Swimming, sailing, tennis, snorkeling from an outrigger canoe. Sunrise, noon heat and humidity, fine sand like hot velvet to her bare feet, sweat, torrents of rain, cool baths. A wardrobe to die for, selected in the resort's boutique. Torchlit evenings, guitars, dancing, good-looking boys, all of them hitting on her. But she couldn't; she knew Victor wouldn't approve. Tropical darkness lit by distant storms, star burn and yellow moon, long waves spilling across the reefs. All of this was a satisfying blur in her mind. She couldn't have said how long she'd been there. She had an even, deep tan. Days, weeks? What did it matter?

"Having a good time?" Victor Wilding asked indulgently.

"Oh, I love it here!" She looked at him as if she were afraid the query was a prelude to bad news. "I don't have to leave yet, do I?"

"Stay as long as you like, Eden."

She smiled gratefully. "What are we having for lunch?" She looked at the laden table. Sliced pineapple, melons, small red bananas, other fruits she couldn't identify. Mahimahi filets, Thai chicken curry, and garlic prawns simmered in copper chafing dishes.

"Help yourself," Wilding invited her.

"What can I give you?" the dpg said, remembering her manners.

"I think I'll just have a little of the broiled fish, and some sweet potato too, Eden."

Her smile faded a little. She was used to having him call her by that name, but still she couldn't help feeling like an impostor. Too bad she couldn't remember her own name. Or where she had come from. She wanted Victor to like her for herself alone, not because she reminded him of someone. But the uneasiness was just something that lay under the surface of bright, enjoyable things like a school of tiny dark fish packed together but easily scattered when she waved a hand through the water.

They ate and chatted, and the dpg looked up from time to time with her happy smile as she was greeted by other friends passing their table. She had made so many friends since she'd been at the Reef Club.

"Do you have anything planned for this afternoon?" Wilding asked casually.

"Steve and Gerry. You know them, they're here on their honeymoon?"

"From Australia."

"Yes. They said something about the three of us jeeping over to Tiara Falls later. Do you think that would be okay?"

"Fine with me, Eden. I hoped we might go for a walk after lunch. There's someone I'd like for you to meet."

The Turtle Airways seaplane from Nadi was coming in to land on the calm surface of the lagoon, bringing new guests to this small island retreat on the Koro Sea, picking up those whose vacation time was over.

"Oh, is he coming in on the plane?"

Wilding shook his head. "No. He's been here on Muronga for many years. His place is down the road about half a mile."

"Sure, Victor. No problem." The dpg cut into a saucy chicken breast on her plate.

Marcus Woolwine, seated next to Victor Wilding, said, "Time out."

Wilding said, "Eden?"

She looked up, fork halfway to her mouth. She smiled tentatively.

Wilding said, "Red light."

A change came over her. Nothing dramatic. Her movements slowed somewhat. She chewed the bite of chicken she had taken from her plate, still looking at Wilding, and through him with the expression in her eyes that Robert Louis Stevenson, also a sojourner in these and other Pacific isles, had described as "A fine state of haze." The dpg was not aware, nor had she ever been aware, that Marcus Woolwine was at the table with them intently monitoring what he considered to be his creation through his mirrored sunglasses.

She was, in fact, in an ordinary cafeteria setting, one of several identical, except for thematic decorations, cafeterias found throughout the Plenty Coups facility. It was no closer to the South Seas than some framed reproductions of paintings by Paul Gauguin that broke up the monotony of the surrounding concrete walls. The food she ate was real. Everything else she saw and felt relative to her environment had been provided for her by Woolwine. Yet he wasn't quite satisfied.

"Is something wrong?" Wilding asked.

"I can't be sure. I thought I detected a slight hesitancy when you address her by name, almost as if she isn't certain whom you're speaking to. Haven't you noticed it?"

"A time or two. Just now. That momentary blank look. But it's as if, you know, I'm breaking into her thoughts. Everybody's like that. And she does get those little spells of blankness even when I'm not talking to her. They're like petit mal seizures."

"Oh, yes," Woolwine said a bit huffily, "that will often happen, when we're doing a massive sensory override. It's a matter of fine-tuning the psychoactive drug protocol."

"Otherwise she seems fine to me," Wilding said in a mollifying tone. "Remarkable. But when will we know if she's retained her powers?"

"We'll know more after Phase One is completed this afternoon. But I shouldn't worry. In the meantime we might as well let the dear girl finish her lunch."

Wilding looked at Eden Waring's doppelganger again. She had swallowed the bite of chicken. The hand with the fork rested on the table beside her plate. Her lips were parted. She was rocking, from the waist up, ever so slightly, still with that look of somnolent delight in her half-closed eyes.

"Eden, green light."

With no visible indication that she had been in a state of hypnotic suspension, the dpg transferred her fork to her left hand, picked up a knife, and cut another piece of chicken. Marcus Woolwine, who still did not exist for her on her present level of consciousness, continued to watch her carefully, reaching up to slowly paw his sunlamped bald head. As if he had stored something on a back shelf of his own mind, and now was unable to locate it.

"What's his name?" the doppelganger asked Wilding.

"Excuse me?" Wilding said, his own thoughts interrupted. "Oh, you mean—his name is Robin."

The dpg flashed a smile at an imaginary someone walking past their table, waved to someone equally imaginary coming in from the nonexistent beach wearing a sarong and an orange flower in her hair.

"Any friend of yours is a friend of mine," she said.

Eden had been in the city for less than an hour when she realized, with feelings of intense disappointment and burgeoning panic, that they were in the wrong place.

From the terrace of the top-floor suite of their hotel she had a wide view to the north and west. There was good sailing weather today, and more boats than she could count were tacking across Lake Mendota. The sun was reflected from the dome of the University of Wisconsin's observatory. The campus was huge, several square miles of it along the shore, a mix of ivied old brick and colonnaded limestone buildings and newer, steel-and-glass high-rises. Awesome, compared to Cal Shasta, which had not existed thirty years ago. But Wisconsin wasn't the university she had seen during Dreamtime. The lake, largest of the two within the city limits, was the wrong size and color, blue instead of greenish brown. And it was in the wrong place, too close to the campus.

Eden rubbed her temples, closed her smarting eyes, and tried to concentrate. It wasn't the kind of headache that accompanied her periods but the kind that usually resulted from being in the hot sun too long. Yesterday and this morning it had been mild and not sunny in southern California, with low clouds most of the day. She had left California with Tom Sherard before nine A.M., in a Citation jet from Santa Barbara airport. She had dozed part of the way, dreamed of swaying gently in a hammock on the patio at home while Winky, her aging Lab, lapped at her dangling hand with his warm wet tongue. Then she had awakened to a full-blown and scary hallucination.

A man she'd never seen before was sitting opposite her in one of the deep leather swivel chairs aboard the Citation X. An old man, but fit-looking. He had a bald head tanned cinnamon-brown and he wore mirrored sunglasses, in which Eden saw her reflection clearly. His mouth moved as if he were speaking to her, but she couldn't hear a word. They were at twenty-eight thousand feet over the Midwest. Other than Tom and herself, she knew there were only two pilots and a flight attendant aboard the corporate jet. According to her reflected image, she was wearing a lei of red and white hibiscus flowers.

Eden jumped as if electrified and the hallucination ended. Tom Sherard gave her a perplexed look. She didn't tell him what she'd seen, but she knew it wasn't something left over from Dreamtime. The man was real.

Who he was or what he meant to her was inexplicable. She was left with a numskulled nauseated feeling to go with the headache behind her eyes.

Eden walked in off the terrace rubbing her eyes. In the suite's large living room Bertie Nkambe was on her cellular phone talking to her booking agent. Tom Sherard waited for Eden with a trace of anxiety in his normally stoic hunter's face.

"It isn't here," she said, too loudly, her voice barely under control. "We're in the wrong city. Maybe the device was supposed to come here, and Portia Darkfeather told me true. But if MORG changed their plans since she passed on, Portia wouldn't have known."

Bertie told her agent she'd call him back. She walked over to Eden and put an arm around her. Eden trembled.

"What do we do now?" Sherard asked.

"*I don't know,*" Eden said, desperation in her face.

PLENTY COUPS, MONTANA · JUNE 6 · 3:05 P.M. MDT

Eden's doppelganger strolled barefoot with Victor Wilding half a mile down the Jeep road south of the Muronga Reef Club, past a Fijian market and homely Methodist church. They came to a bungalow down a lane in a grove of coconut palms. Fallen green-hulled fruit littered the dooryard. There were chickens in a fenced coop. They walked up to the shaded veranda. No one seemed to be around, but the dpg had the odd feeling that they were being watched by several persons. She heard a vaporous hissing sound that she couldn't identify; it came from inside the bungalow. So did a draft of cold air through the open doorway.

The doppelganger looked curiously at Wilding, who seemed to be under a strain.

"Is anyone home?"

"He's always at home," Wilding replied. "It's okay, you can come closer—I mean, go on in."

He put a hand between her shoulders, guiding her through the doorway. The room inside was furnished in bamboo and rattan, colorful cushions and pillows, mats on the polished stone floor. The louvers on the windows were nearly closed. Shut away from the sun and deep in the grove, the bungalow should have been quite dark inside. But there was low even illumination everywhere, and a small spotlight was aimed down through a hole in the tapa cloth that covered the high thatched ceiling. It was focused on a hammock, and in the hammock lay Victor Wilding's friend Robin, who appeared to be sound asleep.

"He looks like you, Victor."

"We're . . . identical twins."

"Oh!" The dpg looked from Wilding's healthy face to the pale death mask likeness upturned in the hammock. "Is this a bad time?" she whispered.

"No," Wilding said with a sigh that seemed to cause him pain. "He's always asleep."

She didn't understand.

"He was hurt in a fall. A head injury. He can't wake up."

"Shouldn't you get a doctor?"

"He's had the best. There was this thing, deep in his brain—you've seen it, you know what it looks like."

"I do?"

"The crown of thorns starfish. The reef destroyer. I thought . . . I was told that Mark showed you one when he certified you the other day."

"Oh, that ugly . . . yes, he did." Mark was her diving instructor, kind of a neat guy except she didn't care for his shaved head and know-it-all manner. She shuddered, visualizing the voracious alien-ugly crown of thorns that had been pointed out to her. They were like small brown bushes with cactusy spines and tensile arms that clung to brain coral, eating the soft tissues until the coral died. She looked at Robin again, moved slowly closer to him. She heard that hissing, breathy noise she'd heard as she came into the bungalow, saw a cloud of vapor issuing from the transparent mask fitted over the lower part of Robin's face. Odd that she hadn't noticed it before.

Victor Wilding said, his voice now dim to her ears, "The neurosurgeons removed it all, of course, and some portions of the destroyed brain. But his coma has lasted to this day."

She whipped her head around and saw bow-legged, deeply tanned Mark, wearing those steely mirrored glasses even indoors, standing a few feet to one side of Victor Wilding.

"Go ahead, Eden," Mark said. "Dive in. See what you can find out, and tell us about it."

"Okay." She looked away from him, toward the sun that was directly overhead, and adjusted the fit of her own mask. Then, as she had been taught, she did a back-fall out of the low boat and sank down flippers-first into an altogether-different environment, not the sea but similar in its saline composition: the warm fluid within Robin's brain. The crinkled reeflike lobes were immense, scary in scale, laced with deep-red veins and filled with flickerings, intense pale blue flashes, storms not of the sky but of the spirit that still lived amid the wastelands. And there was, unexpectedly, a lot of noise. Static-y crackles, kettledrums, whistles, and poppings. She swam slowly around, needing only an occasional kick to maintain her momentum in this universe, looking into the deep crevasses, lost where she was but afraid to become even more lost by slipping into one of those convoluted canyons. She needed to explore but also she could use some help now that she had arrived, and she asked for it.

Robin? I'm here. Are you listening?

NASHVILLE, TENNESSEE · JUNE 6-7 · 3:10 P.M.-12:26 A.M. CDT

Old Hickory Lake, just to the east of Music City, USA, is a nearly one-hundred-mile-long impoundment of the Cumberland River, with over four hundred miles of wooded shore. It looks, from several thousand feet up, like a crinkly paper dragon in a Chinese New Year's parade. Old Hickory is a center of the power- and houseboat culture common on the man-made lakes and rivers of the South. Some of the houseboats complementing the mansions on Old Hickory's bluffs that belonged to Country recording artists and Music Row executives are upward of a hundred feet in length and fancy enough to cost in the hundreds of thousands of dollars.

The houseboat on which Randy and Herb, recently of Plenty Coups, Montana, were to spend the night with their one-kiloton nuclear device was tied up to a dock in a finger cove down a private road patrolled by MORG security specialists. No one except members of the team assigned to guarantee their safety and anonymity knew that Randy and Herb were there. The boys had stopped on the way down to gas the truck at a Texaco by exit 38 on the Pennyrile Parkway in southwestern Kentucky, where they also had picked up their guide, a MORG Homefolks agent who had been raised in Gallatin and knew every foot of Old Hickory's saw-toothed shoreline. He didn't know what Randy and Herb had with them besides their fishing gear. He had obtained the proper licenses, and after they'd settled in he took them out after largemouth in the bass boat included in the short-term lease.

When they returned to the dock around six-thirty, the sun flashing low through tall hickories and pin oaks on the west bank, two good-looking women were grilling steaks in the large galley. One was from the Los Angeles office of Homefolks; the other worked out of Washington. They introduced themselves as Cheryl and Sandi. Cheryl had school-girl frosted bangs, a sexy overbite, and a slight stutter. Sandi was a big febrile blond with a total lack of artifice, the sort usually known as "a man's woman." They had flown into Nashville during the afternoon, and would be leaving on early flights the next day. Another MORG agent who had brought the women to the houseboat drove the fishing guide away. He would never lay eyes on Randy and Herb again.

The women were not so fortunate.

After ribeyes rare, home fries and a tossed salad the women cleaned up the galley while Randy and Herb showered and changed clothes. They spent the next three hours playing canasta in the big salon, which was decorated and furnished with all the joie de vivre of a Danish mortuary. There was no drinking. None of them talked about themselves; they were on the job and personal histories were irrelevant. They didn't listen to music. Sandi told two jokes and discovered that Randy and Herb, whose banter was quick and hip but laced with jailhouse idiom, lacked real humor. Well, Jesus. Cheryl's cutesy stutter got on Sandi's nerves to where she wanted to clock Cheryl with the heel of her sandal. She took to nibbling her voluptuous lower lip during the card game. Through the in-slanted bow window they could see a vivid streak of lake like fire underwater and a moon three days from the full.

About eleven o'clock Randy, who had dark slick-backed hair and frowsy sideburns, threw in his cards and yawned. He went into one of the staterooms. After another minute Sandi also got up, drifted to the galley for a drink of water, then followed Randy.

He had already undressed except for his socks. He was sitting on the edge of the double-size bunk. Sandi wondered if there was something about his feet he was protective of; but socks were all to the good, she hated the toe-sucking so many guys were into. She glanced at the scars that clung to his hide like pale leeches. He had taken quite a few hits, nine-millimeter or .40 caliber just as a guess. He had a penis smaller than her thumb. Without preamble Sandi pulled off her halter top.

"You don't have to get undressed," Randy told her, as if he felt overmatched by her bountiful upstart jugs. "I don't need all that much."

And at ten past the hour Cheryl snuggled naked beside Herb in the other stateroom, hoping his sexual preferences wouldn't g-g-gross her out.

By midnight the last growlings of boat traffic had faded from the lake. They were all asleep except for Sandi, who had two problems: she was an insomniac, and after giving Randy the blowjob he'd required, she was seriously turned on. Randy being the fastidious kind of guy, in spite of his rough looks, who really didn't care all that much for pussy or its companion orifice. Sandi tried bringing herself off but flopped. Victim of a puritanical upbringing, she'd always been a little ashamed about masturbating.

A couple of stiff shots of black label would've calmed her, but there was no booze aboard. And she wasn't going to get any sleep next to Randy, who had clogged sinuses. No place to go except for a short walk around the houseboat's two decks. Nothing to read but the collected works of the Reverend Billy Graham and magazines for the outdoorsman. Men with space-age hunting bows, camouflaged to the eyeballs, holding up the heads of unsuspecting deer they'd whacked. The music library consisted of white gospel music. Her tastes were classical. She played viola in a chamber group at home in Fairfax County. Satellite TV presented a digital jigsaw puzzle. The message on the screen read, indefinitely, SEARCHING FOR SIGNAL. What was she supposed to do, turn the damn houseboat around? Shaping up to be one of those nights. Solitaire and gummy freezer pizza at three A.M. She was prohibited from making phone calls. She missed Toddie, her Yorkshire terrier.

She wondered what Randy and Herb were doing here. What the assignment was.

None of her business, of course.

But short of running naked in the woods and howling at the moon there was nothing else to do but think about Randy and Herb, a curious pair. Unusual types for MORG agents. Intel was her customary game, MORG's Russian desk. Speculation was a difficult habit to break.

The guys didn't have much gear with them. Two or three gym bags. They were in the stateroom with Randy and Herb. The fishing stuff, including that big tackle box (more on the order of the toolboxes that itinerant auto mechanics, like her father, took with them from job to job), was there in the salon, close to the galley, in an alcove where rods were stored with waders, creels, and a spare trolling motor for the bass boat. Randy and Herb's box was padlocked. More lock than the contents—hooks, lures, line, extra reels—seemed to call for.

If that was all they had in there.

Sandi prowled around and around, soft-footed, pausing to glance at the tackle box. Then for no good reason, probably because she was bored, she picked it up.

Well, Jesus. Heavier than she'd thought it would be. She had to drop the box, yanking a bare foot back out of the way, and the sound of the box hitting the deck crisped the blond furze along her naked spine. She backed away, mouth going dry, into the galley. She ran a glass of water for herself and leaned a haunch against the sink, seeing herself like a pink-and-cream nudie calendar pinup in a black window. She gave the tackle box more glances. Still none of her business.

But now she had to know.

It was a good lock, but Sandi had worked better ones, with whatever tools were at her disposal. She needed forty-three seconds to open the lock. She took it off and raised the heavy lid, saw at once why the box weighed so much. It was sheathed with lead inside, quarter-inch thickness, and within this lead casket was a Russian-made yellow carrier bag, property of the Strategic Rocket Forces. She didn't touch the sealed bag. She had a strong hunch about its contents: a plutonium-implosion bomb. Given its size, Sandi estimated the bomb to be a KT'er. Assuming a surface blast, forget survival up to four-tenths of a mile from ground zero. Serious damage to exposed human beings as far as seven and a half miles away.

Her first reaction was alarm, her second total confusion.

If Randy and Herb were MORG agents, what were they doing with— *Portland.*

And now Nashville?

Good God. The company she'd worked twelve years for. *Why?*

Sandi closed the lid of the tackle box and, hunkered down with goose-flesh rising on her thighs and forearms, she tried to replace the padlock with shaky hands.

Get out of here!

Sandi felt an inquiring touch on one shoulder and jumped up with a shriek. She had a glimpse of Randy, socks and bare ass, reacted by throwing a karate fist at his chin. He moved his head two inches with the reflexes of a mongoose and the short blow only grazed his jawline. He struck hard to her solar plexus with stiffened fingers and Sandi's big body sprawled on the galley floor. Wind knocked out of her. Randy was on her immediately, seizing the hand that held the padlock, stepping inside her elbow with his right foot. He twisted her fist sharply toward her body; her arm couldn't move and the torque snapped both wrist bones. She dropped the lock and lost control of her bladder. All of the fillings in her back teeth were visible but Sandi couldn't breathe, couldn't scream. He backed away from her and looked around as Herb came out of his stateroom towing fumble-footed Cheryl. She still had sleep in her eyes and wasn't resisting him. But she balked at the sight of Sandi writhing on the deck.

"Whatever this is about," she said, "I d-d-d-d—"

Randy glanced from Herb to Sandi and said, "Sweet Patootie had herself a look at *Babycakes.* I'll take care of it."

Herb clamped a hand over Cheryl's mouth as she struggled, terror bolting into her eyes.

"What about this one?"

Randy allotted Cheryl a few seconds' thought, then nodded.

"Don't make any more mess," he said. "It's a fuckin' rental."

MADISON, WISCONSIN · JUNE 7 · 2:35 A.M. CDT

With her nervous system hotwired from all the caffeine she'd swallowed—pills and colas—in order to stay halfway alert, Eden Waring pushed her chair back from the desk where she'd been staring at the screen of a laptop computer and said quietly, "Found it."

Bertie Nkambe was curled up asleep on a sofa. Tom Sherard put down the book he was reading, walked over to Eden, and stood behind her chair looking, from her angle, at the active matrix screen.

"Sure?"

"This is definitely the school I saw when I was dreaming. The same style of buildings, either old-time collegiate or boxy-modern. Vandy has an observatory too, but it's smaller than Wisconsin's."

"Vanderbilt University?" She had tapped into their Web site, which featured an introduction to the school, a tour of the campus. "Where is it?" Sherard asked.

"Nashville. Another state capital, like Madison. Let's see if they have a Web site. We'll find out what the city looks like and hope there's a big lake in the neighborhood. Then I'll know for sure."

The best source the search engine found for Eden was the Tennessee Film Commission's site, which provided information and photos for Hollywood production managers looking for locations in the area. She printed out a photo of the Greek-revival capitol building near downtown Nashville, studied it, walked outside onto the balcony to get some fresh air and have another look at the city of Madison, lucent but nearly motionless at this hour against a dark-bodied lake.

"The capitol buildings are different," she said, looking at Sherard with reddened, transfixed eyes in the hush of night. "Madison's capitol has a dome. Nashville's doesn't. There are big stadiums in both cities. The lake I saw must be Old Hickory. Okay. Now I'm sure. It's Nashville. But that's all I know. God help those people down there. I don't think I can."

The assassin who now called himself Corey DeSales had spent the better part of the week making himself available in the San Francisco area. Days and nights on the move, taking little time to sleep in his hideaway in Sausalito. Riding BART across the Bay. Strolling through Berkeley by the university, browsing in the bookstalls on Telegraph. Making his way through the summer crowd around the street-cart bazaar fronting Sproul Plaza. Always alert for the contact he was confident would come now that he was available again. The assassin had a new identity, but They would know him. Although he had prudently changed his face his vibes hadn't changed; they were as individual as fingerprints. Impact Sector, he knew, had his vibrations on file. They had developed a machine, now scanning the earth from a proprietary spy satellite, that could locate him in a matter of minutes.

In San Francisco he rode cablecars, hung out at the Marina and Ghirardelli Square, the Embarcadero and Golden Gate Park. The weather was fair most days after noon, the nights mild until the fog returned.

At least once a night he made it over to Chinatown. For one thing, he liked the food. For another, he liked to shop for little things to brighten up his digs. And then there was the girl who sold watercolors down the block from the Ya Lin restaurant—the "Elegant Forest"—in that part of Chinatown known as the Alleys.

She'd always had a smile for him, even before he bought a couple of her works—an impressionistic view of Grant Avenue; three grinning effigies, Chinese household gods. The assassin thought she had talent. Her name was Lu Ping, and during the day she studied to be an architect. He didn't know much else about her. They talked mostly about art. On his fourth or fifth visit she recommended, because he appeared to be very interested in Chinese *objets*, that he not miss a new collection in the Chinese gallery of the Asian Art Museum.

Then she looked him in the eyes for one of the few times since he'd taken to dropping around her sidewalk place of business, and suggested when. Four-thirty on Saturday, half an hour before the museum closed and the crowd would be thinning out. She turned to smile at a potential new customer, who had a question about the subject of one of her watercolors.

The assassin reacted with a slight nod following Lu Ping's suggestion. He didn't linger. He walked down the alley and turned right on Clay Street. There was a restaurant near Stockton he favored. On his way up to the second floor in an atmosphere heavy with wok oil and sizzling rice, he encountered a blind old man with a cane making his way down the rubber-treaded stairs. The assassin moved aside to let the old man pass, not taking his eyes off him. The assassin carefully watched everyone, blind or not, he encountered in close quarters.

The Chinese man, sensing his presence, paused and nodded, a smile adding new creases to the fragile paper lantern of his face.

"Chinese music developed from a five-note scale," he said, speaking slowly.

The assassin didn't reply and resumed climbing the stairs. He heard the old man's cane lightly tapping the wall on his way down.

Sometimes it happened that way. A young woman selling watercolors in a Chinatown alley. A blind man with a cane. He had been contacted. Impact Sector was putting him back to work. Afterward he couldn't remember what he'd eaten for dinner, but he slept deeply in his aerie on the barge above Poppa Too Sweets', oblivious of the bistro's hull-rocking tempos that lasted until three A.M.

Lu Ping drank from a second cup of the Shu Mal White Ebony tea prepared by Chien-Chi in the antique-filled apartment her uncle maintained on Jackson Square. Then she rubbed her temples and said, "What an ordeal. I hope he couldn't tell I was shaking inside."

"You did good," Danny Cheng assured her.

"I couldn't begin to tell you what it's like peeping that mind. I have been like weirded-out for days. If rattlesnakes had memories—"

"It's over now. For you, kiddo. But I want you to stay away from the Alleys for a week or so. Until we know he's out of the Bay Area." He peeled off fifteen one-hundred-dollar bills from the inch-thick billfold in his pants and handed them across the table to Lu Ping. "Buy yourself something pretty." He added a one-ounce gold panda coin. "This is for luck on your exams."

"That is so sweet of you, Uncle! Did I tell you he's carrying a gun? I can't think of anything else that might help. What do you want with this turdball? A cross-dressing government hit man? I mean, like I already told you. He is totally insane."

"That's what makes him so wonderful," Danny said, glancing at the screen of his ever-present laptop. Fingering the keys. Adding to his storehouse of knowledge. Danny Cheng, the information man. "Even madmen have their motives."

"Chinese music developed from a five-note scale," Chien-Chi said, chuckling softly to himself.

At 4:34 Saturday afternoon Danny, wearing one of his gray shantung suits that swarmed with flash like an aquarium tank, walked into the hall of the Chinese gallery that housed the latest exhibit, a donated collection of old Chinese musical instruments from the estate of a San Francisco lawyer with Mob ties. Danny was studying the catalogue through glasses as black as the enameled ornamentation on a T'ang dynasty guitar. There were a dozen other browsers in the gallery, including a thirtyish young man whose thatch of brown hair, brown mustache that hung over his upper lip, and brown eyebrows seemed too perfectly toned to be natural. He also wore glasses, a heavy horn frame resting on a high-bridged nose.

The assassin glanced at Danny Cheng, and didn't look at him again. Danny kept his nose down to his catalogue as he circled the display cases on the floor. A fifteen-minute warning was sounded. Only four other visitors and the guards remained.

Danny glanced up at the reflection of the assassin on a thick sheet of glass protecting fragile gongs and drums. He didn't look around at him.

"Chinese music developed from a five-note scale," the assassin said in a conversational tone.

"Without semitones," Danny added, giving a slight nod of approval. Then he folded his program, put it under one arm, glanced at the blue face of his Breitling wristwatch and said, "Tan limousine on Tea Garden Drive. Five minutes."

He walked briskly out of the gallery while the assassin remained in contemplation of the tall case containing gongs and drums.

Five minutes later he emerged into the sunshine and breezy chill of Golden Gate Park. Temperature in the mid-sixties. The limousine was where he had been told to expect it. A chauffeured driver stood beside a rear door, looking at him.

The assassin had never been contacted in this manner before, by someone obviously of rank in the Bureau's Impact Sector. Perhaps The Man himself. He was both excited and wary. This change in routine could be about his approval rating. Or else he was wanted for something extremely important, unprecedented in his career.

He walked to the limo. The door was opened for him.

Danny Cheng waved the assassin to a jump seat. Danny watched him for a few moments behind the impenetrable dark glasses. Then he held out a hand, palm up, a request.

"Current identification."

The assassin handed over his wallet without hesitation. Danny looked at a driver's license, credit and business cards, put them back, and returned the wallet.

"Those will be okay, Mr. D. But we'll need photos for additional documentation that may be useful. Hold still, please, keep your chin up, and continue to look this way."

There was a bright flash, from a concealed camera in the back of the limo. The assassin blinked afterward. When he could see again, Danny Cheng was holding out a letter-sized envelope, sealed with tape.

"Five thousand in cash," he said.

The assassin nodded, took the envelope, and put it away. He smiled slightly, at ease now, his pulse rate down. He waited.

"Anxious to get back into show business?" Danny Cheng asked. He pressed a button on a console under his left hand. The door of a cabinet beside his knee slid back, revealing a small television screen. The assassin turned slightly on the jump seat to see it better. "Here's the show," Danny said. "And here's our star."

The tape ran for only a couple of minutes. More than enough time. The assassin was stunned as the tape began; then he experienced a cold wave of exhilaration. The audacity. He stopped watching before it was over. He was already thinking, not about what They were asking him to do, but how it might be done. He could refuse, of course. Step out of the beige limousine without another word. The limo would drive away. He was in Golden Gate Park. The sniper might be anywhere—on a roof of the museum or atop the California Academy of Sciences Building on the other side of the Music Concourse. On a wooded knoll nearby. He would be killed before he took a dozen steps.

Either way he was a dead man. Even if he completed his assignment. But if he made good, his approval rating would reflect that final triumph. One that would be whispered about for a very long time. They could be cruel, it was the nature of Impact Sector's business. But They had not written him off after his failure. He had been given the opportunity to redeem himself, to leave this life justified. On his terms. On a stage of his choosing.

Face would appreciate that.

W*ake up, dammit!*

Eden Waring's doppelganger stirred in the hammock in which she had been blissfully asleep and tried to ignore the pestering sound, now sharp in her mind, then receding like an echo in a dark-walled dream as she willfully pushed the voice toward oblivion without yielding to its demand. There. For a few moments, silence.

Don't go back to sleep!

The hammock began to sway and then to rock. "Stop!" she cried, but she couldn't hold on and was thrown to the mat-covered floor of her *bure* at the Muronga Reef Club. She sat up groggily, rubbing a bruised buttock, and tried to climb back into the low-slung hammock, resume her rest. Shut the intruder out of her mind.

Instead she found herself on her feet as if yanked upright by the power of an ancient god she had unwittingly offended during her stay in Fiji. She trembled superstitiously, looking around in bewilderment, hearing the familiar, distant booming of surf on the reef that surrounded—

Snap out of it! You're not in a tropical paradise. They've drugged you. And it's been hell for me too, I haven't slept in forty hours.

"Go away."

Immediately the dpg went lurching helplessly across the *bure* to the bathroom. She tried to dig in and resist, spraddle-legged, head down like a donkey's, bare feet skidding over the woven grass mats. She clung to the door frame and was jerked loose; momentum caused her to sprawl into the bathtub. An elbow rang against porcelain.

"Owww!"

That hurt me too, my elbow's numb. Stop fighting me, you asshole!

"Why can't you leave me alone? I was h-having so much fun! And I d-don't need you anymore!"

What you need is a cold shower.

The dpg tried to huddle in the tub with her hands in her armpits. One hand was pulled loose. Her arm shot up. She gritted her teeth and made a fist, refusing to grasp the shower lever.

"No . . . I . . . won't."

Yes . . . you . . . will.

Her hand flew open, then closed on the handle. Water gushed from the showerhead, soaking the shorty pajamas she wore. The shower turned to a needle spray. She couldn't get away from it, or her tormentor.

Call me anything you like, but you're going to sober up before I let you out of there.

"I'm not drunk!"

You're worse than that. But it's not your fault.

Fifteen minutes later Eden Waring's doppelganger was sitting on the bathroom floor wearing a towel and nothing else, her head sagging.

Okay, one more time. Where are you?

Sobbing. "I . . . I don't know anymore."

You're in MORG'S underground facility at Plenty Coups, Montana.

"But . . ."

Fiji is some kind of hallucination they designed for you. To keep you in a happy frame of mind so you'd cooperate with them.

"Who? Are you talking about Victor and Mark?"

Victor? Maybe that's Victor Wilding. What has he asked you to do for him?

"Nothing! He's just a friend! We have lunch together every day."

What do you talk about?

"I don't know. I don't remember."

Think!

"Stop! You're hurting my head. It hurts enough already."

Drink more water. Flush the drugs they've given you out of your system.

"All that water has me peeing like a pig!"

Good. Now what is it Victor Wilding asked you to do?

"Nothing! He's so nice. He's been nicer to me than you've ever been." Eden's doppelganger obeyed a stern nudge in her mind by picking up the liter bottle of spring water. She had a few more swallows, even though she felt bloated. She choked, and some of the water spilled down her chin. "I went with him to see Robin," the dpg said drearily. She took her time focusing on that visit. "I remember that Mark was there too."

Robin? Robin Sandza?

"No, his name is Wilding. He's Victor's twin brother. He was hurt in a fall and he's been unconscious since . . . oh, it's a long time, Victor said. Twenty years."

Twenty years in a coma. I had a vision of Robin a week ago. And I've been told everything that was done to him. Victor Wilding isn't his brother. I believe Wilding was a doppelganger. Maybe he still is, that's why he's anxious to keep Robin alive.

Eden's dpg shuddered. "A doppelganger? Couldn't be. It t-takes one to k-know one."

If you were in your right mind, sweetie. You saw Robin, but did you make contact with him?

"Of course I did. I called him, and he came. We went walking . . . on the reef together. The reef that's been half destroyed by the crown of thorns."

I don't know what you mean.

"I held his hand. He's a sweet boy. But he was . . . too far gone to talk to me while we were together. He told me what he wanted, though. He touched his forehead, then . . . pointed to the sky. He wants them to let him go."

Did you tell that to Victor Wilding?

"No. I just couldn't. He loves his bro—he loves Robin so much."

It's his own existence he's concerned about. What did you say to Wilding?

"I told him I'd have to spend more time with Robin before I knew anything. Can I get up now? It's almost dawn. I want to put some clothes on. And I'm hungry."

I don't want you to get dressed. If you're not wearing anything, they can't see you.

"But they're my fr—"

Get this straight, okay? They think you're me, the one and only original Eden Waring. They took me—you—to Plenty Coups hoping you can heal Robin's damaged brain. Give him back his life. But Robin wants to die.

"Yes."

Can you find him? Go there without anyone knowing?

"I think so. He was just down the road about half a mile from the Reef Club."

Oh, shit. You've got to stop hallucinating.

"I'm trying! You can be such a bitch. If I had my own name, I would never be anyone remotely like—"

Shut up and listen. I'm tired. In a day or two, maybe just a few hours, a couple of hundred thousand people will die if I don't do something to prevent it. I don't know if you can help. Maybe. First I want you to find Robin again. He's somewhere in that hole in the ground. Find him, and pull the plug.

"*Kill* him?"

Release him. It's what he wants from you. Us. Me.

"Yes," the dpg conceded. "Poor guy. But . . . what about Victor?"

Sorry I can't be there to see his face when he hears the news.

The Citation X jet bringing Eden, Tom Sherard, and Bertie Nkambe from the upper Midwest touched down at Nashville's International Airport at 9:18 A.M., flying low over Old Hickory Lake in order to make the approach to a north-south runway.

Bertie had spent most of the flight talking on the phone, to her mother who was at home in Kenya, and to her brother Kieti in Paris. Tom Sherard used the other, encrypted phone aboard the jet to keep Buck Hannafin and Wanda Chevrille up-to-date. Eden, after the lengthy skull-splitting session with her doppelganger, conducted in secret, was at last able to go get some sleep in a deep soft glove-leather seat with an ice pack at the back of her neck.

In the glittering lake they had flown over at two thousand feet, Randy and Herb were relaxing on the lower deck of the houseboat reading the sports pages of the Sunday *Tennessean* after an early two hours of fishing the nearby coves. They'd cleaned their catch, iced down the filets, and cooked their own breakfasts. Microwaved sausage and scrambled eggs, black coffee. The bodies of Cheryl and Sandi, individually wrapped in blue tarps, were long gone from the houseboat, courtesy of a Homefolks CD (casualty dispersal) team. Forensic investigators could not have found evidence that the women had ever been aboard.

Randy and Herb still had most of the day to take it easy.

A limousine picked up Eden, Bertie, and Tom Sherard and drove them to a hotel on West End opposite the Vanderbilt University campus. On the way to midtown Nashville Eden kept her eyes open long enough to take in a billboard with Garth Brooks's face on it. In concert Sunday, June 7, at seven-thirty P.M. His first Nashville appearance, according to the grandmotherly limo driver, in many years, not counting a visit to Fan Fare during which he had signed autographs for twenty-three hours straight. Trisha Yearwood also was appearing with Brooks, and the venue was huge: Adelphia Coliseum.

Eden yawned. She never listened to country music.

"I need a workout," she said, "or I can't function. Does this hotel have a gym?"

They had a terraced suite on the top floor of the hotel. Nashville was jammed with Brooks fans, but Sherard had encountered no difficulty booking the suite on short notice. One of Katharine Bellaver's trusts owned a fourteen percent interest in the chain.

No one was hungry except Bertie, who was hungry all the time. She ate a couple of high-energy granola bars from her traveling stash of health foods and accompanied Eden to the gym.

Sherard rode the elevator down three floors to another, smaller suite he had reserved.

The two men who were still unpacking after a hasty trip from Washington aboard a Department of Energy jet were Russian-born, former colonels from the Twelfth Department of the Russian General Staff. They were nuclear weapons specialists, trained at NPO Impulse in Stalingrad before the end of the Cold War. Now they were part of an international crisis team devoted to tracking down nuclear warheads, artillery shells, and bombs that had been in the Soviet Republic's arsenal and were now unaccounted for. They were dressed in Banana Republic casual wear and carried DE credentials, Threat Assessment Intel. Mikhail, who said call me Mike, had gruff features and black hair thick as a garden hedge. Alyosha, who said call me Alex, had high color, a lazy habitual smile, and quick-temper blue eyes.

They had with them a twin of what they hoped was the device that MORG had purchased in a terrorists' bazaar on the bleak steppes thousands of kilometers from Krasnoyarsk 26 and now planned to detonate in Tennessee. Their device was exact in every detail except for the plutonium package, which when included was about the size of a softball and weighed seventy-two pounds. Alex told Sherard this with the hostile smirk an expert in mass destruction might be expected to have for the uninitiated.

When Eden, rosy and refreshed from a hard workout on the StairMaster, came to the Russians' suite with Bertie, the visitors looked at Bertie in lustful admiration and looked at Eden with total skepticism.

"Where is your crystal ball, honey?" Alex said, his complexion turning redder.

"Do I have to listen to this?" Eden said crossly to Tom Sherard.

"Give her some space, fellas," Tom cautioned.

"Why not?" Mike said. "It's only our asses that are on the line here. Asses to ashes, if you're not for real."

"I don't believe in this ESP," Alex said. "What is it they say in the good old USA? If it ain't shit, it must be Shinola."

"How did you lose part of your ring finger?" Eden asked, glancing casually at his left hand.

"Car door, *honey*."

"Mind if I see?" Eden held out her left hand, palm up. Alex smirked, but he laid his four-and-a-half-digit hand in hers. Eden looked thoughtful. She withdrew her hand.

"You're running a low-grade fever," she said.

"I'm in perfect health," Alex scoffed.

"Not the kind of fever I mean. How long has it been, a few years? Even though she took a pair of scissors to you, you're still crazy about her. Maybe that's the part you liked best in the relationship."

Alex's smile vanished; he looked bewildered. "It was only a puncture through the nail. I neglected it, and infection set in. How could you—"

Eden said, "At least Nadya didn't damage the goodies she was really after, huh, Alex?"

Bertie was looking at him with half-closed eyes, a sidelong glance. Alex's eyes were flicking back and forth between the two of them.

She said to Eden, "You missed something."

"You mean where she tried to hack his throat and hit the collarbone instead? A tip of one of the scissor blades broke off, didn't it?"

"Uh-huh. Still in there. His aura's a little tarnished in that area."

Alex stammered, "B-but—"

Both women turned to Mike, who backed off a step, holding up his hands in a gesture of mock-conciliation.

"Hey, not me! My life is an open book. I'll tell you anything you want to know."

Bertie smiled and gave Mike a reassuring pat on the shoulder. Sherard looked curiously at Bertie and then at Eden, who seemed momentarily to have lost focus. He would have thought her mind was wandering, but by now he knew her better than that.

"Maybe we ought to get down to business now," Sherard said. He turned to Alex. "Where did you fellas stash the dummy device Eden needs to look at?"

"In the bedroom," Alex said. He was still trying to retain his composure, his eyes fixed on Eden.

There were double doors between the sitting room of the suite and the large bedroom. They all went inside. Bertie looked around, then went to the terrace door, parted the sheer curtain and pushed the door back. They heard church bells.

"Lovely morning," she said.

The device that the Russians had brought with them was in a titanium case two and a half feet square and a foot high. Mike put the case on a round table under a hanging light fixture and unlocked it. The device was in a carrier bag, also locked. Mike selected another key from his ring. Eden, still a little dreamy, gazed at the carrier bag. Bertie stood just outside the room on the terrace looking east toward downtown Nashville and the stadium on the Cumberland River a few blocks away from the hotel. She took some deep breaths. Eden looked slowly around at her. Sherard felt uneasy, knowing something was going on between the two women. But he couldn't say anything.

Mike removed the dummy nuke from the carrier bag. It resembled an overweight laptop computer, but the case was polished steel, and the detonator, keyboard labeled in Cyrillic, nested in a vault of armored glass. Someone had placed a happy-face sticker on the rectangle of glass. Russians were the best at gallows humor.

Eden took one look at the device and collapsed with a gurgling noise to the floor, as if she were having a seizure.

"Oh, *God!*" Bertie said, hurrying to kneel beside her. "Oh, my God, what happened?"

"I don't know," Sherard said. "Let's get her off the floor."

Alex helped him pick Eden up and carry her to one of the twin beds. Her eyes were half-closed, her face congested. The gurgling had become a desperate throat rattle as she struggled for air.

Bertie turned to Mike. "Poor kid, she's diabetic." Sherard glanced up swiftly; this was news to him but he caught Bertie's look and acted on the hint.

"Can you get her something from the minibar? Fruit juice is best."

"Sure, I'll be right back."

"Alex, would you fetch a cold cloth from the bathroom?"

Alex nodded. Bertie was holding Eden down on the bed. Mike had gone into the sitting room. When Bertie heard water splashing in the bathroom she left Eden's side and took four quick steps to the bedroom door, closed it. Turned back to Sherard. Whispered.

"Do you have Danny Cheng's Glock on you?"

"Sure."

"When he comes back, stick it in his ear. Put him down but don't shoot him."

"Who do you mean, Alex?"

"No, he's okay, it's just his attitude. Mike's the bad apple."

Alex came out of the bathroom with a washcloth and said to Bertie, "What should I do?"

"Has she swallowed her tongue?"

"How would I know?"

Eden sat up suddenly, eyes rolled up in her head. She clamped her arms around Alex. She gagged as if she were going to vomit in his face. Alex jerked his head aside. He didn't see Mike returning. Mike saw Bertie wailing at the foot of the bed and Eden apparently convulsing. He wasn't aware of Sherard stepping in behind him. Sherard thumped Mike on the side of his skull above the ear with the steel slide of the Glock pistol.

Mike staggered a step, went down on one knee with a muted groan, and Sherard hit him again, getting more muscle into his side-arm swing. Alex yelled something. Mike pitched forward on his face and didn't move. He was still holding the unopened bottle of orange juice. Alex tried to get off the bed but Eden clung to him until Bertie intervened, thrust the long pale palm of one hand to within an inch of his forehead. If Alex could have deciphered the lines in her palm, he would have discovered a very old soul in a young woman's body.

"Do you like your brains fried or scrambled, Alex? Just settle down until you've heard us out. Eden, I think you can let Alex go now."

"Gladly," Eden said, exhaling explosively. She pushed him away. Bertie held Alex's attention with her outstretched hand. There was a moment when Alex might have come up fighting, but something in Bertie's eyes, the tone of her body, the sum and power of her *chi*, discouraged him.

Sherard stepped over Mike, moving where he could see both men, and aimed the Glock at Alex. Alex swore at them in Russian, his face darkening with bad blood.

Eden picked up the washcloth and mopped her own face.

"For a little while there I thought I *really* would lose it. Was I as good as Julia Roberts in *Steel Magnolias*?"

"Didn't see that one, but you were great," Bertie assured her. "Now we'd better get organized, on the double."

"What's up?" Sherard asked.

Bertie withdrew the hand she was holding next to Alex's head and pulled off one of the enameled copper bracelets she wore on her other wrist. She moved away from Alex, knelt beside Mike, and pressed the curved bracelet to the bone beneath his right ear.

"Implant," she said. "Barely a trace of a scar. Remember Rory Whetstone, Hannafin's right-hand man? Same deal. MORG got to both of them. I saw Mike's implant when I scanned his aura. Difference is, Mike is two-way. I just took him off the air." She slipped the bracelet back with the others on her wrist. "Magnets," she said. "Probably too late, though. My hunch is a lot of MORG guys are on the way over here already. What happens next depends on who they are. Gunmen, or MMF. I think I prefer the gunmen."

"I don't," Sherard said with a nod to the Glock in his hand. "This is all we have, unless Alex—"

"No I don't have a gun, and what is all this fuhkeeng nonsense about implants!?"

Bertie got up from one knee. "I could do a little surgery with a pocket-knife and show it to you."

"We don't have time," Eden said.

"Right, what am I thinking. Alex, get your dummy nuke and let's be on our way. Both Eden and I have left signatures in this suite the MMF can follow like a neon rainbow."

"I'll make a stand here," Sherard said. "The rest of you get out."

"No good, Tom. You'll get two or three, sure; then you're a goner. Besides, we need one of them if we're to have any hope of coming up with that live nuke. Alex, are you a believer yet?"

Sherard said, "I think we had better leave the Russians behind."

"Good idea. Then *you* disarm the fuhkeeng bomb, if you find it in time."

"He believes," Eden said, with an encouraging look at Alex.

Alex glanced at Mike and said to Bertie, "Since you seem to have all the answers, has he betrayed us?"

"No, he didn't know about the bug they snuck into his skull. Probably while he was having dental surgery. That's the beauty, and the terror of it."

"Then let me tie his hands, at least. If they, whoever *they* are, find him bound and unconscious, they may not execute him."

"Do it," Sherard said, and to Bertie: "What about those telepathic signatures, footprints we'll be leaving in the air?"

"We do nothing. Let 'em follow us."

"Where are we going?"

Bertie didn't answer him. She seemed to have drifted away momentarily, attracted by other sounds, another's voice.

Sherard tensed, also listening. But he heard nothing except the nearby tolling of church bells.

PLENTY COUPS, MONTANA • JUNE 7 • 6:25-7:40 A.M. MDT

Even though she couldn't be seen, by human or optical eyes, Eden Waring's doppelganger soon discovered in her forays down the long bright passages of the underground facility that there were areas where she couldn't go without tripping a hullabaloo and razzamatazz of alarms. Flashing red lights and massive steel gates rising out of the floors she could deal with. But she drew the line at fogs of lethal gas and unleashed killer dogs. These rewards for unauthorized MORG employees who might have an itch to explore were graphically posted in the red zones.

And she was still hallucinating (which was what Eden had called it) although her visions of paradise became more ephemeral with each recurrence. It was during the flashbacks to what had never been that she had violated a couple of minimum-security zones while trying to orient herself. But no one had come to investigate; obviously no evidence of her presence had shown up on the TV monitors. After thirty seconds the warning lights had stopped flashing, the entrapment gates had been withdrawn with a clang of super-hardened steel.

She was cold and hungry. Eden, for practical reasons, had forbidden her to eat. Ingested substances remained visible in her digestive tract. There was nothing on her stomach. She had emptied her telltale bowels and, one last time, her bladder before venturing out.

Sunday morning, very early. The Plenty Coups facility seemed nearly deserted. And endless. And totally confusing in the businesslike sameness of its corridors. She longed for Fiji, coconut palms, blue water. She was barefoot, and the floors were cold. She shuddered almost every step of the way. After fifteen minutes and two nerve-jolting alarms she was ready to give up and retreat to her hammock—the South Seas furnishings in her suite were real, at least—and coddle herself with a picturesque dream.

And Eden would be so angry with her that she would never achieve the only dream she had that truly mattered: her desire to be *named,* and be granted a life of her own.

Then she could spend the rest of that life in Polynesia, if she damned well wanted to.

There was no choice. Eden had to be obeyed.

Get it done, the doppelganger thought drearily. Help Robin Sandza find his eternal rest. Easy enough to accomplish. A few circuits to disconnect. Robin already had shown her how to do this, on his guided tour through his own brain.

But where *was* he?

Just before eight-thirty Sunday morning Air Force One touched down on the recently extended (to ten thousand feet) runway at Bozeman's Gallatin airport, under the protection of MORG security: three helicopters in the air, perimeter patrols on the ground. Another, identical 747 with limousines, trailers, and logistical support aboard had arrived half an hour earlier. The First Lady had banned from Air Force One the traveling press corps and nearly everyone else, excepting the new MORG presidential security detail and the military crew from the 89th Airlift Wing. The press corps, which was billeted in Bozeman, was due to arrive on a third plane after the President had disembarked and was on his way to the western White House.

Clint Harvester had been sedated for the trip to his home state, although not so heavily that he needed help walking down the steps from the door of Air Force One to the waiting limo. There wasn't much of a crowd on hand for their early arrival; Bozeman is a small city of about thirty-five thousand people when Montana State University is in regular session. Rona saw a few signs and banners half a mile away at the airport terminal. She nudged Clint's elbow, a signal for him to wave, and hoped nobody with a camera had caught him yawning.

He dozed in the limousine on the thirty-mile trip down to the ranch. Roadblocks, cars and pickups pulled over, some flags waving, Boy Scouts in uniform, backpackers, old-timers and babes in arms behind barricades at crossroads hamlets with names like Lingo and Beaver Hut. Friendly faces for the most part; but then you could never, in Rona's book, tell what an Indian was thinking. She had the window down on her side and showed a cheery face, a perky thumbs-up. The caravan was traveling at thirty-eight miles an hour, fast enough so that none of the onlookers could catch more than a shadowy glimpse of their President.

Keeping up appearances in Washington for the past week had been an ordeal, and Rona was happy to be home, in near isolation on eighteen thousand acres of summer range, subalpine meadows, hanging valleys, and forested cirques. Roadless terrain. Mountain peaks wherever one looked. Fast clear water and huge red cedars; animal trails dense with needle-pack and hard crusts of snow year-round. Twelve feet of snow in ordinary winters, twenty to thirty feet when the weather turned savage.

Soon there was no one left to wave to, but Rona kept the window open. The hard road ended; a newly graded dirt-and-scree road slanted through an upcountry pass. Pure, stunning rush of wind on her face. The breath of deep woodland—larch, Rocky Mountain maple, fir, a dozen varieties of pine growing close to the road. Ambush country for road agents, she thought whimsically. The old Bardstown stage. *Stand and deliver.* But she wanted the smoke-toned window down. She recalled campaign trips in Clint's pickup: mud and manure, sweaty leather and woolens, plug tobacco and snoose, effluvium that no amount of hosing-down could remove. Cow-country cologne. Not all that bad until you tried to wolf down a Big Mac on the go with the windows closed in a thunderstorm. Visiting pool halls and post offices, body shops and beauty parlors, beet dumps and feed lots. No vote too remote to track down. Singing along at the tops of their voices with Hank Junior, Buck Owens, John R's dark and melancholy baritone. Pulling over by the side of the road when the urge was upon them. Doing it at high noon standing up behind an old barn. Chaff and finely rotted wood sifting down into her hair as they banged the boards. Or after midnight in a high place, damn near halfway to the moon on Acapulco Gold, shuddering butt-naked together on the blanketed ground, his balls tight as prunes from the cold. Three, four hours sleep a night. Exhausting. But on a high, on a roll. Clint was a winner and they knew it, even before his first landslide. Fun, fun, fun all the way. It occurred to Rona with an unexpected twinge of nostalgia that her life wasn't fun anymore. But that was one of the expected forfeitures when destiny took over.

Small lake with half-sunk deadwood on its placid shores, then the treeline dwindling to rocky meadow and sunlit rangeland spotted like a bobcat's pelt with flowering cushion plants. She saw white-faced calves and riders in a slow string from the Broken Wheel guest ranch that lay next to Big Country. Almost there.

Clint Harvester made waking-up sounds, clearing his throat. The chill morning air had revived him. Rona glanced at Clint. He was looking past her, his eyes filled with the daze of blue distance. Then he appeared to focus on something, or someone, out there on the range. Rona turned her head. Early summer vacationers, dudes on horseback. A couple of pack mules. At the head of the file of a dozen riders was a young woman wearing a white or cream-colored Stetson. Abundant black hair swayed on her shoulders as she rode. Rona knew most of the female guides who worked at the Broken Wheel, but she didn't think she'd seen this one before. Even so, there was something about her, in profile, that was startlingly familiar.

Clint had moved across the seat and was next to Rona. She glanced at him again. He was still looking past her, out the window, and she could hear him breathing excitedly even as a rush of sorrow suffused his face. His hand came up. He pointed.

"*Linda!*" he said.

The main house at Big Country Ranch was two years old; it replaced the homely one-story log house at the entrance to a box canyon that Clint Harvester's grandfather had built, almost single-handedly, in 1909. The ranch manager, Cletus Huckey, now lived in the old family home with his wife. The Huckeys were in their sixties, and Cletus liked to joke that they'd been married for so long they were on their second bottle of Tabasco. Clint and Rona's new digs half a mile away occupied a rocky promontory on the northeast corner of the ranch. The house was eight thousand square feet of cedar and stone amid old pine and fir trees, a waterfall, a swimming pond, and gardens. There were extensive decks on several levels. The floor plan was open, with mountain and valley views from the great room. The free-form granite and soapstone fireplaces had built-in bake ovens, and the one nearest the kitchen area contained a stove. The dining room, with yet another Red Moss Rock fireplace, could seat twenty-four for dinner. There were four bedroom suites upstairs. The lower level of the house was dedicated to games and an exercise area with a Jacuzzi and steam showers. There was a granite-lined lap pool for Clint.

A bomb shelter designed to withstand anything short of as a direct hit by an ICBM lay in the granite beneath the house. A disguised radar installation on Silverdust Peak six miles away was there to give the President time to reach the shelter in the event of unexpected hostilities.

Within easy walking distance of the main house and away from the barns and stock pens four well-appointed guest lodges and offices of the western White House were scattered among the lofty conifers and creekside poplars, separated from one another by the meandering trout stream. The White House Communications Agency had installed three uplink dishes next to the office building, which contained a fully equipped television studio. Two generators of the type used for movie location work, enough emergency power for the entire ranch complex, were parked beside the studio in bomb-proof trucks, protected around the clock by members of MORG's Elite Force. Several more members of the force rode the range day and night equipped with sniper rifles and night-vision scopes. There were dozens of surveillance cameras on the property, but an expert eye was needed to spot most of them. Two helicopter gunships stationed in Bozeman were combat-ready and twelve minutes away. The ranch's water supply was tested four times a day. Rona had decided that it was just too medieval to have a food-taster on the premises. MORG used two of the ranch's Border collies for that chore. They remained in robust health.

Rona loved the pomp and circumstance of the heritage-laden White House, but she loved her downtime on the ranch even more.

On arrival she parked Clint downstairs with two MORG agents and a personal trainer to supervise his session with the Nautilus machine. She changed into her shit-kicker duds, substituting sneakers for boots, which hurt her feet when she wore them only once in a while. She left the house and, unaccompanied, drove a golf cart down to the largest of the guest lodges, two stone chimneys on either end and a deep screened porch across the front. Two more MORG agents, still in city clothes but with their jackets off, were on the porch. Rona gave them a jaunty wave and went inside.

Victor Wilding was having brunch on another sunny porch at the back of the lodge. He smiled in a relaxed way at Rona, who wiped a bit of egg from his lower lip and kissed him fervently. Then she plopped into a padded chair and sighed.

"Made it."

"Care for something to eat?"

"No thanks. These jeans are snugger than the last time I had them on. How's everything?"

"Fine. How about you?"

"Oh, fine. Now that you're here."

Wilding spread apple butter on corn bread. "Thought I noticed a frown just then."

"I wasn't frowning, I was squinting. Bright in here." Rona adjusted the angle of her chair away from the windows. Then she reached impulsively for the apple butter and ate some with a spoon. "Oh, boy. Nobody puts up better apple butter than Jonquil Huckey, bless her heart." She enjoyed another spoonful from the canning jar, licked her lips, and sighed. "Clint gave me kind of a jolt on the way down here," she finally admitted.

"Really? How?"

"When we passed the Broken Wheel he saw a string of riders and, in particular, one of the ranch hands leading them into the mountains on a pack trip. The guide I'm talking about had, you know, Linda's shape and profile and wore her hair like the first and late Mrs. Harvester."

"What about it?"

"He said her *name*. With this look in his eye. God damn it, Clint *remembered*. He remembered being married to or at least knowing her twenty-three years ago."

Wilding said after a few moments, "An isolated flashback. Doesn't signify that he's coming out of it."

"But there has always been that possibility. Lately he's been fucking *uncanny* with Rubik's Cube. Solves it in a couple of minutes. That's memory too, isn't it? And I caught him yesterday moving pieces around on the gold and jade chessboard one of the sand nigger sheiks gave him for his fifty-third birthday. Clint looked as if he was trying . . . to figure out a move."

"I wouldn't worry about it," Wilding advised. "He won't suddenly recover all of his faculties." He paused, looking her in the eye. "Not in the time he has left. Marcus Woolwine assured me of that."

Rona bit her lip and shrugged. "I was a little creeped out, I guess. I've been on edge. Speaking of Woolwine, how's our Shaman-in-Chief doing with Eden Waring?"

"Remarkable results."

"Can she heal Robin Sandza?"

"Don't know yet. Marcus and I introduced her to Robin two days ago. We're certain they've made contact on some level of apprehension. Quoting Marcus. But she's a kid still, not the experienced Avatar and neurosurgeon Kelane Cheng was. It's too soon to tell what she may be able to do for him, or how long it will take. After Eden's visit, he appeared to rally. That's encouraging."

"It certainly is. Have you almost finished eating? Not that I'm rushing you, but I want to get into your pants. Like I said, I've been terribly on edge."

Wilding smiled. "We should touch base on the important stuff."

"Your cock is important." She moved her chair closer to him. Put a hand even closer, under the table. "Go ahead," she told him. "While I'm getting you ready. When's the blastoff?"

"Eleven-fifteen P.M. CDT."

"I'd say in about ten minutes, way it feels now."

"What about the help in the k-kitchen?" Wilding said, looking over one shoulder.

"They see me doing this, they better *stay* in the kitchen. Damn this zipper! Okay, next."

"One hour later we start our spring roundup. Washington, New York. Pretext is a phone call from a spokesman for H-Hamas, threatening total extinction of the white capitalist devils of the West and their client state in the Mideast. The t-tape will subsequently be released to all the m-media."

"Am I giving you the stutters?" Rona asked with a devilish expression, working his penis free of his Jockey shorts. "Everyone accounted for?"

"No, but we'll have ninety percent of the members of the executive and judicial branches iced within an hour. Some important exceptions. We haven't been able to keep track of Buck Hannafin since his Chief of Staff resigned. Buck's canceled appointments and committee meetings. There's a rumor he checked into the Mayo Clinic under another name. Prostate cancer."

"Yeah, right. If Buck's being surreptitious, something's up. Buck Hannafin is a problem for us. Major problem. You'd better find him."

"We will. Wanda Chevrille is her usual elusive self; may be on a religious retreat, that cloister she favors in western Maryland. The Veep is in Bonn trying to talk the Krauts out of withdrawing from NATO. AG is at the bedside of her sick mother in Maine. Admiral S-Sobieski left yesterday for O-Oh!-Oceania to dedicate the Navy's new super-carrier, c-can't touch him there. Jesus, Zeph, I was going to have a second cup of c-coffee."

Rona's face was snuggled naughtily in his lap. "Uh-uh," she murmured.

"The tapes are ready. Clint addressing the nation from the western White House. Clint invoking his executive powers. The d-disinformation will come thick and fast from around the world. Who is it? Who else is involved in this conspiracy? London, Paris, Israel, Seoul. Everyone will be on full military alert. Washington is rumored to be the next target. Pandemonium. Mass exodus. And then the really b-bad news." He inhaled sharply. "The P-president of the United States is—*God,* Zeph!"

She looked up with a grin. One hand still clutching the empurpled stalk.

"And a new legend for our time arises in the darkness of fear and turmoil, twelve feet tall with thunderbolts flashing from the tip of her swift sword." Rona gave Wilding a downstroke and a series of slow squeezes that took him close to a peak of ecstasy. "Don't suppose we could borrow Excalibur from the British Museum. Now *there* is a goddamn sword. No negative comparisons intended, lover. Or maybe Excalibur is in the Tower with all of the family jewels." With her thumb she gave Wilding's engorged jewels a little nudge, then unexpectedly relaxed her hand.

"Excalibur is a m-myth, I'm afraid. You're not going to *leave* me like this?"

Of course not. La la la la la! That's enough business talk. Come along, darling, play with li'l Ron-er till it's time to pull on the chain mail."

Rona knew they were being peeked at from the kitchen while she elevated Victor Wilding from his chair, Victor laughing with the roots of his short hairs a-sizzle, Rona towing him playfully by his extended penis toward the master suite of the lodge. God help her, she did love it so, as General George S. Patton reportedly had remarked in a different context. Her hand on a willing weenie, and the rest of the nation soon to follow.

The fourteen riders from the Broken Wheel Ranch took a break at the Mahoon Falls meadow. From that elevation there were exceptional views of three mountain ranges, national forests, and the ranches in the Black Alder Valley below. Forty-three square miles in all. Good photo opportunities.

Buck Hannafin walked about half a mile higher through a grove of old-growth cedar and fir with three of the men who had accompanied him up the trail. They followed a pack mule and a woman named Courtney Shyla, whom Clint Harvester had glimpsed in passing an hour ago and had mistaken for his first wife. Courtney had worked at the Broken Wheel a decade ago during her summer breaks from college. She had studied biology and ecology at the University of Montana, then opted for adventure in her life. Her current employer was the United States Army. She held the rank of major in the Special Forces.

Her boss was Lieutenant General Royce Destrahan, in charge of the U.S. Special Operations Command, which had jurisdiction over all of the armed forces' elite military units. These included Shyla's group and the Navy's SEALs. Destrahan also was Buck Hannafin's son-in-law. One of the other two men with them was Nick Grella of the Secret Service, who knew all of the security arrangements at Big Country Ranch. The last man was a Special Forces noncom, the best long-range sniper in the Army.

"Good place for a BASE jump," Courtney commented when they reached the cliff she had selected for their reconnaissance. "Watch your footing, everyone. Follow the mule."

The huge cliff, with a pitch of twelve degrees, was more than four thousand feet above the valley floor. The footing was mostly loose talus rock partly held in place by bear grass and huckleberry. There was enough sun-dappled lodgepole and spruce growing there to afford concealment if anyone was looking their way through binoculars.

Destrahan had studied satellite photos of the Big Country Ranch layout, but he wanted to see if MORG had installed any surprises. Courtney Shyla unpacked the telescope the mule had carried up and installed the fork mount on a field tripod. The twelve-inch Astro-type scope was motor-driven and could pick out a tenth magnitude smudge in the sky. Aimed toward the ranch, the lenses magnified a barbed-wire scar on a cow's behind at ten thousand yards. Courtney hooked up the telescope to a CCD camera, a laptop computer, and an ink-jet printer.

The sniper had a pair of 40X150 Japanese-made, military-spec binoculars to do his own reconnaissance. Buck was frowned at by Courtney the ecologist, and guiltily put it away. Nick Grella labeled the photos as they came from the printer.

"Did you ever rodeo?" Buck asked Courtney.

She swatted a biting fly away from one cheek. "Yes, sir. I was Little Britches' National Champ three years in a row before I got more interested in boys than barrel-racing."

"While you were working summers at the Broken Wheel, did you ever get over to Big Country?"

"No, sir, never did, they kept me too busy where I was."

Buck smiled. Down at the meadow she had taken off the wig of dark abundant curls that was part of her cowgirl pose. The wig was hot and made her sweat. He assumed that the severe military bob of her natural hair was necessary in her line of work, but damn she sure had been something special in all those curls.

"So nobody over there would know you, didn't date any of the cowboys?"

"No, sir."

Buck nodded vaguely, watched a couple of golden kestrels riding a thermal. Then he said, "If you boys have had yourself a good enough look, listen up here for a minute." When he had their full attention Buck looked at his son-in-law. "Just give me the bottom line, Royce."

"It can be done."

The sniper said with deadpan relish, "Fifteen hundred yards downrange, night, moving targets. Affirm, initial phase is do-able, sir."

"Well, sure; but done tidy, or done with a whole lot of unnecessary bloodshed on both sides? Seems to me that when you attack their perimeter, the perimeter collapses around 'Rawhide,' and he's hustled forthwith into that rockbound shelter. Which there is no way to breech without putting his life in jeopardy. Am I telling you true?"

"That's the way it works," Nick Grella said.

"Buck, it's all in how you coordinate the strike! There are multiple assault points, from the ground and the air simultaneously. Casualties, I can't sugarcoat that. Eight, maybe ten of ours. *All* of theirs, guarantee. I don't hold MORG's Elite Force in such high regard."

"And if one of them has instructions to turn his weapon on the President at the first indication of trouble?"

General Destrahan took a breath, let it out, finally nodded.

"That's the drag coefficient we can't afford."

"So maybe the best way to get Clint out of there is not to mount a hellfire assault, but to work stealthy from the inside. Inside the house, where they all feel the most secure. Those guys guarding the First Family are new on the job. Whatever Rona was thinking when she put MORG in charge of the POTUS detail, experience still counts. Isn't that a fact, Nick? So what is the most relaxed time of the day for most folks? Right around supper, dark-thirty, after the happy hour."

"Oh, no, Buck. No, no, no, I couldn't face Reggie if she found out that I let her father—"

"Why not? Has to be *me*, Royce. For certain you're not goin' in there with all your hard-ass ninja types. Or even by yourself. They'll scope General Royce Destrahan two hundred yards from the front door. 'Sorry, sir, the President and Mrs. Harvester are indisposed, we'll let them know you paid them a call.' On the other hand—" Buck looked at Courtney Shyla. "We fix up the major here with a pair of horn-rims and a cell phone, I can pass her off as one of my staff."

"Doesn't matter, Mrs. Harvester won't let you in either."

"Yes she will. Know why? Because Rona's cooking up something big, and I'm the fly in her soufflé. What is it the old Mafia hands used to say? Keep your friends close and your enemies closer. Hell, it'll make Rona's day to see me on her doorstep."

"With what? You'll never get a weapon past them. This isn't a good idea, Buck. Now let's get serious about—"

"General Destrahan?"

"Yes, Major?"

"Begging the General's pardon, but I believe Senator Hannafin's idea has merit."

"Major, I've already—"

"Let her talk, Royce."

Destrahan nodded, but folded his arms.

"Well, sir, there wouldn't be any need to try to get a gun into the house, because I'm sure there are some inside already. Although probably not close by while everyone is having dinner. The element of surprise is central to all of our operations. I know that at some point I would have an opportunity to—obtain a gun from one of the MORG guys." She smiled. "Once I have one, then I'll have them all. Sir."

"She's making sense to me, Royce," Buck Hannafin said. "And you told me not two hours ago that you had a lot of confidence in this young woman."

"I have confidence in a well-made plan with second and third options. If even a single shot is fired inside that house, the game is lost."

Courtney Shyla responded by pulling a prehistoric obsidian knife from a boot scabbard. She passed one edge of the knife through a hanging alder leaf. The leaf barely stirred on the branch as it was sliced in two.

"Whisper-quiet, sir."

"We're gonna be a hell of a team," Buck said, beaming.

"Buck, nothing personal, but you're not as fast as you used to be."

"You haven't seen me on a dance floor lately. It's footwork, not foot speed that counts. Audacity and a little pluck can succeed where an entire company of Rangers might fail. I just have a bad feeling. Therefore I'm invitin' myself to dinner tonight at the western White House. Be nice to have your approval, Royce; but as you well know it ain't essential."

Destrahan chewed over the proposition, looking from Buck to Courtney Shyla. He couldn't completely sell himself, but finally he nodded his concession.

"All right, Major. I'll agree that you can probably pull it off, up to a point. How do you get the President out of there, and into safe hands?"

"Well—I think—we declare a medical emergency, sir. POTUS has a fainting spell, vertigo or something. A little chloral hydrate would do the trick."

"Go on."

Courtney looked at Nick Grella. "Which hospital in the area has been prepped to receive the President in case of an accident or sudden illness?"

"Bozeman. Twelve minutes by chopper. Medevac team from Mountain Home Air Force Base. The helicopter is on the pad at Deaconness Hospital. The team includes a cardiologist and a flight surgeon, and they're on twenty-four-hour call."

"Once the President is at the hospital, a Secret Service team already in place can seal it off from everyone, including MORG, long enough for the psychiatric exam to be completed."

"Okay," Destrahan said. "Here's my part of it. A diversionary thrust at the perimeter on Major Shyla's signal from inside the house. We'll make it look like right-wing nutballs operating out of the back of a pickup truck."

"Aw-dacious," Buck said admiringly.

"Still leaves a hell of a lot of variables. Not the least of which is the First Lady."

Buck's attention seemed to wander. He reached absently for the cigar that Courtney Shyla had disapproved of earlier, twiddled it between his fingers, took out his cutter and trimmed one end, fished for a kitchen match that he struck on one of the hand-tooled silver studs that ran down the sides of his leather chaps. He took his time, putting on a show that had everyone's attention, looking smug as only a man lighting a fifty-dollar cigar can look. He took a few puffs. Then he spoke.

"As for Miss Rona—Fate does have a way of taking a hand," he said.

NASHVILLE, TENNESSEE · JUNE 7 · 11:20 A.M. CDT

When Eden, Tom Sherard, and Bertie Nkambe reached the Beloved Souls Church three blocks up West End from their hotel, they lingered outside while Bertie freshened their trail by peeping two churchgoers as they walked up the steps. She had done this a couple of times already, in the lobby of the hotel and during the short walk to church. The blue-haired lady she peeped first was oblivious, but her husband paused and looked around uneasily through thick glasses. Bertie smiled at him. Poor guy. Needed a new liver, but he was far down on the transplant list. Both of their minds were on miracles today.

Eden got in the way of three teenagers who were chatting and didn't see her. She faked a stumble down the steps and one of the boys rescued her. Eden clung to him for a few seconds, laughing, apologetic, then let him go when she'd seen enough, left her own signature for the MMF to pick up. Nice kid. Born-again, but he'd slipped with his girlfriend last night and had a brand-new sin on his conscience after being forgiven for the old ones. He also had a slight nosebleed as he rejoined his friends, and that was on Eden's conscience. She didn't have Bertie's ability to read an aura from a distance or overwhelm another's mind with her *chi*. If an incipient event was powerful and close enough in time she could visualize it. But in order to read a human being, a power that had been revealed to her during the phenomenal stress of recent days and extraordinary events, she had to rely on touch. The paranormal energy she channeled wasn't controllable yet. She had been taught that during her Dreamtime she was dangerous to the susceptible. Which, unfortunately, didn't include trained telepaths and Mind-Fuckers.

She looked at Tom Sherard.

"You're sure you want to do this?" he asked.

Eden showed him the clenched jaw and determined fist from team huddles during close basketball games. *Just give me the ball and box-out.* "I can handle it. I've had some practice, remember? Let's smoke out the rats."

She put on the jogger's blue headband Bertie had given to her at the hotel. It seemed a little out of place with her pleated skirt and silk blouse.

The church buildings were new; the style of the sanctuary, which smelled agreeably of recently completed carpentry and acres of paint, could only be described as avant-Biblical. The sanctuary was soaring steel and glass with stained-glass skylights that featured doves of peace. Vermilion pile carpeting throughout. A painted crucifix twenty feet high, mid-Renaissance in concept and execution, hung from the topmost point of the vaulted ceiling like a chime in a clock cabinet. Jesus and the cross were turning slowly; one complete turn might take several minutes. It was a startling sight.

"New Testament Baptists," Eden whispered for Sherard's benefit. "The Old Testament is a hard sell these days."

There was a resounding organ with tiers of pipes and a ninety-voice choir behind the altar. Seating was theater style. The service was being televised locally and taped for a Sunday-night showing on the Trinity Broadcasting Network, which had a banner hanging from the balcony.

Apparently the eleven-thirty was the big draw of the three worship services offered on Sundays. Most of the thirty-five hundred seats were already full, but they hadn't planned to sit together. Eden was ushered to a seat on the left-side aisle six rows from the altar. Bertie went up to the balcony. Sherard chose standing room at the back of the first floor, although a young girl, seeing the man with a cane, offered him her seat. He thanked her, explained he was waiting for someone.

Nice people in Nashville, he thought. His skin was quite cold and his mouth was dry. Everything was at risk, *right now.* If they failed, they were likely to be vaporized or burnt to the quick along with a sizable chunk of the population. No way to know how much time was left: a day, an hour, a minute. He looked down toward the altar and saw the blue headband. Eden's head was bowed in prayer. Sherard had no gods to pray to. All he had was a rather shaky faith in Eden Waring and in the other young woman he loved. And he had a gun, tight against his side beneath his suit coat. It made him feel all the more futile, considering the powers that might soon be unleashed inside this sanctuary.

The service began with chimes, then the Prelude: "All Glory Be to God on High." A smiling usher with a boutonniere handed Sherard a hymnal. He wasn't the only standee; there were other late arrivals, but plenty of room remained for them in the wide aisle behind the last row of seats. Ushers were quietly setting out folding chairs. Sherard looked up and spotted Bertie at the far end of the curved balcony. She was in the front row, singing along with everyone else but scanning the congregation both visually and with all of her senses that lay beyond the fifth.

He tried to do his part, keeping an eye on latecomers, no idea what or whom to expect. Young couple with a toddler, all of them blond as butter cookies and the mother pregnant again. Teenagers: black, white, and Asian. Tall balding young man pushing a bewigged woman with a sideways lean in her wheelchair. She seemed folded into a secret drowse. A couple of middle-aged gays in Prada suits, good tans. A fat man with speckled eyes and a disdainful crimp to his mouth. His wife was thin, nervous, and kept a balled handkerchief close to her nose, sneezing like a cat.

During the Associate Pastor's welcome and announcements there appeared a slender woman in her thirties. Black hair in a psyche knot, pinstriped pants suit, rimless glasses with octagonal tinted lenses. She looked at Sherard as soon as she entered. When he looked back at her she smiled, not really interested, picked up a hymnal, and sat on the edge of one of the folding chairs next to the motionless woman in the wheelchair. The tall man standing behind the wheelchair looked straight at the outsized suspended body of Christ, the pierced wrists and ankles, the uplifted eyes. Still turning almost imperceptibly above the worshipers seated in the first few rows before the altar.

Sherard found Eden again. Her head was still bowed. He looked for Bertie. She had moved from her seat in the balcony; he couldn't find her. That troubled him. He resisted an ominous impulse of panic.

The Hymn of Praise was "O for a Thousand Tongues to Sing."

While the congregation was singing Sherard got that panicky feeling again—a sense of dissociation from the sanctuary and the people around him. He felt as if his brain had been pried open and something dark had slipped inside, like a black cat easing through a door space. Entering *him*. Making itself at home, looking curiously around with a low satisfied purring. Groping his mind with a paw as if it were teasing a mouse it had found. The mouse quivering, numb with terror.

So it's Eden Waring, is it? That's a bonus. You just wait right there, big boy.

He had lost touch with his body. As easily as he might move a pawn on a chessboard he was pushed back two feet and pinned to the wall behind him. Helpless. He could move his head a little, move his eyes. Breathe. His vision lacked color and depth. His ears seemed to be plugged.

The woman who had lately come into the sanctuary was standing next to him, hymnal in hand. She had joined in the singing. He could barely hear the words from her lips, but another voice was clear in his mind, a husky contralto. Her voice, he supposed, but not the first voice he had heard, saying *So it's Eden . . .* That had been the voice of a much older woman. Reedy, a slight quaver to it.

Why don't I just take that gun you're carrying, Tom?

Not that he could do anything about it. The flap of her black shoulder bag was open. She held the hymnal where it blocked the view of the usher standing a few feet away, lifted the Glock by the butt and dropped it into her large purse.

Sherard looked past her to the other latecomers at the back of the sanctuary: the blond young couple with their child, the teenagers, the ancient nearly comatose woman in the wheelchair who appeared to be a victim of a wasting disease. The gay couple. The fat man. His thin wife who seemed allergic to everything, including her husband. The tall balding young man dutifully attending the wheelchair-bound woman. A grandson, nephew perhaps—no, actually he wasn't related to her at all. They only worked together.

And as Sherard realized this, Big Baldy turned his head for a curious glance at him.

Catch that? He read me. Latent ability, perhaps.

Then another, fourth voice in his captive mind, as all of their heads—all except for the blond couple's two-year-old toddler, who was snoozing in his daddy's arms—turned briefly toward him: *Everybody's a latent, Franc. Shut up and concentrate. Help Mae out. She's having a tough time. The girl's resisting.*

And still more voices, like half a dozen radios playing simultaneously in Sherard's mind.

Penny's right.

All of you, concentrate.

Break her down.

She's the Avatar. All of us together can't sandbag an Avatar. We need to regroup and wait for new instructions.

The old woman's voice. *You are not running this operation, Joel. I am. Let us get a grip, shall we? Thankew.*

It's the church. We're no good in a church! The vibes are bad for us. And I'm getting a bitch of a migraine.

Sherard saw the fat man's wife sneeze again. She was miserable. The fat man stared at her, his eyes filled with broken veins.

Should have left you on the team bus, Heidi.

Fuck you, Gordo! I've always pulled my weight.

It's her headband. Mae came to this conclusion after the hymn and the last reverberations from the organ had ended. The congregation recited the *Gloria Patri.* Sherard saw no movement in the wheelchair; the old woman's eyes looked vacant, but her voice continued strongly: *She has got something in that headband she's wearing. One of those copper bracelets, p'raps. Copper also blocks thought transmission. I'm simply unable to bang my way through it.*

The woman standing next to Sherard had a suggestion.

Speaking of banging—

That would *be on* your *mind, Roxanne.*

Up yours, fudge-packer. I've got Tommy's Glock. Suppose I hand it back to him, march him down the aisle, and have him blow her head off.

We haven't clearance to kill an Avatar! Mae responded crossly. *But you've given me an idea. If we are unable to get into her head., then we shall get to the girl through her heart. Mr. Sherard! Have you heard me? Merely nod. Good. Now Roxanne is going to relax her pinch sufficiently for you to walk down to where the girl is sitting. You are to bring her back up here. Then we all will leave quietly together. Oh, yes. She* will *do it, ducky. Otherwise I promise that the Second Coming will cause enormous havoc in the first couple of rows.*

Sherard looked at the hanging Jesus. Even with his constricted mental and visual capacity he could tell that the crucifix had begun to revolve more quickly on the cable that anchored it to steel roof beams. Together the martyred figure with its crown of thorns and the twenty-foot cross, both carved from solid wood, must have weighed nearly half a ton.

Unexpectedly he felt his feet under him again. He was given a slight forward push, almost stumbled but kept himself from falling by leaning on his cane. The rest of the congregation was engaged in silent prayer, all heads bowed, eyes closed. He looked up again at the crucified Christ. Revolving faster now. The stark tormented eyes, each the size of a turkey's egg, whipped around and around until the motion blurred into a surrealistic stare. A few worshipers looked up and gasped.

Sherard heard sardonic laughter in his mind from the MMF delegation behind his back.

Better hurry, Tom.

Roxanne still had a telepathic grip on him, just in case, but some of his mind was functioning lucidly again. He could walk, his vision had cleared. His hearing was sharper. Underlying their laughter he detected urgency, even fear.

MORG Mind-Fuckers. Bad Souls, Bertie had called them. The condemned of heaven. In God's house, which they had dishonored by entering, the only strength the Mind-Fuckers possessed lay in their numbers.

Whirling Jesus had almost everyone's attention as Sherard increased his pace down the aisle. Eden was half out of her seat, looking up. Then she turned quickly, eyes sweeping his face. She seemed to grasp most of what was happening.

Bring her to us!

Eden stepped out into the aisle. Many in the congregation were standing. A few were screaming as the Pastor came forward, Bible in hand, gesturing for them to be calm. The organist began to play, for reasons known only to him, "The Battle Hymn of the Republic." The organ went haywire, pipes emitting terrible shrieks and groans that caused the worshipers to hold their ears in pain.

Bring her!

Eden reached out, touched Tom's forehead. Her eyes flashed; her mouth was set in an angry line. She glared at the MMF arrayed at the back of the sanctuary. They were moments away from pandemonium.

"Tom, give me your cane!"

Roxanne tried to block him, disconnect mind and body again, but she'd given him a little too much freedom. With an effort Sherard handed the cane to Eden. Instead of taking it she swiftly ran her left hand across the burled ironwood and the gold head of the lion.

"Now give it to them. Give it to them good, Tom!"

She touched his forehead again, banishing Roxanne. Tom felt all of his strength return, flowing into him like a fountainhead. He didn't have to ask Eden what to do. He turned and raised the cane and hurled it through the air over the heads of the congregation, those who had stayed in their seats weeping with hands clenched in prayer.

The cane flew, swooped, and darted, missing innocent heads and bodies. It hovered a few feet in front of the Mind-Fuckers, who backed away or tried to work their own spells, turning the hard wood into splinters or sawdust. Then the lion snarled and the cane began to flail and punish. It cracked heads and bones, chewed ears and noses in attacks too deft to defend against. As the cane did its work driving the Mind-Fuckers from the sanctuary, the crucifix came to a sudden stop in the air and trembled on its cable.

"Come on!" Eden said, pulling Sherard toward an exit at one side of the altar.

"Wait, I don't know where Bertie is!"

"She can take care of herself. I *need* one of them, Tom! Before they all get away."

"Get going, I'll find you."

"Where are you—"

"I want my cane back. Will it come if I whistle?"

"Goof," Eden said with a fleeting smile, and she disappeared on the run.

When the old woman in the wheelchair saw Eden with Sherard's cane, she recognized the special properties invested in it and came to the conclusion that things were about to go badly. Her decision to do a bunk was also a measure of how much respect she'd gained for Eden Waring in just a short time.

Without waiting for her escort to wheel her out of there, Mae cut in the mental afterburners and willed it to happen. The standard-issue hand-propelled chair did a one-eighty and went flying through the padded doors to the vestibule, picking up speed across the plush carpet while she sat like a mummy in a go-to-meeting silk dress, wighair wisping on her skull in the faint breeze of her passage, the old flesh from hairline to collarbones resembling candle dribble. Only a yellow slit of one eye provided proof that her body was slightly more alive than dead. But her mind didn't have any flies on it.

So they'd underestimated the powers Eden could summon and the others were now paying for it. She heard them bawling and calling for help as the African cane beat them mercilessly. Not for Mae, thankew. Ta-ta, darlings. The younger telepaths *did* require a setback now and then to underscore the seriousness of their education.

Some parishioners were trying to leave the church with Mae. They cluttered the wide entranceway, bleating like lost lambs. All new souls, probably, Mae assumed. Put on a little show for them, they lose what few wits they possess. And they had no regard for an old woman in a wheelchair who needed to get to her invalid coach, her two husky and devoted male nurses, have something intravenously for lunch and put on her thinking cap. She'd seen Eden Waring at work. Quite splendid, actually. But Mae had been around in one guise or another since sorcery was in its infancy. She could show that cocky kid a thing or two.

Just keeping the wheelchair in motion was a severe demand on her resources, and she couldn't manage at the same time the people who stood in her way, unless she chose to drop each in his tracks with no pulse. A crude approach. She did have a scruple or two. Mae decided to get airborne.

No sooner thought than done. Eight feet was enough elevation, she decided; the church doors were a massive fourteen feet in height. In contrast to the hip architecture the church entrance had the traditional shape of a woman's vulva: *enter and be reborn.* Both doors, fortunately, stood open. The wheelchair lifted off the carpet and flew above the heads of parishioners, giving them a more severe fright than they'd received from the whirling crucifix.

Mae exited the church and zoomed straight into the wrathful *chi* of Bertie

Nkambe, who stood with folded arms on the walkway between the borders of late-blooming azaleas.

Mae had intended to bank to the right and land the wheelchair gracefully a block up the street where the invalid coach, double-parked, was waiting for her. Instead Mae discovered that she had no control at all. The attitude of the flying wheelchair had changed; she was headed up. And *up*, with a whoosh of wind in her partially paralyzed face.

Mae fought back as she crossed West End Avenue at forty miles an hour and climbing. The driver of a delivery van, catching sight of the airborne wheelchair, was disconnected from his wits and the van plowed into the back of a city bus. Mae was experiencing hot spots in her brain as if several minor blood vessels had popped simultaneously. Outrage further diminished her capacity to retake control.

Who are you? You cannot do this to me!

A flock of birds scattered from the boughs of a sycamore inside the black iron fence that separated West End from Vandy's campus. The wheelchair, now at rooftop level of two turn-of-the-century brick buildings separated by a small parking lot, began to slow down. There was a quadrangle and some tall spreading oaks ahead. The campus, between graduation and the start of summer sessions, was lightly populated on this Sunday morning.

The wheelchair stopped above the center of the broad quadrangle, hovering fifty feet in the air. Mae made a last effort to communicate with the superior young mind that had overwhelmed hers.

Got to run. Bye-bye, Mae.

Wait. You cawn't leave me like this!

Oh. Well, if you insist.

The wheelchair dropped, but only a few feet. It crashed through the densely leaved crown of a venerable oak and came stunningly to rest, upright, on a bough the thickness of a sewer pipe. The wheels hung over either side of the bough, spinning uselessly. Smaller limbs and leaves embraced and enfolded Mae like a shy nymph in a Victorian children's book.

I will get you for this, lovely. Rest assured. But Mae had the dismal feeling that she no longer was powerful enough to be heard, let alone reckoned with.

The Pastor had restored order if not tranquillity to his flock by coaxing them to join the choir in singing another hymn. About a third of the congregation had decided they'd had enough spiritual sustenance for one Sunday.

Few of those choosing to leave actually believed what they had seen. In spite of their professions of faith they had little capacity for acknowledging the miraculous in their lives. Some parishioners had witnessed Tom Sherard hurling his lion's-head cane in the direction of the Mind-Fuckers. *What? What was he doing? What did that mean?* Others, already distracted by the incomprehensible, namely the spinning crucifix, had witnessed the drubbing and rout of the MMFers. But when the senses are overloaded, the mind simply shuts down or fast-forwards to the next moments of comparative sanity, where the cane-beating could be explained away as some sort of irrational scuffle. Teenagers involved, a flurry of juvenile hysteria.

(Everybody was afraid that crucifix was gonna fall, hey, it was *scary*, man.)

Because Tom Sherard was only one of many leaving the sanctuary, he didn't draw unusual attention. The exodus was quiet for the most part; stunned faces, a few embarrassed smiles. Young children whining in their parents' arms. The Mind-Fuckers were nowhere to be seen. A woman fainted in the vestibule, revealing to passersby that she didn't wear underwear even to church. Sherard heard sirens, still a mile or so away. He saw his cane lying inconspicuously on the carpet against the wall. He picked it up and took a side exit to the parking lot.

The cane felt different to him. He had a tingling sensation from the palm of his hand to the elbow. He was bemused, but he had to smile. Whatever Eden had done, the knobbly wood seemed to have been permanently transmuted into something . . . livelier. Invested (his old friend and mentor Joseph Nkambe might have said) with Eden's considerable juju. He had the feeling that should it become necessary, he could employ his cane to cleave granite with a blow.

On West End a police car had pulled up behind the accident involving the bus. Sherard heard Eden call him. He looked around. She was in the front seat of the van the Russians had rented at the airport when they arrived. Alex was driving.

A side door of the van slid open as he approached. Bertie Nkambe was inside. She smiled happily at him.

"Hey, look what we've got."

Sherard heard a series of muted sneezes. The thin woman named Heidi was hunched over in the rearmost seat. She raised her rabbity face from her sodden handkerchief and glared.

"You *wouldn't* have me except I came down with a migraine. It whiteouts my powers. On good days I'm better than you are, Toots."

"Maybe you'll get a chance to prove that," Bertie said nonchalantly. "Meantime your headache could get a lot worse, Heidi. If you really want me to work at it."

"I told you already. I don't know where the device is! Not our department. We were here for backup, in case it was needed."

"So tell us something new," Eden said as Alex drove out of the parking lot.

"If I don't get a shot of Demerol damn soon, I'll start hurling all over this van."

"Try again, Heidi honey," Alex said.

Silence. The woman groaned. "Hang a right," she said suddenly.

Alex turned on a red light and headed up West End.

"Vanderbilt has a med school and a hospital," Heidi said in a subdued tone. "I have insurance. And a plane ticket out of town. Three o'clock this afternoon."

"No chance," Sherard said, looking tensely at his wristwatch. It was ten minutes to noon.

"Maybe," Heidi said, "I do know something that'll make it worth your while to let me catch my flight. I've been thinking about it. So maybe it all fits in somehow."

The others waited for Heidi to elaborate. At Twenty-fourth Street Alex turned left, guided by a blue sign with a white H on it.

"I flew down from Dulles yesterday with Gordo and a couple of the kids. Mae travels by flying ambulance, and the others are from places around the country. Like I said, we were backup. We knew what was going down would be nuclear, but that's all."

"Didn't know shit from Shinola," Alex said, employing his favorite American expression.

"Shut up. I don't feel like talking anyway. Let me get this over with. Anyway, Gordo and me were boarded already when somebody I knew from college got on. Sandi Goldfarb. She worked for MORG too, the Russian desk. We'd run into each a few times around the company. You know, it was a casual relationship, catch up on old times."

"Where are you going with this, honey?" Alex said over his shoulder.

"Over there, where it says Emergency? They ought to be able to give me a shot. Where am I going with it? Yesterday Sandi's on the plane with me, today she's dead."

"How do you know?" Bertie asked.

"How do *you* know anything? A casual touch, that's all. Precognition, girl. I saw Sandi dead. Broken neck. Murdered, probably. Because she wasn't in a hearse. She was lying on a floor somewhere, lying naked on a blue tarp. Eyes open. Shit. No matter how many times it happens, you almost jump out of your skin."

"What does this have to do with our problem?" Sherard asked.

Heidi was holding her head, eyes shut. Tears drained down her cheeks. "I don't know! Sandi said she was meeting another girl and they were spending the night in Nashville. Company business. If she knew what it was about, she couldn't tell me, but she said she hoped she'd have a chance to do some waterskiing. Later when she got up to use the john I had a peek at the airline ticket in her tote. She was booked on a return flight out of here, eight-thirty this morning. But I know she didn't make it."

"This doesn't do any of us any good," Bertie told her.

"Think about it. Company business. Just down for the night. I got that she was down here to screw a guy, one of ours. Either he turned out to be a homicidal maniac, or—Sandi came across something she wasn't supposed to know about, and drew a quick death sentence."

"You said she was on MORG's Russian desk?" Eden asked. "Did she speak Russian?"

"Sure, her major at Rutgers."

"It's a Russian device. We know that much. That's why Alex is here."

"I wouldn't tell her a fuhkeeng thing," Alex cautioned.

"Okay, that makes a little sense," Heidi said as Alex pulled up to the hospital's emergency entrance. "Listen, I'm trying to cooperate now. I mean I don't want to be stuck here in Music City when there's a major kablooey scheduled."

"We still have nothing to go on," Sherard said.

"I was trying to remember one other thing. Pre-cog is funny; sometimes there's only a vague flash, other times you get details. There was some writing on that tarp I saw, in one corner. Black paint, a stencil I guess. It said *Holly Marie, Hendersonville, TN*—for Tennessee."

Silence in the van. Heidi clenched her forehead tightly, crying in pain.

"You still don't get it? Sandi hoped she could go waterskiing. The *Holly Marie*. That must be the name of a boat. She was killed on a boat! And it has to be registered somewhere. Doesn't it?"

PLENTY COUPS, MONTANA · JUNE 7 · 5:15 P.M. MDT

Eden Waring's doppelganger had been wandering around the Plenty Coups facility for most of the day. During the first hour she had become lost. From the second hour she'd been footsore, and since well before noon hunger pangs had steadily worsened her mood. The scent of food from a cafeteria steam table or the sight of a vending machine was almost enough to fetch tears. But hunger didn't bother her as much as isolation. Her long stretch of invisibility. She was neither human nor ghost. Her aloneness was absolute. Now even the day-to-day routine of shadowing Eden, her left-handed homebody, seemed more appealing to her than hours of trudge through the facility, this bright technologically precise but emotionally neutral construct, climate-controlled, with one cheerless perspective after another, a deadness to each footfall. It would have depressed the soul of a rat. In her bleakness she entertained small fears that she might never leave. It had come to her, dropped into her mind like a seed from the beak of a bird that had flown for a thousand miles, that Eden was in great danger, from a totally unexpected source. What was the fate of a doppelganger without its homebody? The terror of nothingness, beyond her ability to define or endure.

She wondered what Robin Sandza had to look forward to, once she released him. But he had been eloquent in his signaled appeal to her, finger touching his forehead, then pointing to the sky.

Miles of walking, sore feet, flagging energy. But a renewed sense of urgency.

Find him. And get it done.

While Eden was still alive, and could reward her dpg by setting her free.

The doppelganger had already selected the name she wanted for herself. It perked her up, silently repeating to herself the lovely, longed-for, all-important *name* as she made the rounds of forbidden places in the underground facility, numbly searching for Robin Sandza. Imagining social situations. Introducing herself. The joy, the *magic*, in those three syllables.

Hi! I'm Guinevere!

OLD HICKORY LAKE, TENNESSEE · JUNE 7 · 6:35 P.M. CDT

Well, I know I have seen it in this end of the lake," the TWRA officer said, piloting his Wildlife Resources Agency's patrol boat, a thirty-two-foot Whaler with twin 250-horse Johnson outboards, as close to the shoreline as its draft would permit. "Fact is I may have stopped it for some small infraction. They do know how to party on these big-ass showboats, specially college kids on spring break. Gang of 'em will pool their money to rent one for a week. The rowdier kind make a deal of work for us. Figure how they're out on the water, the ordinary rules of human behavior do not apply. Or they get themselves drowned. Sometimes sheriff's divers can't locate the bodies; lake's forty–fifty foot in a high-water year, and it's dark down there. Now a houseboat, it don't go nowheres fast but it does take some experience to drive one and not run it over snags or into 'nother boat. Do us a big favor they just leave 'em tied to the dock. *Holly Marie*. Tell you how that name stuck in my mem'ry. My oldest sister named one of her twins Holly and the other 'un Hallie, or maybe it was Hayley. Say you don't have no idea where the boat might be anchored at?"

Tom Sherard said, "All we had was the owner's name. Windcastle Marine, Inc., and the registration information you looked up."

"Weren't enough to ring a bell," the safety officer said. His name was Carlisle. First name. He was in his early thirties, with sun freckles and wrinkles, new pink burn on his high cheekbones and around his blue eyes. "Well, we got us some daylight yet; after that I couldn't promise nothing."

In the shade of the cabin, Heidi, the MMFer with the huge headache that a shot of Demerol hadn't much diminished, groaned and shifted the icebag she was holding to her forehead. The only word she'd uttered for the last two hours was "fuhkoff." She had refused to wear a flotation vest. Bertie Nkambe and Eden Waring had theirs on. They were in the bow of the whaler, studying the shore, the many small coves they passed. Alex had stretched out on a couple of flotation cushions and was staring at the sky, smoking.

There was a floating dock or boatshed in nearly half of the coves. Speedboats, Jet Skis, a few sailboats, homely pontoon and paddleboats. Small kids wearing bright orange floaters around their upper arms were jumping off the ends of docks. Older kids roared down the middle of the lake on Jet Skis, slowing down when they saw the patrol boat with its orange-and-green striped bow.

The story Sherard had told to warrant the use of the TWRA cruiser involved a fictitious stepdaughter of a close friend of Sherard's. She was visiting friends on the *Holly Marie*. There was a family emergency, and the girl's cell phone wasn't working. Sherard said he was in Nashville on business and had volunteered to find the girl.

What the officer made of Heidi and Alex was anyone's guess, but Sherard couldn't afford to park them elsewhere. Heidi might still prove to be useful, and Alex was indispensable, should they find the nuclear device hidden aboard the houseboat.

Carlisle saw someone he knew in a johnboat with a Merc 75 outboard, puttering home with two fishing companions. Carlisle slowed the cruiser and pulled abreast of the johnboat, staying ten feet away.

"This old boy," he said to Sherard, "has lived on Old Hick'ry for twenty years. He knows ever'body. Mind taking the wheel for me, just keep us even with the johnboat."

Carlisle stepped down to the deck and hailed the man in the tatty brimweary hat sitting in the stern with his hand on the tiller of the outboard.

"Hey there, Homebrew."

"That you, Carlisle? How's it hangin', bud?"

"Plumb and dandy. How you doin'?"

"Right pert, thanky. This here's Macon Oldsmar from Kentuck, and his boy Ben, come down here to see what real fishin's all about."

"Pleased to know y'all. Say, Homebrew, reckon you could help me out with something? This gentleman here's on a mission a mercy you might say. We need to locate us a houseboat name of *Holly Marie.*"

"Well, you know I ain't that strong on 'memberin' names nowadays. But give me a description, she's on the lake I just might be able to tell you whur."

Carlisle pulled out his shirt-pocket notebook. "She's seventy-four foot, built by McAllan boatworks in Bowling Green. Barge hull, sixteen-foot beam, two upper decks, raked, and a fly bridge, which I allow is kind a unusual."

"Yeah, you trailer them boogers, they don't fit the overpasses. Well, all right, sir. Seen one like it four–five weeks ago at Marvin's, in for a overhaul and paint job. They was paintin' it just the prettiest shade a yeller. You give Marvin a call, he can prob'ly tell you where it's docked at now."

8:15 P.M. CDT

Sunset.

The TWRA whaler coasted around a shadowy bend of Old Hickory Lake into darker water, leaving the bright surface of mid-lake behind. Finger coves, where the last light of day was blocked by a long rocky bluff behind them, penetrated fifty to a hundred yards into the hilly wooded terrain. There were a few lights showing through the trees, homes above or along the shoreline. A couple of fishing boats lingered beneath the bluff.

"Good bass fishing there," Carlisle pointed out. "Plenty of submerged structure. Crankbait's your best bet, this time a evenin'."

Bertie, standing in the bow with binoculars, said, "Yellow houseboat. To the right, that next inlet or whatever you call it."

"Good enough," Carlisle said, giving the wheel a turn. "We were gettin' a little low on gas."

"No lights showing on the houseboat," Bertie reported. "There's a road, a fence, and a gate. Padlocked."

"Looks like ever'body's gone off to dinner or to Garth Brooks," Carlisle said, taking the cruiser into the unroofed dock opposite the big houseboat, idling there with the bow against the dock fender.

"I'll leave a note," Sherard said curtly.

"Yes, sir. Would one of you young ladies tie us up?"

Eden made the jump to the dock with the length of dacron line secured to a bow cleat. She wrapped it around a post.

"Let's just make sure we don't disturb nobody," Carlisle said, giving the cruiser's siren a tap. The only light that had come on was the motion detector on the top of the post that Eden had triggered. They waited. There was no response to the siren. The houseboat was buttoned down tight.

Tom and Bertie joined Eden on the dock. Alex got up, stretched, glanced at Heidi, still comforting herself with the icebag.

"Coming, *honey*?"

"Fuhkoff."

Carlisle said a trifle nervously, "Need to remind y'all that this is private property."

Alex pulled his folder and showed Carlisle his bona fides. Although the sun had gone down, it was hot and still in the cove, and Alex had a film of sweat on his face. "Department of Energy, your government, Threat Assessment Intelligence Division. What it means, I am head guy here, not you."

"You're not an American, are you?" Carlisle asked, with growing unease.

"Russian. Take it easy, Carlisle. We are not the Black Hats anymore."

"I thought—"

"You come with us. Stay off your fuhkeeng radio."

Sherard had boarded the houseboat and was walking around, looking for a way in.

"Locked," he reported. "Probably alarmed."

"We'll break in," Bertie suggested, a note of strain in her voice.

"Now just a minute—" Carlisle said.

Alex gave him a pat on the shoulder. Carlisle pulled angrily away.

"I don't know who y'all think you are, but you're about to commit a serious—"

"Carlisle, there is stolen nuclear device with one-kiloton capability, could be armed and ticking fifty feet from where we stand. That is powerful enough weapon to vaporize this end of the lake. Is also very bad for the wildlife population. I am not shitting you, honey. I don't know if we have five hours or five minutes to disarm. Where is your piece?"

"Uh, TWRA personnel don't carry sidearms."

"Then grab a wrench and break some glass. Now."

"My God. My God," Carlisle said, beginning to perceive that Alex was on the level.

The houseboat alarm hadn't been activated. Sherard located a light switch inside the door with the smoked-glass panel Carlisle had broken through. They went down four steps to the salon, turning on more lights. It was hot inside. Bertie and Eden were behind Sherard. They looked around. Eden walked slowly through the salon to the galley, but not in a straight line. She appeared to be walking around something on the deck, her face growing taut. Bertie went the other way, into one of the staterooms.

Carlisle said, "What's going on? What are they doing?"

Eden walked back into the salon, taking the same little detour, glancing at the floor. She was breathing hard.

"It's not here," she said. "It *was* here, but they took it away." She pointed to the alcove where cases of fishing rods and a trolling motor were stored. "Not too long ago, though."

"What was on the floor in the galley?" Sherard asked. "Where you didn't want to walk."

"Body. A woman's body. Her neck's broken. Heidi was right."

Bertie came out of the second stateroom.

"Two women. Both dead. I don't get it, though. I sense fear. That was one of the women. She died right here." Bertie leaned over, passing a spread hand above the deck carpeting. "But *him*. No emotion. No anger or pleasure. Casual as wringing a dove's neck. He's blond. Five-eleven, six feet. Not bad-looking, except he has arms as long as an ape's." Bertie held up something in her other hand. "Throwaway razor. Whoever cleaned up after these two missed it. I don't care much for the aftershave the blond guy uses. I forgot to mention. He has tattoos. Barbed wire, a sailing ship below his right shoulder."

Carlisle's eyes were huge. "W-who *are* you people?"

"You said *two* men, honey," Alex said to Bertie.

"Right. There were two women and two men. Don't have a fix on the other guy yet."

"Dump," Eden said, looking as if she was about to gag. "Oh Jesus.

They're buried in a dump! Burning garbage. Oh shit." She walked swiftly upstairs, Carlisle literally jumping out of her way, and went outside.

"I need to use the bathroom," Carlisle pleaded. There were beads of sweat on his forehead and chin. His eyes had sunk back into his head.

Alex nodded to him, looked at Tom Sherard.

"Just wait," Tom said, his eyes on Bertie. She was prowling around the salon. Studying objects with her hands, not actually touching anything. The furniture, the projection TV, the table where Randy and Herb and their doomed guests had whiled away the time playing canasta. Two decks of cards were on the table. Bertie picked up a deck, shuffled thoughtfully, replaced it. She had a long look at the TV, then passed into the galley, taking a giant step over the place where the body of Sandi Goldfarb had lain.

When she came back she stood a few feet from the TV again, staring.

"Turn it on for me, Tom."

"Can't you?"

"No. Not permitted. You. Please."

He walked past her, picked up the remote control, and pushed the button marked POWER.

Nothing happened. A spot of light appeared in the center of the screen but there was no picture, no sound. As far as his own senses could detect.

Bertie went reeling back with her hands clasping her ears, a scream of pain hung up in her throat. She fell, writhing.

"Turn it off!"

Sherard thumbed the OFF button. The blip of light faded from the screen. Bertie struggled to her feet, the heel of one hand pressed against her forehead.

"Oh. Damn. *Damn,* did that ever hurt!"

"Bertie, what happened?"

She looked at him. Tenderly touched her ears. "What? I'm sorry. Can't hear. The crowd, it's the biggest, loudest—I'm almost deaf."

Alex looked at Sherard. "How often does she get like this?"

"Only when she's on high-burn."

Eden came back down the steps into the salon, two at a time. She glanced at Bertie. *What's up?* she asked subvocally.

"Huge crowd. Lights. That big stadium we saw, on the river in town. That's where they went."

Eden said excitedly to Alex and Sherard, "In a red pickup, maybe an SUV; I couldn't tell. It's a big one. Whoever's driving had trouble getting through the gate."

"ESP?" Sherard asked her.

"No, logical deduction." She held up her right hand. There were flecks of red paint on her fingertips.

"What? What did you say, Eden? I'm deaf."

Eden showed them what she had in her left hand. A shard of thick curved plastic.

"He must have popped a parking light when he sideswiped the gate. So we want a red truck, minor fender damage, left front unless he was backing out."

Bertie shook her head a couple of times as if to clear her mind.

"Where's the biggest show in Nashville tonight?" she asked Carlisle, who had come unsteadily out of the bathroom blotting his face with a towel.

"Garth Brooks. Sold out. Seventy thousand tickets." He glanced at his chronometer. "Started at seven-thirty." He had a sickly smile. "Wish that's where I was."

"You're going," Eden said, grabbing his shirtsleeve. "We need your boat." When he was slow to budge Eden released him and dashed up the stairs again.

Tom Sherard was closest to Eden when he heard the shot. She stopped suddenly outside on the lower deck of the houseboat, looking in surprise at someone on the dock to her right. Eden's hands rose slowly, an attitude of vulnerability. And Sherard was thrust back in time to a New York street, to gunshots and screams, Gillian down and already beyond his help.

Not again. Not to Eden!

He pushed off on his good leg and lunged with a yell through the doorway, throwing himself at the motionless girl. He didn't hear a second shot as he tackled her, lifted her off her feet, his momentum carrying her out of the line of fire. They sprawled together on the deck, rolled over. The only pain he felt was in the shoulder and elbow he landed on. He pinned the stunned girl to the deck, shielding her body with his own, and looked back.

Heidi was on the dock with a rifle, efficiently working the bolt, chambering another round. She fired again. Sherard knew he'd been hit but the impact was slight, near the middle of his back.

"Gun!" he shouted, warning the others. Winchester, perhaps, about a twenty-inch barrel, probably .223 caliber. The size of the magazine told him she had several rounds left.

There was nothing he could do. Heidi was too far away. She would drop him before he took three steps in her direction. And Eden wasn't moving. If anyone tried to come to their rescue, Heidi had a clear line of sight.

Heidi jacked another cartridge into the chamber. Her thin face looked drawn from migraine, but her expression was calm. She moved a step closer. Sherard judged, with a faint feeling of regret, that the range was about fifteen yards. Heidi would go for the head shot now, put him away, then continue rapid-fire until the magazine was empty and Eden also lay dead in his arms.

He had a glimpse of someone else on deck, near the doorway. Heidi was seeing him down the barrel of the rifle but she also caught the movement and was distracted. Her fourth shot struck a chrome railing a few inches above Sherard's head.

Then Heidi didn't have the rifle anymore. For an instant it appeared that she had tossed it away. Both of her hands were clutching air. The blue steel barrel of the rifle caught light from one of the overhead floods as it rose a good ten feet above Heidi's head, spinning like a propeller, then came down muzzle-first toward Heidi's upturned face. Heidi was gaping in astonishment. The rifle barrel struck her with great force as shattered teeth flew from her mouth. Heidi's body jerked and turned rigid while the barrel, like a second, steel spine, penetrated her body—down her throat, through the esophagus, into the stomach.

Heidi trembled, hands still outstretched, feet on the deck as if they had been nailed. Her eyes bulged from her head. Blood burbled like a slow fountain from her stretched gummy mouth.

The bolt of the rifle snicked back, rammed a cartridge into the breech.

Sherard, still crouched over Eden, looked away and into the face of Alberta Nkambe. The Nilotic strain in her mixed-blood features was more prominent than he'd ever seen; the planes of her face looked as harsh as a killer god's. Her eyes gleamed with unearthly life. It was a memorable sight, equal to the memory of a lion bursting out of high grass and charging in ten-yard bounds, coming in three blinks of an eye so close that he could, forever after, smell the animal's blood heat and rage.

It seemed to him that he could smell Bertie's rage now—an odor like acetylene-melted steel or lightning in a seething sky—as she turned all of her *chi* on the transfixed, luckless Heidi.

The rifle she had half swallowed began firing in Heidi's gut, shots coming so quickly the action of the bolt and trigger were only a blur. The shots couldn't be heard, only followed as puckers appeared all over the front of Heidi's pleated pants near the crotch, the cloth staining red. Then her feet came unstuck and Heidi did a little feckless flopping dance that reminded Sherard of a secretary bird chopping up a grounded snake with its claws. All movement ceased abruptly as she stepped off the end of the dock and plunged out of sight.

Sherard sat up slowly. Only then did he pay attention to the back of his neck, which was numb on the right side, warm and bloody. He reached up carefully and found where the bullet had entered. It was still there in the muscle meat of his neck and, hopefully, hadn't fragmented; how close it had come to the spinal cord or the vital hindbrain he didn't know.

The other bullet had plowed at an angle through the flotation vest he hadn't had time to remove. He took it off now but couldn't find the bullet with a prodding finger. Doing something, anything, reduced the trembles and diverted his thoughts from how close the other one had come to killing him.

Regardless, the little bullet in his neck meant trouble and he knew it.

Eden's eyes had opened. She wasn't focusing very well. She made sounds but not words.

Bertie, her face relaxed now, knelt beside Sherard and looked at his wound. He knew from her face what she thought, but she said cheerily, "Hey, it's nothing, a nick from a *panga*, Tom."

"Yeah, I've been hurt worse in thornbush." He turned his head and spat some blood onto the deck, clenched and unclenched his hands, alert for any sign of weakness. Then he stood with Bertie's help. Eden sat up slowly, still looking blankly at the two of them, trying to get her bearings.

Carlisle cleared his throat several times. "I've got a first aid kit aboard my boat."

"Where did the rifle come from?" Sherard asked. There was a slow seep of blood onto the back of his tongue.

"It's my varmint rifle. Use it for snakes, mostly. She wouldn't've had no trouble finding it. I'm sorry."

"Not your fault." Sherard was growing woozy. No time for that. But he feared going into shock. "You have any snakebite medicine in that kit of yours?" he asked Carlisle.

"Yes, sir. Hundred-proof bourbon."

"Let's get to it, then."

Carlisle looked as if he were about to cry. "I have to report this. God *damn*. How do I explain a woman gut-shot from the inside out with the barrel of my rifle stuffed down her throat?"

"Unfortunate accident," Bertie said. "But it cured her migraine. And she's down there in the deep for good. So is your rifle. Unless you want it back, Carlisle."

"What are you saying?"

Alex draped an arm around Carlisle's shoulders. "She is saying you don't have to worry about something that never happened. If nobody saw, then it didn't happen, honey. That is one bitchin' Russian philosophy. Now we need to haul *ass*. Did I say that right? Haul our lovely asses out of here."

"Can you take us by boat all the way to Nashville?" Bertie asked.

"W-where y'all wantin' to go?" Carlisle asked, looking as if he dreaded spending another moment in their company.

"The stadium," Bertie said. "Garth Brooks is about to bomb for the first time in his career. Tom, I'll patch you up as well as I can. But you ought to—"

"No hospital. Not yet. What's become of my cane? Oh, thank you, Alex." Sherard's face had turned cold, along with his hands. He gripped the lion's-head cane tightly, made an effort not to breathe too fast. His shirt collar was sticky with blood. "How are you feeling, Eden?"

"I'm okay," she said, holding the back of her head, staring in horror at Tom. "Who shot you? Would someone *please* tell me—"

"I'll post it on the Astral Internet," Bertie said, giving her a nudge toward the cruiser. "You can read while we're under way. It's good practice for you."

BIG COUNTRY RANCH, MONTANA · JUNE 7 · 8:15 P.M. MDT

Buck Hannafin! As I live and breathe! You're about the *last* person I would have expected to show up on our doorstep tonight."

Buck and Courtney Shyla had been announced, so Rona had had the time to get over her surprise. The fact that she was now greeting them personally confirmed to Buck that, serendipity aside, Rona had calculated having him there was a piece of luck she could make good use of. *Keep your friends close . . .*

"I do humbly apologize for the intrusion, Rona, but as I happened to be right next door—"

"At the Broken Wheel?" Rona waved away all explanations as unnecessary, though Buck saw an instant of calculation in her eyes. Replaced by feminine curiosity as Rona turned her attention to Courtney with her most appealing smile and said, "Come in, come in, don't be strange! You *will* join us for dinner? I'll have one of the boys grain your horses." She looked sharply past Courtney to the hitching post at the foot of the steps. "Three horses? Is someone else with you, Buck?"

Buck and Courtney both removed their Stetsons as they stepped across the threshold. Buck gave Rona a brief embrace and the customary air-kisses near her cheeks.

Courtney said, "The piebald's name is Ezekiel, Mrs. Harvester. We picked him up at the vet's a little while ago, he's been limping and needed hock surgery." She held out a gloved hand. "I'm Courtney Shyla." Her Adam's apple bobbed nervously. "This is just the greatest honor of my life, meeting you, Mrs. Harvester."

"Pleasure's all mine, Courtney. Are you and Buck related?"

"Courtney is my half brother Max's oldest girl," Buck said. Having been officially welcomed, Buck and Courtney began to unbuckle their chaps.

"Wonderful," Rona said with the briefest glance at Buck, her smile shading to amusement. "So you've been over to the Broken Wheel, enjoying some R and R? Some of our people have been trying to locate you for *days,* Bucklin." She put an arm around Courtney's slim waist, separating her subtly from Hannafin, and walked them both toward the great room.

"That so?"

"Regarding S. 723. We wanted your input." Off his brief look she clarified, "Clint and I. But we won't talk legislation or policy tonight, even though I seldom have such a marvelous opportunity to hear your side of things. Now that we're four, we can play bridge after dinner. Do you play, Courtney?"

"Yes, ma'am." Courtney looked around the generously proportioned, multistoried foyer, her lips parted, childlike wonder in her eyes. There was a Marine captain ten paces away sitting on a bench with his back to the wall, one hand on a black attaché case. He was the man with the so-called "nuclear football"—the case contained a code book with strike options for intercontinental ballistics and submarine-based missiles. Seeing him, and knowing what kind of shape her President was in, gave Courtney a sinking feeling, down to the heels of her boots. She wondered if it was Rona who now carried the coded authentication card that identified the President of the United States in an emergency. There was another man, probably MORG security, standing one flight up on the helical stairway. She counted three surveillance cameras. "You have such a fabulous home, Mrs. Harvester."

"Thank you. Clint and I put a lot of thought and effort into what we wanted for our sunset years. —And call me Rona, please," the First Lady insisted, squeezing Courtney's waist above the belt line. Nothing but hard muscle there. "It will be you and me against the boys tonight." Another squeeze, higher. "Oh, Courtney, what I wouldn't give to be in the shape you're in! Or near your age again, for that matter."

Buck said, "Been looking forward to spending a little time with Clint. Didn't want to rush him, you understand."

"We're eternally grateful for the thoughtfulness of our good friends. But I'm sorry to say Clint is indisposed tonight. He retired early."

"Indisposed? Nothing serious, I hope."

"It's fatigue, mostly. I'm sure you understand."

"Then who's our fourth for bridge?"

Victor Wilding, drink in hand, got up from his fireside seat as they entered the great room. His wavy red hair was slicked back, still wet from a sauna and shower. The tip of his snubbed nose and his cheekbones glowed like new pennies from the heat of the log fire.

"You and Victor have met, haven't you?" Rona said casually to Buck.

"On two widely separated occasions," Buck said, recovering from a brief hitch in his stride. "How're you tonight, Mr. Wilding?"

"Fine. Nice to see you again, Senator."

"And this is Courtney, Shiloh, did you say?—*Shyla*, I didn't hear you correctly. She is, somewhere in the thickets of Hannafin genealogy, related to Buck."

"Very nice to meet you, Courtney."

The ritual of politesse and false good cheer made Buck want to spit on the terra-cotta floor. He'd seen the First Lady like this before and knew how thin the façade was; she was wound tight as an old dollar watch and on some kind of ego binge; hell, they both were. Wilding's gestures were a shade too precise, and he smiled like a man who had started his drinking early in the day. With no real capacity for the hard stuff. A shine in his eyes like the peephole into the heart of a blast furnace. Both of them were keyed to some high expectation. It was bound to be a night to remember, Buck thought. If they lived through it.

There was a houseboy standing by the bar. Buck named his potion. Courtney asked for a Coke. Rona, who drank no spirits, kept Courtney close to her while arranging more intimate seating, dragging an ottoman closer to the soapstone hearth. The pre-dinner gab was animated but perfunctory. Buck and Victor Wilding eyed each other with little regard. Buck had always wondered how someone so youthful-looking could have been running an organization like MORG going on ten years now. Both Wanda Cheville and the (presumably) late Robert Hyde had collected data that was mostly conjecture. Wilding had gained his reputation within Multiphasic Operations and Research Group by greatly expanding MORG's presence in the worldwide arms trade, thereby enhancing the exchequer by several billions of dollars. The technique of moving rapidly up the ladder is the same in any business or government. Acquire a mentor, secretly turn his followers against him, then depose him. The most successful monsters in the intelligence game were both snake charmers and blood workers. Buck wasn't all that offended by bloody hands, he'd been around too long. The bad apples eventually rotted themselves to the core. What he disliked most about Wilding was the man's steady assault on Appropriations, looking for fresh billions for empire-building while arrogantly refusing to accommodate the various oversight committees on the Hill.

Rona asked Courtney, who had opted for a starry-eyed routine and a naive personality, a lot of questions. Courtney seemed happy to play to Rona while she conducted her recon of household security. The First Lady had okay'd a complex of perimeter alarms well beyond the house, but the system depended heavily on infrared cameras. Motion detectors had been tried, but in a wildlife area filled with elk, mule deer, brown and black bears, badgers, and the occasional cougar, all of them nocturnal prowlers, such alarms were useless. Inside the house Rona liked her privacy. The Secret Service had limited their security efforts to cameras and motion detectors that covered areas of access on the first floor, six in all. The motion detectors were never turned on until everyone had retired for the night, which often was the hour before dawn. While in residence at Big Country the President and First Lady were supposed to wear tracking devices, but Nick Grella had said they almost never remembered them.

Courtney spoke under her breath as they walked together. A camera full on her face could not have seen her lips move. The hearing aid Buck had substituted for the one he usually wore could pick up a whisper through a cement wall.

"POTUS is down for the night."

"Then it's a miss."

"No, I can bat from the other side of the plate."

"Come again?"

"FLOTUS is hot for me."

"Noticed that."

"She'll invite us to spend the night. Wilding is half-bombed already. You fake it. Pass out early. Then it's me and FLOTUS, and she'll be ready to boogie. When we're alone it's all my play."

"Can't ask you to—"

"Like I said. I'm a switch-hitter."

"Oh."

Outside the baronial dining room, with its twenty-five-foot vaulted ceiling and rustic chimney stack, the temperature had fallen into the low fifties. A fire of seasoned hickory blazed on the hearth. The solar-gain windows framed a panorama of mountain peaks. The moon was golden in a misty nimbus. A meteor flickered in the far, far dark.

They were halfway through a meal of poached trout, elk steak, and wild rice when Clint Harvester appeared, wearing only his pj's. The top half was mostly unbuttoned. He had put on sneakers, on the wrong feet, and the laces were untied. A MORG security man with a harried expression came up behind Clint as he hesitated in the doorway fifty feet from where Rona was sitting, her back to him.

Victor Wilding noticed Clint first and nudged Rona. The others looked up as she turned, a glass of cabernet sauvignon halfway to her lips.

Buck Hannafin saw her hand tremble. He seized the moment and stood, pushing his chair back from the table, and before anyone else could move or speak he strode across the floor with a glad smile, his hand out.

"Mr. President! Wonderful to see you again. Rona said you were a little under the weather tonight."

Rona recovered her wits, put down the wineglass and said, "Buck, don't."

Buck ignored her. When Clint failed to respond, only stood there with a slight swaying of his body and a mildly puzzled expression, Buck seized his right hand and pumped it enthusiastically, looking intently into Clint Harvester's eyes.

The MORG guy behind the President said, "Mrs. Harvester, I'm sorry, but he heard voices—"

"Should be asleep by now," Rona finished, biting her underlip in exasperation. She smiled at Courtney, excused herself, and went swiftly to her husband's side.

Buck was saying, "Don't you know me, Mr. President? It's Buck Hannafin."

Clint's eyes were moving, but not as if he were trying to track something inside the room. He appeared to be deeply engrossed, like a very young child sitting on the ground, counting marbles as he put them into a sack. He made a windy sound.

"Hafffn."

Rona linked arms with her husband as if giving him desperately needed support, and faced Buck with a set defiant face and a half smile that dared him to take a fatal step.

"He doesn't know you, Buck. Why not let it go at that for now? We were having such a good time."

Buck's eyes turned flinty but he smiled, more for Clint than Rona as he reluctantly let go of Clint's hand. He glanced over his shoulder. Victor

Wilding was pouring himself another glass of wine, his third or fourth since they'd all sat down to dinner. He was content to let Rona handle the situation. There was a warning in Courtney's eyes.

"Why'd you put on a show, Buck?" Rona asked. "No point in confirming what I'm sure you already knew. Being Buck Hannafin."

He looked at Rona, his shoulders falling slightly. "I thought he might have made some progress. I thought maybe seeing an old—seeing a friendly face—"

She shook her head. "I'm going to take Clint upstairs now. Finish your dinner. I can't promise when your next meal might be."

A cell phone began to ring.

Courtney burst into sobs. "Is the President sick? What's going on? I don't understand!"

Buck looked quickly at her, realizing she was about to make an impromptu move. He wished he knew what was on her mind.

Victor Wilding picked up the cell phone next to his plate with a grimace of annoyance, flipped it open.

In desperation Buck put a hand on Rona's arm as she was turning her husband around in the doorway.

"Let me speak to him again, Rona! Let me try, I think Clint recognized me."

"Don't ever touch me, Buck!" Rona snarled, and jerked her head toward Clint's MORG nanny. "What are you standing there for? Get this old bastard out of my face!"

Courtney wailed hysterically, holding a napkin to her mouth, slumping out of her chair as if she didn't have a bone in her body. Buck knew she was going for the flint knife in her boot. It was blowing up, here, *now*, right in their faces. He tugged at Rona's arm again. The MORG agent, mindful that he was dealing with a United States Senator, tried to separate Buck and Rona.

Victor Wilding rose from his seat, cell phone to his ear.

"What? WHAT?!"

His face went slack. Nothing but the whites of his eyes showed, as if he had taken a knockout punch and was on his way to the canvas.

Clint Harvester, in obviously good physical shape, wrestled free of Rona and, for the first time, looked directly into Buck's eyes.

"Help me," he said.

Joy welled up in Buck's heart. He let go of Rona and backed away. He was looking at Rona, and she was staring past him at Victor Wilding.

Clint's left arm jerked up. It seemed to Buck to be an involuntary movement. His elbow hit Rona in the face, breaking her nose. She staggered back a couple of steps and sat down hard.

They all heard an anguished moan that rose in pitch to a scream, but it didn't come from Rona.

Victor Wilding had dropped the cell phone and was clutching at his throat in a paroxysm of solitary violence. He fell over a serving cart and rolled in scattered food and chafing dishes on the floor, making terrible scalded animal noises. Courtney Shyla was crouched on the same side of the table with the flint knife held low in fighting attitude, but she was distracted, as they all were, by the sight of Wilding writhing in mortal agony. Especially Rona, in shock herself, what remained of her nose pushed gruesomely to one side, almost lying on her right cheek, blood flowing.

She said in a choked voice, "Gahh—wha's wrong . . . Victor?"

Three other MORG agents and half the household staff came on a dead run. Courtney saw guns in too many hands and slipped the knife back into her boot. She was the closest to Wilding and the first one to get to him.

"Bring me morphine!" she yelled, in order to be heard over Wilding's shrieks. "Then get medevac here fast! This man's burning up!"

The numbers flashing on Victor Wilding's digital watch read 9:26.

PLENTY COUPS, MONTANA · JUNE 7 · 8:44–9:24 P.M. MDT

Eden Waring's doppelganger had nearly given up finding Robin Sandza when she saw Dr. Marcus Woolwine coming her way in one of the many look-alike corridors of MORG's underground facility.

It gave her some hope that he might be on his way to look in on Robin before calling it a night. She followed him.

Card key unlocked a private elevator. Snug in there, but she hugged a back corner of the elevator during the slow ride down. Woolwine, with the dpg slipping out behind him, entered what looked like a maximum-security unit of a communicable disease control laboratory. Air-lock doors with a "clean" room in between. Woolwine was sanitized, gowned, gloved, and masked by a technician. The procedure seemed to bore him. He had little to say to anyone working there.

The dpg, stifling an urge to yawn, drifted to a window with a full view of what had been Robin Sandza's world for the past several years.

Nothing very homey about the room in which he lay, not in a bed but on a cushion of air, no part of his body actually touching anything. Warm air, she hoped, because his pathetically pale, thin body was nude. What hair he had left on his scarred head was white as moondust. There was a respirator mask on his face. He was attached by wires and drip lines to several monitoring machines and life-support systems. Because he was fed like a hydroponic tomato he needed a catheter, but his bowels were perennially empty.

But when she went inside after Marcus Woolwine she saw the other Robin Sandza, the athletic, vital boy of twenty years ago, leaning against one blank wall of his cavernlike sterile crypt.

Robin was bored too. But glad that she had come back. He grinned and walked over to her.

Took you long enough, he chided.

Just all day. Sorry, I couldn't bring flowers.

Your eye is turning in. Gillian's eye used to do that, when she was tired. Has she ever come to visit you?

No. But we'll see each other again. Once this is over with.

The dpg glanced at Marcus Woolwine, who was studying a printout from one of the machines.

Do you have any idea how to do this? Should I just pull some plugs after he leaves?

Wouldn't work. They have backup life-support systems. And backup for the backup. You'll have to go into the brain again. The hindbrain, did I show it to you before?

I remember. Where all life begins in the womb.

And ends. Go in there, shut off the power. It'll just take a few seconds.

Eden's doppelganger looked at Woolwine again. He had a peculiar smile, as if he were savoring a joke. It had to be a coincidence, but he was looking right at her. Then he turned to the viewing window and signaled someone.

Oh-oh. Robin said, and suddenly he wasn't by her side anymore.

The recessed ceiling lights went out. For a few seconds it was nearly dark. But the power hadn't failed. She could still see the luminous, nocturnal blink and scrawl on the screens of Robin's monitors, hear the rhythmic whoosh of his respirator.

Then light returned, a stealthy alarming ultraviolet glow that took her breath away.

Black light.

The dpg felt energy draining from her body. Her lungs seized up. Her knees were as weak as if she had spent the last couple of hours climbing steps in a dream-tower. She saw her hands. They trembled.

If *she* saw them, Marcus Woolwine could see as well. All of her. Helpless. Panicked.

He was smiling again.

"As I suspected all along: when the lab couldn't find the blood sample we took from you. The vial was empty. Your blood seemed to have vanished overnight. Also I noticed at table that you favored your right, not your left hand. I knew from studying videotapes of Eden Waring that *she* was left-handed. So the new Avatar fooled us, sent her doppelganger in her stead. To what purpose? Just what mischief are you up to?"

"Can't . . . breathe. Turn off . . . that light."

"And have you disappear again? I won't take the chance. Now that I know who—*what* you are, I want to study you. Very closely. Black light is not fatal to doppelgangers. Nothing short of the death of your homebody can end your own existence. Ultraviolet or infrared only makes you very, very weak. Causes some discomfort as well, no doubt."

The doppelganger was on her hands and knees. "Yes . . . it hurts me. *Please* turn it off!"

"If you're cooperative I will let you dress yourself and then, once you've been suitably shackled, you may leave. With me. But what brought you back to Robin? Nothing but the truth, now."

"Robin . . . wants to . . . die."

"Out of the question. It has been my responsibility to keep him alive, and I never fail. We won't expose you to Robin Sandza again. Victor will simply have to accept that it is too much of a risk. Take a last look at Robin if it pleases you, Eden. Oh, my mistake. *You* have no name. No existence except at the discretion of your homebody. You are cunningly made, but of no consequence. A soulless facade, a fake, a nonbeing."

"I have . . . a name. And I will . . . be someone . . . that you could never . . . deal with!"

She heard Robin's voice.

We can end this now.

How? I can't move. I'm stuck to the damn floor.

I'll help you.

The doppelganger raised her head. It felt as if there were a yoke of iron on her neck. She looked at the still body of Robin Sandza, suspended in a puppet's snarl of wires and drip lines, a violet glow around his body. Where his head and face should be she saw a different aura, light as distant as that from a nebula in space. But the light exploded into the sterile room with the speed of thought.

One of the ultraviolet spots overhead shattered smokily. Woolwine looked up, then stared accusingly at the dpg.

"What are you up to? Do you need a pacifier?"

Two more lights broke, showering his bald head with hot fragments. Woolwine threw up his arms to protect himself and scowled.

"Stop this, bitch!" He fumbled in a pocket of his long white coat for a hypodermic.

With the load on her body lessened, the doppelganger struggled to her feet, located the remaining sources of the black light, and popped those bulbs.

Woolwine dropped the vial from which he had withdrawn a powerful hypnotic and started toward the dpg. But without the glow of black light he couldn't find her.

"Seal the room!" he shouted to someone beyond the viewing glass.

The dpg slapped Woolwine hard across the face, and he staggered back, glasses askew on his face, one shocked eye revealed.

The EKG machine that monitored Robin Sandza's heart rate began to beep in emergency cadence.

Woolwine recovered from the smack in the face and lunged forward with the needle held like a stubby rapier. Poised to jab flesh he couldn't see. Jab, jab—nothing there, or *there,* or behind him. The room was glowing now from Robin's funerary light. Woolwine raised his head sharply toward the cat's cradle containing Robin's slight body. He saw Robin float free of all restraints, rise toward the domed ceiling. His face was a luminous death mask. But Robin's eyes were open. They were free of pain, ecstatic.

"No! No! No!"

Eden's dpg gave the doctor a hard shove from his left side. Woolwine tripped himself up and sprawled, the hypodermic in his hand crumpling beneath him.

Robin?

I'm almost there. I could use a push too. But take it easy. You don't know your own strength. The shining blue cord—cut it for me, please.

Where are you going?

Can't make that out yet. Too far away. But I know it's where I want to go. I can feel gravity pulling me. Just cut the cord.

Done. Good-bye, Robin.

Marcus Woolwine was on his feet again, minus his mirror sunglasses. The doppelganger watched his eyes as he looked at the flat-line EKG. There was no supportive whoosh from the respirator. Saline solution and drops of chemical sustenance dripped uselessly from the ends of dangling IV lines. He saw Robin's body, white and weightless as an egret's feather, float higher, begin to glow translucently, dissipate atom by atom.

Good-bye—Guinevere. Good luck. Tell Eden I said . . . you deserve to be free. It's what we all deserve . . . for being, and trying.

The door to Robin's former prison stood open, and medical technicians were milling about, gazing in wonder at the all-consuming but pacific drift of light that had replaced Robin's body. There was nothing visibly left of him except for a fine drift of sparky ash. Marcus Woolwine, in a grunting fit of rage, struck at everyone who stood helplessly near him. Bloody saliva flew from his mouth. He had bitten his tongue.

Eden Waring's doppelganger walked away. Nothing left for her to do there. She felt weightless herself. She took four or five climbing steps and found herself a welcome distance from the underground facility. On the surface, good Montana ground, on a rise a mile or so away from the fake brightly illuminated fort that marked the site of Plenty Coups. She sipped a rush of raw wind through clenched teeth, basked in starlight. There was a storm in heaven, off to the west, as beautiful and slashingly violent as a Van Gogh painting. A rumble like chariots across the sky, arriving with a pantheon of gods for a celestial inquiry. She felt that it had something to do with Robin, part of his redemption. Or was it about the condemnation of those who had used him, and his powers, so badly?

She waited for Eden to take notice of her, and bring her home.

BIG COUNTRY RANCH · JUNE 7 · 9:54 P.M. MDT

The medevac helicopter from Bozeman had arrived just ahead of the storm that had banged its way down from the mountains and was traveling full-throttle across the Big Country range like an old-time Mallet, the behemoth of long-haul locomotives.

Two physicians and two paramedics were aboard the chopper. A paramedic tried to attend to Rona Harvester's devastated nose, but she kept throwing him off and crawling to where Victor Wilding lay on the floor. They'd had to restrain him to keep him quiet long enough to thump up a vein and insert an IV. He'd already had morphine from one of the RNs on duty at the ranch's small infirmary. His temperature was 106, pulse 180. His blood pressure was systolic 270, diastolic 150. The higher figure was a crisis number. Wilding was in imminent danger of blowing out every valve in his heart, a major blood vessel in his brain.

Rona coughed blood from her throat. "Victor! It doesn't matter! You know it doesn't matter that Robin is dead! Don't *do* this to yourself! Victor, Godddd, *I need you!*"

The cardiologist with the med team recommended a sedative. Two of them held Rona while the intramuscular dose was administered. Rona still wouldn't stop screaming, when she wasn't spitting gobbets of blood. Her hysteria, the window-rattling thunder, and the big flaring bolts that turned the room's every face and object into a gothic frieze scraped their nerves.

Clint Harvester, however, didn't seem to be upset. He sat patiently in a chair while everyone else was running for something. His eyes went to Victor Wilding's flushed, engorged head on which his features were etched like an intaglio to the scary display outside. Part of his demeanor may have been due to Buck Hannafin, who stood behind Clint with a hand on his shoulder. Until he heard another helicopter coming down through the torrent, miraculously unstruck by lightning, Buck didn't know where Courtney Shyla had disappeared to.

With the IV in and Wilding packed in bags of ice, he was rushed outside. A second medevac helicopter had landed a hundred yards away in a clearing uphill from the house. Nearly everyone in the Harvester household—MORG agents included—followed the stretcher bearers as far as the deck outside the front entrance, where they were pelted with rain and hail and flying leaves.

Courtney had reentered the house by another door. She was wearing a poncho with a hood that dripped rain. From the hall outside the dining room she silently got Buck's attention and when he turned she used hand signals to tell him what she wanted. The paramedic and nurse who were trying to get Rona to lie down on another stretcher failed to notice when Buck left the room with Clint Harvester.

The MORG agent whose job it was to keep his eyes on both Rona and Clint moved to intercept them. "Sir—"

Buck said with a wave of his hand, "For God's sake, I'm just gonna get the President looking decent. You stick with Miss Rona, lend a hand if need be. We'll be back in a jiffy."

Outside the four men taking Victor Wilding down the series of right-angle steps from the house dropped him when lightning sheared the top out of a larch tree fifty feet from them, a torrent of sparks shooting through the low clouds. A smoking bough sailed onto the lower deck of the house, burying a MORG agent and a couple of houseboys. Windows were shattered.

Wilding's stretcher skittered down another twenty steps, where it stopped falling and stood, momentarily, upright. Wilding's face appeared to glow with a pale blue light, like the corona of a gas flame. His heavy-lidded eyes were expressionless. His temple bones stood out, and there were swollen veins across his forehead, in his neck. With his dark sodden clothing and rain-slicked hair, his wrists and ankles in leather restraints, he had more than a passing resemblance to the just-unwrapped monster in the classic movie version of *Frankenstein.*

No one who saw it was sure of what happened next. Most witnesses believed that another lightning strike to the metal frame of the stretcher had electrocuted Victor Wilding.

Lightning has the power to stop hearts and carbonize lungs, just as it had the theoretical power to animate the fanciful creature in James Whale's movie. But no one had ever seen or heard of a victim of lightning almost fully consumed within his clothing—not just burned beyond recognition but *gone,* except for a few bits of heel and toe bones in his Timberland hiking boots. The boots, like Wilding's clothing, were otherwise intact, not a single lace singed by heat that had, for seconds, reached several thousand degrees Fahrenheit. A spontaneous combustion as bright and hot as an exploding star.

Courtney Shyla escorted the stretcher on which Rona Harvester lay, covered against the fury of the storm and quieted by an intramuscular shot of Adavan, to the second medevac helicopter, a venerable Jolly Green Giant that could accommodate up to fifteen stretchers. The MORG agent assigned to Rona climbed in after her and was greeted with a blow to the back of the neck by one of Royce Destrahan's paramilitary operatives.

Courtney returned to the house by a side door, walked up the steps to the bedroom floor, and found another MORG agent outside the President's suite. He looked overexcited. He was holding a bullpup, but the safety was on. D-U-M-B, she thought.

"President's getting dressed. What are you doing up here?"

Courtney didn't want to go hand-to-hand even with an obvious incompetent. She shot him in the knee with the silenced HK Mark 23 she was holding beneath the poncho, and when he collapsed, in so much pain he couldn't scream, she used her slap-daddy, a leather truncheon filled with double-aught buck, to anesthetize him, dragged him into another bedroom and shut the door.

Buck Hannafin had appeared with Clint Harvester after getting him dressed and into his boots. Courtney gave each of them a hooded poncho.

Buck clamped a Stetson on Clint's head and they went downstairs, Courtney with her finger on the trigger of the .45. But nobody showed up to challenge them. They left by the side door and walked a hundred yards through drenched woods to the waiting helicopter. The rain had lost some of its sideways sting and fury.

"Shame we won't get to ride tonight," Buck said to Courtney as they boarded the helo. "But this works out better."

Rona Harvester looked at them with dulled eyes from her stretcher on the deck. Clint got on first, glancing at her. There was a clear shield taped down from cheek to cheek to prevent more damage to her nose. Behind the shield her eyes were swelling shut, turning black.

"Shame," Clint said. To no one in particular; he was just mimicking what Buck had said. He was led to a seat. Nick Grella helped him into his harness.

"Okay, Mr. President?"

Clint looked up at him with a faint smile, but not as if he knew who Nick was. "Candy?" he said.

One of the paramilitaries aboard came up with some M&Ms for the President. He sat there munching contentedly.

"Any serious change in plans?" Buck asked.

Royce Destrahan looked back at them from the right-hand seat in the cockpit. "No, sir. We'll change aircraft in Bozeman, shoot down across the Bitterroots to Hailey."

The rotors were turning. Buck said, "Idaho. Isn't there a first-class private hospital over Sun Valley way? Sure. They do some of the best reconstructive surgery you'll find this side of Lausanne, Switzerland. Guess that's a plus for Miss Rona. What's all the uproar out front?"

"Lightning hit a tree. Also the dude on the stretcher, according to the radio."

"Victor Wilding," Courtney cut in.

"That a fact? Well, they're gonna be looking for a new head of operations around Plenty Coups."

Rona moaned from the depths of the twilight to which she'd been consigned.

"MORG won't need nobody," Buck said grimly. "Once I get done rolling the rock off that nest of vipers. Maybe we need to wait 'nother few minutes until this Montana monsoon passes through."

"Can't wait long. They see the President's missing, we'll have shit for rain. Amazing how these storms just blow up out of nowhere."

"Fortuitous," Buck said, settling into a seat with a winded sigh, smiling sideways at Clint Harvester. He resisted an urge to reach out and wipe a gob of chocolate from the soon to be ex-President's chin. Not that Clint would recognize what an indignity the gesture represented. But Buck knew, and his heart felt hollow enough already.

NASHVILLE, TENNESSEE · JUNE 7 · 9:22 P.M. CDT

Carlisle tied up his cruiser at the marina by Adelphia Coliseum across the Cumberland River from downtown Nashville. The blended voices of Garth Brooks and Trisha Yearwood singing "In Another's Eyes" seemed to float on the bright cloud of light above the stadium bowl.

There were two parking lots that they could see, and a six-level parking structure that looked to be full. Thousands of cars, campers, trucks of all types. For a few moments after they'd left the boat they all simply stood unmoving on the riverbank, staring, disheartened.

Tom Sherard saw Metro police cars on the street. He had turned up the collar of his jacket so his bloody neck and shirt collar wouldn't be too obvious. He had shifted the lion's-head cane to his left hand, because his right hand had gone numb and there was no feeling in the forearm almost to his elbow. Every move he made seemed to press the bullet closer to his spinal cord. But he could still walk.

"How long do these shows usually last?" Tom Sherard asked Carlisle.

"Hard to say. Probably started at seven-thirty. Garth likes to give 'em their money's worth. Reckon he's good for another twenty minutes."

"Where do we start?" Bertie asked, with a slow benumbed shake of her head. The parking lots seemed infinite from their perspective. The stadium was huge.

"There's five of us," Carlisle said. He had become part of the team, and now he felt called upon to make a contribution. "We could split up, each take a section of the lots and the decks. What about the police?"

Alex was carrying the dummy device in its case. "Leave them out of this. Too much to explain. No time."

"I need Alex with me," Eden said. She nodded toward the case. "And that. The rest of you—" She couldn't stop a jet of tears. "Get back in Carlisle's boat. Clear out of here. Tom, you should be in the hospital. Alex and I—we can do this."

"Not a chance," Bertie said. "Alex is right, no time. Carlisle, where's your flashlight?" He held up a three-battery steel Maglite. "Good. You take the lot over there. If you find the truck first, climb on the roof and signal. Three short flashes. Tom and I will take the other lot. Alex and Eden—"

"Let's go," Eden said.

On the first floor of the parking decks Alex said, "Up or down?"

Eden was silent for a few moments, then pushed the elevator button for the roof.

"Start at the top."

Garth Brooks was singing "Ain't Goin' Down 'Til the Sun Comes Up." The concrete and steel decks seemed to be vibrating slightly from the power of his amps.

In the slow elevator Eden rubbed her temples and fidgeted.

Alex said, "You have a boyfriend?"

"Not anymore."

"Maybe you and me, then."

"Oh, great, Alex, is that all you have on your mind right now?"

"Better than the alternative," he said with a shrug.

They stepped off the elevator onto the roof under sodium vapor lights. The stadium was rocking. Eden closed her eyes briefly, turning her head slowly.

"Better start looking," Alex advised.

"I am. Shut up. Please."

She was rubbing the thumb of her right hand back and forth over her fingertips. Then her head nodded forward.

Alex took out a pack of cigarettes. Eden straightened and opened her eyes.

"Don't smoke, it'll mess me up."

"I thought you were falling asleep."

"It's not up here. Let's go down."

They took the stairs to the next level. There was wild cheering from the stadium.

Eden repeated the exercise she had begun on the roof. Results negative.

"Maybe," Alex said, "they changed trucks somewhere. Then how could you know what you are looking for? Or they might have dropped the device into a trash can."

"It would leave a signature. What do you want from me, Alex?"

"You are already an angel. Me, I would have some explaining to do if I go boom tonight."

Eden was already out the door and down the steps to the next level. Alex took a deep breath, decided to smoke after all. Probably they were doomed. He thought about Eden, and shrugged again. Too bad they couldn't die while making love. American bitches, too many hangups.

"*Alexxx!*"

He banged a shin with the metal case getting down the steps to the level below. When he opened the door he didn't see her.

"Where are you?"

"Over here!" Her voice reverberated; he couldn't tell where it was coming from.

"That's no help!" he shouted.

"We're on the blue level and, uh, section G. To your left from the stairs."

Alex hobbled in that direction with his case.

The red club cab pickup had been parked at an angle in a corner of the deck, facing the river and the lights of Nashville on the other side. Eden was looking at the left front fender, but she didn't touch it. She glanced at him, pointed.

"Scraped. And the parking light is broken." She was going through her pockets. "Now what did I do with that piece of—"

"Never mind, if you are sure." Alex set the titanium case down. The bed of the deluxe pickup had a removable metal cover that matched the rest of the truck for a streamlined effect. There was a key-entry lock.

Alex took a folder of tools and a small flashlight from his jacket pocket. He selected a lock pick. His hand was trembling. He leaned against the back of the truck and there was a crackling sound, a blue flash. Alex was thrown back five feet to the concrete floor. His eyes were closed but the lids twitched. He didn't make a sound.

"Alex!" Eden knelt beside him. Was he breathing? She put a hand to her damp forehead, looked up at numerals on a post with a blue stripe.

Bertie. Get here fast.

She didn't waste time trying to find a pulse. She put the heel of her right hand on the lower third of Alex's sternum, covered it with her left, the approved position for CPR. She began to rapidly compress Alex's chest. Five compressions, pause to ventilate, resume compression. So they'd booby-trapped the truck before abandoning it. She settled into the routine of CPR, sweat stinging her eyes. *I'm yours, Alex; you want me, I'm yours. Just breathe, God damn it!*

Eden couldn't have said how long she'd been working on Alex when she heard the stairwell door bang open, heard running footsteps.

"Bertie!"

Her shoulders ached as she continued the routine of trying to bring Alex around, glanced up as Bertie arrived.

"What happened?"

"Don't touch the truck. Electrified."

Alex suddenly trembled under her hands, gasped, and retched. Bertie reached down and moved his head to one side so he wouldn't aspirate his vomit.

Eden sat up and wiped her face. "Where's Tom and Carlisle?"

"Coming. Alex? Hey, Alex! Do you hear me?"

"Huh."

Bertie helped him sit up.

"Thirsty. Where am I?"

"Truck zapped you," Eden said.

"Headache," he complained.

"I just got your heart started; you'll have to deal with the headache yourself."

They propped Alex against a pillar and conferred.

"Is the device in the truck?" Bertie asked.

"I'm sure of it. But there's an electrical field in my way. A shield. I can't break through to find the device."

"What if I could, you know, push that shield out of your way? Hold it back for a little while?"

"But if you let it slip—"

"I know. The shield will bounce your *chi* straight back at you, and you'll wind up on the deck like Alex. Or worse."

"Gotta do it. Alex! Need your help."

They heard the elevator door.

Eden said, "I hope that's Tom. Stadium will be emptying out any minute now. Once this building fills up with people getting their cars, there'll be so much noise neither one of us can function."

"Right back," Bertie said, and she sprinted in the direction of the elevator.

"What do you want, honey? Alex doesn't feel good."

"I know. I'm sorry. But you have to get the duplicate device up and running for me. Can you manage that?"

"Sure. No problem."

"Set the timer, let's make it four minutes from now."

"Timer, sure." Alex opened the titanium case and took out the yellow carrier bag with the dummy nuke inside. He was fumbling, bleary-eyed. "What do you do then, honey?"

"I follow my usual procedure for disarming nuclear bombs."

"Bravo. Did I tell you I want you to be my woman?"

"Yes, Alex. Stop staring at me and set the damn timer."

Bertie came running back.

"Carlisle says Brooks is halfway through his encore number, and he only does one. He and Tom will try to keep people off this floor, by virture of the absolute authority invested in Carlisle through the Wildlife Resources Agency."

Eden grinned tautly. "Let's do this."

Bertie faced the red truck. She extended her hands, not quite touching metal. Then she placed her steepled hands against her face, bowed her head slightly as if in prayer. She trembled.

"Ready," she said to Eden. "Say when."

Eden said, "Alex?"

"One little jiffy. Okay . . . timer is set. Four minutes and counting. So what?"

Eden ignored him. "Go, Bertie," she said softly.

Bertie made an incomprehensible sound. She appeared to be straining forward, under excruciating tension. The planes of her face glistened, and it seemed as if every bone in her skull were aglow beneath the stretched skin.

"*Yeah!*" she screamed.

Eden saw the high-energy field around the truck. A writhing, pulsating entity. She was afraid of it. But she had to channel her own force, slip through that net of enormous power into the neutral zone Bertie was providing at huge cost to herself.

"How do you *do* that?" Alex said. His hair was standing on end. He backed away as if he were looking at Death Itself.

Eden probed, was pushed back. *Afraid, afraid.* Ten days ago all she'd been thinking about was getting her diploma. Bertie moaned sorrowfully, holding on, keeping the gap in the field open. Couldn't let Bertie down, even if it meant the destruction of her own mind.

She heard it ticking. Backseat of the club cab. She pressed closer. There it was. A twin of the other device, with one lethal exception.

Just a little more time, Bertie.

Mentally Eden pounced on the dummy device outside the truck. The timer read two minutes fifty-eight seconds.

Inside the stadium Garth Brooks yelled, "Good night, Nashville!"

Good night, Nashville. Show's over. Except, perhaps, for the fireworks.

Eden stopped the timer on the dummy at two minutes forty-nine seconds.

Easy when you know how. You look up into a clear sky, see a plane that isn't there, but know it's coming and when it does it will crash. Couldn't stop the DC-10 in midair. But a little old digital clock, that was a cinch. She was the fuckin' Avatar, was she not?

Feeling bold and skillful, Eden probed the cab of the truck again.

I'm slipping, Bertie said faintly in Eden's mind.

Almost done. Easy when you know how. Except she didn't. She just kind of interfered with the mechanism in some way, by wanting to. Figure it out later. Just do the other timer, stop it cold, get Bertie off the hook.

It didn't work this time.

Whoops.

What's wrong?

Shit.

Again, again!

Not working.

"Alex! I can't . . . it won't shut off like the other timer!"

The stadium was beginning to empty out. A couple of thousand people would be coming for their cars.

Please, Eden, Bertie said in her mind.

"How much time?" Alex's voice. "There must be a fail-safe. I would have to see it to know exactly what they have done."

How much time? This, urgently, from Bertie.

An hour. But if I pull out now I won't get back to it!

Eden, I'm almost done. Can't hold the shield. Get away!

No! I've got to do this!

Whatever you're going to do . . . do it now!

Eden stared at the bomb on the backseat of the truck. The timer that refused to stop. Fifty-nine minutes. No immediate jeopardy. But it didn't matter. She couldn't do anything. It seemed to Eden that her body and mind had locked up. That hadn't happened to her since she was in the sixth grade. On the line with seconds left to play, but she couldn't shoot her free throw. On the line now but that long-ago game, and this game, *all* the games were over. She'd failed the world this time, not just a handful of teammates.

Then she felt as if steel fingers were sinking into her jammed, frozen mind. The fingers dug in and yanked her back through the gap in the shield an instant before it closed in a zigzag of brilliant blinding energy.

For a few moments she was out of touch with her body, senses depleted, adrift, a poor naked soul in a bright void.

She felt a slap, her head was rocked, she opened her eyes and perceived Bertie's glistening face inches from hers.

"WHATINTHEHELL were you waiting for!?"

"I couldn't . . . I . . . sweet Jesus! I've really fucked up. *It's going to blow!*"

"The device?" Alex said with his infuriating smirk. He was on one knee wrestling the dummy nuke back into the carrier bag.

"Yes!" Eden screamed at him. "The nuclear goddamn bomb! The bomb in the truck we spent all day trying—"

Bertie pressed a hand across her mouth. "Hey, not so loud. Just calm down. Okay? No more yelling."

Eden's heart was pounding like a sledge against the chest wall. She blinked at Bertie, showering a few tears over the hand that sealed her mouth.

Bertie moved her hand and stroked Eden's wet forehead. Eden crept tremblingly into her arms. Bertie held her, rocked her gently, smiled.

"You were unconscious for a couple of minutes after I pulled you back through the shield."

Eden sobbed. "Failed . . . we're going to . . ."

Bertie turned her head. "Alex, give Eden a look at what you have there."

Alex opened the bag again. Wide enough for Eden to see the bright digital numerals on the detonator timer.

Fifty-four minutes eight seconds. And counting.

"But—"

Bertie shook her exuberantly. "*That's* the device that was in the pickup truck, Eden!" Eden, skin cold from shock, heart still beating with massive blows, didn't understand. Bertie said, "Alex needs about three minutes to disarm it when you guys get back to the boat."

"But—"

"You switched them, Eden."

"I did *what*?"

"The devices were identical, except one was loaded and the other wasn't. You couldn't shut the other timer down. So you switched them."

"How?"

"If I knew the answer, if I could pull it off, then I'd be the Avatar. But I'm not that good, and besides I don't want to *be* the Avatar."

"Neither do I."

"That's something we really should talk about. Later. Beginning to get crowded up here. And I'm hungry."

"Miss Nkambe?" Carlisle said.

Eden and Bertie turned. He was standing about fifteen feet away, as if he wasn't sure it was all right to come any closer. A car trying to back out almost bumped into him. The parking decks trembled from the weight of cars headed for the exits.

"What's wrong, Carlisle?" Bertie said, but from her expression it was clear she already knew.

"Mr. Sherard's down. He can't move. I've got an ambulance started, but he needs you."

Even before he finished Bertie had run past him, with Eden close behind.

Rona Harvester awoke to sunshine and flowers in her suite at the Camberlane Clinic. There was an IV in the back of her right hand, a leather strap attached to the bed around her wrist. Her left hand was similarly restrained. She had a taste of old blood in the back of her throat. Her eyelids felt as if they were stuck together. She was able to get the right eye open a little more, but still she only had a slit to see through. When she licked a dry underlip she felt the taut pull of surgical tape on her cheeks.

There was a nurse in the room wearing a pink smock. She was looking for a place to put yet another basket of flowers. She heard Rona trying to speak, smiled over her shoulder.

"Good morning, Mrs. Harvester."

Rona trembled. Breathing nasally stung like fury. She breathed through her mouth instead. Her throat was sore and her tongue dry.

"Water."

The nurse brought her a cup with an angled straw. She sipped.

"Doctor will be with you in just a few moments," the nurse said. She had Southeast Asian features, a slip of a body. She wore her hair in a ponytail. Rona coughed and tried to moisten her lips again. She was wearing what looked like a rubber thimble on her right index finger. The nurse glanced at her blood pressure readout on a monitor screen.

"Where am I?" Devastating memories were trying to take shape in Rona's mind. She had only flashes of coherence.

"This is the Camberlane Clinic, Mrs. Harvester. You're in Sun Valley. You were brought here from Montana last night after your horse threw you."

"Horse? I don't . . . remember."

Another face in the room. Black man, young, small mouth, toothy smile, mustache.

"Good morning, Mrs. Harvester. I'm Dr. Wheeler. How are we doing today?"

"Why . . . am I tied down?"

"You've had reconstructive surgery on your nose. There's a protective shield, but while you slept you might have inadvertently—"

"Victor. Where's Victor? Something ha-happened to *Victor*! I remember he . . . there was a phone call. Then . . . oh, shit!"

Wheeler grimaced sympathetically but shook his head. "I'm afraid I don't know who you mean. Senator Hannafin may be able to help you. If you feel up to having a visitor."

"Buck . . . Hannafin?"

"Yes. He arrived very early this morning."

"What . . . day is this?"

"Monday, Mrs. Harvester."

"Is there a TV in here? Turn on the TV! I want to see . . . the news. CNN."

"Certainly. Should I tell Senator Hannafin that you'd rather not—"

"No. Get him in here. *Now.*"

Rona heard one of CNN's anchorpersons and turned her head on the flat pillow. While she waited for Buck to appear she tried, with a violently racing heart, to put together a sequence of events from the night before. It was too much of an effort. They'd sedated her with something very powerful. She stared at the TV screen, momentarily seeing a double image. News footage. Ramstein Air Force Base in Germany. Something to do with Allen Dunbar. A shot of Air Force Two on the ground. Dawn there, would have been . . . hours ago. The plane was taking off. What was *that* all about? Rona realized, after a memory jolt, that the news this morning should have been totally focused on what remained of Nashville, Tennessee. A nation in shock again.

"Hello, Rona. Sorry about your accident, but I understand they're taking real good care of you here."

She turned her head again. "Buck." Image of Hannafin on her doorstep with the young cowgirl type from the Broken Wheel Ranch. "I don't fall off horses." Then she remembered. The melee in the dining room. Clint's elbow in her face. "Where's my husband?"

"Clint checked into Walter Reed about an hour ago, following his psychiatric examination."

"Psy—? On whose orders!?"

"It'll take a long time, of course, but because there doesn't seem to be anything organically wrong with his brain, Clint should recover fully. Call it a bad case of amnesia. Official word is, the former President suffered another stroke, but it isn't life-threatening and he's resting comfortably."

"*Former* President?"

Buck glanced at the TV mounted on the wall opposite Rona's bed. Saw himself behind a bank of microphones at one of Sun Valley's resort hotels. He turned down the volume, looked at Rona. His eyes had a touch of red in them. There remained in his breast a hard knot of anger that would have busted the teeth off a sawmill blade.

"Allen Dunbar took his oath as the new President of the United States by Chief Justice Rumsill at five o'clock this morning aboard Air Force One in Germany. President Dunbar arrived at the White House forty minutes ago, and will be addressing the country in just a little while. Stock market dropped about three hundred points after the opening, but it's been recovering nicely. Oh. That nuclear device somebody carelessly left in a Nashville parking facility was recovered and disarmed by a NEST team. That won't be in the news, but I thought you'd want to know. I guess you could say it's all over, Rona."

In spite of her agitation she remembered to smile, as if she'd just heard an unfriendly question at one of her news conferences. "I haven't the slightest idea what you're—"

Buck smiled too, glanced at the monitor beside her bed. " 'Fraid I've overstayed this visit. Appears your pulse is way up."

"I want to talk to Victor!" Rona yelled. "Get me a phone! *Somebody bring me a fucking phone!*" In times of great stress Rona's voice became as hoarse as a goose honk.

The expression on Buck Hannafin's face cut short her rant.

"No. Oh, *no*. What do you mean? Victor? Dead? I don't *believe* you! That is—you're trying—you're messing with my head, but it won't—" Her voice failed completely. She tried to stare Buck down, but the harsh truth was in his eyes. Tears squeezed through the slits of her own eyes.

"*You*," she said, whispering. "You set it all up! Some kind of ambush, wasn't it? Inviting yourself into *my* house! What have you done with *Victorrrrr*?"

"He's dead," Buck said ruthlessly, "and you'll never lay eyes on him again because there wasn't enough of him left to show a spark in hell." His lips compressed into a thin line. Rona flinched. Her pulse rate in spite of the sedatives in her system broke 130, according to the Critikon readout. She began to tremble as Buck went on, "My concern was Clint. Only Clint. I had nothing to do with Wilding's . . . timely demise. Appears he did it all to himself." Buck snapped his fingers. "Spontaneous combustion, I hear. One of the mysteries of nature. Like Wilding himself."

Rona made incoherent grieving sounds. He stared implacably at her, distanced from her sorrow.

"You might say Fate took a hand. By the way, one of our new President's first official acts will be to name Nick Grella as acting head of the FBI, until Bob Hyde shows up. That would seem to be the dimmest of possibilities, since he disappeared in the wilderness over a week ago. One of Nick's, and Justice's priorities, will be the dismantling of the Multiphasic Operations and Research Group. Reckon that won't leave you many friends on either side of the government. Rona, it would be a pure pleasure to strip your treacherous hide, currycomb the meat from your bones, and nail your skeleton to the shithouse door. But in the end that might prove hurtful to Clint. We'll leave it up to him to deal with you, once he's recovered and is able to understand what you had done to him and tried to do to our nation. Until that day comes, I'm sure you'll enjoy a comfortable retirement at Big Country. Don't bother showing up at the White House, you won't get in. Your staff is packing up your things and they'll be sent out directly. Good morning to you."

Buck walked out of the room and down the hall that opened onto to a terrace and a fine view of the Sawtooth Mountains. There were several patients in wheelchairs on the terrace, where they'd been enjoying the cool breezy morning. Now they were distracted by a disturbance going on, inside the clinic. Buck put on his Stetson and took a full minute getting a cigar going. Then he walked down the flagstone steps to the circular drive and a waiting limousine.

He hesitated before getting in. Listened. Even at that distance from the clinic he could hear Rona Harvester screaming. Buck shook his head, knowing he was enjoying this moment too much. But what the hell. He started to laugh. Great gusts of belly-heaving laughter that brought tears to his eyes.

NASHVILLE, TENNESSEE · JUNE 9 · 3:40 A.M. CDT

Tom Sherard awoke in the dead of night feeling as if he were floating vertically underwater. But water wasn't the element he found himself in, because he could breathe normally, without the nasal cannula that had been inserted after the surgery on his neck to remove a small chunk of lead pressing close to the *medulla oblongata*—that point where his brain was joined to the spinal cord. He had come within a sixteenth of an inch of dying on the floor of the parking garage by the Nashville stadium. The partial paralysis caused by inflamation should have kept him pinned to his bed in the critical care facility of Vanderbilt University Hospital, and he was—had been—on an IV line. But he could lift both arms freely and make slow swimming motions toward the light that glazed the surface of the element in which he was almost free to move about at will. A fluid element, as colorless as a predawn sky, neither cold nor hot: it had the temperature of his blood. The motions of his arms and his free leg caused the element to ripple and take on rainbow hues. He was fascinated.

Come on, Tom. A little more effort now.

He heard the voice inside his head, and knew who it was.

Where are you?

Just keep moving. Straight up.

I'm stuck.

No, you're not. It's the basic fear everyone has, of leaving the body. But you can return, whenever you want. You'll just be Visiting me, for a little while. Probably the last chance we'll have for a long time.

Leave his body? He looked down and there he was, or *it* was, as he hovered several feet above the bed in the otherwise cramped hospital unit. High enough to bump his head against the Celotex paneled ceiling. But the ceiling wasn't there. Only the opaque Element with its ghost surround, a lovely pacific light, existed above him. There was a cord of blue light, thin as boot stitching and cool as neon, connecting his noncorporeal body to the sleeping body at the base of the spine. What a neat trick. He felt reassured. And with reassurance came the final upward thrust into another, remembered world.

Sunlight so brilliant his eyes closed involuntarily. He felt a touch of vertigo, staggered a couple of steps to regain his balance. He heard an elephant and a treeful of birds. He breathed the chilly air of the land in which he had been born. He opened his eyes on miles of thick yellow grass and baobab, finger-groves of acacia and fever trees, a brown river with sluggish hippos lying on its banks or immersed to the knobs of their eyes in the dry-season pools, babies clinging to their mothers' backs. He was home again, deep in the Masai Mara, the wild country of his boyhood.

Just past eight o'clock by the angle of the sun. Sherard knew where Gillian would be, and all the others. He was close enough to camp to hear them talking and smell the coffee as breakfast was set out by his father's sturdy old safari cook, who had only two-thirds of a face due to the proclivity of hyenas to seize a sleeping victim by the head. Sherard walked that way, more aware of the blue flies buzzing up from a dung heap at his passing than he was of the thin flexible cord wavering behind him like a strand of spider's silk in a gentle breeze. He walked easily, without a limp, his legs feeling fresh and young.

Mojo, his father's Alsatian watchdog, last owner of the spiked brass collar generations of Sherard dogs had worn, saw Tom first and rose stiffly to greet him. His mother looked up with a smile. She had died at the age of twenty-eight beneath an overturned lorry; her only child was just two years old. Tom had inherited her angular body and long legs, but not her tightly curled copper hair.

"Good morning, my boy."

"Mother, it's wonderful to see you."

Tom kissed her cheek and turned to his father, who had risen from his camp chair with one of the corncob pipes he crafted himself gripped in his left hand. Donal Sherard looked as Tom remembered him just before his death in '61. His father's body finally had given in to the massive insults it had suffered during the Mau Mau uprisings and a lifetime of hunting big game, his broken heart irreparable after Deborah's passing. At the time of their marriage he had been thirty-one years older than his wife. Donal's heavily pouched gray eyes, the eyes of a man who missed nothing and forgave no weakness in other men, were also Tom's eyes.

As always Donal had been out hunting before sunrise. His crepe-soled desert boots stood unlaced behind his chair and he was wearing felt carpet slippers, a concession in his later years to the aching often-broken bones in both feet.

"So they've dug another bullet out of you. Thought you'd be joining us permanently this time."

"I wish—" Tom said, but didn't complete the thought. He was looking at Gillian, who was seated in the third camp chair around the morning fire. Whole again, slender, with peaceful but penetrating eyes.

He felt his father release his hand. "You bloody well don't," Donal said. "Too much at stake yet. You'll be going back, and no nonsense about it. I do sympathize. As Pease wrote in his fine book on lion, 'You go out to Africa to see savages, and you find them only on your return.' "

"This is the world I want," Sherard said, staring at Gillian.

Gillian answered for all of them. "But this isn't a destination, Tom."

"What is it, then?"

"The country of memory. The 'mind-forest' of the old tribes. I thought you would be more comfortable meeting here than on the Astral plane; much too busy there. Too many distractions, some of them unpleasant if you haven't been much exposed to Astral travel."

"How long can I stay here?"

"Time isn't relevant," his father said, filling his pipe with Turkish tobacco, and his mother nodded.

"Time isn't linear either," Gillian said. "Then, Now, and There all exist simultaneously."

"You can see the future?" Tom asked, his eyes going from one face to another. "When will we all be together—I mean, can it be for as long as we want?"

"We have other lives now, Tom," his mother said gently. She made a motion with her spread hand and he saw the memory-earth vanish beneath her booted feet, saw a universe of nebulae glowing with life. "Out there," she said. Deborah looked at her husband. "As a matter of fact, I think we should be going. Tom and Gillian have a great deal to talk about."

Donal nodded and glanced down at the pipe he'd been about to light.

"Yes, of course, you're right. But I was looking forward to a few puffs on the old corncob. Well." He put the pipe back into a pocket of his bush jacket and held out his hand again to Tom. The old watchdog barked hoarsely, and turned into a nebula himself.

His father disappeared as Tom was clinging to his hand. He turned to his mother, seeing only her smiling elliptical eyes in a dazzle of starlight. He whispered something, longingly. Then he felt Gillian's arm slip inside his.

"Do you have another life?" he asked desperately. "Are you going to disappear on me too? Tell me who you are, and where in the world I can find you. I *will* find you."

She laughed. "No, Tom. I'm still Gillian. But not for much longer. My stay in the Astral is almost over. Then I'll choose—whatever life is most useful to the growth of my soul. Then, or There."

"Then? The past?"

"I can as easily be born five hundred years ago—earth time—as five hundred years in the future. Then or There, it's all the same, really: the same battles we fight over and over. Only the hellish technology changes, never the lusts and social ambitions. Our earthly tribulations seem to be ordained by genetics, no matter how hard the Enlightened Ones work to straighten out the human race." She shook her head in a moment of despair. "No, you won't find me. You'll be earthbound in Now for a while. But . . . I make that sound much harder and gloomier than it deserves to be." Gillian smiled. "There's always love, Tom, and the children I couldn't give to you."

"I don't know what you—"

"Shall I show you some of your future, Tom? Do you seriously want to know?"

"Did you realize that you were going to die that day in New York?"

"Consciously, no. But I'd been preparing myself since the birth of Eden."

"You didn't know about her!"

She turned to face him. "It wasn't needful for me to know Eden during my earth-span. I would have been a danger to her when she didn't have the means to defend herself. Instead I tutored her on the Astral plane. She has great soul-strength, loyal friends, and a purpose, if only she will accept it. That's where you come in, Tom. You have *two* women in your life now. Beautiful, headstrong, gifted. Both need you. One of them you will marry."

"One—? But—I thought—who are you talking—"

Gillian kissed him. He was sure of that. But when he tried to pull her closer she wasn't there anymore. He heard only the whisper of her voice; or was that too just another memory, fading along with the landscape, a ghostly flight of egrets from the river's edge, the waning sun?

Tom?"

Two anxious faces in Sherard's hospital cubicle, dawn at the window.

"Where've I been?" he asked thickly, remembering so little.

"You were moving your toes," Bertie said, ecstatic tears on her face.

"You'll be out of here in no time," Eden Waring confirmed. She looked as if she hadn't slept for a couple of days. Exhausted, the left eye turning in, she was still a beauty. Made in the image of her mother. The face he had adored for twelve years, and would never tire of seeing.

Bertie held one of his hands, Eden the other.

His life, Sherard knew, could become very complicated if he wasn't careful. *Stalwart* was the word Katharine Bellaver had used.

Nothing like a serious dilemma of the heart to bring out the iron in a man's character.

He smiled gratefully at the women, and concentrated on moving his toes.

BIG COUNTRY RANCH · JUNE 14TH · 7:20 A.M. MDT

Rona was leading her roan filly Sun Dancer out of the barn when she heard the Secret Service agent named Bannister calling her. She put her foot in the stirrup and swung into the saddle, looked down at Bannister as he hurried to catch up. The other agent on the morning detail, Gorman, followed Bannister. They wore new Wranglers and western-style shirts with mother-of-pearl snap buttons. It was obvious from their expressions that running in new pairs of boots hurt their feet.

"Where're we riding to this morning?" Bannister asked her with a friendly smile. Wasn't even as old as her son Joshua.

"*I'm* doing the riding, and I don't want company. I told you and I told your boss, I'll tolerate having you on the place as long as you don't get in my way. Otherwise I'm not obligated."

"Yes, ma'am. We thought—"

"And I don't believe either of you has ever been on a horse in his life.

While you're hanging around Big Country, take a few lessons. Jess will fix you up with mounts you can handle."

"When can we expect you back, Mrs. Harvester?" Gorman asked.

"For the last time. This is *my* ranch. I come and go as I please, and I can take care of myself."

"Yes, ma'am."

Rona walked Sun Dancer to the pipe gate across the road. Gorman hastened to open it. They and the others hadn't been posted to Big Country to protect her, Rona knew that. They were there to spy on her. But she wasn't fooled.

Sun Dancer knew what Rona wanted on her morning rides, which trails to take. Three or four miles of cantering, then a level gallop for another two miles to Gunflint Spring, which fed one of the creeks flowing across the Big Country range. Easy work for Sun Dancer, who was an Arabian and Russian Orlov cross, bred for endurance racing and difficult terrain.

Thirty-six hours ago it had snowed, a late-spring storm. The snow was half-gone already. The sun was about to rise to join the last-quarter moon in a dawn-pink sky.

Yesterday the bandages had been removed from her rebuilt nose. Beneath the brim of the Stetson her glum eyes were still rimmed in yellow and streaky purple. Rona hadn't wanted to look at herself in any mirror. Her morale was at the vanishing point already although she still had fits of rage, like a badger she'd seen once. Three days with his hind feet locked in a poaching trap, wearing down but still snapping at the steel, snarling at the odor and sight of men and horses. The rage was bad, she knew that, not only an ordeal for the heart but it kept her from thinking of a way out of the trap Buck Hannafin had sprung on her.

Rona was wearing a scarf around her head under her Stetson with the beaded headband, a red and black lumber jacket. Sun Dancer wore a turquoise blanket and breast plate. Temperature was in the mid-thirties, breath of horse and rider steaming as Sun Dancer's hooves crunched through the frozen patches of snow remaining on the ground. But the lupine spikes and buttercups already in profusion had weathered the brief storm. The stock had not been bothered much either. She heard a saw-whet owl, bedding down for the day in a stand of gambel oak. The grama grass was tipped with frost beginning to dazzle as daylight came to the range.

She was only forty-seven. She could go where Clint had gone before her. Run for office in her home state. Free herself from the trap, one foot at a time. Then try for the presidency. They couldn't just throw her out of the White House like a common indigent, like trailer trash, and get away with it. *That was not her destiny.* The American people believed in Rona Har-

vester. They would come to her rescue. Even without Victor she knew . . .
But first she had to kill Buck Hannafin. Kill him, kill him! AND STOMP
HIS GLOATING FACE UNTIL HIS BLOOD WAS HALFWAY TO
HER KNEES NOTHING LEFT NOT AN EYEBALL OR A PIECE
OF BRIDGEWORK FROM HIS FAT INSULTING MOUTH—

Rona's heartbeat had accelerated madly. Now wait. *Don't go off like that.*
Maybe it was the stuff they were giving her for pain. She didn't know if
she needed Percocet anymore, but she craved it. For the pain of her crippled
psyche.

Another horseman caught her attention, probably because he wasn't
moving. His chestnut mount snorted smoke-breath along a ridge of black
alder perhaps a quarter of a mile away. She didn't recognize the rider's lean
silhouette, but there were no fat working cowboys in this country. It was
the flat-crowned hat he wore. None of the Big Country's hands owned
such a hat. The chestnut had a white face, she could tell that much at the
distance. He wasn't from their remuda. So it was someone cutting across
their range, which wasn't unusual. Was he watching her? Hard to say, but
she felt a deeper chill next to the bone.

She spurred Sun Dancer away from the ridge and the unknown horseman
and into their finishing run down to the cottonwoods by the spring, the
small pond dotted with wood ducks. A flock of partridge blew out of the
tall grass beside the trail as Sun Dancer passed. Wind whipped Rona's sore
eyes, drew tears, momentarily blinded her as she leaned over his neck and
gave herself to the thrill of the gallop.

When she dismounted the sun was full and flashing through the lacy pale
green boughs of the tall cottonwoods. No wind yet. Ice still caked the
spring spillway, the sedges that grew in the small pond below. Rona broke
a thin layer of ice with the heel of her boot so that Sun Dancer could drink.
There was a flare of light across the misted, ghostly surface of the partially
iced pond. Some heifers with calves trailing them were on the move a hundred yards to the east. Rona glanced down, saw an exquisitely frosted dragonfly frozen to a blade of grass. Then she caught a glimpse of herself, a
bright reflection off rim ice, and turned quickly away, looking back through
the cottonwoods.

Her heart jumped. The chestnut with the white blaze she had noticed
ten minutes ago was now fifty yards away, standing in the same attitude as
if teleported, but riderless now. The chestnut was half-concealed by the
trunks of the cottonwoods and buckbrush where the pond drained across
a beaver dam and flowed south as Gunflint Creek. Robins flickered in and
out of the hazy sunlight.

She heard a crunch of boots in thin crusts of snow. Sun Dancer raised his dripping muzzle from the pond and looked around, whinnied softly. The riderless chestnut answered.

"Hello?" Rona said cautiously.

Someone walked toward her out of the trees, backlighted by the brightening sun. She recognized the flat-crowned hat.

Rona stepped nearer her horse and the .30-.30 rifle sheathed behind the saddle.

"Oh, dear. I've startled you. I'm sorry."

A lightweight voice; he sounded gay.

"Who are you?"

When he spoke again, his voice had changed: it sounded as if he were mimicking her. Rona's blood simmered in annoyance.

"But how could you not know?"

"Why don't you just stay right where you are?" Rona said, a hand on the familiar nicked stock of the carbine.

"Oh! Oh, my God! What *happened*? The eyes. Oh! No no no! Our beautiful face! Who *did* this to us?"

Rona trembled from shock, as if an earthquake had rumbled beneath her feet.

"I said, who are you?"

"Oh, don't try to sell me *that*. You know very well."

A gloved hand came up and swept off the flat-crowned hat. Then the other hand went to work, busy, busy, unpinning the tightly bunned hair. A shake of the head to settle the ash-blond tresses around the face.

"That's better. Now you simply mustn't tease any longer by pretending that you don't *know*." A stylish sideways move, turn of the head, face finding the light of the sun and taking on a basking glow.

"I'm *you*," the assassin temporarily known as Rona Harvester said, waving both gloved hands prettily, prancing a little on the snow-crisp ground. "And you're *me*, except for those awful bruises. And the two of us—" He danced closer to Rona. "We're . . . *wheeeeee!*"

Rona had the rifle out of its fringed leather scabbard and was lever-cocking it as she turned back to the apparition with *her* face—so faithfully and uncannily reproduced. Something hit her solidly in the chest, a flat rock from the heft of it; she was knocked backward and sat down through the ice at the edge of the pond.

"*Mustn't,*" the assassin chided as he sprang toward her and twisted the carbine from Rona's gloved hands. Rona gasped for breath, turning cold to the roots of her hair. The assassin stepped back and emptied the rifle, twinkling brass falling to the ground. "Now if you'll just change that tune, I'll be happy to *tanggg-go.*"

"Get away . . . from me you . . . fuckin' freak. Help! Help! *Some*body! Help me!"

The assassin took off his riding gloves. Displayed his shapely painted nails.

"Like 'em? I went through *reams* of magazine articles and finally telephoned one of the R Team to find out the *exact* shade to use."

"Fuck you fuckyoufuck—"

"Oh, darling, if only I could, I would be in *bliss* forever. Unfortunately, and this is just between we, it's so *small* it hangs out the back. Now what do we think? Honest opinion, please. Have we *ever* seen us done up so beautifully? No, no! Now you must stop that screaming." The assassin gave Rona a long thoughtful look. "It is time to embrace the facts. Because, realistically, there can only be one of us. So I'll leave it up to . . . you . . . to choose . . . who."

He seized Rona by the shoulders and dragged her a few feet along the pond to where the ice still formed an unbroken reflective surface. He turned her, a hand gripping the back of her neck, pushed her down close to her sad discolored image on the ice.

Then the face she'd had before her nose was shattered appeared over one shoulder like the moon rising past a dusky bluff. A double image of Rona Harvester registered in her shocked mind. Before. After.

"I know it hurts you to look," he said soothingly, his breath in her cold ear. "But don't you worry. I shall do everything I can to perpetuate our legend. Too bad you can't be there to see it—" The position of his hands changed. One hand gripped her chin. The other was pressed flat against the side of her head away from him. "When we make our debut in Vegas."

Rona Harvester heard a hawk cry out. She felt the tension building at the top of her spine. But this couldn't happen! He/she didn't look strong enough to—

She heard her neck snap. It was the last sound she heard as a red the color of blood lit up her eyes. Followed, almost instantaneously, by eternal darkness.

E-mail message
Betts Waring to Eden Waring

Good morning! Or, I guess, while it's still sleepytime here must be afternoon over there. The videotapes were, as always, wonderful. I look at the new ones every night, not without a few tears I have to admit. I know, I have my tickets already and I can't stop flappin' my wings. I've handed over my patients to Zan Fortner, the legal stuff is almost concluded. I've already packed your diploma. About all the animals. Giraffes and zebras and even those cheetahs that come around at night I can take in stride. But isn't it just a little dangerous, hippos grazing so close to the house? Does the colobus monkey you seem to be wearing on your shoulder in most of your close-ups have a name? He looks unsettlingly like my late uncle Norbert. Maybe there is something to transmigration.

You know that Africa was always Riley's dream destination. Wouldn't be surprised if he wangles a weekend pass from the Gatekeeper and drops by while I'm there. If he does, I'll know somehow.

Eden looked up from the E-mail printout she was reading on the veranda of the lakeside house that, apparently, was forever going to be under construction and wiped an eye, gazed for a few moments at the blue folds of the low mountains across a mile of lake. The screech of a fish eagle sounded above the racket of hammering and sawing on the guest wing of the house. The construction crew was sheathing the framework in Kenyan cypress. The copper for the roof had just arrived on a lorry and was being unloaded. Up to her to do the supervising, while Tom Sherard was in Nairobi visiting his physical therapist and Bertie was in Mombasa on a shoot for the Spanish *Vogue*.

There were servants at Shungwaya to look after her, and an assortment of large dogs for protection, but she had been lonely the night before, missing Betts and everyone else, staying up late to read Dinesen's *Shadow on the Grass* and something by Joy Adamson, an epitaph for a beloved lion that spoke poignantly of Africa's true magic:

The wind, the wind,
the heavenly child,
Softly going over the stone,
It strokes and kisses the lonesome night
In which a deep secret lies bewitched.

Eden sniffed back tears, felt a tiny buzz inside her navel. She frowned and chopped a hand sharply through the air.
I'm busy. Not now.
She resumed rereading Betts's E-mail.

No, not a sign of or a word from Geoff McTyer, but then he wouldn't dare, would he? Don't know why you still give him so much as a passing thought. As time goes by memories of last May grow fainter here in Innisfall. Not to say you've been forgotten. The legend, or myth, or whatever you want to call it, continues to grow. The pitiful ones still come around, stand in the road and stare at the house. Some leave notes asking for miracles. A few have tried to come over the fence, but the Blackwelder people put a quick stop to that activity.

And sometimes there are watchers of a different kind.

They keep their distance, but I see a flash of sun off a lens, I hear helicopters in the night. They find ways to get into my office when I'm not there. If there truly are Malterrans—but I know this makes you cringe. I'll get off the subject.

Meg Pardo is still hurt because I won't give her your E-mail address, but I told her it's best under the circumstances if I pass on any messages. Meg has been as good a friend to me as she is to you. Helped me get through some difficult nights. Sorry sorry sorry. Don't want to burden you. Let me remind you again, none of it was ever your fault.

Better go now. Ten days before I board that plane at SFO, and lots to do. Can't wait, truly. I'll be a gibbering mess soon as I lay eyes on you, but I promise to shape up fast.

Cheerio, dear one.

"What are you bawling about?" Eden's doppelganger asked. She was sitting on a railing of the veranda letting Eden's pet monkey nibble a piece of fruit from her fingers.
"I'm not bawling. I just got a little homesick for a while. I don't need you right now."
"*Sure,* that's why I'm here, in the flesh. Can I borrow some clothes?"

"I can see you, and nobody else around here needs to."

"Old monkeyface sees me too." She chucked the black-and-white colobus under the chin, and he stood up, chittering, long tail forming a question mark. "So Betts is coming for a visit. Are you going to introduce me?"

"And scare her into a coronary?"

"She's read your dreambooks. She knows I exist. Betts would like me. How's this for an idea? I could spend some of my lonely downtime in California keeping Betts company while you're busy organizing the Psi Resistance. You'll have Tom and Bertie looking out for you."

Eden flicked a crawling insect like an emaciated beetle off her wrist, careful not to damage it, which would raise a caustic blister on her skin. Africa, or that part of Kenya she'd become familiar with, was close to heaven. Except for the *dudu*. A bull giraffe went striding by, ten yards from the veranda. They were seeing more giraffes lately in the game preserve; she needed to make a note of it for Tom.

"By the way—do you know who he is? The one who keeps showing up in your dreams these days?" The dpg dropped her a significant look.

Eden glanced at her own face. Better than having a mirror, sometimes. She could see that she needed to trim her hair, which had grown out in its natural color.

"No. I don't know who he is. What are you doing poking around in my dreams?"

"He's on your mind when you're awake too. Good-looking guy. Know what I think? He could be *your* Robin Sandza. I mean, Robin before they destroyed his sanity at Psi Faculty."

Eden got up from her cane rocking chair, shouldered the AK-47 she carried everywhere because of the *Shifta*, Somalian gangs of poachers who sometimes infiltrated the Naivasha Preserve. The Kenyan Wildlife Service rangers lately had been doing a good job of patroling their area, and Tom Sherard had his own security force utilizing two fast helicopters, but disturbing incidents of violence throughout the country were reported every day. Eden could shoot very well and wouldn't hesitate. That was something new in her heart, and in her face.

"Where're you going?" the dpg asked as Eden strolled away.

"I want to retrieve some film, find out if the leopard that's been leaving pug marks in the *lugga* showed up again last night. Also I need to get away from the hammering. It's giving me a headache."

"*Us* a headache. Want some company?"

Eden hesitated on the steps. "Sure. Glad to have you. If you don't mind the dogs."

She put two fingers in the corners of her mouth and whistled shrilly.

"Dogs?!"

Two of Tom Sherard's mixed-breed watchdogs appeared on the run, then took off ahead of Eden. She turned and grinned at her doppelganger on the porch.

"Nothing to worry about. We both have the same, uh, body odor, so they probably won't even notice you."

The dpg fidgeted, then lifted her chin and said with a touch of defiance, "Name's Guinevere. I've decided. Or Gwen for short."

"Not yet it isn't. I still need you. Just the way you are."

"A bitter disappointment." Nonetheless her doppelganger joined Eden in the yard. They were followed by the colobus monkey, begging for the security of a shoulder to ride on. Eden paused and scooped him up. "I'm sorry to bring this to your attention," the dpg continued, "But your life expectancy—I get chills thinking about it. Here you are, walking around in shorts and sandals with wild beasts everywhere. Jeez, what are *those* over there with the tusks going every which way?"

"Some kind of warthog. They leave potholes all over the place but otherwise they're no bother."

"Three weeks ago you ran a temperature of a hundred and four from a little tick bite. High enough to boil both our brains."

Eden shrugged, with an expression of contentment.

"Tom says I should have seen Shungwaya thirty years ago," she mused as they crossed a nearly dried-up creek. "But it's plenty good enough for paradise now. What's a bite, a fever, a rash now and then? I want to stay forever. Bertie's father Joseph told me—"

" 'The best part of having lived in a beautiful but hard land is knowing that you never gave in.' "

"How do you know that?"

"I know what you know, of course. So—are we staying?"

Eden drew a pensive breath, didn't reply. She watched an African hoopoe, magnificent in orange with an orange and black crest, drift down as if leaving the orbit of the sun to light up the shady side of a baobab tree. She raised the binoculars that she wore around her neck and focused on a small herd of kudu moving single file through a *donga* a quarter of a mile away. The lead bull was huge, probably more than six hundred pounds, with a gray coat smooth as flannel, thin vertical white stripes on his body behind the shoulder and a long tuft of white on his spine. His horns were long and spiraling, two and a half twists to rapier points.

Tom had told her of the time he had come across two such bulls near a grove of *acacia albida,* one of kudus' prime feeding grounds. They were both kneeling on the red earth facing each other, bodies torn and black with flies at the bloody places, eyes growing dim in death, their twisted horns locked fatally together after a rutting bout. Bateleur vultures had begun their wheeling stalk in the sky. Each bull had fought as he was born to fight, and neither had given in. The heat of their struggle was still vivid in the air. It was a lonely, bleak, but untellably beautiful scene: the essence of life, the pride in death.

Eden lowered the binoculars.

"We're going back," she said. "I don't know about this new guy. If there's goodness in him, or pure evil. All I know is, the vultures had better keep their distance."

Eden Waring, Tom Sherard, and Bertie Nkambe will return in
THE FURY AND THE POWER.